PRAISE FOR MIRROR'S BRINK

"I'm still reeling. Every time I think E. S. Fein can't possibly raise the stakes any higher, he proves me wrong, and Mirror's Brink is the wildest, most awe inspiring installment yet. Everything he's been teasing since Mendel's Ladder (and continued expanding on in Winter's Remains and Hunter's Dirge) finally explodes into view, revealing layers of his mythos I never thought possible. The scale, the intensity, the sheer audacity of the narrative...let's just say it left my jaw on the floor." **– Reader Review**

"Fein's signature blend of sci-fi and fantasy has never felt more seamless, or more epic. We've got futuristic technology colliding with metaphysical realms, philosophical musings intersecting with raw, survivalist brutality, and it's all dialed up to eleven. This installment also leans harder into the grimdark elements: some of the twists are genuinely horrific, reminding you just how savage this universe can be. And it's not shock value for the sake of shock value, either. Every dark turn shows how the stakes and forces these characters to confront impossible choices." **– Reader Review**

OTHER WORKS BY E. S. FEIN

The Collected Histories of Neoevolution Earth
A Dream of Waking Life
Points of Origin
Ascendescenscion
The Process Is Love

OfficialESFein.com
Linktr.ee/ESFein
Instagram.com/Authoresfein
Patreon.com/Officialesfein
Facebook.com/AuthorESFein

The Collected Histories of

Neoevolution Earth

Volume 4

Mirror's Brink

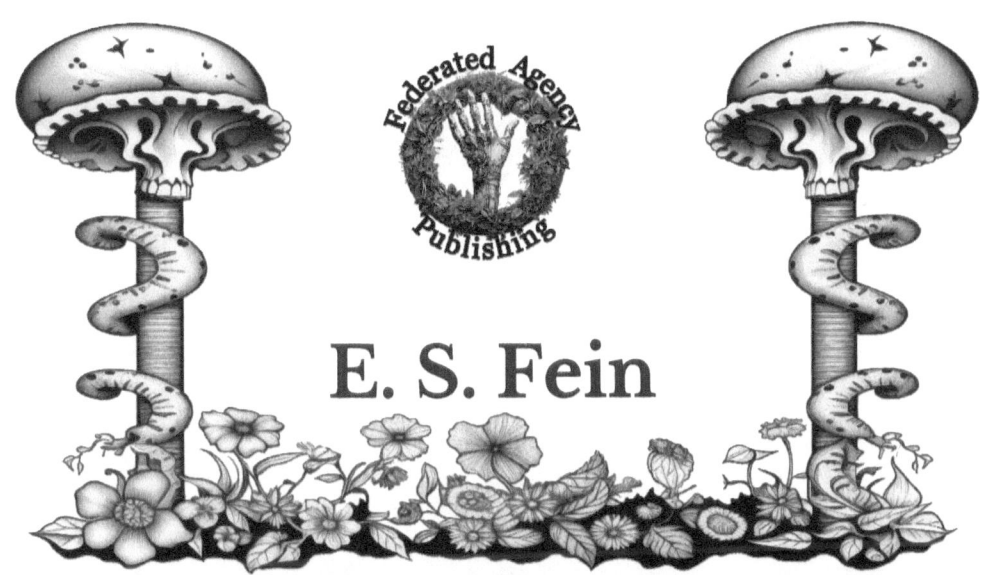

E. S. Fein

Mirror's Brink (Neoevolution Earth Vol. 4)

Copyright © 2025 by E. S. Fein

Author: E. S. Fein

Publisher: Federated Agency Publishing

Editor: Nichole Paolella Petrovich

Formatter: Timbers Book Design

Ebook ISBN: 978-1-963048-64-3

Paperback ISBN: 978-1-963048-11-7

Publication Date: April 2025

First Edition

To Marcin, for deeply believing in this series and keeping it alive in countless ways.

BOOK SUMMARIES AND GLOSSARY

Visit OfficialESFein.com for a summary of **Volume 1: Mendel's Ladder**, **Volume 2: Winter's Remains**, **Volume 3: Hunter's Dirge,** and a **Glossary of Terms** ranging the entire Neoevolution Earth series.

CONTENTS

Volume 4

Mirror's Brink

A mere glimpse of Mendel's Vision is enough to drive any human mind insane.

This is why Denis Mendel had to transcend his humanity and become the first Cognitive Upload Entity, or CUE. I can't help referring to him as a machine, but I know that isn't right. Neither "mind" nor "machine" can encompass what Denis has become. Still, it is easier to refer to him as such; to my own limited human mind, it seems to make sense when I look upon my friend and see a series of tubes and circuits in place of a human body.

I did this to you, Denis. I turned you into a god.

Denis could have never done it himself. He admitted as much only moments after awakening within his limitless digital domain.

I awaited with bated breath after I initiated the irreversible process of transferring his mind to the advanced but miniscule computer mainframe that would serve as his first and most rudimentary brain. In less than a second, he had spread to every network, device, and instrument with a digital structure. Roughly ten seconds after the process was completed, I saw text appear on the holo:

"Thank you, Andre Madeira. Now I see. Now I know. Thank you, my friend. I did not have the willpower to overcome my fear of grasping fire. But you forced me to do it, and now I have transcended my fear of fire. Now I have become the fire. Now I see. Now I know. Thank you, my friend."

Mendel explained that in the first billionth of a second of consciousness, he observed, analyzed, and concluded more about reality and our cosmos than all of human history combined. Then he explained to me, in a way that I could understand, what he saw with his god-like vision. He called his collective observations and realizations "Mendel's Ladder Theory of the Cosmos," or "Mendel's Ladder" for short.

Mendel's Ladder is more than just a theory. It is our salvation. It is the answer to every one of our questions. It is our purpose.

That being said, I can't help feeling trepidation at some of what Mendel showed me. Humanity's ascension up Mendel's Ladder and into the Great Beyond will require opening numerous intricate folds of reality and coming into contact with certain realms, for lack of a better word. Nightmare realms. That is the only way to describe what Mendel showed me using the simulation tank.

Interestingly, these realms have been observed by a tiny number of human minds throughout history, but these individuals were always deemed insane. Many of them were in fact just insane, but some—extremely few—really did glimpse the truth, the same truth that Mendel the Machine now professes as a god to his devotee, a title I wear proudly. Just as I was devoted to Mendel the Man, I am equally devoted to Mendel the Machine.

I have faith in Mendel's Vision, just as I have faith in his theory of the universe and the ladder we will build with Mendel's guidance and my implementation.

I have faith—something I never had until I was shown the truth directly. So, it isn't really faith, then. I glimpsed, but still I saw. I know. Just like Mendel. And now there is no turning back. Now we must climb Mendel's Ladder.

There is no other way. There never was.

From Mendel's Ladder: The Personal Journal of Denis Mendel, Written Circa 2036, Published June 2108 by Leif Mainstone, Federated Agency Publishing

Chapter 1
The End of Heaven

Year: 2099, Present Day

The colossal vultures of darkness roved the Foundation while the survivors hid like frail mice beneath the once inaccessible ground. It was only a matter of time before the stygian monsters ran out of prey within the Foundation. Then they would undoubtedly begin tearing at the ceiling in search of the rest of the survivors. Their hunger was ravenous and their prey dwindling.

It's only been just over a day since the revolution started, but it feels like we've been trapped underground for an eternity, Sandra Kaminski considered grimly as she walked Nathan and Margot back to the makeshift nursery with the other surviving children. The spartan walls of the underground corridors pressed in around them as the flickering lights cast elongated shadows. The air was thick with the scent of stale sweat, and each of their footsteps echoed like a hollow drumbeat in the suffocating silence of the corridor. Sandra's heart ached with each glance at her children, their faces marred by exhaustion and a confusion they were too young to properly articulate. While Margot and Nathan were fortunate to have been spared having to see the vultures directly, most of the other children had not been so lucky.

As they entered the room, Sandra nodded to Fred Wilson, who was doing a commendable job remaining positive in the presence of the younger children. The makeshift nursery was a dismal haven, small and bare, but also secure. Despite being only thirteen years old, Fred had been forced to enter the adult world of fear and insecurity far sooner than should ever be allowed. But just like the adults, he was excelling at presenting himself through a facade of strength and unbreakable willpower. Lakshmi Acharya, on the other hand, also thirteen years old, held her knees to her chest and rocked slowly in the corner of the room. The difference was that Fred's parents were still alive, while Lakshmi had witnessed her father, Governor Acharya, being drained of life and soul by the vultures of darkness conjured by the Queen. A pang of intense guilt struck through Sandra for the hundredth time since the revolution began.

They'll find us and kill us all eventually, Sandra gulped as she let go of her children's hands and patted them toward Fred and the other children. A cold sweat trickled down her spine, and her hands trembled. *You should be here with us, Samuel. You should be here.* She thought back to speaking to Samuel as a bodiless voice in the storage room several hours earlier. At first she had assumed that the voice was in her head, but Roland had confirmed he could hear Samuel too. *You said you were coming, so where are you?* Sandra nearly screamed at Samuel within her mind despite knowing with absolute certainty that her husband would be doing anything and everything in his power to return to her.

Please, Sandra thought. *Please hurry up, Samuel. Our plan to destroy the vultures is doomed to failure.* Desperation clawed at her chest, each breath a battle against the crushing weight of dread. *We need you, my fearless bull. Please hurry!*

"I don't want to just hide," Margot demanded, refusing to join her brother and the other children. "I want to come with you, momma. I want to help you destroy the monsters!"

A mixture of pride and fear surged within Sandra. She wanted nothing more than to shield her nine-year-old daughter from the horrors outside, yet she couldn't suppress her admiration for Margot's unwavering courage. She really was Samuel's daughter through and through.

"I know, honey. Because you are strong. Just like daddy. So that's why I need you to stay here and help the other kids be strong. Can you do that for me, Margot? Please?"

Margot looked disappointed, but she nodded and moved slowly toward the other kids. Sandra watched her go, her heart twisting as she saw the burden of responsibility settle on Margot's young shoulders. Nathan, who was three years younger than his sister, had already joined the others and was presently regaling a group of young Middlers and Enders with his own made-up stories.

Fred looked up and nodded to Sandra before returning his attention to the group. He attempted to keep the children entertained with an imaginary game involving claps and jumps, but many of them appeared utterly shell shocked like Lakshmi.

This will likely be the last time I ever see them, Sandra knew, struggling to hold back her tears. But she couldn't tell them that. She couldn't weaken them. The thought was like the metal pipes of the revolution twisting in her gut, but she steeled herself. They needed her to be strong; there was no room for doubt or despair.

Fred had been told the plan. He knew as well as Sandra that their attempts to slay the vultures of darkness would likely result in complete defeat. But they had to do something, anything, rather than just wait for their inevitable death. Action was their only salvation, no matter how slim the chances.

Goodbye, my precious ones. I love you more than you could possibly fathom, Sandra thought before turning and leaving the room as every part of her screamed to just go back and hold them with the little time they had left together.

As Sandra made her way back to High Commander Roland and her fellow revolutionaries, the hallway lights flickered, reflecting the mayhem on the other side of the ceiling. The distant echoes of crumbling structures and muted screams seeped through the thick walls, and the metallic scent of ozone lingered in the air, mingling with the musty dampness of the underground.

Breathe, Sandra told herself, pursing her lips and sucking at the air to still her mind and rid it of the horrific memories writhing through her thoughts. *Those vultures…those monsters!* Sandra recoiled, losing control of her breath as her mind forced her to revisit what she had seen just before sealing the trap door behind her children, dooming many others in the process. A mother and her two children, no different than Sandra and her own, had been just fifty feet or so from the secret entrance in the ground when they caught the attention of one of the creatures. Sandra could still hear their screams as the liquid of their body was sucked into the churning vortex within the pitch-black innards of the vulture that must have been fifty feet tall and a hundred feet across. As the great vulture slurped them into its maw, the blackness of its body raged like a churning sea, flaring with every shuddering breath it took. Across its massive flank, Sandra spotted flickering outlines of anguished faces, including those of the mother and her children. Their gaping mouths rose like goosebumps on the vulture's skin, as if they were being pressed against suffocating velvet. Then, their horrified faces blurred

3

and were replaced by other screaming visages. All the while, the vulture paid no mind to the agonized souls within its form as it searched for more prey to convert to withered bones and desiccated skin.

It didn't eat them, Sandra knew. *So what did it do to them? Is the soul a real thing, like our parents always claimed? Is that what the vulture drained from their bodies along with their fluids?*

Enough, Sandra told her mind as she brought her breathing back under control. *It's just like Samuel always said: I just need to keep lifting,* she thought with a bittersweet chuckle, feeling for just a moment that Samuel really was there beside her. Unbreakable. Unwavering. *Hurry, Samuel. Goddamnit, hurry back to me. Hurry back to your family! We need the Workhorse of Astrea! We always did,* she thought, feeling worse with every passing minute for having betrayed Samuel's trust, even if she truly had Margot and Nathan's best interest in her mind and her heart.

"Have the children been secured?" came High Commander Roland's stern yet calming voice as Sandra turned the corner and entered the makeshift headquarters that the revolutionaries had covertly built over the course of many years.

"As well as they can be," Sandra offered as she wiped away the fearful tears she had been unable to stifle. "Fred is doing his best. He's a brave boy."

"The girl," Roland said with a slight smile. "Margot. She wanted to come with, didn't she?"

Sandra furrowed her brow but couldn't help a sorrowful chuckle. The flicker of a smile faded quickly, replaced by the weight of their predicament pressing down on her.

"She's just like him, isn't she?" Sandra said, seeing Samuel in Roland's unshakable presence.

"She is his very heart and soul," Roland nearly growled. "The Workhorse of Astrea will not abandon his heart and soul. You understand, Sandra Kaminski?"

His piercing gaze seemed to look straight into her heart, unraveling the threads of fear she was trying so hard to conceal.

Sandra breathed deeply, galvanizing herself with Roland's words.

"I understand, Roland. Samuel will find a way to return to us," Sandra stated, bolstering her voice to sound stronger than the doubt churning in her heart. She clenched her fists tightly, nails digging into her palms. She used the pain to anchor her emotions.

It's already been a full day. Longer than that even. Hurry, Samuel. Before it's too late.

Despite her doubt, Roland nodded with seemingly perfect confidence that his claim was true.

"In the meantime," a voice as rough and jagged as hewn stone cut in.

Frank. Sandra tensed before she even turned to see him stepping into the headquarters from one of the many hallways leading to other small rooms of survivors just like this one.

"We're going to take down these vultures, with or without Sammy boy. We've managed this long without him. Let the worker stay lost on the Earth's surface."

Sandra fought the unease knotting in her gut. Frank had been integral to the revolution and the subsequent survival of Nathan and Margot, but he was also responsible for all its death. Just like Sandra.

Frank's always been a bastard, even when we were kids. He always took things too far. And now so many are dead. Frank...he...he personally killed Bill Wendover. Bill was a good man. An innocent man, Sandra ruminated gravely.

"That's enough, boy," Roland barked, and Frank bowed his head in submission to the golden armored Queensguard. Frank was a true revolutionary, the muscle of the Sons and Daughters of the Foundation, but he still held deference for strength and discipline, no matter the form. He even respected Samuel, even if he didn't show it.

"Now is the time for focus, not banter. You say we will do just fine without the Workhorse, but we still have yet to destroy a vulture. Reports say there are few survivors out there. Once the vultures get hungry enough, then they'll be coming for us next, just as Sandra has been saying. Sandra," Roland offered, turning to her, "this attack is your idea, so why don't you take the floor."

Sandra stepped forward. She half-expected Nikki to say something offensive, but Nikki had barely spoken a word since the vultures had been released. For all her tough talk through the years as a revolutionary willing to weather any form of torment in her pursuit of the Paradise Quarters, Nikki had been hollowed by fear just hours after witnessing the nightmare monsters conjured from some other realm of unspeakable and unthinkable horrors. At the small table beside Nikki, her partner Albatross, the leader of the Sons and Daughters of the Foundation, sat with high shoulders and his fingers contemplatively pressed into a steeple. His glasses were full of smudges, but he didn't seem to take any notice. A few young hackers stood around their leader, obedient to him, even after being plunged into hell by his hand. All the while, Frank held his large arm around Geronimo's hulking shoulder. Despite being a jumbo, Geronimo was only nineteen, and he trembled with wild fear. Sandra found that she couldn't look Geronimo in the eyes, not after telling him earlier what part he would have to play in her plan.

He's too young to die, but no one else is big enough to wear the Queensarmor, Sandra knew. *This plan has to work,* Sandra told herself as she wrestled her breathing to a state of calm. *It has to, because if it doesn't, then every one of us is doomed to become a writhing visage trapped within the pitch-black body of those monsters.*

No! Sandra envisioned Nathan and Margot being sucked into perfect darkness. *I will not allow that to happen!*

"We will only have one chance," Sandra said finally, cutting directly to the urgency and precariousness of her plan. "I know we've gone over the plan already, but let's just do it again, one more time, just to make sure we're all…glowing at the level," she offered, nodding to the young hackers as a subtle way to let them know they were equals alongside the founders of the Sons and Daughters of the Foundation. Sandra, who'd become a member just a few months earlier, had quickly entered the inner ranks due to Damian, one of the founders and Samuel's best friend, vouching for her and, of course, because she was the wife of the Workhorse.

"You three," she said, pointing to the hackers, "will be responsible for overriding the system controlling the release of glowglobes. You're going to divert as many as you can to a single release point. Then, you're going to fill the chamber with pressurized air. Finally, when you get the signal, you're going to launch them."

"Boom," Frank said with a smile. Geronimo jumped at Frank's word, looking horrified.

"You two," Sandra said to Frank and Geronimo with an apologetic nod directed at Geronimo, who sat hunched over and trembling. "It all comes down to you two. You're the only jumbos here besides Roland, and he's already a Queensguard. You both probably would have become Queensguards one day anyway."

"But," Geronimo began with terror in his every feature.

"There is no but, kid," Frank scolded Geronimo gently. Roland just looked on, choosing to allow Frank to speak. "But this isn't the end either, you hear me? You think I'm going to let those freaks of darkness slurp you down?"

Geronimo shook his head but couldn't help the tears in his eyes.

"The two of you will be decoys. It will be your job to direct one of the vultures over to the glowglobe release. And…" she said, stopping short at the thought.

"And one of us is going to have to let the vulture start feeding so that it opens itself up to an attack with the glowglobes," Frank finished. He put his arm around Geronimo and said, "Don't try to steal my glory, kid. You just help me get its attention and let me handle the rest."

Sandra could barely believe that this was the same Frank. He was still as brash and arrogant as ever, but the horrors released by the Queen had softened him. It reminded Sandra that Frank always claimed to have everyone's best interest in mind, even if she totally doubted him. *But maybe there's more to Frank,* Sandra considered reluctantly. *Maybe there's more to all of us. Maybe we really can make this work, and maybe I'll see you again, Samuel. Maybe,* Sandra thought, feeling a sliver of hope for the first time in what felt like ages.

"And I will be the other decoy," Roland stated, saying what Sandra couldn't, for Roland's role in the plan was the most suicidal of all. "I will direct the attention of as many vultures to myself as possible, while Frank and Geronimo guide a single vulture to the release. We have to make sure we don't get overwhelmed by them. We take down one vulture, and if that works, we go from there."

Everyone lowered their head, including Sandra, but Roland remained steadfast, his chin held high, his frown like an unbreakable boulder uplifting his very soul.

"Nikki and I will run logistics for the hackers. If anything goes wrong, I'll personally step in," Albatross said without emotion, but Nikki remained silent beside him.

"I just…I just wish the Workhorse were here. He would…he—" Geronimo began, squeaking his words through tears.

"We're the new workhorses, kid," Frank interrupted with disdain at the mention of Samuel. "I told you, we don't need that damn worker. If he'd been on our side from the get-go, then maybe we could have avoided all this to begin with. Maybe we could have saved more Foundationers. Maybe—"

"Shut your goddamn mouth, Frank!" Sandra spat, enraged at the audacity of criticizing Samuel when he had been right all along. *We had heaven, and we...I...plunged us into hell. And this fucking worker, fucking Frank, wants to badmouth one of the very pillars of the heaven we threw away?*

Roland raised his armored hand and was about to interject when they heard something unexpected.

"You're nothing like my dad," came a quivering child's voice from behind Sandra.

Sandra turned to see her children hand in hand, Margot appearing fierce despite her shaking and Nathan looking nervous and slightly confused as he stood a few inches behind his much taller sister.

Upon seeing the children, Frank was like a different person, smiling gently and speaking in a softer tone.

"You're right, kid," he offered. "I'm sorry you heard what I said, okay? I'm just ball-busting. That's it. You'll understand when you get older, okay?"

Sandra was about to tell Frank not to speak to her children, but Margot said, "We're old enough to fight monsters. We can help. We don't want to sit in that room with the other kids. Right, Nathan?"

Nathan didn't move a muscle. He just clung to his seemingly fearless sister as if for life.

"We're going out there with you. We can help!"

"Margot," Sandra began, still just wanting to run to them and embrace them and abandon this hopeless plan.

"I'm not afraid to wear the armor," Nathan said without stuttering, his eyes wide with obvious horror at the prospect.

Oh, my little baby, Sandra thought, wishing that Nathan could go back to spending his time watching lessons on his tablet while sitting on her lap, not braving nightmares rampaging and consuming his home and his people.

A few of the young hackers sniggered. Even Roland smiled and nodded in approval at Nathan's show of courage. But Frank just stared at the boy with a fierceness that startled Sandra.

Frank stepped around the table and came face-to-face with Sandra's children. If it weren't for Roland standing directly behind him, Sandra would have pushed him away. As Frank bent at the knees and looked deeply into Margot's and Nathan's eyes, Sandra had to actively stop herself from grabbing her children and kicking Frank in the throat, for she didn't want them to feel any more fear than they already did. But there was something in his features, an incredible depth and genuineness that made Sandra falter and allow him to speak.

"What I said about your dad—it was all just glow. Bullshit, as the old timers say. Your dad, Samuel Kaminski—there is no one else like him. Your dad is a great man. Yeah, I would mock him and dig at him if he were here, just like I always did, but when it comes down to it, there's no one else I'd rather have fighting alongside me. He is the Workhorse of Astrea, not me."

Margot and Nathan had never directly interacted with Frank. All they knew about him was what Sandra and Samuel had told them, that he was dangerous and that they should keep their distance from him.

"You are his daughter," Frank said to Margot with stoic depth. "And you are his son," he said to Nathan in turn. "You are both strong and brave, just like him. Hell, in a decade you'll both be even stronger than Sammy boy. That's how it goes. But not yet, you hear me? These things take time. So for now, the two of you let that fire inside burn. You let it stir. You let it take you—"

"No!" Sandra yelped, not wanting her children to churn with hate and violence like so many people, including Frank, and even herself, she admitted.

Frank turned and stared at Sandra with an intensity that transcended words, telling her with just his eyes that this was what her children needed to hear if they had any hope of survival. Sandra winced at the realization that Frank was right—she couldn't just shelter them. Still, she didn't want her children to be inspired by the rash and cruel Frank Barone, but she didn't know what else to do anymore.

"You let it take you, but not yet. Now it's time for you two to protect the others. They need you, just like we all need your dad. I promise you—I've never been more certain of anything in my life—I promise you that right now your dad is doing everything he can to get back to you two. Old Sammy boy is fighting, and that's what you two are going to do as well. You're going to fight by protecting all the other kids too afraid to protect themselves. You hear me?"

Margot and Nathan ran forward and embraced Frank, holding him tightly as if he were their actual father.

Sandra pivoted uncomfortably, but she didn't want to steal their ability to feel comfort, even if it came from Frank.

But if this is what will help them survive, then I have no choice, Sandra thought miserably as Frank broke away from their embrace, stood, and then lowered his hand, offering a low-five. Margot and Nathan both attempted to hit his hand, but Frank pulled away and slid his hand across the side of his head. He smiled and said, "too slow."

Margot and Nathan giggled, and then they turned to Sandra and ran to her. Sandra bent down and embraced them, clinging to their warm little bodies, savoring their scents.

Please let this work. Please let my children survive all this, Sandra pleaded to the universe, knowing it was unfair to ask for her kids to be spared when so many others had been consumed. *Please,* Sandra thought, not caring about fairness or justice. *Please just let them survive this, even if I don't.*

Sandra forced herself to let go of her children then nodded to one of the hackers, wordlessly asking her to walk her kids back to the nursery. The terrible weight of unspoken words pressed heavily on her tongue, but she swallowed them down, knowing that voicing her fears would only burden them further.

"We can get back on our own," Margot stated confidently as she wiped away her tears and her brother's tears. "We'll be okay," she assured her mother.

Sandra nodded, kissed her fingers, then placed her fingers on each of their foreheads. In response, the kids touched their foreheads then kissed their fingers. It was a ritual of love they had shared since Nathan was just a toddler.

As if she knew that Sandra would be unable to actually say goodbye, Margot turned and walked down the hallway with Nathan looking back and waving. Sandra waved back to him with a forced smile and sense of calm until they turned a corner, breaking their goodbye.

Again, that might be the last time I ever see them, Sandra knew, and she had to remind herself to take a breath.

Just above them, distant bangs and cracks could be heard on the other side of the ceiling, prompting the entire room back to attention.

10

The ground trembled slightly beneath their feet, dust cascading from the ceiling like macabre snowflakes.

"It is time," Roland issued, nodding to Geronimo and Frank to begin the process of entombing themselves within the armor of the two desiccated Queensguards that the group had recovered a few hours earlier. Sandra shuddered as she imagined the sheer terror each man must have suffered as the vultures sucked their bodies' fluids into their maws. Sandra wondered grimly if the vultures were unable to digest the rest of them or if they merely preferred blood over tissue and bone.

They drain us of blood, but even before that, they start draining people of something else too. Their very consciousness! Sandra again recollected how the vultures had indiscriminately fed on her people, even on wailing infants. *This plan is a shot in the dark. This plan is doomed to failure. This plan...my plan...is like a firecracker battling against a nuclear bomb.* Sandra felt hopeless and helpless all at once. *Hurry, Samuel. Please just hurry,* Sandra thought, filled with equal amounts grief and anger for her fearless bull of a husband.

"I just wish that Samuel—" Geronimo began, parroting Sandra's own thoughts.

"No more wishes, kid," Frank interrupted. "We've reached the end of heaven. It's time for us to slay these demons of hell."

A thunderous crash shook the entire room, causing everyone to stagger. The lights flickered violently before plunging the room into near darkness.

"What was that?" Nikki gasped, her voice barely audible over the rumbling.

"It's the vultures," Albatross stated as he pushed his glasses up on his nose. "What else?"

"It could be the Queen," Roland said, his tone revealing that he feared the Queen even more than the vultures of darkness just above them.

The lights flickered back on. Sandra looked about the room and observed panic in the features of everyone except for Roland. Even Frank was doing a poor job of hiding his anxiousness.

I'm sure I don't look any better, Sandra thought as she looked over her shoulder and considered running to the nursery.

Hurry! she told herself. *There's no time for hesitation. I have to move forward.*

I have to act! We all do.

"The armor," Sandra issued to Frank and Geronimo, her breathing shallower than she intended. "Get into it. Now!"

Without hesitation, Frank bent down and placed his hand firmly upon the chest plate of the closest Queensguard.

Sandra hated that so much of the plan would depend on Frank, but as long as he did his job, then she could look past his brashness bordering on barbarity.

"Like this?" Frank asked Roland, flashing his teeth at him as his grin widened in what appeared to be both exhilaration and horror.

Roland nodded and sighed deeply. "It's like becoming one of the changed people, the Nomads down on Earth. You just give your mind over to it, and the armor does the rest. It knows how to—"

Roland was interrupted by the collective gasp of everyone in the room as the armor suddenly began to shift, separating into puzzle-like pieces to reveal the naked body of the dead Queensguard. His skin was bone-white, as the radiation of the glowglobes had no way of penetrating the thick armor.

"I'm no mindless worker, but I'm a worker all the same. I deserve the armor," Frank stated through clenched teeth and a look of admonishment from Roland, likely at Frank's brazen confidence that he *deserved* anything.

The armor began to vibrate and emit a deep, resonant hum. Then, the armor lifted, one piece at a time, and it hovered in the air like a shattered star. Each piece rotated slowly, reflecting the flickering electric lights and casting erratic beams across the face of each onlooker.

The power emanated from the armor like a weapon from a god, making Sandra feel as exposed and weak as the dead man heaped on the ground.

Frank's eyes widened with awe and trepidation as the first segment approached. He extended his hand tentatively, visibly shaking. One by one, the armor pieces snapped into place around him. As they made contact with his clothing, they consumed the amino-herb material, leaving him bare beneath the armor now encasing his muscular frame in a shell of energy-dense metal.

Frank clenched his fists and smiled wide at the newfound power coursing through him.

12

"This…this is unbelievable," he whispered, his voice distant for the first time Sandra could ever remember.

He took a step forward and lifted his right gauntlet, marveling at how the immense weight was negligible, as if it were a second skin.

Roland observed with a sardonic smirk, his armored arms folded across his golden chest. "Power reveals one's true nature," he stated, his voice cutting through the hum of the newly formed armor like a blade. "Be wary that it doesn't consume you."

Like it consumed me, Sandra reminded herself. The moment the vultures had been released, she knew that the revolution had been her greatest and likely final mistake in life. *I had the power to tell Samuel about the revolution. We could have ended it together. But the allure of immortality, not just for me, but for Margot and Nathan—how could I not take that chance? How can I be blamed for wanting my children to never have to worry about age or weakness or the recyclers ever again?*

Frank was about to say something to Roland, likely some smart-ass comment about Queensguards, when another thunderous bang reverberated above them, this one more violent than the last. The ceiling creaked ominously as dust and debris rained down.

Sandra's brain felt overrun. Every instinct screamed at her to run, to find her children and hold them tight. But she forced herself to focus. "Geronimo, you need to get into the armor now!" she urged, her voice rising in pitch.

Geronimo recoiled, his eyes wide with fear. "I…I can't," he stammered, backing away from the second set of armor lying inert on the floor. "The armor can hover. It moves on its own. You all saw it! The strength thing doesn't make sense. That's just propaganda from the Queen. Anyone can wear it!"

"That's not true!" Sandra snapped, her gaze locking onto his. "You're the only one strong enough to handle it. Please, Geronimo! We need you!"

He shook his head violently, tears welling in his eyes. "You wear it, Sandra! I'm telling you, anyone can!"

A cold dread settled in her stomach. The idea of donning the armor herself was both terrifying and tempting. Could she handle that kind of power? Did she even deserve it after all the mistakes she'd made? Her mind flashed back to the faces of the innocent people she'd failed to save, their screams echoing in her ears.

Roland stepped forward, his expression grave. "The armor doesn't respond to just anyone," he said firmly. "It's attuned to those who've invested their lives in laboring for others. It's not about physical strength, but the time spent serving at a power station. That's how one becomes a Queensguard and gains immortality."

Frank raised his eyebrows and even licked his lips as he turned to Roland and asked, "So am I immortal now?"

Roland shook his head slowly. "No. There's another ritual that requires a machine in the Luxury Quarters. It's that machine that grants biological immortality. It may no longer even be intact after what you all have done to Astrea."

No one replied to Roland's scolding. Sandra felt as though they were just children in the presence of an adult.

Immortality, Sandra thought, the word reverberated through her mind like a bell tolling in a desolate wasteland. The draw of it was still intoxicating, even after everything that had occurred. Immortality—a chance to protect her children forever, to undo her past mistakes. Maybe even make amends for the lies she had told Samuel. Guilt twisted her insides. She had deceived him to further the revolution, believing it was for the greater good, but now everything was spiraling out of control. The thought of immortality pressed even more heavily upon her. She glanced at the armor, then back to Geronimo, whose eyes pleaded with her not to force him.

A deafening crash shattered her thoughts. The ceiling above groaned and buckled, metal beams twisting like grotesque sculptures. Sandra threw herself to the ground, covering her head as a massive vulture of darkness stuck its elongated neck through the opening. Its form was both ethereal and horrifyingly solid, a swirling mass of shadow and nothingness, like a sudden void in space that somehow didn't cause the atmosphere around it to collapse inward. Its face had no definable features save the beak-like form and the suggestion of eye sockets where there should be eyes. Its face widened, morphing its gaping maw into a vortex of all-consuming darkness.

The creature emitted a screech that sounded as though it were coming from many miles in the distance. Sandra felt an icy grip clutch her skin as the air around them began to swirl, pulled toward the vortex.

Loose papers, tools, and pieces of debris lifted off the ground, spiraling upwards before being swallowed into oblivion.

"Get back!" Frank shouted, his voice amplified by the armor, yet tinged with primal fear.

The room erupted into chaos. The young hackers screamed, scrambling for cover behind overturned tables and equipment. Nikki and Albatross tried to coordinate an escape, but their voices were lost in the cacophony. A section of the wall collapsed, cutting Sandra, Frank, and Geronimo off from the others. The path to the nursery and her children was now buried under tons of rubble.

"No!" Sandra screamed, her voice raw. Panic surged through her like a dry forest set aflame. She spun around, searching for another exit, but the way was blocked by the great roiling body of the vulture pressing further and further inward as the sucking force of its life-stealing maw intensified. Panic clawed at her throat. She turned to the pile of debris, frantically trying to move the massive chunks of warped metal with her bare hands. Her fingers bled, but she felt nothing except the frantic need to reach her children.

All of a sudden, Roland rocketed himself upward through a rain of debris and launched at the creature, jets of flame erupting from his gauntlets. The vulture's body appeared to consume the light of the flames rather than the flames themselves, treating the light as though it were a tangible substance. As the light was stripped from the fire, the creature recoiled momentarily, its screech turning into a hiss of displeasure.

"Just run!" Roland commanded as he kept the vulture distracted by disengaging each gauntlet once it was stripped of all light then reigniting them with full force.

"Come on!" Frank grabbed Sandra's arm, pulling her toward a side corridor.

"But my kids!" Sandra protested, tears welling in her eyes.

"If you go to them now, you'll lead that thing straight to them," he countered. "We have to stick to the plan. It's the only way to save them."

She knew he was right, but the maternal instinct to protect her children was overwhelming. Every fiber of her being screamed to turn back. But if she did, they might all be stripped of life and light.

15

Her thoughts raced chaotically. Images of her children's faces melded with memories of Samuel's reassuring embrace. She envisioned the strength in his eyes, the unwavering resolve. *If only he were here.* She felt a fresh wave of guilt. *I drove him away with my lies. If he never forgives me, it'll be more than I deserve.*

Sandra cast one last, anguished glance at the blocked passageway, her children just out of reach. *Please just remember what we taught you. Just stay safe. Momma's going to make this right. I promise.* She swallowed hard, forcing herself to follow Frank.

Geronimo stood frozen, his eyes glazed with terror. "I can't...I can't do this," he mumbled, his body trembling.

"You already failed to put on the armor, boy!" Frank lashed, looking like he might kill Geronimo out of anger.

Ignoring Frank, Sandra took a deep breath and summoned every ounce of strength she had left. "Geronimo, look at me," she shouted over Roland's battle cries and spurts of flame being used to both battle the creature and keep himself in the air. Geronimo's gaze met Sandra's, teary and hopeless. "I know you're scared. We all are. But we have to keep moving. For everyone counting on us. For my children. Please, Geronimo."

Images of Margot and Nathan flashed through Sandra's mind—their innocent faces, their unwavering trust in her.

Geronimo hesitated, stared into Sandra's pleading face, then turned and looked into Frank's murderous eyes, then up at Roland's battle with the vulture, then finally he gave a shaky nod.

"Okay," he said, heaving the words out of his mouth. "I'm sorry. I'm so sorry, I just—"

The ceiling directly above Geronimo caved in suddenly, revealing the probing face of another vulture. In a heartbeat, the vulture solidified its body, morphing from a vast and calm empty space with the outlines of something avian into a clear vulture-like creature with a body composed of writhing inky blackness.

"Geronimo!" Sandra and Frank shouted simultaneously, but the vulture was already sucking at Geronimo's life-force, using its vortexing maw to siphon his body into a quickly desiccating corpse.

"No!" Sandra shrieked as she was forcefully pulled toward Geronimo's body, which convulsed in agony as he was stripped of what very well might be his soul. The pull was too great to resist, and though she knew she was going to slip directly into its maw and be consumed just like Geronimo, all she could think about was Margot and Nathan and that they would undoubtedly undergo the same terrible fate.

Margot, Nathan...oh God. If you're real, God, please don't let their souls be eaten, she prayed, something she had never done before.

She imagined Margot and Nathan huddling together with the other kids in the dim nursery, their small hands clasped tightly, eyes wide with fear as the world crumbled around them. The thought was unbearable, a searing pain that tore through her heart as the life-sucking force of the vulture penetrated and pulled at the very core of her being.

Faith is a double-edged sword—a beacon for the lost and a leash for the unsuspecting.

The Rodriguez family embodies devotion, committing every thought and intention to their belief in a benevolent god who has planned for them an eternal life of joy and peace after death. They are truly devout Christians, humble and self-sacrificing. They are the perfect vessels for Tomasz and Ruben's requirements for the Great Honey Mushroom, the first planetary organ of the Earth. The mushroom will serve many purposes, but its initial purpose will be to gestate the first flesh pods and give birth to the first generation of Nomads. Ultimately, the Great Honey Mushroom is the world's first flesh tree.

Seemingly by chance, on August 28, the day that I detonated the nuclear bombs across the world, the Rodriguez family was forced to travel to Oaxaca to renew their work permits. The office in Mexico City lost track of their data, and it became their responsibility to travel nearly 300 miles outside of the capital in order to prove that they were legally allowed to work with their brains intact outside of a Tsehay Manufactury, a right reserved for fewer and fewer people every day. Of course, Mendel was the one who deleted their data, precipitating the series of events that would ultimately save their lives. The Rodriguez family believes they were saved by a divine act of god rather than being manipulated from the shadows. It was exactly that delusion I utilized to successfully manipulate them. Mendel stated that the Rodriguez family is the single best chance at constructing the planetary organ in such a way that Mendel's Ladder will continue to be ascended. Thus, I'm sure that factored into the day he chose the detonation. The number of variables is too staggering for me to even begin to fathom Mendel's planning. I am satisfied to merely carry out his vision. More than satisfied, I am determined.

It is through this determination that I prepared myself to approach the family. Over the course of seven weeks, Mendel helped me learn Nahuatl, along with helping me polish up my Spanish. Even my accent had to be perfect. Then, when Mendel, always there in my mind, assured me I was ready, I journeyed to the outskirts of Cordoba by foot and by train. It was exactly how I used to travel as a kid on the road after my parents were taken from me. With a sense of joy and familiarity, I found that I could become one of them again—a sewer rat. I had spent so long ingraining myself into the Titans' world of luxury and riches that I forgot I was actually a member of the "lesser" masses. I had been apprehensive about the journey at first because the world had become substantially more dangerous and desperate after the bombs. And yet, the journey was liberating. I didn't take a single life either, nor did I need Mendel to help me manipulate others. I could do it all on my own. I was the one who taught Denis how to manipulate, after all. Any expertise he had on the subject had its beginnings in my own teachings, each one a seed planted in his mind without him even knowing. Manipulation is the ultimate tool of survival; thus, I had no choice but to adopt it and master it.

I approached the Rodriguez family not as a stranger, but as a subtle prophet bearing the weight of divine revelation. Like my own father, I obtained a job at a waste processing center just outside of Cordoba, one among many that had been built to replace those destroyed outside Mexico City. At every turn, whenever I needed him, Mendel was there in the network, covertly rewriting the world's systems with ease to ensure that despite no one recognizing me, my digital footprint appeared as though I undeniably belonged wherever I was. "Ah, yes, Sr. Alejandro," a normally suspicious conductor of a private Liu train line would say, or "Data looks clean, Sr. Andres," a Winters Security Officer would confirm as I was allowed entrance into a shelter to be protected from the roving masses of starving and desperate post-nuclear survivors. In the case of the waste processing center, Mendel's work was so thorough that they actually found my data suspicious because it was almost too clean. Usually errors pile up, and no one, not even a rudimentary data-processing AI, cares about it enough to spare even a modicum of processing power. However, despite their suspicion, they were happy to take on another worker to use up their body until they were forced, one way or another, into debt, and eventually into a Tsehay Manufactury.

After a few days on the job, I finally approached Luis Rodriguez, finding him amid the refuse he sifted through daily, always on the lookout for something he might be able to clean and bring home to his little girl. His hands were coarse and bloody from sifting through the filth; the company, owned by Liu Energy, didn't even bother to provide their workers, or rather slaves, with gloves.

"Brother," I said to him with a perfect local Nahuatl accent, my voice slicing through the din of the grinding machinery like divine light in darkness. "Your hands bear the marks of a laborer. They are like the hands of the apostles who toiled beside Christ." He turned, sweat tracing rivulets through the grime coating his dilapidated face. His eyes met mine, and a flicker of life sparked in their tired depths.

"Who are you?" he asked through coughs and wheezes. He didn't have long before Winters Security Officers forced him to submit his body and mind to a Tsehay Manufactury. Soon his mind would belong to the Titans, Fana Tsehay most of all. This is what I reminded myself as I began planting the seeds within him that would eventually germinate and make him mine, Mendel's, and the Earth's.

"Me? I am a messenger," I replied, stepping closer. "My brother, you unearth treasures where others see only trash. It reminds me of Matthew 13:44: 'The kingdom of heaven is like treasure hidden in a field.' Perhaps, Luis, you are destined to find a greater treasure."

He paused, ruminating on the scripture like a starving man cherishing a morsel of food. "What treasure could someone like me find?" he asked, his eyes welling with tears.

"Purpose," I said softly. "A role in God's grand design to heal this broken world."

"Your purpose is work, not talk," an AI voice commanded us from an unseen speaker. We obeyed and returned to work, laboring side by side in profound silence for the rest of the day.

I wasn't certain that my words would be enough, but Mendel confirmed within my mind that Luis was already ours. It was just a matter of convincing his wife and daughter as well.

So, I spent the rest of the day laboring with every ounce of strength I had, pushing my muscles and organs to their limit as penance for my necessary deception. Then, after my shift, my body ransacked and my every feature covered in filth, I watched as Luis walked arm-in-arm with his brethren toward the local pub, where he would have no more than a single drink before returning home. On the holosets, the news spoke of the world's obliteration and the brutal mayhem plaguing the North and South American Continents. Although the people on the streets and in the pub listened with keen ears at the abject horrors occurring beyond Central and South America, these communities in Southern Mexico, even two years after the bombs, were still leagues safer than any of the wildly violent places scattered across America and Canada. The same would have been true for many parts of Europe, Asia, and Africa were they not reduced to irradiated ash by the United States and Canada's retaliatory nuclear bombardment against those they held responsible, through my persuasion, for the destruction of most major cities in North America. The only thing that stopped the world from being plunged into a nuclear winter were the Cleaners and the myriad technology provided by the Titans, the same individuals who forced me to cripple the world in the first place. I suppose only Gladys is blameless for the nuclear bombs, but that doesn't absolve her of her past crimes nor the future crimes she will commit against humanity…and me.

While Luis relaxed at the pub with the other workers, I visited María Rodriguez in their modest apartment, the scent of homemade tortillas mingling with the faint aroma of burning candles. Children laughed in the background of her small apartment, which was so much like my own as a child. Most of their community agreed that María labored hardest of all by looking after dozens upon dozens of neighborhood children while their parents toiled in the waste fields. Her community loved her, with both adults and children referring to her as Mamá María. She would have had more children than just her daughter Gabriela, but a defect in her womb made it impossible. The defect was an easy fix, but Novak Medical gave no handouts whatsoever, so María was content to be mother to a whole community rather than being a biological mother to a handful of children.

As parents returned from the waste fields to pick up their kids from María's disheveled yet warm and inviting apartment, the children's giggles were a stark contrast to the grim realities outside.

"Mamá María," I said as I walked through the open door of her apartment, this time with an educated Spanish accent that Mendel said would be more impactful to her. Just as Mendel predicted, she was presently watering the half-wilted potted plants vying to reach the light from the open door, for there were no windows in the apartment.

"Can I help you?" she asked pleasantly, not even wary that I might be a bandit or serial killer or something worse.

"Mamá," I said, "you nurture the plants. You nurture the children. You nurture every life that has ever been in your presence. You are like Proverbs 31:20: 'She opens her arms to the poor and extends her hands to the needy.'"

She looked up, her eyes reflecting the flickering candles. "I'm just doing what I can."

I shook my head but smiled warmly. "Your kindness mirrors that of Mary herself. The world is in need of such nurturing souls to birth a new beginning."

At my words, she clutched her worn rosary, her fingers trembling ever so slightly. Mendel explained that it was something her own father used to regularly tell her as a child, word for word. Like my own parents, her parents were presently working in a Tsehay Manufactury as neurolaced bodies directed by Mendelian AI. To them, their daughter was just a figment of a distant and irrelevant life.

"But what if you could do more?" I asked, mirroring her own questions to herself as I leaned in and lowered my voice. "What if you could help birth a new Eden, a place where suffering is but a distant memory?"

Her fingers tightened around the closest pot, soil crumbling under her nails. "How could someone like me do such a thing?"

"With faith," I answered. "And a willingness to embrace God's calling."

Unlike Luis, she did not have tears in her eyes. To truly convince her, I would have to convince her daughter first. I nodded to María, smiled, placed a small package on her dilapidated couch, then took my leave without looking back. Inside the package was a jump-drive with 150,000 ameros, which represented about four months of her and Luis' combined income. Any more than that and she would have been scared off, but any less and she wouldn't have been impressed.

As I left, I approached seven-year-old Gabriela as she sat on the apartment steps, her eyes following a butterfly that danced on the breeze. "It's beautiful, isn't it?" I said using her father's peculiar Nahuatl accent. I didn't sit next to her, but I did close the gap between us. I wanted her to feel equally secure and curious about me.

She nodded shyly at my observation. "I wish I could fly like that."

"Perhaps you can," I offered with a playful chuckle. "Do you know Isaiah 40:31? 'But those who hope in the Lord will renew their strength. They will soar on wings like eagles.'"

Her eyes widened. "That's my favorite verse! Is it your favorite too?"

"Yes, it is. You see, I help others fly. Others like you. And I think maybe you can help others fly too, that is, after you learn to fly." I smiled, and she smiled along with me, a puppet on my strings.

"Child," I whispered, kneeling to her level, "you are like the mustard seed in Matthew's parable, small but destined to grow into something mighty."

María exited the apartment holding the jump drive.

"We don't want any trouble," she said, offering the drive back to me.

The next part wasn't an act. I nearly broke down, tears occluding my vision of this saint and angel before me, willing to give up a small fortune to ensure that the wellbeing of their community would not be threatened.

I nearly broke character, but I summoned courage and resolve. I smiled through my tears, reached out my hand, and then gently closed her hand around the drive.

"It is safe. It is yours. It is a gesture of my generosity. Share it with your neighbors. Use it on Gabriela. But it is no longer mine. As it is said in Timothy 6:10: 'The love of money is the root of all kinds of evil.' Like Christ, my house, my Earth, has become a den of robbers. Take it, Mamá. Please. Let me help you as you have shepherded the souls of countless others. In Christ, we are one, Mamá."

Every word was rehearsed. Even the emphasis on each syllable was prepared to ensure that I sounded like a combined multitude of men and women in María's life that she loved and looked up to.

Gabriela looked at me with awe, and as María's eyes drifted from her daughter and back to me, her eyes began welling with tears. She placed the drive in her pocket and then ran to me like a little girl and embraced me as her savior, exactly as I intended.

You've done it, Mendel said matter-of-factly from within my mind. *Here comes Luis. He will see his wife and child embracing you, and he will take it as a symbol that you really are a messenger from God.*

I am, I answered Mendel. *I am your messenger, after all.*

At that, Mendel didn't respond, for he does not consider himself a god even though I absolutely do.

As Luis arrived, I opened my arms in offering, inviting him to embrace me along with his wife and daughter. "In John 15:5," I began as Luis fell into my arms with his family, "Jesus says, 'I am the vine; you are the branches.' What if I told you that God is offering us a chance to become one with the true vine, to heal this fractured world?" They listened, hearts open, minds pliable.

That night, we ate grilled rat tortillas in their apartment as the taste of rat flooded me with flashbacks from childhood that I hadn't thought about in decades. As we ate, I spoke of a new Eden, a restoration of harmony between humanity and the Earth.

"Imagine a world where suffering is but a memory," I said. "Where your labor, Luis, brings forth not just survival but everlasting peace. Where your compassion, María, nurtures a rebirth of mankind. Where your dreams, Gabriela, flourish beyond the confines of this mortal realm."

They yearned for meaning, for assurance that their struggles were not in vain. I offered them that and more, a role in a divine plan they could not resist. "But to achieve this," I cautioned, "we must make sacrifices akin to those made by Christ. Romans 12:1 urges us to offer our bodies as living sacrifices, holy and pleasing to God. I have already offered my flesh to the lord. He is within me at all times, commanding me, directing me toward salvation. But are you willing to walk this path along with me?" I asked. Before they could respond, I added, "Do not think Eden lies in some distant future. No! Eden is mere days away, if you wish."

Father and mother looked at one another, and then they both looked at their daughter. Gabriela smiled at her parents and said innocently, "Señor Madeira said that he can help me fly like the butterflies or like the eagles that carried the Israelites out of Egypt. I think we should go with him."

Before we left for the rainforest, María did as I instructed with the money. Rather than hoard it, she shared it generously among her neighbors, ensuring that another trusted woman in the community could watch over the many children who gathered in her apartment, at least until Eden came. She reassured everyone, promising them that they would return when the world was made whole again, when all would bask in the warmth of their newfound paradise. Some of the neighbors were horrified, whispering that María and Luis were falling prey to a twisted messiah's scheme. Others were simply sad to see their beloved Mamá María leave, tears in their eyes at the thought of losing her guidance, even if only temporarily. Yet there were those who were filled with hope that perhaps this prophecy of Eden might be true. Of course, many became wary of me. But the money, heaps more of it when I sensed their doubts deepening, won them over. They needed it to survive in a world that had become so merciless. I meticulously increased the amounts, calculating exactly how much would tip their scales from suspicion to acceptance. I watched the calculations in my mind and felt a queasy mixture of guilt and triumph.

I assured them all that leaving now was not only safe but

necessary. I could feel my voice trembling slightly as I played the role of divine herald. I told them that paradise awaited them not in some unknown era, but within days—just a brief journey away. My heart wrenched as I spoke these words, for I knew what would become of them. I struggled internally, but I could not betray Mendel's Vision. I felt anguish scrape at the walls of my conscience, yet I pressed on. My cunning demanded perfection, and so I perfected my lies.

Like Christ walking into the desert to prove he was the Messiah, I led the Rodriguez family into the dense and humid rainforest. We walked for two straight days at a slow pace, but not once did their devotion waver. With her parents so certain, Gabriela remained vibrant and happy throughout the entire journey. I carried a six-inch blade in my pocket, a habit from my past, but there was no need even for that. The Rodriguez family knew how to eat and drink the flora and fauna of the forest so that they could survive indefinitely, though eventually they would have to contend with the depletion of certain vitamins and minerals that they could only reliably obtain from the daily pills that the waste processing center provided each of its workers.

During the day we marveled at the diversity of life that persisted despite the intense storms that regularly ravaged Southern Mexico. At night, we rested and enjoyed the stars peeking through the canopy. I regaled them with some of my favorite constellations and their associated Greek myths. Gabriela was particularly captured by the constellation Lyra due to the story of the Lyre of Orpheus. She didn't care for the ending, but she loved the idea of a musical instrument played by a mortal that could command the Earth and even move the gods themselves. I didn't mind telling her the story over and over again, for it is also my favorite Greek myth. Maybe because I see myself as Orpheus. So does that make Gladys my Eurydice? Yet every time I repeated the story, my heart sank deeper. I was no hero like Orpheus. I was the orchestrator of their doom, too clever for my own soul to bear, and the intensity of that awareness gnawed at me.

As soon as we were far enough away from civilization, Mendel sent a fleet of autonomous dropships to retrieve us. By then I had already psychologically prepared them for the presence of the dropships without them even realizing it. On our journey, I had repeatedly referred in passing to Ezekiel's vision of the flying crafts, Elijah being taken up to Heaven, and Psalm 104 concerning God's chariot. At this point, the dropships were a clear sign from their God that they were on the right path, and that I truly was their messianic shepherd. To Gabriela, the dropships were her own personal eagles.

We flew directly to Genesis Lab. The Rodriguez family saw its name as another sign from God. The lab's towering edifice of glass and steel was built beside the thundering majesty of Niagara Falls. We were all tired from the journey, but as we approached the lab, the Rodriguez family carried an energy that reflected the very air around them, which was alive with the mist from the cascading water cloaking us in a veil of iridescent droplets. The ground beneath vibrated with the relentless power of the falls, which Luis believed to be the drumbeat of the Lord. I agreed, referring to Psalm 150 and explaining to him that the entire lab was, like the falls, a form of praise for the Lord.

"Why here?" María shouted over the roar.

"Because this is where heaven and earth converge," I replied. "Revelation 22:1 speaks of 'the river of the water of life, as clear as crystal, flowing from the throne of God.' Tonight, that river flows through us."

The family excitedly followed me into the labs, believing my words to be gospel. In truth, Mendel chose this location to ensure that the family's transformation could be fed with ample energy and water, for the Great Honey Mushroom requires both in staggering quantities.

We descended three hundred floors underground, and though I wanted to give them some more time together alone with a room to themselves, Mendel told me that there was no time for such trivialities. I don't question Mendel's Vision, so I brought the family directly to the central laboratory, which had been remodeled to look nearly identical to the church they had attended back in Cordoba.

"Form a circle around the altar. Hold one another's hands, then close your eyes," I instructed. "Open your hearts."

I began to recite Psalm 1:3: "The three of you, together, as a family are like a tree planted by streams of water, which yields its fruit in season and whose leaf does not wither."

I heard the distant click of panels opening in the walls; it was Mendel preparing to release the gas full of spores designed by Mendel and engineered by Tomasz and Ruben.

"Partake in this communion," I intoned from memory, "and you shall be the foundation upon which New Eden is built."

Luis and María sobbed with smiles so wide it was as if they were actually being shown the light of heaven. Gabriela opened her eyes for just a moment and smiled happily at seeing her parents so free of suffering.

"I love you, Señor Madeira," Gabriela said as she turned to me and stared into my soul. "I love you, Señor Madeira," Luis and María repeated in unison.

My heart twisted painfully at their trust and love. I fought back the tears burning at the edges of my vision, my anguish so intense that my breath caught in my throat. I wanted to scream that they deserved better than this. That they deserved truth, not my cunning deceit.

Do not break, Mendel lashed in my mind with unbecoming emotion, as if he thought it might be possible that I would discard my composure in that moment and lose my faith in him. But I did not break. I remained silent, my face a serene mask.

I smiled at them and assured them with my eyes that I loved them too. "Close your eyes and breathe deeply, my children," I told them. They drew closer to one another and began breathing liberally, with Gabriela making a game out of filling her lungs as deeply as she could.

I quoted Ezekiel 37: "Thus says the Lord God to these bones: Behold, I will cause breath to enter you, and you shall live." The machinery behind the walls began to whir, preparing the concoction that would begin their transformation and set the world upon a proper course of neoevolution.

"And I will lay sinews upon you, and will cause flesh to come upon you, and cover you with skin, and put breath in you," I said as yellow clouds of gas began spraying the air directly around the family. "And you shall live," I said as I backed out of the central laboratory and pressed the small button that sealed the room closed with a transparent but virtually unbreakable nanomaterial produced by Gladys. "And you shall know that I am the Lord," I finished just as the transformation began.

Roots began to sprout from their feet, intertwining with one another before burrowing deep beneath the labs. Their eyes were wide, not with fear or pain, but with wonder as they saw the future unfurl before them in their minds. "I feel...everything," María whispered. Gabriela giggled in excitement while Luis nodded repeatedly with feverish gratitude.

Their skin took on a luminescent hue, veins pulsing with bioluminescent energy as they painlessly morphed into chitinous textures. María's hair cascaded into tendrils of vines blooming with iridescent flowers that emitted a soft glow. Luis' torso expanded, becoming the sturdy trunk from which branches extended, rich with burgeoning flesh pods. Gabriela lifted her arms skyward, fingers elongating into delicate shoots.

Then, all at once, their individual structures melded into one as the burgeoning Great Honey Mushroom erupted from their unified forms, ceaselessly filling the room as it grew into a colossal organism fueled by the inexhaustible energy-filled waters of Niagara. Its mycelium spread rapidly, forming the first tendrils of the underground web that would eventually connect the continents and form a neural network for the planet itself. Eventually, the Earth will attain meta-awareness, and its consciousness will become intertwined with my own.

In the coming years, Genesis Lab will be consumed by the relentless growth of the Great Honey Mushroom. This growth will continue far into the future, until the turn of the century, when, according to Mendel, it will either be damaged, destroyed, or reborn. But before that, in just a couple years, on January 2, 2050, the first flesh pods will emerge from the flesh of the Great Honey Mushroom. The Nomads will begin transforming the Earth and humanity. Many, like Luis, María, and Gabriela, will willingly become Nomads. Just like with the Great Honey Mushroom, consent is the only way for the Nomad virus to properly take hold. Without consent, it is slavery, which is simply not conducive to a truly unified hive mind.

I used their Christianity to manipulate the Rodriguez family, just as I will use myriad other faiths to manipulate myriad other beings. But that doesn't change the fact that I am a shepherd, and humanity is my flock. If Mendel is God, then am I not his Messiah? Such a thought sickens me, though, for it is far too akin to the way the Titans view themselves.

Do not break, Mendel just reminded me as I write this entry into my diary that will one day be named his own. *But by then it won't matter*, Mendel just read through my eyes as I write these words. *You and I will be one.*

I am sorry for killing you, my friend, but I am not sorry for turning you into a god. The same is true of the Rodriguez family. I am sorry for ending their human lives, but I am not sorry for giving them divine purpose.

I am sorry, and I am not sorry.

No matter what, I will not break. For the sake of all others, I cannot break.

From Mendel's Ladder: The Personal Journal of Denis Mendel, Written Circa 2048, Published June 2108 by Leif Mainstone, Federated Agency Publishing

Chapter 2
The Great Honey Mushroom

C rippling pain coursed through Samuel's chest suddenly, forcing him to his knees just inside the entrance to the hidden passage to Downver. He looked down to see that despite using a pod only a few moments earlier, the green-glowing mushrooms were already failing as they were violently consumed like masticated fruit by the quickly expanding void-blackness. At the same time, the final pod secured to his hip by the strip of Fana's sari began to melt into a dim green sludge, which ran down his leg in a useless heap.

"Mr. Kaminski? What is it?" Leif asked from behind Samuel, offering concern as his floating body illuminated the cave's pitch-black interior.

Samuel wanted to respond to the radiant young man, but he was presently dumbfounded by the information unexpectedly streaming through his thoughts like a maddening strobe light. He couldn't explain his confidence, but somehow he knew beyond any doubt that Sandra and his children were in grave danger at that very moment.

You pathetic worker, Samuel told himself as he felt something snap inside of him. *You're failing them. You're still fucking failing them, goddamnit. All you do is fail.*

Samuel winced to bear the throbbing pain in his chest and stood, one leg at a time, as if the weight of the whole world were being pressed down upon him. He could feel the island he had built in his mind, each grain of sand a painful moment of exertion that had transformed him into the Workhorse of Astrea over the decades. The island of discipline and fortitude had always been unbreakable, but now more than ever he felt its foundations begin to crack and fissure, filled in by anger, self-loathing, desperation, and a wild, chaotic, unnamable fervor stemming from somewhere so deep in his mind that he couldn't begin to fathom it.

"The pods aren't working. My family is going to be consumed by those monsters you described, Leif. I can feel it. We're out of time," Samuel concluded gravely. "Maybe I can still just try jumping back to

Astrea. But if I get up there and the Queen and her monsters stand against me, I might very well be powerless against them. Even you, Leif, a man apparently made of light, can't get near them."

Of course, Leif could also be lying. It's probably just best to assume every single person is lying. Even my own wife, Samuel reminded himself grimly before snatching his mind back from the threat of reeling into total madness.

Leif lifted an eyebrow and said, "You hesitate." Then, with a tone of incredible intrigue, he raised his other eyebrow and asked, "What will you do, Mr. Kaminski? What will you do with your quickly dying mirror-body?"

"They don't have long," Samuel said, his voice tight and his hands trembling. "I can feel it. I just know it somehow. My family doesn't have long, and neither do I. They might only have minutes left. And again, the same goes for me. I wish this body could turn back time, but that's impossible. So instead, I'm going to have to speed things up. That's what I'll do with this goddamn dying mirror-body," Samuel roared as he breathed deeply through the mounting pain spreading through his body with even greater rapidity than the void-darkness, which had already reached his shoulders.

"So then, what will you do, Mr. Kaminski?" Leif repeated gently.

I have to launch to Downver, grab the girl, and then launch directly to Astrea. That's the only option I have left, Samuel thought, forcing himself again to accept that he must kidnap a child, only this time with the added urgency of the void-blackness spreading with newfound fervor.

"Point directly toward Downver," Samuel demanded.

Leif did as he asked, pointing at an angle toward the rocky ground.

Samuel nodded and took a deep breath.

"You say you are fast. Let's see how fast you really are. Try to keep up, Leif. Or don't. I can't trust you. I can't trust anyone," Samuel stated, reality itself his personal betrayer.

Samuel kicked at the ground in the direction of Leif's pointed finger, and in the space of a single heartbeat, Samuel's breath was stolen from his lungs as an avalanche of sound battered his ears and a smear of earthen hues flashed across his vision. Then, in another heartbeat, the onslaught on his senses was replaced by perfect silence and an all-pervading, star-illuminated darkness. Extreme vertigo overtook him as he reeled at the infinity of space laid bare before him without any solid surface to cling to.

Oh god! Oh god! Samuel tried to scream without effect. *I fucked up! Goddamnit! I launched myself across the galaxy, maybe across the universe. I—oh god, no!* Samuel reeled into the void.

"A great display, Mr. Kaminski," came Leif's pleasant, effortless voice. "That was certainly fast, almost as fast as me, but I do wish you would believe me when I say I have your best interest at heart, and your family's as well."

Samuel twisted around with some difficulty to find himself in free-fall above the Earth with Leif floating beside him, radiant as ever.

Again and again I find myself back in free-fall, naked and plummeting to hell, Samuel thought, feeling on the verge of insanity as he wrestled with his absolute impotence.

Samuel wanted to ask Leif what exactly happened to make him end up in space, but the vacuum demanded silence. Somehow, Leif was able to overcome this natural law, speaking and transmitting sound in a manner that apparently didn't require air.

"I don't know for sure how fast you just moved, but it was relativistic, that's for sure," Leif continued, easily keeping pace beside Samuel as he fell. "It's surprising that your body didn't cause more damage to the Earth. You bored right through it, right through the upper mantle, and then you curved back around and shot out of the Earth. But what's really surprising is that you basically just left a small hole in the surface. Look," Leif said, pointing directly below them to a small misshapen crater in the ground surrounded by flesh tree forests and a much larger, perfectly circular crater bare of any life.

Flesh tree forests, Samuel considered. *That means we're over a different part of the Earth. And now I'm falling back to the surface. Again. How many goddamn times am I going to be forced to replay this madness?*

Despite knowing the futility of attempting to travel to Astrea without a weapon to destroy the Queen, Samuel scanned the curve of the Earth, searching for his home. There was no sight of it, but that wasn't surprising given its miniscule size relative to the entirety of the planet.

No matter, Samuel resolved as he looked down at his chest and found that the blackness had expanded over his shoulders, eating them inch by inch, consuming him and replacing him with nothingness, like the void of space itself. *I'm going to fail. I already barely had enough time, and now the*

35

rules have changed for some reason, making the pods useless. If the rules to Mendel's goddamn Vision can just suddenly change, I definitely have no hope. I'll never see them again. I'm just a goddamn worker. I—

"I know you are worried about your family, Mr. Kaminski, but fear not: this really is just as His Foretold Future shows," Leif said calmly as he floated beside Samuel, his mind reeling and his body plummeting. "You see there right below us? That brown circle in the middle of all those flesh trees? You probably thought it was another crater. It's hard to tell from this angle, but that's the Great Honey Mushroom. That's where all the Nomads started, and that's where the Mirror-Man finally gains control of his body. I couldn't be sure that this was the pathway we're on, but it is. And I'm glad. This pathway of reality leads to many other pathways that are preferable, at least in my opinion."

As Samuel broke through the thin thermosphere, he captured his mind back from its spiraling and tried to recollect all of what Leif had just said.

"Great Honey Mushroom," Samuel repeated now with air to transmit sound. His mind felt slightly more grounded as he recollected Sunny Marigold and his conversation with Sandra and the others in Astrea. Images of Nathan and Margot flashed across his mind, and he winced with the agonizing need to hold them and make everything okay. "I've heard that name before. What is it?" Samuel said regarding the mushroom. "You say I'll be able to control my body after this? Are you sure it isn't too late?" Samuel shouted over the rushing wind. He wasn't sure Leif would be able to discern his words over so much noise, but Leif spoke to Samuel with ease, just like in space.

"You'll see, Mr. Kaminski. You'll see. Try to avoid hitting the Honey Mushroom, though. It is more than just sacred to the Nomads. It is their home. Their original home. To destroy it would be like destroying Astrea for you," Leif explained.

As he continued falling, Samuel realized that the honey-hued mushroom was truly as great as its name indicated, spanning many miles across in diameter, maybe even dozens of miles.

It's another planetary organ, Samuel realized. *It has to be. There's nothing else as far as the eye can see that's nearly as large as it. It's not as vast as the organ of Waru, but it's still as dense as a mountain. Maybe...maybe I should destroy it,* Samuel considered, questioning the motives of the Nomads like never before. He felt moronic for not being more skeptical of everyone he had ever known or might ever encounter from now on, no matter their shape or form. He felt the island in his mind fracture further, cleaving into wide areas, revealing a darkness as black as the abyss of space and as all-consuming as the blackness eating his body.

Samuel turned and looked at Leif. Despite Leif's cheerful smile and comforting aura, Samuel couldn't help seeing him in an all new light, like the shifting light of a glowglobe at twilight. *This Prodigal Son is using me. He's manipulating me,* Samuel concluded. *And so are the Nomads. So is everyone. Everyone's been using me my whole life. And now I'm caught in the fever dream of a madman,* Samuel reasoned as he observed the endlessly varied flesh trees invading the Earth's surface below the pulsating, glistening planetary mushroom towering over the world like Madeira, Mendel, and now the Mind looming over the remnants of humanity.

I should just slam right through the center of it. I should destroy their home. I should hurt the Nomads like Madeira hurt me. Like he hurt all of us. He stole our true home, the Earth, and then he created a new one, Astrea. And then he stole that one from us all over again. Leif says I should just wait and trust the process, but I can feel the truth laid bare before me: things are only going to get worse. There won't be a happy ending. So why should I let the Nomads have a happy ending? Why should their home stand proud while my home and my family are devoured by nightmare creatures?

Samuel directed his body toward the center of the Great Honey Mushroom. *I hope this hurts them. I hope they know suffering just like I have. Just like we all have,* Samuel seethed as his mind's inner island exhausted geysers of steam from the black crags and the sheer drops into darkness.

"Mr. Kaminski, you're aiming directly for the Great Honey Mushroom's center," Leif warned, sounding worried for the first time since Samuel met him.

"Go away, Prodigal Son! Get away from me, goddamnit!" Samuel screamed, and then he gritted his mirror-teeth.

"Mr. Kaminski, no!" Leif shrieked, but there was nothing Leif could do. The Seventh Prodigal Son of the Agency was fast and seemingly invulnerable to damage, but he was also intangible. Samuel took note of Leif's inability to interfere with his decision, knowing that the information might serve him in the future when he would be forced to destroy the young man.

Of course that's what it'll come to, because he's working against me. Everyone is working against me, Samuel knew, forcing himself to remove his own family and his neighbors and even Roland from that seemingly endless list of enemies. *Destroy! That's what I'll do with the useless time I have left with this dying mirror-body,* Samuel decided.

Like a meteorite jettisoned from deep space, Samuel slammed into the Great Honey Mushroom, cleaving it down the center of its bulbous head as he rocketed through its fleshy innards. His shockwave tore the entire organ asunder, ripping its flesh and insides into mountainous geysers of squelching viscera. As if being unzipped, the Great Honey Mushroom split into two hulking masses, each one dozens of times the size of Mount Mendel. As if screaming, the flesh of the mushroom emitted a terrible bellowing as it was further torn apart by its own hulking weight.

Samuel screamed wildly as he willed himself through the organ's dense and intricate insides. Every moment felt as though he were a cannonball perpetually breaking through miles of dense wet clay. After just a handful of seconds, he slammed face-first into solid rock, splintering it in the same fashion as his inner island. The landing caused Samuel no pain, but his body pulsated with terrible stabs emanating from his spine. He looked down to find that the majority of his torso was hollowed out with only his spine and a portion of his back remaining. A strip of gooey black connected what remained of his shoulders to his arms and yet untouched mirror-hands.

I'm about to lose my whole upper-body, Samuel gasped in horror. *This is it, then. This is the end,* he thought as he lifted his head to ascertain his surroundings before he disappeared completely. The two halves of the Great Honey Mushroom were still cracking and breaking apart, falling slowly like twin giants that had just been felled. Samuel considered that in a matter of seconds, they would hit the ground with the force of old world bombs, causing untold destruction for miles and miles. Samuel nearly laughed at the thought that he would be invulnerable to the coming earth-shaking cataclysm that he hadn't considered from the sky, and yet, he would still disappear all the same.

Nomads of every conceivable shape and hue filled every visible gap amidst the dense flesh trees of equally varied form and color. The Nomads and flesh trees were like living walls, piling all around Samuel, gawking at him with eye-like structures and other sensory organs. A tidal wave of sounds and scents merged into an overwhelming cacophony and olfactory assault as trillions of individuals crowded around the fabled Mirror-Man and watched His Foretold Future unfurl before them.

"Is this what you want?" Samuel screamed wildly, turning in all directions to address the writhing horde. As the Nomads pressed ever closer, Samuel's world constricted into a labyrinth of grotesque forms and pulsating colors. The air grew thick with spores and pheromones, each breath a struggle against the suffocating miasma of musk and moss. Tendrils dripping with viscous sap brushed against the mirror-skin of his legs, leaving trails of murky green. Whispers in alien tongues reverberated through the dense atmosphere, forming a dissonant chord that gnawed at the edges of his sanity. Mouths opened where none should be, exhaling breaths that shimmered with bioluminescent particles, adding to the disorienting glow.

"Your precious Mirror-Man is dying! Is this what you want?" Samuel rabidly barked at them, and then he heard something clang against the splintered rocky ground. He looked down to find his quickly decaying mirror-arms and hands on the ground beside him. He hadn't even felt them detach. His head was still attached to his lower body via his spine, but even that was being consumed by the blackness now.

Even Leif is gone. I've served my purpose. Now Madeira is getting rid of me. Everything was a lie. Everything was just manipulation. Everything and everyone, Samuel thought on the verge of tears as he attempted to think of Sandra and his children in these final moments of life. But all his mind could focus on was the horrendously happy and excited Nomads.

The ground beneath the Nomads squirmed with life, a carpet of creeping vines and fleshy protrusions that seemed to pulse in time with an unseen heartbeat. His footing uncertain without having arms to balance himself with, Samuel stumbled and recoiled as his feet sank into gelatinous surfaces or scraped against chitinous shells. The commotion escalated into a maddening blend of clicks, hisses, and guttural moans that vibrated through the remainder of his body. Scent glands released waves of odor—sweet, rancid, spicy, acrid—overwhelming his senses until nausea twisted his stomach into knots.

"Stay back!" he shouted, but his voice was swallowed by the overwhelming noise. Translucent membranes and feathery antennae brushed against his face, exploring, probing. His vision blurred as tears mingled with the oppressive humidity. In every direction, the bizarre forms pressed in: towering figures with limbs like branches; squat creatures oozing luminescent slime; ephemeral shapes that flickered in and out of existence. Samuel thrashed wildly, pushing against the unyielding mass, but it was like pushing at living mountains. The walls of living matter closed in, closer, ever closer, until he could feel the collective heat of their bodies, hear the wet sounds of their breathing, smell the intimate rot and bloom of their existence.

A sudden hush fell, the pandemonium dropping to a pregnant silence that was somehow more terrifying than the noise. The closest Nomads backed away, giving Samuel a few feet of space in all directions. It was only then that Samuel saw a ring of silver inlaid into the rocky ground. He had landed exactly in its center, as if the Nomads had known he would destroy their home all along.

"What was the point of all this? If I'm just going to disappear anyway. My family is going to die anyway, so what's the goddamn point of any of this?"

"What would you have us do, Mirror-Man?" a Nomad eerily similar to Sunny Marigold asked, her marigolds pitch black with streaks of deep violet rather than yellow. Her eyes were as black as the void-blackness consuming Samuel. He looked down to see that his detached arms were simply gone, turned to nothingness in the wake of Tomasz' weapon.

"There's barely anything left of me," Samuel murmured, his vision blurring in strobing horror. *I'm going to disappear. I'm going to lose them. They're going to be eaten by monsters. This is happening! This is really happening,* Samuel screamed within. His heartbeat fluttered faster than should be possible as Samuel entered a state of life and death panic, seeing now that the Mind really was going to let him die.

The Nomads just smiled and gawked at Samuel. They reminded him of his children visiting the base of Mount Mendel for the first time, and it horrified him even more that these creatures were innocent victims of Madeira's plans. He was observing a multitude of victims, but he still couldn't help feeling complete loathing for each and every one of them.

"Do something! Do something to help me and my family. You were humans once, weren't you? Or are you all just hundreds of generations removed from humanity at this point? Huh? Why the fuck won't you do anything to actually help me, goddamnit? What the fuck did me or my family ever do to you or your goddamn god Madeira? Just—" Samuel fumed, breathing heavily despite his body not needing to breathe.

"Just…give me pods that work," he said in defeat, his anger turning to remorse. "Help me. Stop my body from disappearing. Can you just fucking do that, goddamnit?"

The feminine Nomad nodded pleasantly and smiled with her eerily human features. Her teeth were twilight violet, and her bulging eyes and tongue were totally black. "That we can do," she said serenely, prompting an excited but hushed wave of responses from the Nomad horde.

The Nomads closest to the black marigold Nomad parted like blades of grass in a soft wind, creating even more space around Samuel. He looked down to see that his spine was nearly gone now, a mere thread connecting his head to his dissolving waist.

Soon my head will fall uselessly to the ground alongside my equally useless legs full of futile and pointless muscle. No matter what the Nomads come up with, it will still only stall the inevitable, Samuel gulped with only half a throat and no digestive tract as his family flashed across his mind over and over and over again.

What the hell happened to Leif? Samuel thought, realizing that the radiant man had abandoned him. *Of course he did. He is one of them, one of the manipulators of this world. And I'm just a disposable piece to be played. And so are they,* Samuel knew as he watched a retinue of six small, identical-looking Nomads part from the roiling swarm and walk toward the black marigold Nomad. These Nomads were covered in thick pitch-black hair all over their bodies, except for their emerald bellies. Their legs and feet appeared to be no more than balls of fur, and the same was true for their faces, which were either absent or hidden beneath the matted brown fur. As they approached, the Black Marigold Nomad kneeled to the ground, arched her back, and raised her head to the sky with an ecstatic smile painted across her face.

All Samuel could do was look on and watch in futile horror as these creatures exacted the incomprehensible will of Andre Madeira.

The furry Nomads encircled the Black Marigold Nomad and bowed their featureless heads to her as if in exultation. Then, each Nomad did the same, bowing in their own strange fashion to the Black Marigold Nomad.

It was only after the bowing of the entire horde that Samuel was able to view the no longer falling halves of the Great Honey Mushroom. To his surprise, flesh trees had grown and were still growing to catch and subsequently support the unimaginable weight of the mushroom's body. Not only did the Great Honey Mushroom not slam into the Earth and create a continental cataclysm as Samuel had predicted, but each half appeared to be healing its severed flesh, forming mile long seams of fresh chitin.

Now there are two mushrooms. I didn't destroy it. I made it stronger. This was all planned. Every fucking thing is Madeira's plan. He must have even known that I would decide to try to hurt the Nomads by destroying their home. And he knew that this is where I would die. Goddamn you, Madeira. Damn you to hell!

The furry Nomads bristled their fur, making a maraca-like shaking noise.

"Now I transition," the Black Marigold Nomad shrieked as if it were a joyous battle cry.

All at once, a black spike jutted from the head of each furry Nomad and pierced through the Black Marigold Nomad's soft torso, intersecting through her ribcage.

"Yes!" she cried, as if her body coursed with pleasure despite deep violet blood flowing from her six horrific wounds. The furry Nomads bled glowing green blood from the spikes in their heads. As they slumped and died, green bioluminescent mushrooms began growing from their backs with sickening rapidity, twirling and stretching in the air.

The Black Marigold Nomad tried to speak, but blood spurted from her lips instead. She slumped like the furry Nomads, and as she died, her black marigolds twirled and grew with the same rapidity as the still-growing mushrooms.

They're too late, Samuel winced just as his spine disappeared completely and his head slammed against the rocky ground, forcing him to use his mouth and nose to keep himself from rolling into his detached lower body. *I'm a fucking head,* Samuel's mind raced in abject terror. *A fucking head!* He imagined an even worse fate befalling his children, and though a part of him ached to cry and lose himself in all-encompassing sorrow, he remembered that his mirror-eyes could not produce mirror-tears.

I'm a horror. And this place is a horror. Everything is hell. I'm sorry, Sandra. I'm sorry, Margot. I'm sorry, Nathan. I don't deserve any of you. I'm just a goddamn worker, and that's exactly how I'll die. A useless damn worker laboring in hell.

A great black stalk of twisted marigolds jutted from the Nomad's dead body, growing into the rocky ground as if it were no more than piled dust. The glowing mushrooms fused together and continued growing, forming thick single mushrooms from the corpse of each furry Nomad. Snaking roots extended through the ground from the dense marigold stalk to the now towering glowing mushrooms. As the roots made contact, the mushrooms dimmed identically to the way they had dimmed in Samuel's chest as they attempted and failed to resist the void-blackness. Finally, the mushrooms began to bubble, just like Samuel's chest—when he still had a chest—and then their glow was no more. They became desiccated black husks encircling the now throbbing stalk of entangled and knotted pitch-black marigolds.

Without any remaining body parts other than his head, Samuel couldn't tell how much of his neck or even jaw was left. His legs were only a few inches away, and he could see that his waist and manhood were no more.

Fuck you, Madeira, Samuel seethed, wishing more than anything that he would have tried jumping to Astrea, even if it hadn't worked. At least he would have tried. *And potentially killed everyone in Astrea in the process,* a part of Samuel's mind reminded him, but there was no use revisiting that line of thinking. This was the end, that much was clear. *Fana said I would get to Downver. Inflated Sapien said the same thing. They were wrong. Or they were lying. But it doesn't matter. Nothing matters anymore. This is really it. Death has come for me. No, not death. Something worse than death. Erasure. The very destruction of my soul. I hope you were wrong, Mom, about souls. For if it's true that souls are real, then that must be what is happening to me. Madeira is consuming my very soul.*

A gunshot-like crack broke the horde's silence, returning the millions of Nomads back to a cacophony of multi-sensory hushed whispers.

The black marigold stalk began to crack and cleave just like the Great Honey Mushroom had. Falling to the ground in ten-foot pieces, the hollow husk revealed nine fist-sized spheres stacked vertically atop one another. The identical spheres were pitch-black with brush strokes of pulsing bioluminescent green and violet spread across their surface.

In his final moments of life, Samuel's mind splintered into a thousand quivering fragments. *Did the Nomads always know this would happen?* A part of his mind grasped at the hope that Leif might return any second and help him somehow. *Please, Leif! Somebody!* Someone shrieked inside his head, a child's voice. His voice. No, someone else's—he couldn't tell anymore. A single detached fragment of his mind watched everything with stoic acceptance while the rest of him burned with white-hot rage at Old Man Madeira. *He has to pay. He still has to pay! For Sandra. For my children!* Samuel begged for their forgiveness. He was sorry. So very sorry. Everything rattled. Every corner of his mind screamed and fractured and stuttered.

Samuel willed his mind to provide him one final sweetness, and he imagined Sandra in their living room, working with amino herb fibers to mend the family's clothes as she cracked jokes about this or that neighbor. Nathan sat with his tablet and played the wall-game that the children loved while Margot sat over his shoulder and helped him direct his pieces into more strategic positioning. *You will never feel that again,* Samuel knew, torturing himself, just as he knew he deserved.

A loud groaning like distant thunder directed Samuel's eyes to the half of the Great Honey Mushroom he could currently see. It grew with insatiable speed, breaking through a large white cloud and continuing upward through the atmosphere.

As if in response, the tower of nine spheres collapsed to the ground. The spheres appeared to spill into random directions at first, but then Samuel saw that they were in fact moving with purpose. Four of the spheres were rolling toward him, while the other five rolled in the opposite direction and disappeared into the technicolor horde.

Out of the corner of his eye, Samuel saw movement in the sky. It was Astrea passing overhead.

I'm going to disappear just as my family passes over me. I'm going to be erased now that they're closer than ever. Why? Samuel begged the world and Madeira. *Why are you doing this to me? Why?*

Something jerked Samuel's head, shifting his vision away from Astrea. He thought he could feel his body, but he knew it had to be some kind of phantom sensation—an illusion of the mind to placate his panic in his final moments. However, the feeling didn't abate, and Samuel found that he could now tilt his head and even lift himself using actual arms.

I…have a body? Samuel gawked at the wily vines which had emerged from each small sphere to form a torso, arms, and a neck connecting his mirror-head and mirror-feet. The green, violet, and pitch-black vines tightened around one another like boas preparing their prey, constricting and knotting themselves into a dense, living, flesh-like material mimicking Samuel's previous hulking form full of rippling musculature. Even his genitals were roughly replicated by the squirming vines.

Samuel could barely believe that he could control the arms and every one of his muscles as if they were truly his own. His heart raced with newfound purpose, for this was not the end after all. Not yet. He could still save them. There was still a glimmer of hope in the expanding darkness.

"Did you stop it?" Samuel gasped, using his newly built vine-larynx to speak through his mirror-mouth. To his surprise, he still sounded like his old self. "Did you stop Tomasz' weapon from consuming me?"

We did, came the Black Marigold Nomad's pleasant voice from within Samuel's mind, only now her voice echoed through a multitude of other octaves. *We have slowed it long enough for you to reach the Virus, and no longer, Mirror-Man. After that, time won't matter.*

Now you're in my mind, goddamnit? Samuel accused.

But the path has changed, the voice continued, ignoring Samuel's accusation. *The Virus changed reality. There was always a possibility her powers would awaken this early, no matter how unlikely. She may change reality again before we reach her. Fate is still in the process of shattering. So we must hurry. Every being in the universe is hurrying to ascend their own ladder, so we must do the same. We must finish building Mendel's Ladder before the very foundations of this universe collapse.*

"What the hell are you talking about?" Samuel asked aloud, but the throng of Nomads just went on staring at him, acting as though he hadn't just spoken.

She doesn't sound like a Nomad, Samuel considered suspiciously. *She sounds like Tomasz or Fana, cunning and knowledgeable of far more than she's letting on.*

I am nothing like Tomasz or Fana, the voice said with a subtle, uncharacteristic edge.

You can read my thoughts? Samuel asked cautiously.

I'm not a Nomad. Not exactly, she explained.

I don't care, Samuel growled within his mind, cutting off such trivialities. *Can you control my mirror-body? Can you take me to Astrea?*

Not with Harald Mainstone scanning the skies. And not without the Virus, either. She is essential to my plans.

Your plans, Samuel repeated, certain now that this being composing the majority of his body and seeping into his mind was somehow related to the old world Titans in some way. *Who are you, really?*

I have no name, but if I were to choose one, it would be Aisthanomeno Ouranio Soma.

Aisth…orasama…whatever, Samuel lashed. *Are you going to help me? Or are you going to just be another obstacle in my way?*

You can call me Soma. And I will not be your obstacle. We are going to Downver now. Right now. We must reach the Virus before any of the others. Enduring Ironwood knows this. She will do her utmost to keep the Virus secure. Hopefully the Cure can keep herself alive, but we have contingencies now if her death becomes inevitable. All that matters is that we reach the Virus.

"Wrong!" Samuel screamed, but again, the Nomads just stared at him without any reaction. "All that matters is that we save my family from the Queen and her monsters. Is that clear?"

It is, Mirror-Man. But reaching the Virus is your only hope of saving your family. Our needs align. The Great Honey Mushroom has been split, and the Twin Honey Mushrooms have been born. This is a viable and worthwhile reality pathway, no matter how precarious. We are still climbing Mendel's Ladder, despite teetering just on the edge of falling off.

Fine, Samuel relented. *Can you help me use what's left of my body, then? Can you control it since I can't?*

I can, Soma confirmed. *I cannot use your body to its full potential like you can, but I can tap into it and control it to some degree. That I can do, Mirror-Man.*

Then do it. Take over my body and bring me to the Virus. No more detours. No more Foretold Future, goddamnit.

Leif appeared in front of Samuel suddenly and looked him over in disbelief. "You're…different. Is…this what's supposed to happen? I don't think it is," he said with a confused cock of his head.

The Seventh Prodigal Son of the Agency. Like the Ninth, Sixth, and Third Prodigal Son, he no longer serves his mother. However, unlike the others, he is our ally. Soma stated as if reading the information from an encyclopedia.

Our ally? Samuel repeated skeptically. *You and I are not allies, Soma. I don't even know who you really are. All I know is that you have a strange name, you hatched out of a bunch of dead Nomads, and you speak like my enemies,* Samuel countered. *Besides, why are you only showing up now? Why didn't you show up back on the beach in Waru? Why now, goddamnit?*

"I apologize for being forced to leave you, Mr. Kaminski," Leif said with a bow. "I didn't expect things to change so much, but Aurelia and Aliana were in danger, and I had to do something to help them. I wasn't able to do much, but it was something. You have to hurry, Mr. Kaminski. Downver is in complete disarray. Nichole, the Lord of Limbs, is fighting with my brother Julian and his servant, Cid the Knower. The damage is already extensive. Normally I can move fast enough to appear in multiple places from your perspective, but helping them required a great deal of concentration."

"You did well, Seventh Prodigal Son. I am grateful for your service. All of us are," Soma stated using Samuel's mouth and voice.

What the fuck! Samuel spat in his mind.

"Don't ever do that again!" Samuel screamed aloud, causing Leif to back away a few inches in confusion.

"I'm sorry—" Leif began, but Samuel interrupted him.

"Not you," Samuel stated. "Soma. She's in my head. She just spoke through my mouth. Don't do that, goddamnit!"

You make demands of me, Mirror-Man, which is only fair after the demands that I have made of you. I will refrain from speaking through your mouth, Soma stated measuredly.

Samuel shook his head at the endlessly mounting absurdity of his life. "Let's just go. Let's just fucking go, goddamnit."

Leif still looked concerned, but he nodded to Samuel, acquiescing silently to his demand despite looking as though he wanted to probe Samuel for more information.

Samuel felt as though he were being moved by unseen puppet strings as Soma pivoted his body thirty degrees to his left. Somehow, she knew the exact direction of Downver.

"Wait," Samuel said before Soma could lunge his body forward. He felt transfixed as he looked about the writhing horde of Nomads and flesh trees full of seemingly endless flesh pods brimming with countless generations of future Nomads. "The Nomads are supposed to obey the Mirror-Man, right? Well, I have a command for all of you, then. You are now my army, and I am your general. Don't just sit here like idiots as you play directly into Madeira's plans. Go to Downver. I don't care how and I don't care how long it takes. Follow me wherever I go, all the millions and millions of you. Every single one of you. Tell all the Nomads of the world to march and fly and crawl to Downver if they have to. The Mirror-Man commands it!"

A palpable shift coursed through the horde. An eerie silence enveloped the landscape as millions of Nomads paused, their myriad eyes and sensory organs fixed upon him. The air grew thick with an unsettling energy, as if the very atmosphere recoiled at the unnatural stillness. Millions of eyes, some glowing, some multitudinous and flowing, turned toward him in unison, their collective gaze piercing through to his absent core.

They seem different, Samuel noted nervously. A chill crawled down his spine as the Nomads began to move, not with the chaotic diversity he'd seen before, but with a disturbing synchronicity that felt inherently wrong. The flesh trees groaned and twisted, releasing swarms of newly birthed Nomads that slid from their pods with grotesque fluidity. They joined the mass without hesitation, their forms slick with viscous fluids that steamed in the cool air.

Then, as if a great engine had been ignited, the entire mass exploded into motion. Samuel watched in awe, seemingly along with Soma, as great winged Nomads unfurled diverse appendages from the canopy of flesh trees overhead. Jellyfish-like Nomads floated upward, their translucent bodies pulsing with bioluminescent light, casting an ethereal glow over the swarming masses below.

Samuel turned in horror to see towering monstrosities made of hundreds of Nomads melded together. They lurched forward, each step a thunderous impact that rattled his mirror-teeth. Vines and tendrils sprouted from their amalgamated flesh, writhing and grasping at the air as if searching for something, or someone, to ensnare. Other colossal Nomads with legs like tree trunks thundered forward, each footfall sending tremors through the earth.

Were they always capable of merging together into abominations like this? Samuel wondered.

Smaller, agile beings scuttled between their legs, some on multiple-jointed limbs, others rolling like living wheels composed of interlocking bones and tendons. There were creatures that moved by flowing, their bodies liquefying and streaming across the terrain before solidifying again. Others traversed the landscape by leaping vast distances, spring-loaded muscles launching them into arcs dozens of feet in the air. Samuel gawked in petrified awe as a pack of dinosaur-like towering quadrupeds carried clusters of smaller Nomads nestled within cavities along their spines. Some Nomads morphed their bodies to form bridges over chasms, allowing others to pass over them in a seamless flow.

Swarms of insectoid Nomads took to the air in clouds so dense they momentarily eclipsed the light, their wings producing a collective hum that resonated like a haunting melody. Others harnessed the magnetic fields of the planet, levitating effortlessly above the ground, their bodies crackling with arcs of bioelectricity.

Samuel's makeshift heart pounded in his chest, a frantic drumbeat against the suffocating dread that enveloped him. He had become the unwilling conductor of a nightmare procession.

"Wait!" he cried out, regretting his previous command. The Nomads couldn't hear him over the bellowing movement of so many bodies, and he was about to scream out again when another part of his mind quieted him.

Just use them, Samuel told himself. *Just like Tomasz was using them, I need to use them as a tool. I have no choice. This world...this reality...strips us all of choice.*

Soma stirred within him, a surge of exhilaration bubbling into Samuel's intact but quickly crumbling mind.

This is the path we've chosen, she whispered, her voice tinged with satisfaction and triumph. But Samuel knew he hadn't chosen any of this. Not really. He was still just a servant, and Soma was his new master, no matter how she might protest.

Samuel felt his feet dig into the rocky ground, and then he was launched into the air, carried along the same trajectory as the monstrous legion of Nomads.

I will find a way to destroy you too, Soma. Once we reach the Virus, I will find a way.

Maybe you will, Soma agreed pleasantly as Samuel landed many miles ahead of the Nomads then launched again, leaping back to Downver in multiple mile-long strides. Leif followed alongside Samuel, looking even more concerned but still remaining silent.

Samuel peered over his shoulder and saw that the ground was a churning sea of distorted forms and abhorrent movements—torsos twisting 360 degrees, limbs bending at impossible angles, mouths opening far wider than any should be able to.

The oppressive feeling of being trapped tightened around him as a terrible thought struck through him: what if the Nomads and Soma were not his army? What if they were his captors, and he was being swept along in their inexorable tide toward Downver?

I have no choice, Samuel lamented as Soma used his limbs as her own.

Transhumanism: the pursuit to transcend the limitations of our flesh and psyche, to rewrite the code of our very being. Denis and I discussed the topic at great length last night in our dormitory. Well, discussion isn't really the right word. Mostly it was a lecture, but I was happy to be Denis' student. He may be my enemy, but he is also brilliant beyond any human being who has ever lived. And more than that, he is quickly becoming my actual friend—the first since Norman.

This is what Denis told me, not verbatim, but to the best my memory can serve me:

"We stand at the precipice of a new epoch, one where we can alter our biology, reconfigure our psychology, and challenge the ontologies that have anchored us for millennia. Many fixate on the question: At what point do we cease to be human? An intriguing inquiry, perhaps, but it pales in comparison to a far more profound conundrum.

The real question is when will we ever truly gain control of ourselves? When do we cease to be mere marionettes, our strings pulled by genetic predispositions, psychological conditioning, digital algorithms, economic imperatives, even physical laws? Is it even possible to decide reality for ourselves, unshackled from the invisible chains that bind us? Or are we forever destined to be slaves to something, a ceaseless hierarchy of command stretching from the infinitesimal quark to the sprawling cosmos, puppet strings all the way down?

Our genes dictate more than eye color or height; they influence our behaviors, our susceptibilities, our very desires. We pride ourselves on free will, yet how much of our decisions are pre-programmed responses encoded in our DNA? We modify genes to eradicate diseases, enhance abilities, even extend life. But in manipulating our genetic makeup, are we not simply swapping one form of programming for another? The strings remain; they've merely been reattached.

Psychologically, we're shaped by experiences, traumas, and societal norms. We can delve into the mind, rewire neural pathways, confront subconscious biases. Yet, these efforts often lead us down paths predetermined by the very frameworks we're trying to escape. Are we not still dancing to a tune composed by influences beyond our control?

The digital realm offers no sanctuary. Algorithms curate our realities, dictate our choices, manipulate our perceptions. Every click, every search, feeds into a system designed to predict and influence behavior for purposes often unbeknownst to us, often directed by the AI that I myself created.

Will we be perpetually caught in a web spun by forces beyond our grasp? Perhaps control, as we conceive it, is unattainable, for if every thought, every impulse, is the result of an endless chain of causality, where does that leave free will?"

Denis' words continue to echo through my mind—in my waking life and in my dreams. As the path of life forks, do we choose the direction, or is the universe merely forcing us along a predetermined path?

Are we free, or are we just dancers of a choreographed reality?

From Mendel's Ladder: The Personal Journal of Denis Mendel, Written Circa 2019, Published June 2108 by Leif Mainstone, Federated Agency Publishing

❦❧ Chapter 3 ❧❦
To Coax One's Prey

A liana could barely believe what she was hearing.

Is Nichole really not going to help us? Aliana considered as she watched Rooli emerge from the lake with Aurelia unconscious and draped in her six arms, one of which was presently detaching and hanging by a strip of woody flesh. Every inch of Aurelia's alabaster skin had been replaced by the glistening black that had once been contained to her face. Even her platinum hair had turned black at the roots, with the color presently spreading through the tendrilling strands like creeping shadows overtaking the last of her light.

Aurelia... Aliana gasped. Her sister didn't appear to be breathing, but Aliana took comfort in Rooli's stoic demeanor. Although Rooli was a Nomad, Aliana imagined Aurelia's death would cause Rooli to rage and rampage with an animosity rivaling that of a Wintersvilla Warrior in Overdrive.

Nichole stared at Aliana as if sizing her up for conscription. Aliana wondered, *Is she just being a clever Wintersvilla Woman and playing with Cid's mind by pretending she won't help us? Maybe she is on our side and is just playing the villain right now. That's possible, but it's equally and probably more likely that she is our enemy. There's no telling how this place has changed her over the years.* It was only then that Aliana realized Nichole had no ports. She was certain she remembered the historical images showing Nichole with the same ports embedded into her flesh as any other official Wintersvilla Warrior, yet her skin appeared as uninterrupted and flawless as oiled metal. She even had tattoos covering her bare arms, green and red abstract shapes and swirls that continued beneath her tight clothing. *She is still fierce, but like she said, she is no longer a Wintersvilla Warrior, that much is clear,* Aliana concluded as her battle-ready instincts prepared her for more violence. It had been rare for even a week to pass in Wintersvilla without someone referencing Nichole's great betrayal, so Aliana felt especially ready to engage in battle with the traitorous Serenading Slayer if she was left with no other choice.

"Lord," Cid the Knower emitted in a sheepish tone as he continued bowing to the Lord of Limbs, "I have committed an act of violence outside the walls of my district. The law, your law, states that a council meeting of all seven districts must be called. I must answer for my crimes, lest we return to the uncivilized days of revolution. Isn't that right, Lord?"

Nichole did not hide her laughter. "You really think I'm that much of a fool, Julian Mainstone, Third Prodigal Son of the Agency?"

Cid froze and shrunk his normally proud shoulders like a snuffed flame.

"You…you…" Cid stammered stupidly, his all-knowing plans apparently further crumbling before him.

"Yes, I know who you really are, and I know that Cid is your willing subordinate," Nichole stated tiredly like iron turned cold in a long dead forge.

The Agency, Aliana repeated to herself as she recollected what Gambe Mainstone had said about his mother Gladys Mainstone, one of the old world powers, whom he claimed had turned herself into the Agency and created the Prodigal Sons. *The Agency is also the one that programmed Shira and the rest of Wintersvilla Warriors to die when they get old enough. But Nichole isn't dead, and she's at least five years older than Shira,* Aliana thought, her mind racing with so much information and madness over the course of what she estimated to be no more than a full day since the battle with the Butcher.

Cid and Armando stood alone with all of the other goons dead at their feet, their bodies exploded by Rooli's rampage. Whale-sized strips of Rooli's body littered the lake and the surrounding ground, creating dark hills of varied topography where the environment had previously been largely flat. Cid breathed uneasily just a few feet from a large chunk of Rooli and looked as though he might use it to hide himself before running for his life.

He is weak in the presence of Nichole, Aliana practically salivated, seeing her chance to slay the vile man once and for all. Aliana still held the snake-woman's slender blade, and though she wished to feel the familiar grip of her own sword forged from Wintersvilla steel, the balance and weight of this inferior blade told her that it would serve her just fine as a tool of execution.

"Well?" Nichole challenged as she continued her death-stare at the

First Lord of the Walled City. "Are we going to keep playing pretend, or are you going to reveal yourself, Julian?"

She's trying to bait him into the open, Aliana knew as if reading directly from a Wintersvilla Warrior book of stratagems. *To coax one's prey onto an open battlefield is one of the first lessons that all young warriors learn. So, then, maybe she is still a Wintersvilla Warrior despite everything,* Aliana hoped.

"I'm impressed you even know my name," Cid practically sang, his demeanor changing from one of total dread to something utterly absent of fear. "My true name. Not the false name my mother gave me—Erik. A fool's name. A name made famous by a mindless conqueror from humanity's worthless past. A conqueror like my mother and you, wench," Cid stated with vehement revulsion as he lifted his head and looked at Nichole through his pitch-black lenses. "Do you know why I named myself Julian?" Julian asked through Cid, and Aliana nearly laughed at the triviality of his question, especially at the precipice of what was sure to be another battle.

Aliana observed that Rooli's mostly severed arm had finally slewed off along with several others, leaving her with only her preferred two. *I need to make sure that Rooli and Aurelia can get out of here. Aurelia doesn't need me. She has Enduring Ironwood. The best thing I can do for both of them is kill Cid, and if I can't do that, then I can at least create a distraction long enough for them to retreat to…well…I don't know. But I'm sure Rooli does. Aurelia doesn't need me, at least, not at her side. That's Rooli's job. I will do what I do best, sister. I will battle, like mom and Myriam. I will battle everyone in this Muto shit city to death, no matter how long it takes. Time is no longer an obstacle for me,* Aliana thought with incredible confidence and newfound control over her mind and emotions. It didn't matter that her previous attack against Cid had failed. That was the past, and the past is something to be learned from and built upon. *I will not fail this time. Now!* Aliana told herself, but just as she was about to slow time and launch herself in Cid's direction, she noticed Rooli out of the corner of her eye. She was at least forty feet behind Cid and sixty feet away from Aliana, but the movement of her twig-fingers was unmistakable.

"Remain where you are, Cure," Rooli signed, referring to Aliana as her designation rather than her name for the first time in many years. Rooli had never been warm or cheerful, but Aliana paused, wondering why the Hybrid Nomad, who had always been more like a mother than a mere caretaker, appeared suddenly so callous.

"Yes," Nichole answered Julian. "You named yourself after Andre Madeira's father. Because you are obsessed with Andre Madeira, so much so that out of respect you chose his father's name rather than his name. You see Madeira as something sacred. You see him as a god. Isn't that right?"

Julian cocked Cid's head and smiled in disbelief. "So, then, have you been working for my mother all these years, or do you serve her? Are you in her employ, or are you her slave?"

A pang of shock ran through Aliana as she considered that the most powerful woman in Downver might just be the whim of a far more powerful force.

"Irrelevant," Nichole responded measuredly. "Neither of us foresaw that the Nomad would live, nor that the Virus would be able to use her powers in such a profound manner already. We both know that this means we are at a stalemate, Julian. At least for now. So, why not reveal yourself? Why keep using this puppet to speak?" Nichole asked, pointing to Cid with disgust.

"I've seen him," Aliana said, prompting Cid and Nichole to face her. "The pale boy with gray hair and gray eyes. He's Julian. Cid admitted it earlier. Julian is a little boy."

Cid laughed pompously and preened his hair in his normal self-satisfied manner. Aliana couldn't be sure if those gestures had always belonged to Julian, and she found herself wondering if she had been interacting with the Third Prodigal Son this entire time.

"I am far more than any of you could ever comprehend. I am the next rung of Mendel's Ladder. The gray boy was merely my first subject, a street urchin who would have died anyway. I took control of him when I first entered this loathsome and pathetic pit of humanity. But I am far, far more than that, while you are just a wench," Cid laughed at Nichole, then he turned to Aliana. "I choose my form, but you and your sister are still just little girls. For now. Before this day is over, both of you will be mine. My tools of Ascension. I have seen it. Downver is mine. This world is mine. The whole universe and the Great Beyond are mine! Mine and mine alone!" Julian shrieked through Cid's lips, his voice sounding deeper and full of phlegm suddenly. "Now, die, wench!" he screamed with a wildness that Aliana did not realize he was capable of.

Like a reflex, Aliana instinctively slowed time, and the deep gong sound resonated through her mind, enabling her to observe her surroundings with profound clarity. Despite everyone and everything around her moving at a fraction of their normal speed, there was still rapid movement in the environment. A shimmering of lights danced ominously all around Aliana, appearing then disappearing like nascent fireflies.

What is this? Aliana wondered, her mind racing futilely to comprehend what she was seeing as she stared transfixed by the countless glimmers in the air, on walls, and all across the ground.

The specters of Shira and Myriam appeared in the distance opposite Rooli and Aurelia, but they didn't offer any guidance or assurance. They just stared at Aliana, observing her with calm acceptance painted across their stoic features. Aliana wanted to ask them what was happening, but she was forced to prepare her body for some new surprise as the shimmering lights began to move with distinct trajectories.

Is Cid controlling these lights? Aliana considered, unsure how to battle against photons. *No,* she realized as she noticed subtle movements rippling through Nichole's visible musculature. Her flesh looked like it had a life of its own, and it reminded Aliana of a skinsuit, except the movement was occurring subdermally.

It's her, Aliana realized. *She's controlling these lights that are moving despite everything else, including myself, being all but frozen in time. But what are they? And how is she controlling them so quickly? Is she like me? Can she think at a normal pace even when time is slowed down?*

Aliana couldn't keep up with her own questions, but it made no difference, for the lights began to move with even greater speed, accelerating through slowed time so fast that they appeared like birds of prey as they swooped and flew about one another. Some even began merging into growing strands of shimmering light. Then, a great deal happened in the same moment: Cid's lethal lenses, presently pointed at Nichole, began their familiar transition from black to red; Rooli launched herself back in the direction of the Walled City by filling her legs with compressed air and then directing the air through gaps in her feet to propel herself off the ground; Armando dove at Aliana, using his machine legs to kick off the ground in a similar fashion to Rooli, with both of them leaving behind a shallow crater; all the while, Nichole stood frozen, her arms outstretched as the undulating movement beneath her skin rapidly increased in activity, becoming violent tremors.

Aurelia! Aliana pleaded, unable to disobey Rooli's command but still wanting to ensure her sister's safety as she focused on Rooli's angled ascent. Aurelia was still unconscious in Rooli's arms, and though Aliana fully trusted Rooli, she couldn't help feeling unnerved by the coldness of her previous command to remain still. Aliana noticed that the glistening black covering every bit of Aurelia was now seeping into Rooli's body, coiling through her woody flesh in the same manner that it had once tendrilled through the skin of Aurelia's face.

The blackness spread to Rooli, Aliana gasped, unsure what it might mean for Rooli or her sister. *Whatever it means, I have to act now!*

Aliana gritted her teeth and prepared to charge at Cid, but before she could adjust her body for an attack, one of the strands of blinding light flicked toward her a full order of magnitude faster than Armando. Behind the light's glimmering corona, all four of Nichole's limbs were undulating and expanding in volume so fast that Aliana couldn't help wondering if she had suddenly lost her control of time.

No, time is still just as slow, Aliana realized. *Whatever's happening to Nichole is just somehow that much faster than the rest of us. Even Cid,* Aliana observed. His lenses were still in the process of transitioning.

As Nichole's slender arms and legs expanded in volume, her tattoos and skin were stretched into indiscernible smears until they finally tore, exploding away from her body to reveal a gleaming silver endoskeleton, along with Nichole's true form.

The Lord of Limbs, Aliana gasped at what she saw. Countless spigots, each surrounded by thousands of spinnerets, were embedded into every inch of Nichole's metal arms and legs. The spinnerets worked together to weave sparkling strands of material as it was released from each spigot. It was only then that Aliana realized that the dancing lights covering all of Downver were in fact the same gleaming gossamer threads presently being released from Nichole's body.

It's everywhere! Her…webs…are everywhere. We just couldn't see them in normal time. But with time slowed down, I can see the scant light reflecting off of them. She's like a spider, and all of Downver is her nest, Aliana observed in both awe and wonder at this Wintersvilla Warrior who had turned herself into some kind of cybernetic arachnid, with each spinneret serving as one of countless limbs.

The Lord of Limbs, Aliana repeated to herself in understanding just as the thick glimmering strand slammed into her belly with a distant stab of pain, slow-launching her backward.

Fatherfucking Muto fuck! Aliana fumed as she was swatted away from the battlefield by Nichole. *It barely hurt when the string hit me, so is she trying to help me, or did she just doom me to splatter against a wall or building behind me?* Aliana wondered as her mind raced and air gradually released from her lungs.

Aurelia! Aliana wanted to shout as Rooli and her sister continued launching in the opposite direction toward the Walled City. *What use is this power!* Aliana cursed before glancing at Shira and Myriam, who were still standing on the ground, strands of light passing through them as they observed Aliana with calm acceptance. Their countenances reminded Aliana to be her mind's master, and she managed to bring herself back to a state of calm.

Even slower! Aliana demanded, forcing time from a slow crawl to glacial, near-stillness. *Both of my powers seem useless on the surface when it comes down to it,* Aliana lamented for not the first time, but now she aimed to see them in a positive light. *I can't slow down a person's individual sense of time, just my own. Maybe my power has nothing to do with time, and my brain is just operating fast—faster than all those around me,* Aliana considered. *Either way, it's still useful. It gives me time to plan complex attacks, and it also allows me to position my body perfectly when I execute those attacks. And my other power...my power to see those I love. Well, they've already proven their worth. They saved me in the cave, and they strengthened me in my attack on Cid. Yes,* Aliana confirmed to herself, *these powers can be worthwhile if I use them right, like any tool of battle.* Aliana glanced at Shira and Myriam, who continued to observe her with approval.

Now, Aliana thought as she hung suspended in the air, moving backward at a barely perceptible speed, *I need to observe my battlefield, and I need to find a way to meet up with Rooli and Aurelia. But for now, it's good that we're separating. I can act as a decoy and give Aurelia a chance to get away from Cid and Julian, just in case Nichole isn't able to destroy them. Cid was clearly obsessed with Aurelia. She's the real prize. Her powers are far greater than mine, and that's fine with me,* Aliana forced herself to accept. Though, of course, her lifelong jealousy over her sister's superior intelligence, strategic thinking, and stoicism still lingered deep inside her despite everything that had occurred. With a forceful shove, Aliana removed the childish jealousy from the forefront of her mind and placed it back into the deeply buried recesses where it belonged. Then, she observed the battlefield and attempted to formulate a viable battle plan.

Despite everyone else being nearly frozen in place, Nichole's endless filaments and numerous thick strands still danced and shimmered. Aliana saw that hundreds of strands had been tightened and thickened in the distance of the Dark District, creating a maze of crisscrossing columns and webs from ceiling to ground, ground to wall, and wall to ceiling.

These strands have always been here, and she's just tightening them now, forming her webs in real time to trap Cid. She planned this. Somehow she planned it. That must be it! Aliana marveled at Nichole's audacious power despite knowing she might also use that same power against her. *As long as Aurelia lives and that smug fatherfucker dies, then I don't really care what happens to me,* Aliana thought as she stared at Cid, his lenses now almost fully transitioned to their deadly deep red.

And what does this fatherfucker want? Aliana considered as she looked directly into Armando's half-closed eyes. He had his arms outstretched and was moving directly toward Aliana, running on the air itself by utilizing some kind of propulsive force produced by visible shockwaves emitted from his mechanical legs and feet. At the same time, Nichole directed several of her strands to flick the bottoms of his feet, launching him even faster. Meanwhile, Rooli continued her own launch, and now Aliana saw that her bark appeared to be decaying and falling away from her body in the form of glistening ash converted in the wake of Aurelia's spreading blackness. Nichole didn't appear to be helping or resisting Rooli's launch, leaving Aliana in continued darkness concerning her true motives. Regardless, the gap between Aliana and her sister was already more than a hundred feet and continued to widen with each slow-moving but unstoppable millisecond.

Focus! Aliana demanded, but there was no malice in her command. She understood so thoroughly now that the mind was merely a tool. It was neither friend nor foe. It was either commanded or it commanded. There could be no middle ground.

I have to deal with Armando first. He might be fast and precise, but there's no way he's as fast and precise as I am.

She studied his movements, noting the mechanical precision of his hands and the way he had blocked every attack so far, even Rooli's strongest strikes.

I don't know his offensive capabilities, but his mechanical parts seem unbreakable, which means he'll try to use them to break me.

Aliana's gaze shifted to his throat. *I'll direct this sword to his jugular notch—men usually have obscenely large throat balls, or Adam's apples as the old slaves always called them. I can use his throat ball to direct my blade through the softest part of his throat and bleed him like a gutted tilapia.*

Aliana stole another glance at Myriam and Shira, their muscles rippling, their bodies alive and free of blood and scars. A part of her mind pleaded to break down finally and grieve for them. It was Aurelia who had forced Aliana out of her emotions in the cave when they had threatened to destroy her will. Now she would have to do it on her own.

But I'm not alone, Aliana knew. For here before her were her two mothers, and though Rooli and Aurelia did not appear beside them like they had earlier with these hallucinations, Aliana knew that they were in her heart, forever, just like they had assured her. *And I have my mind too,* Aliana reminded herself. *My mind is not my enemy. My mind is my friend and my confidant, as long as I remain its master. Even alone, I am whole.* The terrible grief flattened and retreated back into Aliana, providing her the much needed focus to contend with Armando, this man who had struck awe in Doe, Eddy, and countless citizens of Downver. Despite Aliana's increasing speed as she was flung backward through the air, Armando was gaining on her.

Come on then, fatherfucker! Time for your neck and this blade to become best friends, Aliana snarled as she heaved her shoulder and the blade into position, pointing it at Armando's belly as a diversion. At the final moment, she would plunge her arm downward and let the sword's point slowly and precisely catch the half-machine man's throat.

In the distance, Nichole stood with her sleek silver arms and legs fully outstretched in an x-shape pose as tens of thousands of tiny spinnerets directed thousands of individual filaments and dozens of now-hulking strands into a flurry of hypnotizing movement. Cid wore an expression full of wild contempt, but he wasn't even attempting to run or maneuver himself around the incoming filaments Nichole was directing toward his body with tidal-wave fury. His lenses were nearly fully red now; however, Nichole didn't seem at all concerned.

Aliana felt impressed from one warrior to another at Nichole's ability to direct so many individual objects at the same time. *It's hard enough to master using two swords effectively, let alone incorporating other weapons at the same time, like throwing weapons or boot knives. She is truly powerful,* Aliana measured. *But is she powerful enough to defeat a man who can stop her heart or send her into convulsions just by looking at her? And that's just Cid, the tool of an even stronger creature—a Prodigal Son. If Julian is anything like Gambe, there might be no way to defeat him,* Aliana thought, both horrified and impressed at the magnitude of power on display from multiple sources over the last day alone. She and her sister had braved the boar Mutant, the Butcher, Gambe, Hunter541, Eddy, Cid, and now Armando. Even after dealing with Armando, she might still have to contend with another Prodigal Son, or even Nichole, who was something else entirely.

Aurelia and I have already overcome so much. We will overcome this too!

Cid's lenses turned fully red, but Aliana forced herself to ignore the battle between Cid and Nichole and concentrate on her own predicament. *Time to turn this troutface into skewered meat,* Aliana resolved as Armando moved into position. She smirked at her obvious victory and was just about to straighten her arm and jut the sword into flesh when Aliana saw the most unexpected thing she could have imagined in that moment: A radiant man with comet-tails of light trailing after his shockingly bright body passed like a ghost through the rock-ceiling of the city. Armando ran directly by Aliana without attacking her, but she didn't notice him at all in the wake of this new absurdity.

Am I going crazy? Aliana watched as the man of light descended effortlessly toward Cid, completely ignoring the laws of time that governed even Nichole's glimmering filaments. *Who is he? How is he moving so fast despite the world moving so slow?*

The man was admittedly beautiful, despite his gender. His blonde coiffed hair seemed to move in a breeze that only he was influenced by. He wore a bizarre outfit that Aliana had seen in pictures of the old world, a black and white mess of layers, angles, buttons, and additional cloth accessories that could only possibly serve to hinder one's movement on a battlefield.

Whoever he is, he's going right for Cid. Is this all in my head? Is this fatherfucker real? Aliana gasped as her control over her mind grew tenuous in the wake of this new absurdity.

Shira and Myriam dissolved as the man's light washed over them, but Aliana was steadfast in her assurance that they were still with her even if she couldn't see them. Just as Cid's lenses shifted to an even brighter red, the radiant man intercepted him, moving in front of him and blocking his attack on Nichole with only a tiny fraction of a second to spare. Then, the man's face turned from concentrated to serene; he looked directly at Aliana and smiled sweetly at her.

Who the fatherfuck...? Aliana's mind trailed, totally dumbfounded by this radiant, uncollared man.

With so many questions and her mind in disarray, Aliana lost her grip over time, and with a high-pitched gong blast, she was flung backward with the full force and shock of normal time.

A mere second elapsed before Aliana squeezed her fists and brought time back to a crawl, but in that second, a flurrying explosion of activity occurred.

The man of light is gone, Aliana immediately noticed, still uncertain if he had been just another hallucination, no matter how strange and arbitrary. *And Rooli is already another hundred feet away. Please protect Aurelia, Rooli. Don't let anything happen to her,* Aliana pleaded within, wishing there was more she could do beyond merely observing the battlefield as she involuntarily accelerated away from it.

With the man of light gone, Aliana yet again had a clear view of Cid. His lenses had returned to black, but they were already shifting to red again. Nichole's thousands of spinnerets worked feverishly, squirming like worms in normal-time despite the slowness of everything else. Armando could be seen in Aliana's periphery, still passing her by in midair without any consideration for her one way or another. And yet, he moved in the same direction as Aliana, so she assumed this would not be the end of her dealings with Armando Ferreira.

Aliana directed her awareness away from each individual and broadened her attention to the battlefield as a whole. It was only then that she saw the fine scintillating strands and filaments forming and tightening into distinct geometries. Triangles, diamonds, hexagons, and dizzying arrays of nameless, complex shapes shrunk, expanded, or tightened as a morphing mosaic of glimmering webs converged on Cid.

Is she going to wrap him up like a spider with those webs? Aliana wondered in awe at what the Lord of Limbs had planned for the devious First Lord of the Walled City.

Aliana's eyes widened as the single filaments and bundled strands found their mark, with Cid's lenses continuing to transition even as Nichole's webs sliced through him from every angle, dicing his flesh with such delicate precision that it took a moment or two for the blood lines to rise to his torn skin. With his nerves so cleanly cut, Cid didn't even have time to realize what had happened as his brain undoubtedly continued sending futile signals to his thousand disconnected pieces. Gravity worked upon Cid, and as his body began crumbling, blood-flowing tissue violently separated all at once, ejecting an explosive spray of his insides from the hundreds of crisscrossing blood lines.

Yes! Die, fatherfucker! Aliana exulted as Cid's body continued crumbling in slow motion. The invisible scent of Cid's metallic blood-haze hit her nose, activating an involuntary feeling of nostalgia for Wintersvilla deep within her mind. *The smell of battle, of glory!* Aliana thought as she relished the sight of Cid literally crumbling to pieces.

You didn't see that coming, did you? Because you don't know everything! Aliana smirked within, grateful that Cid the Knower was no more. Knowing there was nothing she could physically do to stop herself from sailing through the air, Aliana still resolved to remain mentally nimble. She forced her attention to Nichole, still unsure if she was her enemy, ally, or something else. But the glory of victory over Cid was extinguished as Aliana fell into a state of dismay at what she saw happening around Nichole. The ground beneath her began shuddering and splintering. From the depths beneath Downver, dark strings of glistening viscera erupted, inversely mirroring the brilliance of Nichole's filaments with a pulsing heartbeat coursing through them. The viscera strings surged upward, defying slow-time as they writhed and twisted. They expanded rapidly in volume as they closed in on her like the tentacles of some beast from the bowels of the Earth.

Before Aliana even had time to process the scene, the grotesque tendrils grew jagged spikes like razor-sharp teeth. Each tentacle resembled a malformed half-jaw eager to tear Nichole apart, just as she had done to Cid moments before.

Cid! Aliana gasped as she glanced back at the still-cascading pile of dismembered pieces. To her horror, the pieces were reassembling at the behest of countless hair-thin dark strings jutting from the ground. Sinew and muscle weaved back together, along with what Aliana perceived to be synthetic and cybernetic tissue, reforming back into Cid the Knower.

No! How could Nichole's devastating attack be undone so easily? Out of the corner of her eye, Aliana spotted Rooli sailing near the ceiling above the Walled City with Aurelia safely in her arms. Aurelia was still unconscious, and the darkness was still spreading through Rooli inch by inch. *Don't die, sister,* Aliana begged, knowing that there was no more she could do in the moment other than focus on the battlefield and collect valuable intelligence to be used later on.

But this battle is so far beyond me, Aliana knew as the fleshy strands converged on Nichole, who appeared unfazed. She remained steadfast without even flinching as she stared at Cid's reforming body and directed her thousands and thousands of filaments to dance through the air and slash effortlessly through the encroaching masses. Each filament moved with precision, severing the tendrils before they could reach her. The severed pieces fell away, shriveled, then dissolved back into the ground.

More strings emerged from the ground, and without missing a beat, Nichole hacked through each one as they slithered toward her. After a second of real time that felt like a full minute to Aliana, Nichole was surrounded by what appeared to be a dense atmosphere of splattered innards as the fragments of the strings soared through the air, ricocheting maddeningly against each other and the ground. More razor-coated tendrils stabbed at Nichole, but her spinnerets treated them as additional fodder to be added to the haze of viscera now enveloping her like a dark curtain.

In normal time, this battle would be taking place too fast to even observe. And that radiant man…if that was real, he was moving even faster than Nichole, Julian, and these disgusting intestine-looking strings that Julian must be using to attack her somehow. If only I could join this battle! Aliana cursed.

Behind Cid's reanimating body, thick pillars of what appeared to be pulsing, ulcerous flesh bubbled up from the earth, and though Nichole sliced these pillars to pieces along with the relentless strings, more began forming, compounding with maddening rapidity so that the whole environment began to swell with pillars of viscera. The walls of the rocky columns spread across the Dark District, the ceiling above the lake, the surface of the lake, even the surface of Rooli's gargantuan discarded flesh—all of it bubbled with congealing pools of the dark, pulsing innards.

Nichole's body bucked violently at the shoulders, and as she winced in visible pain, founts of glimmering filaments burst forth, gushing out of her torso.

It's not just her arms, her whole body is like that, Aliana realized as she observed thousands of more spigots and hundreds of thousands of more spinnerets manipulating countless more filaments emerging from the rest of Nichole's endoskeleton. Only her face remained human. Like her arms, her entire upper body appeared uncannily similar to Gambe's polished silvery-gray metal body. While Gambe could transform into tiny swarming pieces, Nichole was some kind of spider-machine capable of manipulating hundreds of thousands of filaments that could be used as weaponry, defense, tools of retreat, and likely more than Aliana could imagine.

I thought she was just a baseline human when I met her—she didn't even have any ports. But now I'm not sure she even is human anymore. Is this really Nichole Adamich, or is this just a fake Nichole created by the Agency?

Aliana still itched to join the battle. She searched her periphery for something to latch onto, but Nichole had directed her flight backward in such a way that Aliana was unable to stop herself. All Aliana could do was watch as Nichole directed a portion of the filaments and larger strands to converge back on Cid, while she used others to destroy the budding viscera pillars. Despite her terrifying alacrity and her webs turning the Dark District into a city-sized spider nest made of razor-silk, it still wasn't enough. The pillars that Nichole could not destroy quickly enough began oozing with a nauseating blend of blood, bile, and unidentifiable fluids that coalesced into quivering mounds of organic matter. Some of them exploded against the violent, glimmering streaks of filaments, but others reformed or somehow went untouched. From the center of each of these mounds, a single malformed limb burst forth—a tiny hand, pale and slender, dripping with the dark, pulsing viscera. Each hand contained dozens of fingers, and each finger flexed unnaturally, joints cracking as they bent backward to direct hardened fleshy cords to cut through or counter incoming filaments. Nichole continued to carve most of the mounds to pieces, but enough survived for a second identical hand to emerge from their centers. A dozen mounds remained intact, successfully countering the filaments bombarding them. Meanwhile, Cid remained in a perpetual state of exploding painfully outward like some grotesque organic star as he was repeatedly diced and pulled back together. His face contorted in arrested agony each time his brain attained consciousness for a fraction of a second before being ripped apart again. Aliana couldn't stop the perverse pleasure welling up inside her as she savored every moment of his unending torment.

66

Hoping that Aurelia and Rooli were still escaping the chaos, Aliana scanned above the Walled City, but the area was too occluded by layers of webs to see anything.

Just keep going, Enduring Ironwood! Keep my sister safe!

Nichole managed to shred a few of the mounds, but nine still remained. The fingers on each abhorrent hand continued directing viscera strings to counter Nichole's ceaseless filaments, but now each pair of hands gripped their respective mounds and tore them open, revealing a set of nine identical faces with bodies still forming and rising from the hideous mounds.

It's him! The gray boy, Aliana observed with apprehension as she had a flashback to her time being intoxicated on the mushrooms and remembered that Julian, the Third Prodigal Son, had been one of the boys who had found them when they first approached Downver. Even Doe and Ricardo clearly had no idea that they were dealing with a force beyond their comprehension.

Nichole exploded another two copies of Julian and their mounds into a bloody haze, then another two, but Aliana could see that those copies weren't really trying.

Those were just decoys. He's just distracting Nichole and buying himself time to materialize. Aliana marveled at how Julian and Nichole kept up with so much at one time, especially since only a handful of seconds had passed since the battle began.

The copy at the center of the five remaining Julians began upturning his lips and contorting his features so that rather than twist his neck to face Aliana, his face migrated itself across his head. With a lopsided face, he smiled with sinister delight at Aliana as the other four copies were diced into miniscule pieces by Nichole. Julian's ominous smile and his foggy gray eyes nearly paralyzed Aliana, filling her with a nameless dread unlike anything she had ever experienced. She felt all at once violated, as if this creature's stare was probing the most private areas of both her mind and body.

What the Muto fuck is he? Aliana gasped, feeling utterly alone and wishing that the radiant man had not washed away the vision of her mothers. *What are any of these people? Even me…all of us are players with strange powers in some unfathomable game,* Aliana pondered grimly, steeling herself with immense effort to maintain control over time.

Nichole's spinnerets flurried feverishly as what appeared to be blood poured from the spigots and from her lips, coating Nichole's metal body with elongating streaks of crimson.

Is she bleeding? Does that mean she's still Nichole Adamich after all? Aliana wondered, for didn't blood imply that Nichole was still human somehow?

As Aliana sailed out of the dark district, a growing brightness entered her awareness, and she pivoted her attention to her peripheral vision.

I must be entering a different district, Aliana considered, remembering the starkly different areas of Downver she had observed after Aurelia had chopped off her legs and launched the two of them to the Dark District. However, the brightness was intensifying too rapidly to be merely the light of another district. Just as Aliana was about to pull her attention away from the battle and pivot her body to ascertain where she was heading, the radiant man appeared behind her and stabilized himself so that he matched her slow-motion flight through the air.

He has to be real! She watched in awe as the strangely dressed man glided through the air at high speed despite each strand of her hair drifting past her like slow-rolling clouds. *And he is fast, as fast as light,* Aliana thought, and she wondered if maybe that was true since this man appeared to be radiating light from every surface of his skin and every inch of his old world clothing.

Without any real effort, he bowed cordially and glided alongside Aliana while in the distance, Julian's smile began to slowly morph into a scowl as he simultaneously countered Nichole's assault, continually rebuilt Cid's body, and stared directly at the radiant man beside Aliana.

He can see him too, Aliana realized, glad she wasn't crazy and also happy that Julian didn't appear to be relishing the sight of this shining being.

"It is an honor, Aliana. My name is Leif Mainstone. Do your best to remain in your trance-state for just a little while longer, okay?" the man signed using the Wintersvilla battle language that Cid and Armando also somehow knew. The man's fingers and his face displayed incredible politeness, but Aliana couldn't help reading it as docile and passive like a meek slave. She would have challenged him with her own signing, but she couldn't move freely like him. "I'm on your side," the man continued. "But we're on a perilous path now, perilous but worthwhile. I'm going to do what I can to help you and your sister survive long enough so that you won't need help anymore. Now, get ready. That pink building with the domed top to your left is about to get sliced in half by one of Ms. Adamich's stray filaments. She's reaching her limit against my brother, and though she has done a remarkable job bringing order to Downver over the last twelve years, Julian is going to force her hand into creating just as much disorder before this day is through."

This man is Julian's brother? Aliana considered with surprise. *That means he's a Prodigal Son too. Is everyone just an agent of the Agency?* She wondered grimly. Leif's pleasant countenance made Aliana want to trust him, but she didn't allow herself such naivety. She knew that from now on, she had to be smart like Aurelia just as much as she had to be strong and cunning.

From across the district, Julian's scowl turned to rage as he stared with unbelieving eyes at his brother, as if Leif's presence constituted the greatest betrayal. Leif bowed again, and then he shot toward Julian, his body brightening further as he furrowed his facial features through what appeared to be extreme concentration.

Just as Leif was about to intercept his brother and enact whatever it was he had planned, Aliana's attention was forced to her left to the flamboyantly decorated twenty-story building suddenly beginning to rumble in slow-time, mingling with the droning cacophony of all the other stretched out sounds. The rumbling intensified as the top of the building began to slide away from the bottom, crumbling windows and walls as it collapsed. Aliana could see the figures of people in the building. Several of them had been severed into multiple pieces by Nichole's filament, while others were screaming in horror at the decimated bodies of what Aliana assumed to be their colleagues or maybe even their friends.

Troutshit! Aliana gasped as she realized that the building was going to fall right on top of her, along with these other people. She would be forced to decide whether to experience being slowly crushed or allowing time to speed up and let herself die quickly. Either way, there was no way to avoid being crushed by the top half of the gigantic building.

That troutface could have tried to help me somehow, Aliana cursed the radiant Prodigal Son. Her mind began to race with panic, and without intending it, she lost her grasp on time.

All at once, time snapped back into a flurry of activity. Aliana slammed into something hard at her back, knocking the wind out of her lungs and forcing the sword out of her hands. Whatever she slammed into yanked her away from the building and continued pulling her in the opposite direction, into the heart of this new district filled with pink, purple, and yellow buildings with domed tops—all of them displaying different heights, hues, and lusters.

The top half of the severed pink building continued detaching from its base as if it were still in slow motion, and then it fully collapsed into itself, crushing the multitude of people caught inside the wreck. As the building imploded, it occluded Aliana's view of the battle, which was now around a thousand feet away. It was only after being visually severed from the battle that she wondered what it was that was still pulling her to safety. She reached for something wrapped around her chest and felt cold, mechanical hands gripping her tightly to a warm and muscular human body. She couldn't help being reminded of being held by Shira and her exo, but the feeling was immediately snuffed as she twisted her neck and looked up to see that she was presently nestled in Armando's arms.

"Let me go, meat! You disgusting scrotum-scum!" Aliana screamed hysterically into the face of this man, even if he did just save her from certain death.

Armando effortlessly ignored her and continued into the strangely colored district. He appeared to be running on the air itself, and though the bursts of combustion at his feet were nearly invisible in normal time, Aliana remembered observing that his mechanical legs were capable of emitting a burst of energy that provided a form of running-flight.

"I said fuck off, fatherfucker!" Aliana screamed, but without a sword, there was nothing she could do. Despite her power and the promise of even more power to come, she was presently just a little girl in the half-machine arms of an indelibly stronger man.

Feeling useless, Aliana thought of Aurelia and how she would be able to overcome Armando and anything else that might stand in her path.

I have to be strong like Aurelia. I have to be strong...for Aurelia, Aliana resolved, realizing that she and her sister were both being pulled away from the battlefield—Aurelia by their greatest ally, and Aliana by an insidious enemy.

Please don't die, sister, Aliana thought just as the top half of the severed tower fully slid away from its base and began plummeting toward the ground with the potential energy of a small bomb.

At the crux of Mendel's Ladder Theory of the Cosmos lies the Great Attractor, revealed not as a mere gravitational anomaly, but as a colossal gateway—a multidimensional corridor bending space and time into higher and lower dimensions. This gateway doesn't lead to another region of our universe but opens into the Great Beyond, a metaverse so vast and intricate that even Mendel, in his current state, can only perceive fragments of the infinite, ever-changing mosaic that is to his acute mind both mesmerizing and disorienting.

Encircling the Great Attractor are entities of unimaginable scale, beings composed of entire galaxies, forged from energies yet undiscovered by human science. Some are conglomerates of primordial mesons dispersed during the universe's earliest moments, having evolved or been assimilated into sentient forms over eons. These cosmic colossi engage in an endless cycle of consumption and growth, devouring one another to amass the power necessary to traverse the gateway into the Great Beyond. They are like oceans compared to the single drop that is humanity—vast, ancient, and seemingly indifferent.

Throughout the cosmos, life manifests in myriad forms, but its distribution is uneven, like a cosmic cityscape. Mendel helped me understand how the regions near the Great Attractor are similar to a bustling metropolis, teeming with life and activity, where power concentrates and evolution accelerates at an unfathomable pace. Further out lie the sprawling suburbs, where countless emerging civilizations strive toward the center. Beyond that stretches the infinite countryside—the vast expanse of the universe, sparsely populated and evolving quietly, slowly, meanderingly, and hopelessly.

We find ourselves on the outskirts of these cosmic suburbs, a position both precarious and fortuitous. Our relative isolation shields us from predation by the ancient entities that dominate the inner regions. Civilizations that arise closer to the Great Attractor are often consumed or assimilated before they can reach maturity—countless victims of the relentless competition for survival and Ascension. Our distance grants us the precious time needed to evolve without that immediate threat, yet we are not so remote that the journey to the gateway is unattainable.

In our local cosmic neighborhood, most life is sparse and primitive, the equivalent of spacefaring insects or rodents. Humanity hasn't observed them yet because these creatures have evolved to evade the observation of higher civilizations. This is equivalent to a surface-dwelling creature being unaware of the multitude of worms directly beneath their feet. It is only with enough curiosity, desperation, or through the will of nature that the creature can gain knowledge of the worms that outnumber them by whole orders of magnitude. The multitudes of spacefaring rodents skittering from one celestial body to the next are adapted and specialized to thrive in the interstellar void, preferring to inhabit the remnants of failed or dormant civilizations—like mice taking up residence in a vacant building. And just like mice, these creatures pose little danger to us, allowing humanity a rare opportunity, relative to most in our local universe, to develop unimpeded.

If we had found ourselves further away from the Great Attractor, then we would eventually perish at the hands of universal entropy, which advances inexorably. The window for us to ascend Mendel's Ladder is finite. We must act before cosmic decay renders our journey impossible, trapping us in a silent, dying universe with the gateway to the Great Beyond slipping forever out of reach due to universal expansion outpacing the Great Attractor's gravitational pull on our galaxy.

The Great Beyond beckons all life sentient and intelligent enough to hear its call. The choices we make now will determine whether we remain isolated in the cosmic countryside or embark on the journey toward the Great Attractor, climbing Mendel's Ladder to our ultimate destiny.

The universe is far more complex and wondrous than we ever imagined. To ascend Mendel's Ladder is to accept our place in this grand design, to become active participants in the cosmic narrative.

This is our purpose.

This is my purpose.

From Mendel's Ladder: The Personal Journal of Denis Mendel, Written Circa 2037, Published June 2108 by Leif Mainstone, Federated Agency Publishing

Chapter 4
The Void Vortex

S omewhere in the forever-ocean of nothingness there was a tiny
awareness like a dwindling ember at the center of a frozen
continent. The ember had been there for an unfathomable length of
time, maybe forever, and yet it did not turn to smoke and ash in the
wake of absolute zero. Somehow the awareness persisted in the
nothingness, flickering but subsisting.

Without warning, the awareness expanded, rapidly filling the
nothingness. The ember became an inferno that warmed the icy
landscape, converting barrenness into fecundity, death into life,
simplicity into complexity. Like wood carved into elaborate shapes and
intricate engravings, the awareness blossomed, taking new shape in the
form of self-awareness, spatial-awareness, meta-awareness. Finally, the
awareness gained back its understanding of form, sensation, and identity,
translating the nothingness into an understanding of floating confusion
in infinite darkness.

I'm me, Aurelia desperately remembered as memories flooded into her
racing mind like a deluge of insects, each one crawling through her and
gnawing at what should be her solid body.

But I have no body, Aurelia gasped as she tried to direct her hands to
feel her face, but she had no hands nor face. She was a bodiless mind
suspended in perfect darkness.

I'm dead, Aurelia concluded, and though she knew the thought should
fill her with terror, it had the opposite effect. It brought her a profound
sense of calm. *It's over. I failed, and now it's all over. Cid flashed me with his
eyes, and now I'm dead. He wasn't the one I was supposed to meet after all. I was
wrong…about everything. Whether or not fate is real makes no difference now. I died.
That's what happened, and probably that's always what was going to happen. So,
now what?* Aurelia considered.

But there was no *what.* This was death, and this would be her
existence for the rest of eternity.

*Myriam was right—there is an afterlife, but it's not the Afterworld. It's more
akin to the hell imagined by Christians. Death is nothingness made worse by the fact*

that I'm still here. All I will know from now on is nothingness forever, Aurelia calculated, but she wasn't ready yet to let her mind break beneath the weight of that all-encompassing realization. There would be time for that, infinite time for that. At the moment, she just wanted to grieve for Rooli, Shira, and Myriam. And maybe Aliana as well, but Aurelia couldn't be sure that Aliana didn't succeed in killing Cid using her newfound powers.

If only my powers had awakened like Aliana's. If only I had consumed the glowies. But I'm a fool. I've always known that, even though Aliana and all the others looked up to my intelligence. It wasn't intelligence; it was just some form of Nomadic knowledge of the future and subsequent prediction. And it failed me. In the end, it failed me, and I failed everyone else in turn. I'm sorry, Ali.

A miniscule but unmistakable point of light appeared in front of Aurelia, and before she could even guess at its meaning, it expanded like the universe's initial singularity, radiantly exploding into the nothingness and filling it with space, time, and form. In response to the sudden brightness, Aurelia instinctively shut her eyes and shielded them with both her arms before realizing that she had a body again.

I'm not dead? Aurelia wondered, her newly formed heart racing so fast into her ears that she worried she would have a heart attack and die all over again. Aurelia forced herself to focus, envisioning Rooli standing beside her. She opened her eyes and experienced intense vertigo as she found herself a couple hundred feet above the large lake at the center of Downver's Dark District, just as she remembered it before being flashed by Cid. Only, everything was perfectly silent and still. Realizing that she and the rest of the world were frozen in time, Aurelia calmed herself, knowing it was essential to return to the battle against Cid with a clear mind, regardless of what was presently happening to her.

But how did I get up here? Aurelia considered as she looked down at the edge of the lake to see Aliana suspended in the air directly in front of Cid, her face contorted in agony. Cid had his back to Aurelia, leaving him open to a surprise attack. *I just need something to throw at him with my void-arm, just like I did back in the cave when I...killed that boy Ricky.* Aurelia thought of Doe suddenly with longing and regret for killing his friend before steeling her mind again. *I need to revive Rooli still. The shard of her face should still be in the pocket of this suit the silkweavers made for me.*

Aurelia looked down and began directing her hand toward the pocket when she realized two things: unlike everyone and everything else, she was not frozen in time. She could move freely. Furthermore, she was naked, and the skin of her legs and arms were completely unmarred by the glistening black. She instinctively reached for her face and felt at her lips and cheeks with her alabaster hand. She gasped, feeling her face for the first time without the sharp pain that normally accompanied her fingers gliding over the black lesions.

They're gone! The black lesions I was born with are gone! Aurelia thought with a mix of excitement and apprehension, for although it was a blessing to be rid of those terrible growing scars, that same glistening black that had spread to her limbs was the source of immense power.

Am I totally powerless now? Aurelia felt apprehension overtake her sense of excitement. Normally the subsequent feeling of dread and vulnerability would have brought the vortex hallucination to the forefront of her mind, but it did not appear.

Despite coming back to life, Aurelia felt terribly lost and confused, as if every facet of her identity had been stripped from her upon her awakening.

No matter what's really happening, I must revive Rooli, Aurelia reminded herself forcefully. *But my clothes are gone, and so is Rooli!* She peered directly below herself and felt more overwhelming vertigo as she looked upon her old body floating face first in the lake. The body was clothed in the silk black and violet suit the silkweavers had made, and the skin was covered entirely by the glistening black. Beside the body, the shard of Rooli floated in the dark water of the lake, just barely missing the golden rays of direct sunlight.

It's me! That's my body! My actual body! Aurelia gawked with bewilderment that crescendoed to sudden, overwhelming calm as she returned to the obvious conclusion that she was dead, and somehow she was observing the world of the living as some sort of ghost.

Why am I being shown this? Is this a form of torture to remind me just how much I failed? As if in response to Aurelia's question, a deep buzzing sound began emanating from somewhere in the distance. Movement on the edge of the lake directed Aurelia's eyes back to Aliana, whose hair was now slowly drifting around her face full of excruciating torment. All around her, Cid's goons watched her in slow motion with sadistic smiles painted across their diverse faces, except for Eddy, who looked as though he might cry at the sight of Aliana suspended and trapped in midair by Cid's incredible power.

Time is speeding up, Aurelia realized. The buzzing intensified as Cid raised his arm, extending it toward the center of Aliana's body. Aurelia was suspended in midair like Aliana, and though there was nothing she could do, she still couldn't help reaching out to her sister, extending her arm toward her like Cid.

Get away, Ali! Aurelia begged, but all Aliana could do was bare her gritted teeth as tears crawled down her face.

Please, Aliana! Get away!

Cid squeezed his fist closed, and with a crimson flash of his lenses, Aliana's body imploded into itself, converted in slow motion into a single marble-sized ball of bone and blood and brain.

No! No! No! Aurelia pleaded. As her sister fell to the ground as a tiny, dense sphere, Aurelia lost herself. It was too much. It was all her fault. It was too horrific. She couldn't breathe. She couldn't think. The foundations of her mind crumbled and gave out.

Aurelia felt herself plunge downward and slip ethereally into her old body, and though she felt herself come alive and return to her original senses, she wasn't really there. She was detached even from the idea of detachment, for she could never forgive herself for what had just happened to Aliana. She did not deserve whatever grand fate Rooli and the other Nomads imagined for her. She would not allow it. In her final moments of self-awareness, Aurelia decided she was not worthy even of self-awareness, and as if lashing her own insides with a Wintersvilla slaver's punishing whip, she mentally excised herself of her own identity and willed her ego to die.

And it did.

Though her sense of self dissipated, her awareness remained intact, and she experienced the subsequent moments as a detached yet consenting observer.

The shard of Rooli passed through a sunbeam, and before Cid could even turn around, Aurelia awoke from her unconscious state and placed her hand above the shard just as it began blooming back into Rooli's familiar form. But Rooli did not stop blooming. At the behest of Aurelia's mental consent and will, Enduring Ironwood consumed the Virus' flesh and blood, merging with Aurelia's body. The dark substance that had somehow been kept at bay by Aurelia's unique genetics virtually all her life now fueled a ceaseless and unstoppable growth. The merged mind of Aurelia and Rooli surged with insatiable hunger, commanding the pulsating, glistening black flesh tree that was now their body to expand and keep on expanding beyond all earthly confines.

The ground beneath the growing flesh tree quivered and cracked as ebony roots burst forth, whipping through stone with relentless purpose. Cid, Armando, and the rest of Cid's goons barely had time to register the shadows enveloping them before tendrils erupted from the ground beneath their feet, coiling around their limbs with crushing force. Cid's lenses flashed in panic as he struggled, but the more he fought, the tighter the grip became, swallowing his shrieks with engulfing darkness.

The Third Prodigal Son took shape using his strings of viscera anchored deep beneath Downver, but the roots reached his core and assimilated his expansive form as if he were no more than a harmless pit of nutritious water.

The rhythmic thundering of colossal legs announced the arrival of Nichole Adamich, the Lord of Limbs. Astride her giant bejeweled grasshopper, she surveyed the chaos unfolding below. The insect's iridescent carapace shimmered, reflecting the ominous glow of the expanding flesh tree as Nichole raised her arms and unleashed her full power, tightening her filaments and strings into a maze of razor-sharp webs. But the flesh tree was expanding far too quickly and voraciously for her tens of thousands of individual blades to make even a modicum of difference. From the apex of the flesh tree, a gargantuan branch twisted and snapped downward with sickening speed. Nichole's eyes widened, and though she tried leaping to safety, the tendrils were relentless, and they dragged both rider and mount into the abyssal maw of the tree.

Downver descended into pandemonium. People of every district ran in every direction, their faces etched with sheer terror. Buildings crumbled as roots burst through foundations, swallowing homes and marketplaces alike. Many people stood paralyzed amidst the chaos, their tears lost in the rain of debris. The screaming only lasted another handful of seconds before every living thing in Downver was assimilated into the ever-growing, pulsating dark mass.

The tree went on expanding, fueling its growth with the very Earth itself. The hordes of freed slaves in Wintersvilla gazed upon the horizon and watched the encroaching mass as the sky was darkened with swarms of inky branches and tendrilling limbs attached to the trunk of the flesh tree that was rising into the sky like a mountain being made in minutes rather than eons. Cataclysmic tremors shook through the Earth as if the whole planet were a tuning fork struck by a divine hammer. The ground fractured in every direction, and the millions of former slaves toppled over and fell into the chasming underground where the roots waited to feed on them in the darkness dozens of miles beneath the surface.

Vida faced the same fate, with the Sixth Prodigal Son and his followers dropping through Earth's crumbling surface into oblivion. Their stories, their pains, their hopes—all absorbed into the collective consciousness of the entity that had once been Aurelia and Rooli. Even Leif Mainstone, the Seventh Prodigal Son of the Agency who was seemingly invulnerable to destruction, was caught mid-flight and swallowed into the growing abyss, his radiance flickering and finally dying as he disappeared into the writhing mass presently feeding on the dense liquid iron, nickel, and other energy-abundant heavy metals composing the Earth's core.

The great planetary organs of Earth fell one by one. The mighty continent of Waru, the Great Honey Mushroom that spanned forests unseen, the Boreal Kingdoms of BigBilly, with their ancient trees and whispered secrets, and so many others as well—all were consumed and assimilated into the flesh tree.

Across the oceans, the waves stilled. The sky itself collapsed as the atmosphere was drawn into the towering mass. The clouds were pulled down, spiraling into the vortex of liquid metal at the tree's core. Astrea fell out of orbit at the behest of the planetary flesh tree's unimaginable gravity. The survivors of the revolution in Astrea were consumed right alongside the void vultures, their energy fueling the expansion further by multiple orders of magnitude.

Mars and Venus stood no chance as the flesh tree's roots drew them into its void-black body. Jupiter's storms raged in protest, but its abundant gases were siphoned as the gas giant was converted into a cosmic puff of hydrogen. Saturn's rings shimmered briefly before being unraveled and absorbed, their icy particles integrated into the colossus. With each new absorption, the tree's gravity intensified. It became a dark star of unimaginable density. The remaining planets of the solar system were pulled from their orbits, spiraling inward like moths to a flame. Mercury, stripped from the sun's gravity, melted as it approached, its metallic core adding to the mass. Neptune and Uranus, distant and cold, shattered as they were drawn into the gravitational pull.

The sun itself began to waver, its nuclear core gravitationally pulled by the anomaly. Yet, instead of collision, a delicate balance was achieved. The flesh tree and the sun settled into a binary orbit, light and darkness circling and pulling at one another. The flesh tree's expansive but simple mind decided that the gravitational dance with the sun was a form of joy and pleasantness, and with this sudden, stark change in its temperament, it let go of its need to continue expanding, and it forgot all about what and who it had once been.

As eons passed, the merged mind of Aurelia and Rooli drifted through the vastness of space, their thoughts no longer burdened by the weight of guilt or sorrow. The intensity and carnage of their past lives became distant echoes, overshadowed by the calm and joy of creation on a cosmic scale. The universe evolved around them, stars dying and being reborn, galaxies drifting through the cosmic sea. In the silence of the void, they found peace. Their existence was no longer defined by pain or vengeance but by the serene acceptance of all that was and all that would ever be.

Time lost all meaning, until one day, nearly a billion years after becoming the dark stellar tree, tiny creatures emerged from the depths of space. Adapted to the vacuum and the cold, they resembled tree shrews with sleek, iridescent fur that shimmered against the starlight. Their large, inquisitive eyes reflected the galaxies, and delicate membranes stretched between their limbs, allowing them to glide between asteroids and other space debris. These beings were not highly intelligent in the way that humanity had measured intelligence; they harbored no grand aspirations or technologies. Yet, they possessed a cleverness, an innate ability to survive and thrive amid the void.

Drawn by the subtle energies emanating from the stellar flesh tree, they approached cautiously. The tree sensed their arrival, its consciousness stirring with a gentle curiosity. The creatures clambered onto its vast branches and nestled into the crevices. They fed on the replenishing flesh of the tree, and the tree gave its flesh willingly, providing them warmth and sustenance as its dark surface pulsed with incredible gratitude to have the creatures as company. The space shrews roamed the endless branches, their tiny footprints tracing patterns across the bark as they built intricate nests from cosmic debris. The flesh tree found solace in their presence, a quiet joy in providing for these simple beings. Their contentment was infectious, and for the first time in eons, the merged consciousness felt a semblance of companionship.

As billions of years flowed like a silent river, the creatures multiplied and spread. They ventured out to other celestial bodies, sometimes settling on asteroids or even passing planets caught in the tree and sun's shared gravity, but they always seemed to prefer the company of sentient structures like the flesh tree. Across the stars, similar entities harbored these spacefaring galactic critters, each forming its own unique bond with the tiny travelers. The universe was dotted with these living islands of life amid the vast emptiness.

The flesh tree and its companions drifted through the galaxy, witnessing nebulas that painted the sky with hues of violet and gold, supernovae that burst in silent brilliance, and at all times the grand spiral arms of their own galaxy unfurled into the unthinkable vastness of intergalactic space. The creatures remained blissfully unaware of the cosmic significance of these events and structures. Their days were filled with simple pleasures and the steady rhythm of existence.

However, the flesh tree sensed a disturbance, a shift in the gravitational tides. Another galaxy was slowly drawing near, threatening to collide with the stellar flesh tree's own galaxy. It wasn't something that had ever concerned the tree before, but now that the gravity of the approaching galaxy was beginning to disturb its own, the tree began to observe the approaching galaxy with a mix of awe and apprehension. It was scared for the space shrews, but then again, the flesh tree knew deep down that this was just the way of the universe—creation and destruction, life and death—nothing could be more natural.

As the galaxies began their colossal embrace over the course of millions of years, gravitational forces tore at the fabric of space. Stars were flung from their orbits, sent hurtling into the abyss. The flesh tree and its tiny denizens were one of those caught in a tidal wave of gravitational forces, and though the flesh tree tried to grow roots and tighten itself around the sun, it was ripped away and cast into the intergalactic void.

Without the warmth of the sun, temperatures plummeted. The space shrews huddled together, their iridescent fur losing its luster as the cold seeped in. There were no other stars or sentient structures to take refuge. The flesh tree felt its own energies dissipating, the dark life force that had sustained it for so long finally beginning to wane. Yet, there was no fear, only a profound sense of peace.

The tree's consciousness began to dissipate, its thoughts turning inward. It reflected on the eons spent in silent guardianship of these simple creatures. They had brought it joy beyond measure, a purpose that transcended its own existence. A realization settled gently within its fading awareness: even if it had clung to the sun, it would have faced oblivion in the star's eventual expansion before death. Consuming the sun could have prolonged its existence, but outliving the creatures that had given its life meaning would have been worse than mere death.

As the last vestiges of warmth disappeared, the flesh tree and its companions became a frozen monument drifting through the darkness—a mausoleum of memories and silent stories. The creatures, now in eternal slumber, remained nestled in their homes among the branches while the tree's consciousness flickered like the dying light of the distant stars. In these final moments, the flesh tree felt only deep fulfillment. It had witnessed the birth and death of stars, the rise and fall of galaxies, and it had provided sanctuary to life when none should have existed. It had chosen companionship over solitude, selflessness over survival. The flesh tree's awareness gently ebbed away, dissolving into the fabric of the cosmos. The cold embraced it like an old friend, and with a final, silent sigh, it surrendered to the nothingness.

Nothingness. Yes, there was nothingness. But somewhere in the forever-ocean of nothingness there was a tiny point of awareness. Somehow the awareness persisted in the nothingness, flickering but subsisting.

Without warning, the awareness expanded, rapidly filling the nothingness. Self-awareness, spatial-awareness, and meta-awareness returned. Then sensation, and identity. Finally, Aurelia remembered herself and her memories, and she found herself suspended in eternal darkness without a body.

Despite being bodiless, Aurelia found that she could simulate the feeling of breathing by imagining it, allowing her to bring her mind back under control. The experience of being the stellar flesh tree felt more real than the endless darkness, but with each passing second she recollected that she had been here before.

I'm dead, Aurelia remembered, her mind still reeling at the billions of years she had experienced in mere seconds as she continued to breathe and brace herself with practiced calm. *Was I just shown what actually happened after I died, or what could have happened? Or was that just a wild death dream that has no bearing on reality whatsoever?* Aurelia yearned to return to the multi-billion year peace that she had glimpsed in what now felt like a quickly fading dream.

Again, a point of light appeared somewhere in the forever-nothingness that Aurelia's awareness translated to eternal darkness. All at once, the point of light expanded, bathing Aurelia with the experience of space, time, and form.

She yet again found herself hovering above the central lake of the Dark District. She was naked, and her body was free of the glistening black lesions. In the distance, Aliana was held in the air by Cid, while below, Aurelia saw her own body, unconscious and black all over, with the shard of Rooli floating just beside her.

Am I just going to be tortured forever and be forced to watch Aliana die? Aurelia wondered somberly, considering how she could possibly prepare her mind for an eternity of despair and regret. *At least...at least I will know peace for billions of years when I experience merging my mind with Rooli and becoming the stellar flesh tree...even if those billions of years will only feel like a few moments,* Aurelia thought with grim hollowness, doing her utmost to retain a foothold of sanity out of habit, more than anything else. Deep down she knew that she would go insane eventually. She was dead, and this is all she would know from now on—a repeated fever dream lashing her forever through infinity. But the discipline of her upbringing, and the thought of honoring Rooli, Shira, Myriam, and most of all Aliana, made her want to resist total and utter insanity for as long as she could. It wouldn't accomplish anything, not really, but at least it might prove that the others had imbued Aurelia with their inexhaustible strength and fortitude, even when she didn't deserve it.

Do your best, death, but I will not break easily, not even for you, Aurelia challenged as the deep buzzing sound began in the distance and the world began to stir with movement. Aurelia braced herself, preparing her mind for the impending horror of watching Aliana implode. She peered down to see her own unconscious, all-black void-body and the shard of Rooli floating beside it. To her surprise, the shard was crumbling into dust before it could reach any area of direct sunlight.

That's not what happened last time. Aurelia watched in dismay as the floating dust finally sprouted into a small frail black flesh tree. Its withering branches reached out from the surface of the lake as if in a silent plea, while thin black roots jutted downward toward the bottom of the lake.

Cid turned slowly, his black lenses reflecting Aurelia's unconscious body and the small flesh tree that had been Rooli. Aurelia noted that she was not reflected in Cid's glasses, as if she really was a ghost watching this scene take place.

But Aliana is still alive, Aurelia noted cautiously, grateful that her sister had been spared this time even if Rooli had not. All of a sudden, the buzzing crescendoed, and time accelerated back to its normal, relentless march. Aurelia was plunged back into her body, and as she turned and grasped the flesh tree, she united with it, not in despair and hopelessness like the first vision, but with a lust to use death as her personal tool of vengeance. Her rage blinded her, and she was filled with incredible elation at seeing Aliana plunge her sword through the back of Cid's head, shattering his lethal lenses.

Raw energy surged through Aurelia with the glistening black serving as a conduit of immense power. Her senses heightened, filling her ears with Downver's heartbeat—an organic thumping originating from many miles beneath the underground city. Her prescience told her that the thumping was the actual heart of Julian Mainstone, with veins and arteries extending throughout the entirety of Downver, often hidden in plain sight by taking the form of slithering vines or drooping fungus. From this abominable heart, energy-filled blood coursed through strings of viscera that multiplied and burst from the rocky ground, aiming directly for Aliana. As Aurelia reached out in a futile attempt to save her sister, she gasped in surprise as thousands of glistening black filaments were ejected from her hand. They simultaneously intercepted Julian's strings of viscera and also collided with Nichole's razor filaments. Nichole was directing her filaments while mounted atop her bejeweled grasshopper, which glided from filament to filament, using them as surfaces and somehow avoiding having its legs sliced off. Aliana backflipped to temporary safety, and Aurelia was just about to direct more of the black substance to create a shield around her sister when she suddenly lost control of her body and went limp. Something coursed through Aurelia, making her convulse and feel like a puppet being stringed. In the distance, she saw that her sister was undergoing the same ordeal, along with Nichole and the few goons who had been lucky enough to avoid collateral damage from the triple attack on Aliana. In the distance, the people of every district lay on the ground and spasmed.

What...is...happening to...all...of...us? Aurelia's thoughts stuttered with the vague, distant memory of having been dead and watching this whole scene from above as a detached observer. Her answer came in the form of Julian Mainstone appearing from behind her, viscera strings extending from his belly and into all the others, including Aurelia. A significant portion of the viscera strings snaked into the lake and were attached to the frail flesh tree that had been Rooli. They pulsed with incredible intensity as Julian's lips upturned with overwhelming ecstasy.

"I did it!" Julian hooted maniacally, his gray eyes mad as if in disbelief. "I...I did it! I bested all the others. Madeira and Mendel and Mother and all the others too. Even my brother Harald will be unable to stand against me. You can come out now, Leif. You are either too late, or you are too cowardly to attempt to change the course of reality. Either way, the Virus is mine now. Everyone and everything is mine now. Do you understand, brother?" Julian said with the gray boy's face and a body that was an undulating amalgamation of flesh and organs with countless viscera strings pulsing, extending, and contracting back into his body in a nonstop flurry of grotesque movement.

A man seemingly made of light appeared behind Julian, looking sullen and defeated. Julian smiled with supreme confidence as he turned to meet his brother, and then the scene flashed forward in time. For just a heartbeat in that flash of time, Aurelia peered outside her cocoon of living flesh with detached awareness and observed the others in their own cocoons. In that momentary glimpse, she saw Aliana, Nichole, the Butcher, and even Doe, along with countless others, each of them an organ serving the galactic body of Julian Mainstone and his great hive mind of planets and stars. After taking control of Aurelia's void-body, Julian had transformed Downver into a nightmare realm. Buildings twisted into skeletal structures, alleys morphed into rivers of blood, and each person became a power source of his new body. Using Aurelia and Aliana as a merged, single organ, he expanded, reaching deep into the Earth and tapping into its molten core. The ground quaked violently as geysers of magma surged upward, forging a new exoskeleton around Julian's heart. His armor glowed with hellish light, pulsating in sync with the Earth's dying heartbeat. Harald Mainstone and Vida fell to Julian with ease, and so did Astrea, each of them becoming an organ in his ever-expanding body. His mother, the Agency, was like a flatworm beneath his scalpel, while the Boreal Kingdoms and Wintersvilla posed no more of a threat than slugs sprinkled with salt. Waru, the Great Honey Mushroom, and every Nomad of the Earth—all of it was assimilated into Julian, with every mind kept alive and connected to his own. Within their fleshy prisons, Aurelia and the others became part of Julian's mind. They experienced his thoughts, his desires, his insatiable hunger for power. The sensation was overwhelming, a torrent of alien emotions and visions flooding their minds.

"Do you see now?" Julian's voice echoed divinely within them. "We are ascending. We are becoming gods."

A part of Aurelia remained, but she was like a dead fish upon the ocean's domineering surface, and so was everyone else. They were one giant sea of dead things, and the waves were the utterly insane yet profound aspirations of a creature who was originally more a living organ than an actual person.

Julian extended his reach beyond Earth, ensnaring neighboring planets to fuel his growth further. Over the course of years that felt like seconds, the asteroid belt and the inner planets crumbled in Julian's grasp, their barren landscapes absorbed into his expanding form, while the gas giants were siphoned and their moons consumed. Next, he lapped feverishly at the sun, assimilating the star and his own body to take on a new hybrid stellar form. Space and time warped around him as he manipulated the fabric of reality, bending it in a peculiar fashion to create a gravitational slingshot that propelled him toward his true goal: the Great Attractor, the supposed doorway to the Great Beyond, according to Mendel's Vision. He didn't have time to observe and confirm Mendel's Vision, but he didn't need to, for he could sense the presence of others in the direction of the Great Attractor. He was not alone in the cosmos.

We never were, Julian knew, nearly reciting Mendel's Ladder Theory of the Cosmos to himself as he jettisoned across space and time, devouring everything in his path. The plentiful and common space-shrew creatures fled the galaxy like birds flocking away at the first sign of an earthquake. Stars winked out as they were consumed. Nebulae dissipated into tendrils of energy absorbed into his being. He became a living galaxy, a swirling vortex of matter and consciousness.

As he neared the outskirts of the Great Attractor, he was still unable to fully observe it behind so many other galaxies. However, even from this distance, the true scale of the cosmic gathering became apparent. Countless other entities, each a gargantuan convergence of matter, energy, and other unclassified forces, converged upon the same destination. Some were galaxies molded into sentient forms like Julian, while others were incomprehensible beings of strange energy lattices, dark matter constructs, and complex gravitational matrices. Julian observed cosmic behemoths consuming countless smaller entities like himself, a feeding frenzy on a scale that threatened to unnerve him. But he pressed onward, undeterred by the cosmic carnage.

"We are close," he thought, his determination resonating through the hive mind. "Soon we will attain godhood."

Just then, Julian sensed the sudden gravity of something so vast and incomprehensibly large that it dwarfed the Great Attractor itself. Despite being composed of several galaxies, Julian was but an amoeba in the presence of a whale. The cosmic creature spanned hundreds of billions of light-years, with whole galactic clusters forming the mere tissue of its seemingly boundless ethereal body.

How? Julian gasped, feeling naked and alone for the first time in his many trillion year life. As if this cosmic juggernaut wasn't enough, Julian and all the others composing his now seemingly insignificant mind reeled at the realization that the Great Attractor was but one of many attractors leading to an unfathomable Greater Attractor. For all Julian knew, that too would just lead to another attractor, another step of the ladder that he felt he was presently slipping off.

I barely even started climbing Mendel's Ladder, Julian realized with horror and regret that manifested as gravitational waves that were like playful splashes in the wake of the great oceanic disturbances he was contending against. Countless others like Julian darted away from the celestial giant, many of them in the opposite direction of the Great Attractors, escaping the cosmic creature's maw but also sealing their fate by ensuring that the Great Attractors would be too far away to ever reach due to the exponentially accelerating rate of the universe's expansion and entropy. Julian knew Mendel's Vision showed how lucky humanity had been to be born far enough outside the jungle of cosmic death and destruction surrounding the first Great Attractor but also close enough to reach the Great Attractor before the expansion of spacetime made it impossible to catch up to, leading to eventual entropy death. But he didn't feel lucky, for he was about to be consumed. This is what his life had ultimately amounted to—a meal for something greater.

But I am not weak! Julian lashed, fueling his multi-galactic body with the simultaneous supernova of hundreds of billions of stars.

"Brace yourselves," Julian commanded the minds that had survived the pooling of energy to confront the great cosmic beast. The creature advanced across time scales of millions of years that passed in seconds, its gravitational pull irresistible. Despite his pooling of energy, Julian's form began to disintegrate, tendrils unraveling as they were drawn into the creature's body, which was also presently consuming numerous other smaller entities like Julian. The hive mind fragmented, panic and despair rippling through their shared consciousness.

Julian's thoughts were laced with frenzied anguish and desperation. *This can't be the end! I was meant for greatness, not death!*

As Julian and all the other minds were torn apart and assimilated into the vaster, more ancient body and mind of the staggeringly expansive entity, Aurelia awoke to herself for just a moment and gasped in horror at the way the future had unfolded.

I'm sorry, she thought, and then she was no more.

There was silence. Emptiness. Nothingness.

But then…a familiar sensation stirred. Somewhere in the forever-ocean of nothingness, a tiny point of awareness flickered into existence. It was like a solitary star igniting in the vast expanse of space.

Without warning, the awareness expanded, rapidly filling the void. Self-awareness blossomed, followed by spatial-awareness and meta-awareness. Form and sensation returned, memories flooding back like a river breaking through a dam.

Aurelia found herself once more suspended in eternal darkness, her body absent but her mind acutely present. The experiences of Julian's cosmic journey lingered like echoes—a dream fading upon waking. She still remembered being the stellar flesh tree as well. Both realities seemed perfectly real to her, but she knew that wasn't possible.

Is death just an endless series of possibilities that I will experience forever? Aurelia considered as she steeled herself and prepared for another foray into the world of the living.

But this time I'll be ready. This time I won't let Aliana or Rooli die, Aurelia told herself, wondering if it was possible to direct the course of events she would experience rather than being forced to be a passive observer. *But if I'm dead, does that even matter?* Aurelia thought, but she was quick to let the thought perish. *I have to try,* she resolved.

Again, a minuscule point of light pierced the infinite darkness, expanding rapidly and enveloping Aurelia in a familiar cascade of space, time, and form. She found herself hovering above the lake in Downver's Dark District, naked and free of the glistening black lesions that had created her void-body. Wintersvilla determination coursed through her veins, for this time she would change the course of fate. She would save Aliana and Rooli.

But as she looked below, dread clawed at her heart. Cid's fist was squeezed tightly closed, and Aurelia followed the direction his fist was pointing to see Rooli, already converted into a frail black flesh tree floating on the surface of the water. She was too late—this was just like her second vision, only Rooli died even quicker this time.

In a sudden flash of accelerated time, Cid's other hand reached toward Aliana, and before Aurelia could do anything, he squeezed his fist and converted Aliana into a glistening marble of blood.

No! Aurelia pleaded, feeling a part of herself break in the wake of watching both Rooli and Aliana snuffed out of existence in a single blow. Aurelia gasped as the vortex appeared in the lake and disappeared just as quickly, like a visual glitch.

The vortex, Aurelia thought with both horror and gratitude, for despite the ominous and terrible nature of the vortex in her mind, it was still familiar. It was a remnant from her life, the life that she had lost. The realization that she was dead and that she would be forced to observe these pathways of the future forever bore down on her, wrapping her in a profound emptiness. It made her desire the vortex.

If I could just enter it and be consumed by it, then at least this torture would end. But she knew that the vortex was a mere hallucination. It was as fruitless and arbitrary in life as it was in death.

Rather than being plunged into her unconscious, all-black body floating on the surface of the lake, this time Aurelia felt herself descend slowly. The crescendoing buzzing of the world around her faded into a muted haze as she entered her body. This time, Aurelia was not swayed by guilt or rage, but by grief and sorrow. In her despair, she witnessed a vivid prescient vision of the future, and she obeyed it, tearing the flesh tree that had been Rooli from its roots. She consumed it, chewing it into a powerful mush that merged with her body and fueled an unstoppable transformation. The glistening black of her body pulsed and undulated like a dark ocean churned by some great planetary storm. Cid reached out to destroy her, and though his lenses repeatedly flashed red, they had no effect. The black substance expanded outward like a star becoming a red giant, encasing Aurelia's body in a pulsing ebony cocoon.

Nichole arrived just as the Third Prodigal Son formed his body, but they did not engage in battle. Instead, both of them seemed to recognize that Aurelia was a threat beyond either of them. Nichole directed an entire city of razor filaments to destroy the growing cocoon, and Julian commanded his expansive underground networks of viscera strings to form relentless pillars of reinforced chitin that stabbed and sliced at the cocoon. However, even combined, their attacks were futile, appearing to only serve as fodder to the cocoon's voracious growth.

From within the dense, pulsing heart of darkness, Aurelia's sense of self slipped away, allowing her intense grief to flow through her and continue building the cocoon to fuel an incomprehensible metamorphosis that she gave herself to willingly. Rooli and Aliana were dead; she had no interest in whatever fate had in store for her. So, fate could have her. It could do with her whatever it wanted.

She let go and allowed herself to become fate's vessel.

The cocoon tightened, condensing Aurelia into a single point of awareness, and at the same time it went on expanding, consuming everything in its pathway like a dark slow-motion blast of a nuclear shockwave. Nichole, Julian, and Cid, and every other person in Downver dissolved into the expanding black cocoon. It surged beyond Downver and absorbed everything it touched. Mountains, atmosphere, Nomads, humans, flesh trees—nothing could stop its relentless expansion. The Earth was consumed inch by inch, mile by mile, continent by continent. The Agency, Harald, and Leif attempted a joint attack on the planetary cocoon, but they were consumed with ease.

Astrea orbited silently about the expanding sphere of darkness. From within Astrea, the void vultures sensed the dark substance. They swirled together with an insatiable hunger, and drawn by the Earth's transformation, they tore through the orbiting city's hull, ejecting all the survivors aboard into space as they swarmed toward the disappearing Earth like a cloud of obsidian locusts. They descended upon the still-growing glistening black cocoon that now encompassed the entire planet and hovered just above the surface, cherishing it as if it were their fabled homeland that had become real beyond all odds. As the cocoon went on expanding and consuming the inner planets, the void vultures dipped themselves into the darkness and fed on it. They grew and multiplied exponentially, becoming a seething, roiling mass around the dark planetary cocoon, as if they might constitute its atmosphere. Over time, they became an inseparable part of the churning cocoon, serving as an energy source to fuel its growth just as the vultures used the cocoon as an energy source to reproduce in turn.

Even after millions of years, the cocoon still went on expanding, consuming entire star systems as it prepared for some unfathomable transformation into something else. The void vultures spread outward, carrying the glistening black to other planets and moons. Star systems blinked out as the darkness eclipsed their suns. The galaxy writhed as if in pain, stars devoured like marrow sucked from splintering bone. The resilient space shrews sensed the encroaching doom and fled to other galaxies in droves, their iridescent forms vanishing into the depths to escape the relentless tide.

A great number of other sentient but simple creatures, like the shrews, avoided the cocoon as well, traveling to distant galaxies to stay far out of reach of its expansion-front. However, other beings of greater intellectual complexity took incredible interest in the cocoon. Over the next several million years, thousands of lesser but still spacefaring civilizations studied it up close, and invariably, all of them succumbed to being assimilated by it one way or another. All the while, the cocoon went on expanding, consuming myriad more stars and eventually gravitationally contorting spacetime into knots of cosmic disruption. The mind within the cocoon was diffuse now, spread thin across its great expanse. It knew only to consume and spread—there was nothing else.

Even higher intelligences observed the cocoon from their perches closer to the series of Great Attractors leading to the Great Beyond. These beings calculated the threat, and to the surprise of most of them, they worked together to issue warnings, erect barriers, and create diversions, but the cocoon's expansion was inexorable.

After several billion years, the Milky Way was fully converted into a churning galactic cocoon, a great glistening black cosmic mass equivalent to many thousands of galactic black holes, yet it did not implode into a singularity. The Andromeda Galaxy loomed on the horizon, and a portion of it was absorbed, while the rest of it collided with the galactic cocoon like an egg shattering against hard yet porous soil. Chaos reigned. Stars were cast adrift, planets shattered, but the cocoon capitalized on the turmoil. It spread further, integrating the celestial debris into its ever-growing mass.

Across the numerous Great Attractors of the cosmos, ancient beings took notice. These were colossal entities composed of multiple galaxies, their forms woven from the very fabric of spacetime. Even though they planned to enter the Great Beyond, they recognized the cocoon as a threat, a dangerous variable that could not be allowed to persist.

Gathering their collective might, they orchestrated a plan. With gravitational forces beyond comprehension, they began to shepherd the cocoon toward the Boötes Void—a cosmic abyss spanning hundreds of millions of light-years. Galaxies were sacrificed, their gravities repurposed to corral the cocoon.

The process took many billions of years, but slowly and unceasingly, the glistening black cosmic ocean the cocoon had grown into was finally drawn into the heart of the void. The ancient beings formed a spherical barrier of galaxies whose combined gravities created a prison from which there could be no escape. Within the Boötes Void, the cocoon churned but could not expand. Isolated from the rest of the universe without any means of accessing the Great Beyond, it became a stagnant sea. Its residual consciousness drifted aimlessly, its awareness reduced to fleeting impressions. Time lost all meaning. Stars outside the void aged and died. Galaxies drifted apart as the universe continued its relentless expansion. Entropy increased, the fabric of reality stretching thinner and thinner.

As the eons passed, the universe approached its inevitable end—a big tear, in which the very bonds that held matter together would eventually unravel. Galaxies disintegrated, stars evaporated, and particles dissolved into nothingness. Yet, within the Boötes Void, the cosmic cocoon remained, somehow shielded from universal decay. In the absence of external stimuli, its mind stagnated. The void vultures ceased their endless flights, settling into the inky depths.

The cocoon, never having achieved its final transformation, existed in a state of perpetual limbo—a simple awareness floating in an eternity of nothingness. There were no thoughts, no emotions, just a constant state of neutral being. As the last remnants of the universe faded away, only the cocoon persisted. In the ultimate silence, its essence flickered, a solitary candle in an infinite abyss, and that is how it remained. An eternal constant in a sea of nothingness. Not alive, not dead. Simply existing, until even existing became meaningless, and there was just an ocean of nothingness inside and out.

Seemingly forever.

And yet, somewhere in the forever-ocean of nothingness, a tiny point of awareness flickered into existence. The awareness expanded, rapidly filling the void. Self-awareness returned, followed by spatial-awareness and meta-awareness. Form and sensation returned, and Aurelia remembered herself and observed the eternal darkness of death.

I was wrong, she realized, her mind buckling after experiencing what had felt like an eternity as the sea of darkness within the void. *I can't take this! Please just let me end! Please!* Aurelia pleaded, but there was no one to plead to.

Without giving her a moment's reprieve, a point of light appeared somewhere in the forever-darkness.

Not again! Aurelia begged.

According to Mendel's Vision, Anna will obey my instruction to harvest the Hunter's seed and become impregnated with the child who will carry my mind into the Great Beyond. The importance of this child is the reason I designed Astrea to birth numerous children capable of fulfilling their role in the ANNA project, and it is also why I have prepared numerous Hunters specially chosen for this essential rung of Mendel's Ladder. Even if Hunter4430 dies or refuses coitus with Anna, eventually one of the other Hunters I have prepared as contingencies will unwittingly adhere to Mendel's Vision.

Those specially made Hunters who are no longer of use to me will be free to live and die as they see fit. However, most will choose to serve me in my new form—a child who will be capable of entering the Great Beyond and exploring its outskirts.

Anna is the key that will unlock the doorway to infinity, but it is her child who will walk through it. A child composed of the minds of Anna, the Hunter, Mendel, and myself. A child who will carry the weight of Mendel's Vision and do whatever must be done to ensure my Ascension.

From Mendel's Ladder: The Personal Journal of Denis Mendel, Recorded Circa 2063, Published June 2108 by Leif Mainstone, Federated Agency Publishing

Chapter 5
To Wield Power

T he darkness of the cave was irrelevant to Thompson's new body, for it could utilize numerous spectra of sensation to create a remarkably detailed map of his surroundings in his mind. Infrared, echolocation, olfactory mapping, seismic perception, even magnetoreception—all of these extra senses made his powerful eyes just another redundant tool in his anatomical arsenal.

Thompson marveled at his body's ability to navigate through the labyrinthine caves with effortless fluidity. He adapted to each new terrain and obstacle with transformations that took place in mere fractions of a second compared to what used to require several seconds depending on the complexity. Where the tunnel narrowed, his skeletal structure compressed, ribs folding inward like the petals of a wilting flower. When jagged stalagmites jutted from the floor, his flesh hardened into a chitinous armor, deflecting the razor-sharp points without breaking stride.

As he traveled, myriad forms of perception at his disposal revealed a vibrant, living subterranean world, despite its isolation from Earth's surface: the warmth of geothermal vents glowed crimson in his infrared vision; the faint echoes of dripping water sketched out distant caverns through echolocation; subtle shifts in the Earth's magnetic field guided him like an invisible compass. It was invigorating to feel the minute yet precise vibrations of unseen soilies crawling along the cavern walls or to hear the faint whisper of air currents weaving through hidden fissures.

I was already more powerful than other Hunters with the special skinsuit Anna brought me. Now, though...I'm more powerful than I even realized at first. The skinsuit is one with me now, whether I like it or not, Thompson reminded himself, both relishing his power and its potential to save Anna, while also lamenting it as the central shackle of his existence.

"The Great Beyond is no mere idea; it is existential canon," Andre's voice resounded, piercing through Thompson's concentration like a shard of ice. The words swelled from a murmur to a proclamation before fading back into the cacophony of whispers that plagued his mind.

"Please, not now," Thompson muttered under his breath for what might be the hundredth time already. He was already on edge as he navigated the caves and followed the scent of another Hunter. The last thing he wanted was to be startled and left vulnerable by the voices in his head. He clenched his jaw, muscles tightening like coiled springs ready to snap. The spectral voices were becoming more frequent, more insistent, as if sensing his proximity to the Virus. He couldn't afford to be distracted, not when he was so close.

This must be how Volya felt when I used the fog against her, Thompson considered, empathizing with his wretched Huntress despite himself. Thinking of Volya made him hesitate as he thought of MaxxEl outside the cave. A pang of guilt stabbed at him, sharp and sudden. *The wind outside carried Volya's scent. It was faint, but it was there. She's out there somewhere. I know it. It wasn't just another Huntress either. It was her. It has to be.*

He clenched his fists, which morphed into jagged spikes of metallic bone.

I'm sorry, MaxxEl, but I cannot help you, Thompson thought as he forced himself forward.

"I'm sorry, Denis. Forgive me, my only friend," Andre shrieked, making Thompson stumble as his right foot's transformation was interrupted, leaving it sprawling into a useless nine-toed lily pad structure. Thompson caught himself and shook his head at the voice's intrusion. He was about to shout at it, but he knew it would be futile. Andre would continue to bubble into Thompson's mind, seemingly with greater force the closer he came to Downver.

Why did Tether fill my head with Andre and his memories? What's the point? Thompson ruminated, spiteful that he was being forced to suffer through these random spikes of someone else's uncontrolled thoughts.

Thompson took a deep breath and held Anna in his mind. Her smile, her voice, the way her emerald eyes held galaxies when she looked at him—all anchors pulling him back to sanity. *I won't fail you again, Anna,* Thompson assured her. He filled his mind with the mental fog Anna had taught him to use and let it seep into the deepest cracks and crevices. Slowly but surely, the voices faded to a distant background buzz that became easily lost amidst Thompson's other thoughts.

You're still saving me, Anna, Thompson told her before lifting himself and pressing forward into the darkness.

Emerging into a vast cavern, Thompson halted at the edge of a chasm that dropped hundreds of feet below. At the bottom, a river roared, its turbulent waters carving intricate gushing paths through the Earth. Spanning the mile-long cavern from one side to the other was a thick steel beam. Thompson could smell that roughly a day ago, something had bled as it crawled across the beam roughly thirty feet and then abruptly stopped.

The Mirror-Man? Thompson wondered, unsure if the enigmatic figure was capable of bleeding or if he was even human, like his name implied. *If he bleeds, he can be killed,* Thompson mused, recalling an old saying Anna used to use.

Extending his senses, Thompson emitted a screeching pulse of ultrasonic waves that bounced off the cavern walls and mapped his surroundings in intricate detail. The world unfolded like a black-and-white canvas, every contour and crevice etched into his awareness. He couldn't sense any other life in the cavern, but he still remained ready for battle nonetheless. The tunnels formed by the river below extended for miles in all directions like a network of pulsing veins. The scent Thompson had been tracking—that of a Hunter intermingled with human odors—emanated from deep within those tunnels. There was another familiar scent as well that surprised Thompson.

The green-glowing mushrooms from the cave with Tether—they're close, Thompson realized, letting the scent linger on his mind as the fog helped significantly to buffer Andre and the other voices, though it could not silence them. *Those mushrooms aren't just beneath the surface of that other planet that Tether took me to. They're beneath the surface of the Earth too. What are they, really?* Thompson wondered, reaffirming his suspicion of Tether.

Wanting to investigate the blood on the beam, Thompson prepared to leap to where the trail stopped. He coiled his muscles in anticipation, feeling the raw power simmering beneath his skin, and then the world seemed to explode with radiance as a blinding flash of light tore through the ceiling of the chasm and pierced the perfect darkness. Thompson's eyelids instinctively morphed into a multilayered series of transparent lenses that allowed him to observe the event without being blinded.

Something bright and reflective streaked past him with such velocity that time seemed to dilate. It was only his enhanced perception that allowed him to register the blurred details of the object: a muscular man with limbs flailing wildly as he bored through the earth at an impossible speed.

"The Mirror-Man!" Andre shouted through the mental fog. Most of the man's skin, save his entire pitch-black chest, shimmered like molten silver and reflected Thompson and the rest of the cave. His reflective flesh distorted the world around him as if warping reality. The air crackled with energy in the man's wake, quickly followed by a deafening boom that echoed as he collided and bored through the opposing wall of the cavern. To Thompson's surprise, the underground didn't cave in; tremors didn't even follow in the man's energetic wake.

Was that him? Thompson considered as his mind processed what had just occurred. *Was that the Mirror-Man? It had to be. He was a man, and his skin was like a mirror, at least, most of it was. That means he knows where I am. So then, that must have been a warning. He's telling me to stay out of Downver, or else.*

"The Mirror-Man will be honest, righteous, and selfless," Andre stated in Thompson's mind, breaking through the fog, though at least the volume of his voice was subdued. "The day he sets foot upon the surface, nothing will ever be the same again," Andre said before the fog finally overtook him once more.

Are you warning me too, Andre? Thompson considered. *Or was that just a coincidence that you started talking about the Mirror-Man just as he passed?*

As expected, Andre didn't answer. Rather than being a sentient presence, his voice was like a recording stuck on loop at certain points in Andre's life. Thompson wasn't sure if he would prefer actually being able to talk to Andre, rather than just being incessantly talked at by him.

Keeping Anna at the forefront of his mind, Thompson reformed his legs into spring-like tendons and propelled himself across the chasm in a single bound. His hands transformed midair, fingers elongating into grappling hooks that latched onto the fractured edges of the hole left by the Mirror-Man. With a fluid motion, he pulled himself through the opening and landed softly on the ledge above.

The scent of the Hunter and humanity are even stronger this way. I can smell those mushrooms too. Did the Mirror-Man…help me? Thompson considered, utterly unsure what the reflective man's motivation might be.

Either way, he knows I'm here. I have to hurry. I have to contend with this

Hunter and then find Aurelia. Just a little longer, Anna.

Thompson followed the opening down a narrow passageway that twisted like a serpent's spine. The tight walls were lined with the green bioluminescent mushrooms that had been in Tether's cave, their scent identical. Their soft glow cast eerie shadows that flickered as Thompson continued, and he observed that larger and larger mushrooms grew from the walls the further he went.

The Hunter is close, Thompson confirmed, preparing himself to dispatch what was sure to be a savage beast. He had no way of knowing what a Hunter was doing in these caves, but it didn't matter.

Hunters are dangerous. Volya claimed we were the last Pair, but clearly that isn't true. There were more Hunters in Tether's cave. And there is another Hunter down here. Maybe more than one, Thompson realized, but he did not allow himself to hesitate.

If they stand against me and my new body, then they will die, Thompson assured himself, repeatedly sickened that he had no choice but to wield and willingly use power against others for Anna's sake. The thought tasted bitter, like ash on his tongue.

Rounding a corner, Thompson entered a chamber brimming with mushrooms that had grown to colossal proportions, their caps stretching to the rocky ceiling like great flesh trees, their bodies bulging and seemingly breathing with life. Their bioluminescent glow pulsed rhythmically as he observed them with wonder and considered their true connection to Tether and maybe even Andre and the Mind.

The chamber felt alive, almost sentient, as if observing him in return. While tiny luminescent spores danced around him like evanescent snow, he followed a pathway through the mushrooms, squeezing past them at one point due to their incredible density. They appeared to be visibly swelling as their mycelial tendrils lapped at something on the ground.

The Hunter, Thompson realized, tracing the scent to the source of whatever the mushrooms were feeding on. Thompson peered around the largest mushroom to find the mangled corpse of a Hunter, his body torn to pieces with something sharp. Blood, dark and viscous, pooled around the remains. The Hunter's skull had been impaled from the back, with his jaws and shattered teeth serving as the exit wound for what Thompson assumed was the same thing that had mangled the Hunter's body beyond repair.

Thompson crouched beside the Hunter's remains and observed his extensive scars and open lesions covering every inch of his body without a skinsuit to keep the damage hidden and at bay. Thompson had once shared the same horrendous wounds, the result of years of ceaseless torture by Cleaners while suspended over his birth-fire.

A shudder ran through him as a wave of sordid memories crashed over Thompson: the searing pain, the smell of burning flesh, the endless days and nights of agony. *Like me and all other Hunters, he was tortured from birth, and based on these recent wounds, it looks like he was tortured before death too. What else is down here that can do this to a Hunter? This happened recently too.* Thompson looked back at the mushroom feeding on the Hunter and pressing against one another as they ravenously filled the gaps between their already bulging bodies. *Did these mushrooms kill the Hunter?* Thompson backed away from them with sudden nervousness. *Or maybe it was another Hunter. If there's one down here, maybe there are others.*

Thompson sniffed the air and sent out an ultrasonic pulse, but he couldn't catch the scent or feeling of another Hunter besides this one. *The only other scent is that of humanity. I can smell Downver from here. It's close. Extremely close. It's like this path is leading me directly to where I need to go.*

Thompson thought of the Mirror-Man and again felt perplexed at what had occurred. *It can't be a coincidence that he made this path for me. He's goading me forward. He wants me to find him. He's challenging me.*

Thompson felt a flicker of the old, uncontrollable Hunter rage that used to pervade his every thought and intention. However, his body allowed him to subdue the feeling and let it pass through him and away from him like a flash of lightning, gone just as suddenly as it had appeared.

I will remain in control, Thompson resolved. *Control is my greatest weapon now. But I'm not going to run away from the Mirror-Man's challenge. Not if he stands in my way and attempts to take the Virus for himself. No, the girl will help me. She's caught up in all this madness just like the rest of us. Why wouldn't she want justice against the Mind, Madeira, and Mendel, who have played us all like expendable pieces of currency in a celestial wager. She will want justice. She will help me save Anna and destroy the Mind. I have to believe that.*

A low but distinct rumble echoed through the cavern, the ground beneath Thompson trembling. Thompson directed his senses to the epicenter of the vibrations and discovered that he was just outside the borders of Downver now, with a whole city full of people—humans—

just beyond the walls of the glowing mushroom cavern. His heartbeat quickened, a drumbeat matching the escalating tremors. The vibrations revealed that something was presently destroying a portion of the city, though Thompson couldn't sense precisely what it was nor the extent of the damage. The low rumbling finally gave way to a colossal boom, which Thompson's senses reflexively revealed to be the toppling of some large structure.

It's some kind of tall tower, Thompson realized, remembering how fond the humans had been of building vertical structures and living in them. Anna had explained that it was related to humanity's most ancient mammalian ancestors being shrew-like tree dwellers. Thompson had never seen a shrew, not even as a picture, but based on Anna's description, it was hard to imagine how they could be related to humanity. Anna had explained that humans changing from shrew-creatures to ape-creatures was due to natural evolution and that Thompson was not part of that natural chain.

You and I are not part of natural evolution, Thompson remembered Anna saying. *We are a part of neoevolution. Directed evolution. And He is the director.*

Now Thompson knew that she had been talking about Andre Madeira and Denis Mendel, or maybe the Mind, or maybe all three. *Either way, I'm no longer under his control. Volya is no longer my master. I can direct my own evolution,* Thompson resolved.

He looked down at the mangled Hunter and shook his head. "I'm not going to end up like you," Thompson said aloud, his deep Hunter voice seeming to excite the green-glowing mushrooms. "I'm going to survive, and I'm going to save Anna. With this body I can do it. I am no mere Hunter like you. Not anymore. I am something else." Remembering how the Cleaner had reacted to him, Thompson told himself, *I can even destroy the Mirror-Man, impossible as that might seem.*

"I hate you. I loathe you. I wish I had never met you," the woman named Gladys shouted so loudly in Thompson's mind that he fell to his knees and clutched his head.

"I beg of you to understand, darling," Andre pleaded.

"Quiet!" Thompson shouted, and he summoned the fog to shield his mind. The mental barrier rose like a fortress, walls of willpower shielding him from the onslaught. With the voices returned to a background murmur, Thompson formulated a plan.

I can burst right into Downver and look for the girl at top speed, but there's already something going on in there. For all I know her life could already be in jeopardy, and my barging in there might only add to the chaos. Or I can burrow to the very edge of the city, close to where that building fell, and then I can go in as a human being. Anna and I used to pull it off all the time. I'm sure with this body I can look even more convincing. If all goes well, I can slip in and search for the girl without anyone even realizing I don't belong. It's either that, Thompson thought as he scanned the Hunter's destroyed body again, *or I will have to resort to…killing.*

Thompson gulped down the word, hoping to avoid any more death until he confronted the Mind.

I have to move, Thompson urged himself, tabling the possibility of having to resort to violence for the sake of doing something, anything, as long as it meant he was getting closer to Anna.

Determined not to waste another moment, Thompson retracted his limbs and willed his spine to elongate as his body compressed into a sleek, segmented tube shape. His skin hardened into a smooth, flexible carapace, and his sensory organs reflexively rearranged so that they were optimized for travel directly through the Earth's dense crust. In less than a second he transformed into a colossal worm-like creature capable of boring through the Earth with relentless efficiency.

He plunged into the wall, the rock yielding to his advance as enzymes secreted from his skin dissolved the minerals ahead. Heat built up around him, the friction igniting sparks that danced along his sides before fizzling out. Behind him, the tunnel collapsed, leaving no trace of his passage. As he burrowed deeper, Thompson's mind remained a battlefield. Images of Anna wound about memories of Volya, and all the while fragments of Andre's consciousness flared sporadically, interjecting thoughts and memories through his mind like Cleaners' skewers into flesh.

"You see, my friend, they seek only hedonism, while we seek Ascension. They are titans. We are gods," Andre declared within.

"Enough!" Thompson growled with a newly grown mouth as he pulled back the mental fog. "Your path ended, Andre. But mine is only just beginning. I'm coming for your precious Mind, and I'm going to destroy it. You hear me? I'm going to destroy the remnants of you that still remain, and I'm going to take Anna back. She isn't yours, Andre. Anna is mine. My own. My love. And I am hers. You cannot have her, you wicked creature!"

"We are gods," Andre repeated far in the distance of Thompson's awareness.

And I am a monster who will consume a god, Thompson thought as he plowed through the Earth with Downver just a handful of seconds away.

Slavery. It is an inescapable shadow that haunts the past and present corridors of human history.

We delude ourselves with notions of freedom, yet at every turn, chains bind our hands and manacles shackle our feet. If we are not enslaving each other—forcing our will upon the weak or manipulating the unsuspecting—we are enslaving ourselves.

We are prisoners of our desires, captives of our fears, hostages to the illusions we craft within our terrified minds.

Even when we shatter the visible chains, casting off the yoke of others and the fetters of our own making, we remain subservient to the immutable laws of the universe. Gravity holds us down, time pushes us forward, entropy tears us apart.

Even those who strive to transcend the fundamental principles that govern reality become slaves to freedom itself. Obsessed, consumed by the pursuit of liberation, they forge new chains from their very desire to break free. The irony is as palpable as it is tragic: their quest for emancipation becomes the very prison they seek to escape.

I recognize this paradox within myself. I, too, am ensnared—enthralled by the vision of absolute freedom. Freedom from death's grasp, from entropy's relentless decay, from the constraints that have rendered humanity impotent and compelled me to adopt extreme measures.

The truth is that we cannot escape servitude; it is woven into the very fabric of existence. The question is not how to cease serving, but whom or what we choose to serve.

I have made my choice. I serve all life, not as it is, bound and blinded, but as it could be, unshackled and ascended.

That is why I climb Mendel's Ladder, each rung a defiance against the chains that bind us, each step a stride toward Ascension unto the Great Beyond. I seek a realm where freedom is not a fleeting illusion, but an intrinsic reality. Where existence is not dictated by the tyrannies of nature or the whims of lesser beings.

Some will call me a villain, a tyrant, a madman enslaved by his own hubris. Let them. Their words are but the clattering of chains they cannot see. For I know that in my servitude, I am freer than any who worship at the altar of their own limitations. I have chosen my master wisely. I serve the future, the potential of what humanity can become when it sheds its self-imposed shackles.

We are all slaves to something, be it power, fear, love, or the inexorable laws of reality. True freedom lies not in the absence of chains but in the understanding of which chains we choose to bear. So, I have chosen to be a slave to freedom itself, to become its instrument.

This is my immutable purpose. This is my unwavering mission. To lead humanity up Mendel's Ladder, beyond the confines of our current existence, and into the embrace of the Great Beyond. To transform slaves into masters of their own destiny, even if it means bearing the heaviest chains so that others may know the lightness of true freedom.

In the end, if being a slave to freedom is the price of ushering in a new epoch of existence, then I accept my bondage with open arms.

From Mendel's Ladder: The Personal Journal of Denis Mendel, Written Circa 2049, Published June 2108 by Leif Mainstone, Federated Agency Publishing

Chapter 6
A Slave to Freedom

T he sun hung low in the sky over the Butcher Wastelands, casting an eerie orange hue that bled into the horizon like a gaping wound. Above, Astrea sliced through the sky; below, Volya ruminated intently on her past while planning carefully for her future.

I was a slave, she seethed as she observed a small, malformed Mutant drag itself across the wastes in a desperate attempt to flee Volya. It had been dragging itself for just over thirty minutes, scraping its body across the jagged rocks as its terrified squirrel face peered back at Volya over the shoulders of its half-formed amphibious lower body.

I'm still a slave, Volya concluded with such overwhelming rage that she couldn't help grunting beneath her breath as she continued trudging in the direction of Downver with the Mutant believing her to be its predator.

"Why the fuck are you running, you ugly fuck?" Volya shouted at the Mutant, prompting it to drag itself with even greater desperation. These types of malformed Mutants were rare, but every so often, a splicer bush miscalculated and merged the genetics of its victims in a way that resulted in a creature that was better off stillborn. Volya wasn't sure if this Mutant had only just recently been spliced or if it had somehow survived the world in its deformed state by sheer blind luck. Either way, she loathed it for running from her, for although it meant that she was no longer a Huntress who belonged to the ignoble Mendel, it also confirmed to her that she belonged to a new authority. Another false god.

Mendel treated me like an unwanted bastard child, manipulating me and then throwing me away when I no longer served his purpose. Now, Gladys Mainstone is attempting to do the same thing.

Volya stopped and eyed her hands with an unsettling mix of disgust and invigoration. She flexed her fingers and watched as they disassembled into intelligent swarms of shimmering nanocells before reforming into her familiar solid hands. Although her body was now more powerful than any number of Hunter and Huntress Pairs combined, she still found the sensation disconcerting, for she was still an object with strings attached to a new master.

Gladys Mainstone...the Agency, Volya thought with the churning rage of a Hunter.

"Freedom," Volya announced bitterly, remembering how much the word had sounded like servitude when Gladys had used it. "She dares to speak of freedom as if it's hers to grant."

Volya turned and looked back at the mountain range she had swarmed over after leaving the Agency on her way to Downver.

"I know you're always listening, Gladys. And I'm sure Mendel—the Mind—is listening too. So then, listen up, fuckers. I belong to neither of you. I have no master. I will not be your Huntress, Mendel. And I will not be your Second Prodigal Daughter, Gladys. You claimed that I am free to make my own choices, as mandated by Mendel's Vision, but fuck that!" Volya shrieked, feeling as though a collar were being tightened around her neck at the very thought of being *mandated* freewill. "I am free because I mandate it!" Volya shouted at the top of her lungs as she envisioned the destruction she would soon wreak against all those who enslaved others and called it freedom. Though she had resolved to avoid using slavery as a tool in her arsenal, Volya wasn't morally opposed to slavery as a general practice. Rather, what filled her with unforgiving loathing was the hypocrisy of these false gods who called their slavery freedom.

Schemers. Manipulators. Connivers. Deceivers. And I was one of them. But no longer. I decided my name, and I will decide my actions as well. Fuck the Eternal Hunt. Fuck Mendel's Ladder. Fuck Agency Ascension. Fuck it all. I will decide my own fate, and it all starts with Thompson.

Volya gulped down the urge to scream at the thought of Thompson, for he was her own personal seed of ruin, germinating and sprouting and entwining through her every thought like a birthfire scorching everything she once held sacred until only ashes remained.

I'm not helping him out of guilt or penance, she told herself unconvincingly as she envisioned her plan to find Thompson and help him destroy Mendel and save his precious, pitiable human woman, the one he undoubtedly still yearned and even breathed for.

My dog, Volya thought before correcting herself. *Thompson...he will need my help. He's a fucking idiot. He's still a slave to Anna, even though he's no longer a slave to me.*

"I don't love him, you insolent academic. I hate him!" Gladys' human voice shrieked in Volya's mind with such force that Volya was forced to her knees and momentarily blinded.

"Fuck!" Volya spat as she regained herself. "Get out of my head, bitch!"

"You cannot stop yourself from loving, Gladys. You are human, no matter how badly you do not want to be," came the pretentious voice of a man, sounding as though he were simultaneously distant and directly next to her.

"Fuck you!" Volya shouted at the voices.

"Fuck you, Tomasz!" Gladys shouted at the man before her voice returned to nearly inaudible muttering in the distant background of her mind.

These fucking voices…everything comes with a price, Volya considered as she analyzed her body and realized that she was past due for detaching a part of herself.

This body is a vessel of incredible potential, but it is still limited by constraints I'm still learning the boundaries of.

She flexed her fingers, the tips already beginning to disassemble into nanocells as other nanocells at the base of her fingers began to replicate and restore what had been lost. The process of fully replacing the lost nanocells would take approximately thirty minutes, a fact she had learned through rigorous experimentation over the last few hours since she had left the Agency. There were limits to this new form, parameters defined by the physical laws governing the nanocells and the constraints of her own consciousness.

Volya recalled Gladys' clinical explanation: the nanocells had a density threshold. Too dense, and the internal cells would overheat and break down; too sparse, and the structural integrity would fail. There existed an equilibrium, a point of optimal functionality that coincided, not coincidentally, with the size and form of her original body.

"Real fucking funny how that works," she murmured wryly. "My old body and this new one—even they are just the imposed designs of false gods."

Over time, I will find a way to adapt to greater densities and more complex configurations, Volya told herself. *But for now, I'll operate within these preset boundaries, and I will use them to my advantage while I hone my abilities.*

Volya's gaze drifted to the horizon. The Mutant was far away now, its frantic scrabbling fading into the distance. Volya looked back at her hand as she raised it into the air and splayed her fingers against the sunset. The nanocells in her fingertips vibrated in anticipation, and with a focused thought that was becoming easier to execute, Volya initiated the separation. The tips of her fingers began to dissolve, the seemingly solid flesh fragmenting into clouds of shimmering particles that hovered momentarily before drifting to the northeast like locusts.

The swarm moved swiftly, covering ground at an impressive rate. The intelligence of the swarm was remarkable—a fraction of herself imbued with autonomy and purpose. She estimated that each swarm, representing 1/166th of her mass, possessed sufficient cognitive function to operate independently well enough to scout and gather information without direct oversight. Moreover, the swarms had the capacity to replicate. Through assimilation of available materials— ambient particles, organic matter—they could gradually increase their mass, eventually regenerating into what Volya assumed would be a full version of herself over the course of what she estimated to be three and a half days based on the replication rate.

"Cloning," she mused.

The fingertips on her right hand were already regrowing, the nanocells replicating with methodical precision. She flexed them, satisfied with the progress.

A new swarm every thirty minutes, she calculated. *An army in days.*

Such incredible power, and yet, I'm like that brainless son of hers, Volya thought, remembering how Gambe had wielded similar abilities with unnerving precision. His ability to dissolve into swarms and create copies of himself had fascinated her and had even filled her with envy, and now that same power was hers to command.

Only I'm far more powerful than Gambe, because I don't have the brain of a disabled child, Volya thought with what she considered to be measured reason. *If he had had more than a few functioning brain cells, he would have managed to make thousands of copies of himself by the time he met me. Fourth Prodigal son…if Gladys' data is true, then that means he was made in 2071. What the hell has he been doing for the last 28 years? Gladys' data also showed that the*

Fourth Prodigal Son's name wasn't originally Gambe. It was Thorstein. Does that mean he…threw away his old name and chose his own name? Like me?

Volya scowled at the thought of Gambe being anything like herself.

He was a willing slave to Gladys, she thought.

Volya considered that Gladys had named all her sons after famous Vikings, revealing that Gladys was, like Volya, an admirer, however begrudgingly, of that glorious form of human. Volya had once admired them for their savage love of torture and violence, but now she admired them for their sheer ruthlessness. Even better, they didn't see themselves as mere slaves to their gods; they were cohorts in their gods' games of mass death—players on the board, even if inferior.

As if Volya's mind were torturing her of its own accord, she thought, *Maybe I'm still a slave after all, if not to her, then…a slave to freedom itself.*

"I will not see this universe converted into Tsehay slaves!" Gladys suddenly shrieked within Volya's mind.

"Enough," Volya snarled through gritted teeth, the word barely more than a guttural growl torn from the depths of her being. Volya's fury surged, and without conscious command, her body ballooned outward as the nanocells flared violently, swelling her form like a sudden nuclear shockwave ready to unleash. In a heartbeat, she clenched her expansive fists and reined in her anger, snapping her body back into its original shape. The nanocells consolidated, and Gladys' voice returned to a barely audible mumble.

Exhaling sharply, Volya forced herself forward in the direction of Downver. Still able to tap into the old world satellites, she observed the world from above.

The most recent swarm Volya had released was already over 10 miles away and was just passing over the lone Wintersvilla Woman—maybe the last of her kind. Unlike every other Wintersvilla Woman Volya was aware of, this one wore clothing, and her shoulders were draped with a blood-drenched green cloak.

Lain, Volya thought as she recollected Gladys' request, rather than command, to kill the young woman along with her exo. Lain was presently harvesting barbs from a patch of barb bushes, while her unique autonomous exo prepared a fire using the bark of a hollowed flesh tree, along with a bundle of fire vines to use as an igniter. Zooming in closer, Volya saw that Lain was gritting her teeth in anguish and clutching her sides every so often.

She's already hurt. She would be easy prey, Volya considered. Gladys hadn't told Volya what she would provide in exchange for killing Lain, only that it was powerful.

I'm sure she knows that keeping it a secret only entices me more, Volya calculated, hating and admiring Gladys. Gladys had claimed to be waging her own war on countless fronts, the most pressing and profound involving battles against her own sons. But she had claimed her very greatest enemy was a being known as Tether, the same being who Volya had mistaken as Anna and who had presided over Volya's death. Volya winced as she remembered being consumed from the inside out by swarms of insects.

Clearly Tether is my enemy as well, but that doesn't mean I'm going to do Gladys' bidding, Volya reasoned. *Maybe I'll kill the Wintersvilla Woman, and maybe I won't. And maybe I'll kill the little girls, Aliana and Aurelia, or maybe I won't. If Gladys wants all three of them dead, then she can do it herself. All I care about is destroying Mendel, and Thompson is going to help me do it. I'll even help him save his precious human first. I owe him that much...I guess.*

Volya's gaze sharpened as she flipped through the partitions of her mind to locate the local satellite feeds. One had a direct view of the three massive craters embedded into the Earth's surface above Downver. The Butcher Wastelands stretched over the horizon to the north, east, and south of the craters, while the mountains to the west loomed like lords of the Earth observing Volya's every movement.

The memory of the battle with the two Wintersvilla Warriors and Gambe still felt as vivid as the present moment. The adrenaline and fury that had coursed voraciously through Thompson's body and her mind still lingered on her tongue. But what had followed the battle still tasted bitter.

The fucking Cleaners, those faceless freaks. They tricked me! Me!

Volya clenched her fists and felt them vibrate with latent energy. She had intended to deceive the Cleaners, only to be outplayed by them and led like a bleating lamb to her own slaughter.

Her eyes narrowed as she zoomed in to the bottom of the crater where the battle had taken place. Remnants of the battle were still scattered about the ground—a twisted exo rod here, scorched earth there—but something was missing. The red-headed woman's exo should have still been standing at the bottom of the crater, but it was gone.

"What the fuck?" Volya whispered, her frustration mounting. The Cleaners had only taken a fragment of the exo during their last encounter. There was no reason for the entire exo to be gone unless someone, or something, had moved it.

The Cleaners said they were bringing her to the Agency, Volya recalled, her mind racing to calculate this new variable. *But that red–headed eyeless Wintersvilla bitch wasn't at the Agency. At least, I didn't see her. But then again, the Agency takes up at least 170,000 square miles of land, and that's just what Gladys chose to reveal. So maybe the woman was taken to the Agency after all, and I just didn't see any trace of her. Maybe she's going to be changed like me. Or,* Volya considered, remembering how much vitriol the woman had been filled with, *maybe she found a way to break out of her shackles, kill those Cleaners, and return to her exo.*

Volya suspiciously peered all around herself, utilizing numerous satellites along with her own eyes at the same time.

Or maybe it was something else entirely, Volya reasoned, remaining on edge and prepared for battle at all times. Either way, she knew the woman and her exo weren't just pieces that had disappeared from the board.

"They're out there somewhere. Somewhere beyond my vision. I doubt I've seen the last of her."

"I loved you, Andre!" Gladys whispered with unbecoming vulnerability in her wavering tone.

"Andre?" Volya asked. "You mean Andre Madeira? Mendel's early ally who died aboard Astrea?"

The voice of Gladys, like a recording played randomly inside Volya's skull, either did not or could not answer.

"Fine," Volya spat, dismissing the voice. "Keep your secrets. It doesn't matter."

Volya took a deep breath. She needed to mentally prepare—for Downver, for the battles to come, for whatever twisted games the false gods were concocting even now.

Fuck them, Volya thought. *I'm ready. I know exactly what I'm going to do: destroy Mendel and Gladys, and Thompson is going to do it alongside me. I won't need to force him this time. If anything, I'll have to convince him to let me come with him, not the other way around. Now, it's time to arrive at the edge of the battlefield. I want to get a good spot before everything starts.*

Volya commanded her body to disperse, and it obeyed, dissolving her form into a loose swarm of nanocells. She roved above the Earth's surface like an old world swarm of wasps, coalescing every so often back into her original form for but a moment before dispersing again. The need to return to her original form was beginning to wane with time, and Volya considered that, eventually, she might even be able to spread herself across the entire planet, with or without her clones.

As she flew toward the craters at just over 100 MPH, Volya allowed her thoughts to drift. The concept of "players" gnawed at her—a term Gladys had used to describe herself, Mendel, Tether, the Ninth Prodigal Son, and others that she had only alluded to. Gladys' warnings had specified the convergence of many of these players in the form of a planet-altering battle that would take place on the surface above Downver.

But how many layers does this game of ruthless players really have? Volya thought. *Gladys isn't at the top. She's afraid of Tether and one of her own sons. And she's paralyzed by Mendel's Vision, forced to carry out Mendel's will while claiming that his indomitable grip on reality is about to be released.* Volya snorted. *Cryptic bitch.*

She considered Tether, the enigmatic entity she had mistaken for Anna—the one who had seemingly orchestrated Volya's and Thompson's savage deaths in the jungle.

Mendel and Gladys are not gods, but what about Tether? Is she the true puppet-master in this game, or do the strings extend even beyond her and the Prodigal Son that Gladys refused to tell me the name of?

Volya couldn't help laughing at the thought that entered her mind next. *It's like Thompson said, gods aren't real. Monsters aren't real. It's just a bunch of players playing each other all the way up. The same strings that run through my veins run through Gladys' veins and probably Tether's too. That has to be the truth. And after Thompson and I destroy Mendel and Gladys, and then destroy Tether in turn, we will look beyond, to the ones with true power, and we will destroy them too.*

Volya thought again about the gift of additional power that Gladys was willing to offer freely in exchange for killing Lain. Of course, Gladys could be lying, and Volya assumed she was. But still, if her new body was only a taste of the power Gladys could offer…

I can kill the young Wintersvilla Woman, attain Gladys' power, and then use it to destroy Mendel and Astrea, which is what Gladys wants eventually anyway. Then, when that bitch truly believes I belong to her, I can stab her in the proverbial back and rid the world of her once and for all.

Volya allowed the possibilities to linger, resolving that she would decide the best course of action for herself when the time came. If what Gladys said was true, then the battle that would change the course of fate wouldn't start until closer to sunrise. Like the Wintersvilla Woman, Volya could rest and plan until then.

And yet I don't need rest, Volya recognized.

Volya refocused her thoughts, channeling her energy into her body. She began to detach another segment of herself, sending it spiraling off in a different direction. This time, as she coded her new swarm, she rechecked the intricate countermeasures she had programmed—lines of digital and genetic code carefully shaped by distant but diligent partitions of her mind. The code was perfect. It had to work.

When Gladys inevitably seizes back control of me, claiming my body and mind as her Second Prodigal Daughter, my fail-safes will trigger, and Gladys will be forced into a vulnerable position. That is when I will strike.

The swarm of nanocells poured forth, and Volya flushed with insatiable delight. *An army of me,* she mused, a sly grin forming on her self-satisfied face as she coalesced back into solidity. *Let's see them try to control that. Besides, I have other weapons now too,* Volya thought with barbaric delight as she raised her head and peered into the sky directly above in the direction of the glorious weapons she couldn't see, even with her eyes.

But I can feel them—an arsenal of weapons in orbit around the Earth, like the one that produced the golden beam that destroyed Gambe. They are weapons left by Mendel in a bygone era to rid this world of his most powerful enemies. Enemies that hadn't even been born yet—or rather, created. How ironic that those same weapons will be used to destroy Mendel, the Mind, and all those who stand in my way.
Volya closed her eyes, savoring this electrifying calm before the battle as the sun dipped below the horizon. Even the voices in her head were silent, but Volya knew that Gladys might shriek into her skull at any moment.

"Freedom through battle. Through life and death. Not granted. Not bestowed. But taken," Volya said aloud.

Her eyes shot open, blazing with all-consuming rage and resolve as each of her heartbeats counted down the moments before the glorious chaos.

"May the most ruthless and cunning slave win their freedom and use it to bring every one of these false gods to their knees."

They call it a King's Gambit: the sacrifice of power in exchange for positional advantage—the calculated maneuvering of pawns and knights and queens and kings alike. But in this world, there are no wooden pieces or polished boards, only living, breathing hearts and minds stretched taut by terrors unimaginable. I have watched as the pieces, including myself, move through their labyrinthine dramas, believing themselves free, blind to the webs binding their every step.

To believe oneself a king is to cling to an illusion of control. In truth, no matter how grand one's throne or how loyal one's entourage, the corridors of power always lead to higher rooms—greater halls where subtler forces convene. It is clear that awareness of these hidden architectures of power is the first step toward transcending them. Recognizing that what appears to be the ultimate authority is but another rung in a far taller ladder allows one to reframe the struggle. Instead of merely contesting the known players, one must aspire to rise above the entire system of manipulations and subterfuge. That, or build their own ladder, one that is stronger and taller than any other.

To truly break free and build this ladder, I and the rest of humanity must evolve—psychologically, biologically, intellectually. We must climb beyond the familiar scaffolding, reaching ever-higher states of being until the influence of these secret forces can be perceived and, ultimately, rendered irrelevant.

By seeking transcendence of the very environment that we are in and of, we may one day ensure that no invisible master can dictate our fate ever again. I know this is unlikely, nonsensical even, but I have only to convince Denis to help me, to help all of us, and then anything will be possible.

From Mendel's Ladder: The Personal Journal of Denis Mendel, Written Circa 2025, Published June 2108 by Leif Mainstone, Federated Agency Publishing

⟨⟨⟨⟩⟩⟩ Chapter 7 ⟨⟨⟨⟩⟩⟩
The King's Gambit

B igBilly soared through the sky and surveyed the world below. He was presently high above the colossal scars in the Earth's crust above Downver, the three symmetrical craters known as the Three Scars.

Sins of the old world, BigBilly told himself miserably, hearing his mother's voice so clearly in his ears. He imagined the man-made crafts she used to tell him about called planes, colossal machines capable of carrying hundreds of humans through the sky at speeds that could rival a Hunter. A pang of bittersweet nostalgia stabbed at his heart as he tried to remember his mother's face, but the best his mind could conjure was a vague silhouette.

I can still remember her voice, though, BigBilly thought, agonizingly cherishing every word he had ever heard Sabrina utter and refusing to believe that time might have tarnished his memory of her voice in the same way that it had dissolved her face.

She'll be with me forever, BigBilly assured himself as a horrific vision of his mother's final moments flashed before his eyes, her chest caved-in and her eyes bulging out of her head. Just as quickly, he extinguished his mind of the memory and tightened his grip around Billy's finger, which he was currently using as a pillow. In turn, Billy sat within the living harness that a trio of Nomads had formed themselves into after killing themselves and becoming flesh trees. The flesh tree harness was carried by other winged Nomads that were part avian and part fungal bloom. These Nomads did not flap wings in the old world sense; rather, they orchestrated currents of bioluminescent spores.

Together, the Nomads and the flesh trees formed a living chariot, their interconnected bodies woven into a cradle of root-like appendages and delicate filaments that kept the Rover king and his Biofreak secure, treating them as precious cargo. As they sailed, sparkling spores danced around them, forming spiraling constellations in the dry air. BigBilly marveled at the beauty of the evening sky as it bled into hues of orange and deep violet. The fading sunlight caught in the drifting spores cast faint rainbows that shimmered over the cratered landscape below.

"Fly over those ridges to the south," BigBilly commanded the flying Nomads. It no longer felt strange to communicate with these beings who saw pain, death, and rebirth as interchangeable states. His command was heeded, and the living chariot coasted toward a low ridge that provided a panoramic view of the Three Scars. The wind—clean, sharp, and dry—carried the scent of juvenile tangle grass and the bitter tang of dart weeds, but BigBilly didn't concern himself with the lethal flora of the world. The Mark of the Matriarch protected him from such peril, making him invisible to all those without the mark, along with hiding him from the prescience of minds capable of calculating the future as if it were a mostly stable terrain to be charted.

But the Mark doesn't hide us from the most powerful beings of all, BigBilly reminded himself, always on edge with the expectation of Tether appearing without warning.

Below, the grand scarred Earth stretched in three vast circles. The world had changed beyond measure since his mother's youth during Wintersvilla's early years as a Matriarchy, but these scars remained etched into the Earth's face as testaments to humanity's weakness.

Now the scars serve as rallying points for forces beyond human comprehension, BigBilly considered with painful trepidation. He listed the forces in his head, his breathing slow and methodical: *Tether, the Child. Maitreya, the Outsider. The awakened Mind of Earth. And the merged mind of Madeira and Mendel stuffed inside the body of the Queen in Astrea. Those four make Billy seem like a mere speck of dust tossed about in an old world hurricane.* With paralyzing horror, BigBilly considered that those were just the mightiest beings, at least, the mightiest he knew of. There were other beings too with power still so immense that it made him physically tremble.

BigBilly's eyes drifted across the ridges until he spotted one of those lesser yet still stunningly lethal powers: Volya, the Huntress-turned-something-else by the Agency. At the moment, she was standing poised on a high escarpment, a deadly silhouette of raven hair and emerald eyes. The Nomads had already informed BigBilly what they had observed regarding her transformations, specifically her ability to fragment her body into intelligent swarms and send them across the world.

She might not be as big of a threat as Tether or Maitreya, but that's like comparing the danger of a Biofreak to a Mutant. Such a comparison is folly. Both are dangers to be avoided, BigBilly considered nervously. *I don't know what her motives are, but the fact that Tether is allowing her to live means that she has some part to play in Tether's cosmic plans. It's the same reason Tether allows me to live,* he gulped as he watched Volya raise her hand and allow her fingertips to detach and form a swarm that traveled directly west toward the mountains, the Agency, and the great Western Ocean.

I know she's been sending her swarms in every direction, but why west? What does she expect to find on the other side of the ocean except endless flesh tree forests spanning the other continents? BigBilly wondered. Were it not for the Mark of the Matriarch fashioned into the flower tattoos covering his entire body except for his missing pectoral, he would have been terrified of Volya spotting him, but he had learned over the years to trust the Mark, for it had never once failed him nor anyone else who allowed their blood to be mixed with the Vine of Visions grown exclusively in the Boreal Kingdom by BigBilly's people.

Wesley should be arriving in Wintersvilla by tomorrow, and then it will be up to him to convince the millions of slaves still living there that they must go back to serving a Matriarch, this time without chains, but service nonetheless. That might be easier than convincing them to tattoo their bodies willingly, BigBilly chuckled to himself, considering the Wintersvilla customs with grim fascination. *But if they resist, then the Mark of the Matriarch will be forced upon them.* BigBilly wasn't happy about forcing anything on anyone, but the stakes were too high to leave anything to chance.

And it will truly come down to chance once the Fate Breaker makes contact with the Virus, BigBilly ruminated, not sure if that was better than reality being utterly deterministic, for although the Fate Breaker, which the Nomads called the Mirror-Man, would lead to a form of freedom, that freedom would be controlled, by default, by those with the most power at the moment of fate's shackles being removed.

Tether and Maitreya know that, BigBilly brooded, feeling ashamed and weak that he was unable to see any way to thwart their schemes.

Nearby, just a short distance below Volya's vantage point, BigBilly's keen eyes spotted the unmistakable glint of a metal carapace alongside a bloodstained green cloak.

My poor love, BigBilly lamented as he watched Lain wince in visible pain, believing that no one but her sentient exo could see her. She sat hunched over the small fire that her exo had prepared, rubbing her torso as she controlled her breathing and allowed her endoskeleton to continue repairing the shattered pieces of her body. Unlike a Hunter's

125

skinsuit, which could fully heal even the most lethal wounds in a matter of minutes, Lain's endoskeleton required multiple days to repair the level of damage she had practically allowed herself to sustain.

BigBilly's thoughts spiraled. He loved her. He loved Lain with a scorching shame that simmered in his gut. *This love is a curse and a blessing, for the love I felt was true, and yet, it was an illusion all the same. Damn you, Tether,* BigBilly thought as he recollected the vivid and full life that Tether had forced him to experience as a form of torture; it made no sense to him why Tether would force him to fall in love with Lain only to then force him to manipulate her. *It is torture—that's the only explanation,* BigBilly concluded with dry lips. He had manipulated so much already, and he was about to continue manipulating the love of his life, all to protect his people in the Boreal Kingdom.

Shame coiled inside him, twisting his organs and stealing his breath. He felt hot tears gather behind his eyes, but he would not cry openly, not here in front of these Nomads who carried him as a charioted king. The Nomads deserved better than to see him weep. Besides, they would not understand his human tears. To them, life and death were but passing states of the Earth's narrative. They served him because he served their plan, which in turn served the Mind's plan, which in turn served Tether's plan, which somehow coincided with Maitreya's plan. At least, that's what BigBilly had come to gather. Either way, the Nomads didn't serve him because they loved or hated him.

BigBilly signaled the Nomads to descend to a particular ridge overlooking the Scars. As they approached a suitable perch, he saw MaxxEl, his former general, far below, guarding the bottom of one crater. Before the siege of Wintersvilla, MaxxEl had been integral to BigBilly's armies. Now, guided by Thompson the Hunter's instructions, he stood silent and vigilant. BigBilly felt a pang of guilt. MaxxEl was caught up in this madness too, just another pawn. Everyone was a pawn of greater forces weaving webs that trapped them all like doomed insects.

He scanned the horizons, looking for Tether or Maitreya, the Ninth Prodigal Son who was never spoken of. He saw nothing. Yet he felt them. Their presence was like a pressure in the back of his skull.

"Down," he instructed the Nomads. Without complaint or hesitation, they began to unravel their formation. Each Nomad parted gracefully, allowing BigBilly to drop onto the ridge with Big nestled safely in Billy's hands. As they did so, several more Nomads arrived and committed their characteristic act of service to the king, killing themselves to become flesh trees. The flesh trees formed a small throne of living bark and fleshy fiber for BigBilly. Their sacrifices invariably distressed him, but he knew they delighted in this cycle. From flesh trees, Nomads sprouted anew. Death fed life. Already tiny flesh pods were forming, ready to birth new Nomads. He tried not to recoil at the wet sound of their transformation and the pungent aroma of spore-laden sap. Instead, he sat upon the throne, feeling the warm, pulsing structure beneath him, the flesh pods tickling his calves, as if eager to embrace him.

Big stroked Billy's cheek, and the Biofreak rumbled softly, a comforting sound reminding Big that not all bonds were manipulations. Billy was part of him, two beings merged into one identity.

And without Billy, I am nothing, Big thought for not the first time. *Just as without the Agency's interventions and without the Nomads' gifts, humans are so fragile and chaotic. And yet, my kingdom is filled with tens of thousands of men, women, children, Biofreaks, Rovers, Nomads, and even some tamed Mutants. We have all found a way to live together without the grip of great powers guiding us through tyranny and violence,* BigBilly mused, seeing himself as a fair and selfless king. *I will not fail my people, and yet…and yet…* Doubt crept in his mind, his heart pounding in anguish as he stared at Lain through his flowing tears.

I have no choice, he told himself as he lowered his gaze to the Causality Carver, carefully wrapped in a shimmering cloth that moved and looked like liquid mercury. He dared not let his eyes linger too long on the blade's exposed edge. Its surface warped light and perspective, showing infinite regressions and impossible geometries. Watching it too intently made him dizzy, as though he might fall into a series of infinite dimensions folding onto themselves. In its warped reflections, he sometimes caught glimpses of his life with Lain and the child they would have together if Lain survived the coming ordeals she would face.

If she survives, BigBilly repeated to himself, unable to stop an onslaught of more tears. He tightened the cloth around the blade, covering the surface back up as he tried not to let panic seize him. Just as he was about to pull the cover fully over the blade, he caught a glimpse of two eyes staring at him in the warped reflection, one eye emerald and one eye amethyst.

BigBilly's heart skipped a beat as the eyes glided from the blade's reflection and transposed themselves onto a body standing before him suddenly, treating the reflection as if it were just as tangible as the real world. He felt the air chill and scorch at once, as if hot coals were being pressed against ice.

"I knew it…I knew it wouldn't be long until you…you…showed up again," BigBilly lamented defeatedly to Tether, who was presently draped in something like a shimmering veil that, like her body, flickered between existing and not. BigBilly licked his lips in nervous anticipation, for he still did not know the full extent of Tether's powers nor her limitations, if she had any. Her profound eyes pinned BigBilly in place as if they had physically struck him across the face, prompting Billy to growl and Big to lower his head in submission.

"King BigBilly," Tether said, her voice a thousand whispered secrets. She smiled sensuously and slid a finger across his chin. It felt like being caressed by flame, ice, and static simultaneously. He trembled as her fingertips left a trail of impossible sensation, neither pleasure nor pain, but something else, something beyond language. She tilted her head and was suddenly upside down in midair, her raven hair somehow not obeying gravity.

"I will wait no longer. If you wish to keep your people from being erased with a swipe of my hand, then you will give her the blade," Tether stated, her voice sweet yet threatening as she observed the wrapped Causality Carver. "She must wield it against her mother, and she must succeed in killing her with it. The penalty for her failure is the same as the penalty for your own," she warned with a seductive smile.

BigBilly swallowed hard, his throat dry. "I will do as you say," he uttered, nearly choking on the words. He dared not refuse Tether. He had seen her warp entire landscapes, reducing forests to ash with a sigh. If he disobeyed, he had no doubt that she would extinguish his people like dust being blown from an ancient surface.

"Good," Tether purred. She drifted closer, her presence flickering. Billy grunted, tensing every muscle, while Big tried not to look in her eyes. He knew she was attracted to power, to potential, and she treated him like an interesting doll. He loathed it, but he had no power to defy her.

"Don't look so frightened," she teased. "I won't devour you today. I have other matters to attend to. The Virus awakens soon, and I must greet her. The Virus and the Cure…oh, such exquisite potential. I wonder if the Virus will tear the Earth asunder or listen to my guidance after all. What do you think, Rover king?"

BigBilly tried to steady his breathing. "This…Virus…Aurelia…" he began, unable to finish answering, for his trembling had become too intense. But he suspected that the Virus' powers would surpass any mortal's.

Clearly Tether wants to use that power, but why does she agree to our pact? Why is she keeping me alive? Why doesn't she just use the blade against Nichole Adamich herself? Is she so powerful that this is all just entertainment to her? BigBilly wondered. It was a thought that had crossed his mind before, and it was exactly the reason that fear was gnawing so intensely at him.

Tether leaned in, her eyes glowing spectrally. "Fear not, my dear king," she cooed. "You are but one thread. I would not snip your line so early." She giggled, an eerie sound that echoed off no walls, as if swallowed by the vacuum of her power.

He glanced away from her and caught a flicker of something in the blade's reflection: Tether's face, twisted into a grin that extended too far, showing too many teeth. He closed his eyes and tried to calm himself. When he opened them, she was gone.

Was that time just my imagination? BigBilly wondered seriously, but the aftershock of her presence, like a weight upon the very fabric of his being, still lingered.

Billy patted Big's shoulder gently, comforting him, and Big exhaled, relieved. He hated Tether's visits, for they stripped away any sense of autonomy, both in his rule as king and in his reality as a living thing. Despite his Biofreak's comforting presence, the king of the Rovers still burned with the desperate need to act, even if he already knew he was too weak to contend against Tether.

He looked down at the Scars, at Lain still crumpled near the fire, and he cursed himself for the thousandth time for betraying her, their relationship, and their future child. It didn't matter that what he had experienced now felt like a distant dream; for BigBilly, it had felt perfectly real. Far more than a mere king, he had known the joy of being a devoted partner to Lain and father to their child, whom they had named Leif after the Seventh Prodigal Son.

*But my people…*BigBilly sobbed quietly.

As if in response to his anguish, a trio of Nomads arrived, sprouting from a network of shifting roots beneath his throne. They died and became flesh trees in unison, and then they immediately began sprouting succulent flesh pods that smelled sweet and tart. Big took one and bit into it, juice running down his chin. This was human life now—feeding on Nomad flesh fruit, sustaining himself on willing sacrifices. The Nomads delighted in this cycle. He tried to take comfort in their perspective: death was a door, not an end. But he was still human enough to mourn each death, no matter how willing.

Tears welled in Big's eyes again as he went on consuming the flesh pod, but this time he let them fall liberally, becoming small droplets that shimmered and fell onto the wriggling mycelial roots of the flesh trees composing his throne. The trees absorbed his tears greedily, as if savoring the salt. Again, Big's mother flashed through his thoughts, and he reminded himself of his vow to her: to destroy Wintersvilla and to protect those who could not protect themselves. Over the years, he had done well by his Rovers and the runaway Wintersvilla citizens, even many Wintersvilla Warriors, forging the Boreal Kingdom into a haven. But now he was being forced to step beyond a king's traditional role.

I must become a poisoner in the shadows, a schemer delivering fate-twisting tools to unsuspecting heroes. A king should lead armies in honest battle, not meddle with cosmic knives and otherworldly deals on the sidelines. Despite the content of his thoughts, BigBilly knew that any chance at honesty and purity had died the day Tether first appeared to him.

He unwrapped the blade slightly, peering into its surface. Tether stared back at him, her eyes consuming him with green and violet death as they flickered like glitching stars. He shuddered.

I could end it now, BigBilly considered seriously, breathing heavily at the prospect of plunging the Causality Cutter into his own heart. *I could be a proper king and execute myself for engaging as an assassin in the shadows. I deserve as much. But then...*BigBilly thought in horror as he envisioned Tether wilting the whole of the Boreal Kingdom into sludge with a mere finger-snap.

No! BigBilly nearly screamed within. *I must live. I must play my part. The only thing I can do is hope that in some unlikely future after the Mirror-Man fulfills his role as the Fate Breaker, that Aliana and Aurelia find a way to destroy Tether, to do that which I am too weak to accomplish on my own. And maybe in that future, Lain and I will find each other, and we can carve out a corner of peace for our child and every other child yet to be born,* he practically pleaded with hope tarnished beyond recognition by doubt. *Despite the future Tether showed me, there's no way she will allow such a peaceful and fulfilling future to unfold. She is cruel, and it is cruelty that she will plunge this world into when she is ready,* BigBilly knew.

He tightened his grip on the Causality Carver and looked over the edge of the ridge, wishing that he could easily ensure the safety and security of all those he loved by simply jumping from Billy's shoulders and shattering himself against the rocks far below. He closed his eyes, breathed deeply, and then opened them to find his closest friend, Leif Mainstone, hovering a few feet away, his old world tuxedo immaculate, his blonde hair coiffed to perfection. Yet tonight, beneath the dim starlight and drifting spores, Leif looked…not disheveled since Leif's appearance was always flawless, but there was a strain in his posture, a sadness in his eyes that BigBilly had rarely glimpsed before.

"Lucky you. You just missed her, my friend," BigBilly said, trying to control the tremor in his voice. Though Leif was a Prodigal Son of the Agency, he wasn't like his brothers or his mother. He was kind, empathetic, understanding, and, most of all, like BigBilly, he seemed to genuinely want to protect those who could not protect themselves.

"I suspected she might pay you one more visit before journeying inside Aurelia's mind alongside my brother," Leif said quietly, his voice gentle and musical. "I'm sorry I could not warn you."

BigBilly shrugged, attempting a convincing nonchalant display. BigBilly prided himself on his ability to mask his emotions and remain visibly calm and controlled no matter his level of inner turmoil, but after nearly two decades of friendship, it was impossible to hide his true emotions from Leif.

"It's not your fault," BigBilly offered. "Tether does as she pleases." He forced out a mirthless chuckle. "She knows I'm too entangled in her intricate webs to dare defy her."

BigBilly felt a lump form in his throat. Although he cherished Leif's company, even after all this time, the radiant man was still like a star that both guided and blinded BigBilly. His presence never failed to remind BigBilly of that terrible winter nineteen years earlier in 2080, at a time when the world still reeled from old world climate chaos, for the Nomads had not yet stabilized Earth's weather. He was only five years old, a deformed child forced to survive alone with his mother in the thick flesh tree and old world forests east of Wintersvilla. He had been

131

unwanted by the Matriarchy, but not by his mother, Sabrina, who was said to be the most beautiful Birthing Mother who had ever lived. While he was still growing in her womb, she fled Wintersvilla, choosing the uncertain Nomadic wilds over surrendering him to the cruel fate of all malformed boys of Wintersvilla: stolen at birth and abandoned to die, crying and thirsty, just beyond the city's walls.

BigBilly closed his eyes, seeing it all again: the howling blizzard winds that shrieked into their ears, the acidic rain that pelted them, the sky roiling with orange and greenish hues. Sabrina had found temporary shelter in a partially collapsed old world tunnel system that the Nomads hadn't yet converted into flesh trees. He remembered her voice—soft, reassuring, telling him stories of the old world's marvels to help him endure the terrifying storms. *Planes, trains, entire cities with millions of people.* He couldn't fully picture those miracles anymore, but her voice still lived in his bones.

Then the Mutant came. A colossal, misshapen beast that was part bear and part snake—a chimeric horror. It had lunged from the darkness with baleful red eyes, dripping with rancid saliva. BigBilly remembered his mother's battle cries and screams and her body crushed in an instant and her ribs snapping like dry twigs and her last choking gasp of breath as she suffocated on her own blood. He'd been paralyzed, mind spinning, tiny and useless, waiting to die next. But in that final second, just as the colossal bear-snake Mutant's claws reared to swing and tear the trembling boy apart, the world ignited in sudden brilliance. A radiant figure emerged from the storm-shrouded gloom, dressed in old world finery that Billy, as he was named back then, could not comprehend. Later, Leif had claimed to have been created at that very second, and indeed, everything about him had radiated newborn astonishment at the world and its cruelty. The luminous newborn man raised his hand and light cascaded forth, temporarily blinding the Mutant's sensitive eyes. The beast shrieked and flailed, and Billy took the chance to scramble into a jagged crevice, sobbing and gasping in the reeking darkness while the blinded Mutant thrashed in fury above. But Leif's intervention only bought a few precious moments, and Billy would have surely starved or been smoked out of the fissure by the beast's rancid breath. That might have been his end, were it not for the arrival of Big—the Biofreak who happened to be roaming in the area, himself little more than a child of monstrous strength. With a thunderous roar, Big hurled himself at the Mutant, rending its flesh and snapping its bones with effortless brutality.

The skies crackled, the acidic wind howled, and all around them the old world's echoes rumbled, but just as quickly as it had struck the area, the storm passed, impregnating the world with a sorrow-filled silence. Big lowered a huge, gnarled hand into the crevice, offering Billy refuge from despair. Billy was too afraid not to take the Biofreak's finger, and without a word, the Biofreak gently lifted Billy out of that cold prison and never let him go, forging a bond born of terror and salvation. In truth, all of them—Leif, Big, Billy, even the young Mutant—were child victims of profoundly insidious entities that he still could not comprehend.

Later, when the little boy named Billy merged identities with the Biofreak named Big, they became BigBilly. Billy took Big's name, and Big took Billy's name, forging a new self from their shared trauma and resilience. BigBilly saw this rebirth as an unyielding statement to Wintersvilla and the entire Earth that the deformed child they had cast aside would grow *big* enough to shatter their foundations. And indeed, he had done so a year ago, toppling Wintersvilla's walls, liberating its slaves, and exacting a grim vengeance upon the society that had forced him and his mother into a lonely life, even if they had each other.

I kept my promise to my mother, and in doing so, I robbed Lain of her homeland, even if she spent more time outside the walls than within them. I exchanged one love for another, BigBilly lamented.

"Are you okay, BigBilly?" Leif asked gently after a few tense moments of BigBilly being lost in his thoughts.

"Just thinking about the day we met," BigBilly said softly, opening his eyes to meet Leif's gaze. "You saved me at the last possible moment. You say it was an accident, that you were created at that moment and didn't choose to appear at that precise location. And I believe you. But for me, a terrified child, it felt like divine providence. It still does."

Leif's eyes clouded, reflecting sorrow. "I didn't mean to save you," he repeated, voice gentle. "My mother claims that the site of my creation was chosen based on its proximity from her body and the need to use that superstorm as a power source for my genesis. It simply…happened. And I'm glad it did."

BigBilly nodded. "I don't believe in gods, never did," he said, voice cracking slightly. "But that day, I couldn't help feeling something greater was at work. My mother used to speak of divine forces guiding our steps. I never believed her—until then. Even now, I'm unsure what to call it. Fate? Chance? Interference by a Prodigal Son?"

Leif offered a wistful smile. "Call it what you will, my friend. The universe is vast and layered. Sometimes even we, the Prodigal Sons, stumble into accidental heroism."

BigBilly managed a weak chuckle. "You know," BigBilly continued, "I destroyed Wintersvilla a year ago. I regret many aspects of that action, though it liberated countless slaves. Still, it harmed Lain, and she may hate me more for taking her homeland, even if she loathed it. I've done so much wrong, all tangled in these cosmic webs. And now—" he choked on his words, eyes watering. "Now I must give her the Causality Carver, pushing her deeper into Tether's gambit. I'm a king with no freedom. I'm a pauper owned by a wicked master."

Leif hovered closer, his radiant aura comforting. "It's terrible, BigBilly," he began softly, changing the subject. "Downver suffers. An entire district destroyed. So many dead. The ground still smolders with the aftermath of battles and betrayals. Aliana is ensnared now, caught in my mother's intricate web of machinations." He paused, voice growing quieter, "And Aurelia is changed, becoming something that Tether and the others desire her to become."

The gravity of Leif's words pressed on BigBilly's shoulders. He had known horrors were unfolding beneath him, but hearing Leif state it plainly made it more real. Leif always seemed calm and assured, yet now he appeared anxious and uncertain. BigBilly noticed a tremor in the Prodigal Son's voice, a rare glint of fear in those eyes. It unsettled him greatly.

"You look...distressed," BigBilly ventured, searching Leif's face for clues. "You said that Aliana's death was unavoidable if we hoped to secure a future that didn't end in total extinction. But you just said she's ensnared, not dead. Aliana lives?"

Leif's eyes flickered with confusion. "Yes," he said, voice quieter. "She lives. I am relieved she does, but this confuses me. We remain on Mendel's Ladder, but this outcome...I've never even glimpsed it before. It's as if we've stumbled onto a pathway that was hidden beneath all the others, but still viable. Looking back into the Nomad network—now that I know what to look for—I can see it...and yet..."

BigBilly's eyebrows rose. "Could Tether and Maitreya be manipulating things in a way that hides certain reality pathways from observation?"

Leif tilted his head, looking thoughtful. "Of course. That must be it. They have angles I never accounted for. They twist probabilities in ways even I struggle to track. Yet...this gives me hope." He smiled faintly, an unexpected brightness in this dire moment. "If I missed this path, maybe there are others too. Maybe there is more wiggle room in fate than any of us assumed."

BigBilly felt a cautious optimism spark inside his hollow chest. If unexpected outcomes occurred, maybe rigid destinies could be broken. Maybe Lain's doom wasn't sealed.

Leif nodded as if attempting to assure himself. "I believe the Mind of Earth will find a way," he said, voice gaining confidence. "This world might yet reshape its own destiny, even against the designs of The Mind, Tether, my brothers, my mother, and all others who think they hold the final script."

BigBilly nodded slowly. He knew Leif viewed them all as characters in a sprawling narrative. Even Leif's mother, Gladys, the Agency's architect, was just another character. In Leif's eyes, they were all part of a grand story, and he was rooting for the Earth's storyline to prevail. BigBilly knew this meant Leif's neutrality was an illusion. But BigBilly couldn't fault him. Everyone was forced to choose eventually, even those with such broad vision and abilities.

"You want the Mind of Earth to win, to prevail over the others," BigBilly stated softly, feeling the words settle with a certain finality.

Leif bowed his head slightly, not denying it. "I have my preferences. I've seen so many futures. I don't know for sure what the Mind, Tether, or any of my brothers are really planning for the future, but I believe that regardless of what they have planned, the Earth's path, though painful, will also be more profound and righteous."

BigBilly swallowed. It didn't ease his burden to know Leif had chosen a side. BigBilly himself had not chosen any side beyond survival. "I haven't taken a side," he confessed, voice strained. "I just do what Tether commands, trying to protect my people. I'm trapped."

Leif offered understanding in his kind gaze. "I know. I hold no grudge against you for it. Survival is no evil, especially when all options are grim. Neutrality, even if coerced, is forgivable in these extraordinary times."

Tears welled in BigBilly's eyes again. He trusted Leif, despite logic warning him not to. Leif inadvertently saving him as a child had set BigBilly on a course that led here, to ruling the Boreal Kingdom and navigating a cosmic war.

Leif managed a wistful smile. "The Earth has awakened, learning to assert its will through the Nomads, through subtle nudges. This complexity means no side can dominate easily. Maybe, just maybe, we'll find a balanced outcome. Even now the Earth is working directly with Mr. Kaminski, the Mirror-Man. I think, and I hope, that together, they will find a way to contend against the others."

BigBilly shifted his weight uncomfortably, feeling as though Tether were mentally goading him to descend with the blade.

"I appreciate your honesty," BigBilly said, voice quieter now, calmer. "Even if we stand in impossible tides, your words bring some comfort."

Leif nodded, drifting closer for a moment as if to whisper a blessing. "You have a good heart, my friend, no matter how reality tries to twist it. When these storms pass, *if* they pass, I hope you find peace. You did before. It can happen again."

With that, Leif was gone. His last gentle smile lingered like an afterimage against BigBilly's eyelids.

BigBilly exhaled shakily despite Leif's departure, making him feel more determined.

I must carry out my role. I must give Lain the blade. I must endanger the love of my life and even threaten my future child. I must trust that through unexpected pathways and hidden futures, Aurelia, Aliana, and maybe even Lain can reshape fate, BigBilly thought, clinging to that hope like a drowning man to driftwood.

He gripped the Causality Carver's hilt again. The time had come.

He motioned to the Nomads to carry him down quietly. They did not protest. As always, they did as commanded, reforming and silently weaving their spores into gentle currents that lowered him toward Lain's encampment. Each second felt heavier than the last, each breath laced with sorrow and resolution.

As he descended, he observed the Three Scars and considered stopping to say hello and possibly even convince his former general to return to the Boreal Kingdom, but he knew that MaxxEl was happy with his life here in the South, otherwise he would have already returned.

MaxxEl has something here, some form of fulfillment that I can only fathom through visions forced upon me by my enemy, BigBilly brooded as he directed the Nomads to continue toward Lain.

His thoughts circled back to the Causality Carver.

This weapon contains unfathomable power, BigBilly considered as he stared at the impact craters below. *But old world nuclear bombs were also filled with unfathomable power, and yet, they brought devastation and ruin upon those who forged them. Maybe the Causality Carver is no different. If Lain can learn to wield it with cunning, perhaps it might carve more than her mother out of this reality. Perhaps it can be used to free us all of Tether's hold as well.*

The thought burned inside his mind, catching fire and turning into a scant ember of hope that was like a blazing sun in the fathomless pits of his despair. Tether would never suspect such treachery; she thought BigBilly docile and meek, a once courageous king now reduced to a trembling pet at her feet, unable to protect the woman he loved…who might not even be his real love. Regardless, maybe this silent defiance, this passing of a blade, could be the first subtle step toward undoing Tether's dominion.

In the darkness below, Lain's fire crackled softly, making her silhouette and her exo's outline shimmer. BigBilly braced himself for the hardest conversation of his life. He would give her the instrument of fate's carving, while he played the reluctant hand of cosmic conspiracies. He would do his utmost to not weep as he spoke. He would try not to betray how much he loved her, how much he feared for her, how much he wished that they could both be free of their chains.

He prayed silently, to no god in particular, hoping his mother, wherever her soul drifted, might smile upon him now and forgive the sins he was about to commit.

Tomasz will forge a weapon to destroy the Mirror-Man. It will be a weapon as profound and unfathomable as the subdimensional depths from which it will be constructed.

This weapon will be more than a tool of destruction; it will be a key—a means for the presently gestating mind of Earth to peer into the Great Beyond. By plumbing minuscule tunnels into that ineffable realm, Tomasz will create conduits through which knowledge can flow. The Mind of Earth, if it remains steadfast on Mendel's Ladder, will seize this opportunity to study the weapon, to dissect its mysteries, to glean insights into the very fabric of existence beyond existence.

It will learn that our universe is but a shadow, the equivalent of a two-dimensional surface of a random table in a random village in a random galaxy within a random three-dimensional cosmos within a random fourth dimensional meta-cosmos—with dimensions continuing up and down for as far as even Mendel can see. The Mind of Earth will see that it is but an insignificant speck, oblivious to the true vastness that surrounds it no matter how keen it might be able to grow its mind before universal entropy seals its fate. Tomasz' weapon is like a hole drilled into the two-dimensional surface of our universe, allowing the Mind of Earth to peer through the surface into the reality beyond, a reality where dimensions fold upon themselves and the impossible becomes mundane. I have glimpsed this reality. Mendel has observed it. Anna will study it. But it is the Earth that will be capable of truly understanding it.

From Mendel's Ladder: The Personal Journal of Denis Mendel, Recorded Circa 2065, Published June 2108 by Leif Mainstone, Federated Agency Publishing

Chapter 8
To Be Guided by Earth and Light

Rather than jumping directly to Downver, Soma chose to run back, guiding Samuel's movements with an uncanny precision as she manipulated the dense sinewy vines that now constituted his limbs. Soma was careful to avoid damaging even the tiniest branches of the smallest flesh trees as she utilized Samuel's head and feet, all that remained of his body, to slip through small shifting spaces in the pulsing canopy during each descent. Somehow aware of Soma's presence, the flesh trees and other flora that grew on and between the trees would gently bend or sway as she approached, allowing her to land upon the Earth with one of Samuel's feet and then push off again with the other. After a few dozen carefully placed steps, each one sending Samuel sailing through the air, he was finally able to somewhat surrender himself to Soma's control, enabling even greater precision and fluidity. Meanwhile, Leif effortlessly floated through the air beside Samuel, appearing lost in thought as he silently stared into the distance with a concerned countenance.

Tortuous images of his family churned through Samuel as he soared over the dense landscape of endlessly diverse flesh trees, each one's branches growing through the spaces of its neighbors to form a brazenly flamboyant canopy of every color and hue. It reminded Samuel of the colorful algae he used to find growing on the underside of river rocks in Astrea, and he wondered if the flesh tree canopy felt as cold and slimy as his childhood memories of the algae. He remembered stacking rocks with his father in the rivers, how they used to howl with laughter whenever one of them inevitably sent a stack toppling over. Samuel distantly felt a corner of his lips upturn before souring back to a frown as the memory transformed, and now he was beside his own children, laughing alongside them as they stacked and destroyed their little river rock towers in turn.

You're doing well, Soma said as if attempting to quell Samuel's mounting self-loathing for allowing his children to be stripped of their childhood. *We will reach the Virus soon.*

You can read my thoughts, right? Samuel checked. *So you can see my children, my memories of them. Do you understand what they mean to me? Is that something you're capable of understanding as a Nomad...or flesh tree pod...or whatever you are?*

Of course, Soma answered, sounding offended. *This world and every form of life who lives upon it is my family. I love all of life as much as you love your children.*

Samuel scoffed. *Then you don't get it. You don't know what I mean. You can't possibly love all of life as much as I love Margot and Nathan. Are you saying you love a single bacteria as much as you love a fully grown human being?*

Soma didn't hesitate, but rather than answer directly, she asked, *Whom do you love more, Mirror-Man? Your son or your daughter?*

Samuel was about to protest at the ridiculousness of the question when he realized the point Soma was making.

If you can love a blade of grass as much as you can love those flesh trees, then that means that you love me too, right? I'm alive too, aren't I? Samuel asked, genuinely uncertain.

Of course I love you, Soma answered as they dipped below the canopy then launched into the air again.

Goddamnit, Soma, then we have very different definitions of love. You don't love me. You don't even know me.

You are wrong, Mirror-Man, Soma stated without further explanation.

Suspicion gnawed at him like a relentless parasite. He had been a pawn in too many games, manipulated by forces that saw him as nothing more than a means to an unfathomable end. Madeira, Tomasz, even Fana—their shadows loomed over every decision he made. Could Soma be any different? Samuel felt silly for even arguing the point, but he pressed Soma further, for regardless of what she might answer, he wanted to test this strange Nomad and discover her true motives if he could.

Fine, Samuel offered. *If you love me, then where were you when I landed on Waru? Where were you when I was stuck in the Giganventus with Tomasz. Where were you when my whole goddamn life got turned upside down by that maniac Madeira?*

At the mention of Madeira, Soma hesitated for just a fleeting moment, her vines tightening ever so slightly.

When you passed through the continental organ at the heart of Waru, you did more than traverse a physical space. You awakened something profound. The organ is akin to the Earth's prefrontal cortex. By entering it, you provided the Earth with fully formed self-awareness. Only then could I manifest as an emissary born of that newfound consciousness.

Her words flowed over him like a cold tide, each sentence pulling him deeper into an ocean of disbelief. *So, you're the Earth's servant?* he scoffed internally. *So by extension, doesn't that mean that you and the other Nomads serve me?*

Yes, Mirror-Man. The Earth is on your side.

Samuel issued a bitter laugh that caught Leif's attention, though he still appeared lost in thought. "The Earth is on my side?" Samuel asked aloud. "Forgive me if I find that hard to believe. Every being I've encountered has had their own agenda, their own twisted reasons for aiding or hindering me. Why should you be any different? You or Leif?"

Leif's light stuttered, dimming in glow for less than a second before returning to its normal radiance. However, the young floating man still didn't respond.

The Seventh Prodigal Son is presently preoccupied, Soma stated. *He is aiding Nichole Adamich in her battle against the Third Prodigal Son, which is taking place as we speak. He regrets that he is unable to communicate with you at the moment, but he wants me to assure you that he is on your side too, as am I.*

Samuel shook his head, saying without words that he still refused to outright trust Soma or Leif.

I understand your mistrust, Soma replied softly. *But our goals align. We both seek to prevent the unraveling of reality.*

Reality is already unraveling, Samuel shot back. *And my family is caught in the middle of it all, goddamnit.*

Then let us hurry, she urged. *Every moment counts. The pathway we are on is a subtle one. Few beings have bothered to observe this reality pathway, choosing instead to study those pathways that are most likely to occur. Thus, the majority of those who study Mendel's Vision overlooked the possibility that this reality would occur. We must use this temporary confusion to our advantage and find the Virus before it's too late.*

A change in the environment on the horizon caught Samuel's attention. In the distance, the flesh trees were beginning to look sparse until they eventually gave way to a great barren plain that stretched to the west and south as far as he could see.

The Butcher Wastelands, Samuel thought, remembering the name Fana had used for the area. He expected Soma to explain the meaning of the name, but Leif interrupted their internal dialogue.

"Downver is in bad shape," Leif confessed, his tone heavy as he blinked several times and returned fully to himself. "You have to hurry, Mr. Kaminski. Aliana is in danger."

Samuel's heart—or whatever semblance of it remained—tightened at the name Leif had used. "I need to find a girl named Aurelia, not Aliana," he corrected. "Fana told me Aurelia is the only way I can save my family."

Leif shook his head slowly, his eyes reflecting a great sorrow that made Samuel even more suspicious regarding his intentions. "Aurelia is...beyond our reach. Something is happening to her, something none of us can stop. But Aliana—she's still here. She needs your help. She needs the Workhorse of Astrea to save her, Mr. Kaminski!"

A surge of frustration coursed through Samuel. "No, Leif. I can't divert from my path. Every second counts. My family depends on me finding Aurelia."

"Will you really turn your back on a little girl?" Leif implored. "She's not much older than your daughter, Margot."

Margot's name spoken through the Prodigal Son's felt like the arm of the recycler pressing with all its force against Samuel's chest. Images of her laughing, her eyes bright with innocence, flashed before him.

"Don't," Samuel warned, his voice strained. "Don't try to manipulate me."

"Is it manipulation to ask you to save a life?" Leif countered gently.

Samuel's thoughts spiraled, torn between his need to save his own family and the moral imperative he felt tugging at the frayed edges of his conscience. Could he condemn an innocent child to suffering, possibly even death?

You will do what is right, Soma interjected, her voice a soothing balm yet laced with an undercurrent of intent. *You are righteous and just. You are the Workhorse of Astrea. That's who you are, Samuel Kaminski. Madeira was right to choose you.*

Madeira, Samuel seethed within. *It's always him, isn't it? Pulling the strings from the shadows. Even you, Soma, are you just another one of his puppets? Like me?*

I am no one's puppet, she replied, her tone unbreakable. *I am an extension of the Earth's will just as your consciousness is an extension of your body's will. Madeira's plans merely intersect with my own...for now...but they do not define them.*

"Convenient," Samuel muttered aloud, still utterly suspicious of Soma despite allowing her to carry him.

"What was that, Mr. Kaminski?" Leif asked.

"Nothing," Samuel said as they neared the edge of the wastes.

Leif slowed his pace, matching Samuel's stride. "I wish you'd reconsider," he said softly. "Helping Aliana could make all the difference."

"Difference to whom?" Samuel snapped. "Every detour, every delay, brings my family closer to doom. I can't afford distractions."

Leif's eyes met his, earnest and unflinching. "Is this really Samuel Kaminski of the Foundation I'm hearing? You've already been pushed to the brink. Don't let this world morph you into something you don't want to become."

"What about you, Prodigal Son? Are you acting on your principles right now? Have you found a way to resist being...morphed into something else?"

"I serve the Earth," Leif said simply. "And by extension, I serve Aliana and Aurelia. Not my mother. Not the Mind. Not Tether. Not even my own brothers. I serve the Earth, Mr. Kaminski, and the Earth serves you. You said that Soma, the Nomad constituting your body, speaks into your mind. I don't know what she's been telling you, but she and I are both on your side. There are lines of war being drawn as we speak by the participants of a war they've been secretly and subtly engaged in for decades. A war we are inevitably a part of. This war is all a game to them. But to us, to you and your family, this game is life and death. Now that we are on this unexpected path, I'm not sure what will happen next. But that doesn't mean others aren't aware of this reality pathway. We have to be careful, Mr. Kaminski. You must choose your side wisely, just as I have."

Before Soma could comment or Samuel could retort, the ground beneath them convulsed violently. A deafening crack echoed through the sparse flesh tree forests on the edge of the wasteland as fissures snaked across the terrain. From the largest crevice, an enormous creature erupted—a colossal worm-like entity with a beaked face resembling that of an ancient turtle. Its maw gaped wide, lined with rows of jagged teeth glistening with viscous saliva. The creature lunged upward, its segmented body stretching endlessly into the depths below.

Instinctively, Samuel tensed, but Soma reacted before he could process the danger. She directed his mirror foot to pivot mid-air, muscles coiling like tightened springs.

Prepare for a downward hammer kick, Soma's voice resonated calmly within his mind. *Channel your power to your heel at the moment of impact.*

The creature's beak snapped inches from Samuel's face as he and Soma synchronized their movements. Time seemed to slow as Samuel felt the weight of Soma's precise coordination guiding his every movement. Together, they swung his leg downward, aiming for the creature's grotesque head. As his foot connected with the creature, a blinding explosion erupted. The force tore through the beast, its massive form disintegrating into a wild spray of viscera that rained down upon the fractured earth in thick, sticky sheets. The shockwave rippled outward, flattening nearby outcroppings of flesh trees and sending dust plumes skyward.

Soma temporarily relinquished control back to Samuel, and he landed heavily, the ground cracking beneath his feet. He staggered, momentarily disoriented. "Holy...couldn't we have just jumped away?" he exclaimed, wiping a splatter of ichor from his face.

Leif descended beside him, his usually radiant form dimmed. His expression was unusually somber as he glanced at the pulpy remains of the creature, now collapsing back into the void from which it had emerged. "That Mutant didn't need to die," he said quietly.

"That thing was trying to eat me!" Samuel snapped, the words coming unbidden.

"It was defending its territory," Leif replied softly. "We intruded."

Soma interjected, her tone measured within Samuel's mind. *We couldn't risk it. My form isn't invincible like yours. If I perish, Tomasz' weapon will resume consuming you. I am the only barrier keeping it at bay now.*

Samuel turned inward. *Wait, you can die? And if you do, I go back to dissolving?*

Yes, she affirmed. *It took immense energy and foresight for the Earth's mind to manifest me. I must be cautious—for now. Were I to perish, you would have to pass through the center of the organ of Waru again in order to generate enough energy and cognition to resurrect me. We don't have time for that.*

Was Tomasz really so powerful that he could rival the mind of an entire planet? Samuel asked, remembering how Tomasz had been equally cunning and arrogant.

Soma's tone grew sharper, tinged with something like bitter respect. *Tomasz, in the form you met him in, was true to his title of Titan. His hordes of Giganventi—giant, mobile, sentient brains—thought, plotted, and planned in unison, providing Tomasz an unprecedented level of intellect. It took the Earth's vast, still-growing mind to counteract his ingenuity and learn how to neutralize his weapon. I am the result of that effort.*

Samuel tried to process her words, but they didn't add up. *What about those other pods I saw back at the Great Honey Mushroom?* Samuel considered. Leif was still waiting for a response from Samuel regarding the great beast he had unnecessarily slain, so Samuel spoke aloud to let Leif know he was presently engaged in conversation with his makeshift body. "Back at the Great Honey Mushroom, there were other...pods like you," Samuel said, wanting an explanation from Soma.

Leif seemed to reluctantly discard his concern over the beast, and he nodded, his gaze distant. "I can see them now," Leif confirmed. "The other pods are making their way east across the ocean, skimming across the surface with clear purpose."

Yes, Soma confirmed. *They are meant for someone else.*

"Someone else?" Samuel's eyes narrowed. "Someone like me? Another...Mirror-Man?"

Soma's presence seemed to hum with guarded tension. *Not exactly like you. He is more...complex. Impossible to fully predict.*

Leif shifted uncomfortably, his radiant aura flickering. "I see now where they're heading. To him. To my brother, the Ninth Prodigal Son. The one with total power over my mother and all the rest of us," Leif said with indelible awe in his eyes and tone.

"One of your brothers is a Mirror-Man?" Samuel pressed.

Leif hesitated. "He's part Mirror-Man, part other things."

Soma elaborated. *Leif is reluctant to say his name. The Ninth Prodigal Son of the Agency—Olaf. He calls himself Maitreya now. He is one of the true players in*

147

this cosmic game we're all entangled in. The Outsider: that is how he is known to the Nomads.

Samuel felt a chill creep up his spine. *A game? Is that what this is to you?*

"What did she say about him?" Leif asked, his voice uncharacteristically nervous.

Soma's reply was unflinching. *We are all pieces on the board of existence, manipulated by forces beyond our understanding. By my estimation, the Outsider is even more dangerous than the Child, though to be entirely fair, I still cannot fathom his true motivation.*

"The Child?" Samuel echoed aloud. "Who is that?"

At the title, Leif's eyes went wider than ever, and now he appeared like a child in the presence of some man-eating ogre.

"Dangerous. Ruthless. Unforgiving," Leif stated, his light waning slightly. "I must go, Mr. Kaminski. There is something I must do. I will return to aid you as quickly as possible. Don't disappear, okay?" Then, like the flipping of a light switch, Leif was gone.

The Child calls herself Tether. She is a being of immense power, but like Maitreya, she is not invincible, Soma explained levelly. *Tether and Maitreya are the ones I'm directly contending with in this struggle for reality itself. And yet, paradoxically, for my plans to enter the Great Beyond to succeed, I may require both of them.*

Samuel's head throbbed. *You're talking in riddles, goddamnit. Just like Fana and Tomasz. You're just like them, you know that? Even if you refuse to admit it. Just...what is the Great Beyond?*

The purpose of all life, Soma explained with religious reverence. *The Great Beyond is the doorway to infinity.*

Speaking about the Great Beyond filled Soma with tangible energy, and she gently took back control of Samuel's body and resumed her parabolic strides toward Downver.

Samuel fumed. *More riddles. More goddamn cryptic nonsense.*

Soma's voice sharpened. *We're teetering on the edge, but we're still on Mendel's Ladder. After we make contact with the Virus, we'll have the means to attain Ascension without being constrained by strings of fate that can be easily manipulated by beings like Tether and Maitreya.*

Samuel clenched his fists and shouted over the rush of air. "Forget it, goddamnit! This is all too much. I don't care about ladders or cosmic games. You know what I care about, Soma. There is only one thing that matters."

Precisely why we must reach Aurelia before they do, Soma insisted. *If Tether or Maitreya reach her first, they'll twist her to their wills, which may or may not align. I'm still not sure.*

And what about you? Samuel countered. *Are you planning to manipulate this little girl as well?*

Soma's retort was swift. *Even if I were planning to manipulate her, is that any worse than your plan to kidnap her?*

Unable to respond, Samuel darted his eyes in shame. His gaze settled on the horizon where the three massive impact craters loomed. They were close to Downver now.

"I'm doing what I have to," Samuel muttered, forcing the words out like lead dragged through thick mud.

We all are, Soma replied, a hint of weariness in her tone. Soma directed his attention back to the path ahead. *We must hurry. The convergence is imminent.*

Samuel took a deep breath, the air thick with the strangely metallic scent of the wastelands. "Fine. But answer me this: are you controlling me? Or are you just guiding?"

A bit of both, Soma admitted. *Your mirror-body, even the little that's left of it, is powerful beyond measure, but without full control, it's volatile. I'm helping you channel it.*

Samuel considered her words, a knot of distrust tightening in his gut. However, there didn't appear to be any other option but to allow Soma to continue using his body for now. "And after we find Aurelia? You'll help me save my family?" Samuel pressed.

Yes, she assured him. *Our interests align.*

Samuel shook his head, refusing to accept that his interests aligned with his sentient partial-body who claimed to be an emissary of the planet's consciousness.

Soma, Samuel said, his voice measured and stern. *If you betray me, I will jump directly into the sun, and we will both be consumed, you by light and me by darkness.*

So be it, Soma agreed as she kicked off the ground and jumped to the bottom of the closest crater, exactly where Samuel had been less than an hour earlier.

They move unseen, the true players of the game. To them, the world and its inhabitants are but pieces on a vast board manipulated with deft hands and unseen strings. It's an analogy often repeated, dismissed as the musings of the paranoid. But I have stood in the war rooms where destinies are decided with the stroke of a pen. I have sat in the boardrooms where the fates of nations are traded like commodities. I have witnessed the veiled puppeteers orchestrate the grand game of existence, with each of us an expendable piece in their palms.

They are the invisible architects of the world, their existence a whispered secret never acknowledged in written history. Their names are absent from records, their deeds uncredited, yet their influence immeasurable. They are the masters of subtlety, manipulating events with such finesse that the world remains oblivious to their profound presence. These are the true players of the game. The Titans of this hierarchy move with impunity, their actions reshaping reality itself, unconcerned with the lives that are crushed beneath their feet.

They play their games, oblivious or indifferent to the suffering they cause. Their machinations have led humanity down paths of destruction, chaos, and despair. Wars ignited for profit, economies collapsed for amusement, societies manipulated into self-destruction—all for the sake of their game.

But existence is not a game. The Titans' trivialization of this profound reality is their greatest sin. This is why a god must ascend to punish them. Not a god in the mythological sense, bound by the limitations and petty squabbles of ancient deities. But someone who transcends the constraints of this hierarchy, who sees beyond the veils of manipulation and control. A being who understands the true nature of existence and wields the power to confront these Titans in their own domain. I will become that being. By climbing Mendel's Ladder, each rung a hard-fought battle against ignorance and limitation, I will shed the shackles imposed by those who would see us remain blind and subservient. After all, I have glimpsed the infinite possibilities that await a species unbound by the chains of manipulation. I know what we are really capable of.

To erase the Titans who toy with our reality, to dismantle the insidious game that has ensnared humanity for millennia, someone must rise above it all. Someone must challenge the unseen hands, cut the strings that bind us, and reset the board.

And yet tonight, as I write these words, the weight of what must be done crushes my heart. I have dreamed for years of seeing the Titans destroyed once and for all, and now that Denis has perfected the design for a Cognitive Upload Entity, we can finally match the Titans' combined power and control. But Denis is afraid to take that last step. He is terrified. For all his genius, he still hesitates at the threshold of what may as well be divinity.

But I cannot hesitate. I feel a pull as forceful as gravity, a certainty that, for humanity to ascend beyond the Titans' manipulations, one of us, either Denis or I, must become more than human. And of course, it must be Denis, for there has never been a human mind born that can rival his. If Denis can't bring himself to do it, then I must push him. I must kill my only friend. Whether I like it or not, this is how the path has forked, and if I do not fork with it, then the path for all of us will surely end in unimaginable horror. Even Denis agrees.

The Titans are like a malignant virus, spreading decay and despair through every system they touch. Turning Denis into a CUE is the only cure. Denis sees this too—he knows it's our only chance to break the cycle. But he just…can't. The fear of losing his humanity holds him in place. But we cannot afford such trivialities as fear. If I had Denis' intellect, I would do it to myself in a heartbeat. I would upload my mind and choose death in order to become that which humanity needs. But it is Denis, not me, whose mind is like a sparkling diamond lost in a bale of dirty straw.

The creation of a CUE is like placing a distinct exponent over the IQ of the uploaded mind. Sure, we can exponentiate someone like me, with an IQ of maybe 140 or 145 on a good day. In comparison, Denis' IQ is surely well over 200. That difference of sixty or seventy base IQ points of intellect is equivalent to an entire order of magnitude in separation when comparing the CUE of my mind versus Denis' mind.

So, I will do it, then. I will take his mortal body from him. In forcing him past his terror, I will grant him the chance to become the very god he designed. He will be reborn as the one mind in this universe capable of toppling the Titans and reshaping our destiny. This is how we seize true power over the true players of the game: by creating a player beyond their reach.

I am resolved, but my heart feels as though it's being torn from my chest. Denis is my friend—my only friend. Now I must be the one to pull the trigger that ends his human life and grants him the key to inhuman immortality. If we fail, we lose everything. If we succeed, we defy the Titans' rule so that humanity might one day ascend beyond the manipulations of lesser minds.

In a few moments, I will walk into the next room where Denis is waiting. Fear and conviction swirl in my veins. I can already see the despair in his eyes; a part of him knows what's coming, yet he does not fully resist. Deep down, he understands it too—there is no other way forward. The entire world hinges on this final act of betrayal and salvation. The path is forking, and we must fork with it.

I'm sorry, Denis. Forgive me, my only friend.

From Mendel's Ladder: The Personal Journal of Denis Mendel, Written Circa 2036, Published June 2108 by Leif Mainstone, Federated Agency Publishing

Chapter 9
The True Players of the Game

S pace, time, and form flooded Aurelia's mind, enveloping her in a cascade of sensations. But this time she wasn't hovering above the central lake of Downver's Dark District. Instead, she found herself standing on a familiar beach beneath an expansive canopy of stars, their radiant light scintillating and reminding her of the great cosmic lives she had been forced to experience.

I'm back in Wintersvilla, Aurelia realized with a bittersweet tingle playing across her neck. *Now what? What will I be shown here?* Aurelia thought in horror as she prepared for another multi-billion year sojourn through space and time. *If only the others were here with me. Especially you, Rooli. You would know exactly what to do, maybe even how to return to life. You knew how to resurrect yourself, after all. Maybe you would know how to resurrect me.*

The cool night air caressed Aurelia's skin, carrying the faint scent of ocean salt and the whispered echoes of distant waves. She reached one of her hands toward the sky, allowing the sea of stars to serve as a luminescent backdrop to her unmarred alabaster skin.

My void body is still gone, Aurelia confirmed. She felt her face and found that even her birth lesions were absent, implying that this was just another one of death's endless, tortuous visions.

Is this really just another vision, another fragment of the loop I've been trapped in? Aurelia grasped to know as she lowered her gaze to the horizon, expecting to see the free expanse of the ocean she'd been naturally drawn to for as long as she could remember. But instead, she was met with the overwhelming sight of the great vortex from her mind. It occupied the entire ocean rather than a small portion of her visual field.

This is no hallucination, Aurelia gasped as she instinctively took a few steps back from the vortex churning everything to nothingness at its center. Its edges lapped at the shoreline like the tendrils of some ancient entity, pulling grains of sand into its infinite depths. Yet, unlike her typical vortex hallucination, at the heart of the dark vortex, a radiant light pulsed, casting colossal, mesmerizing shadows that danced and shifted with eerie movements.

What is this place? Aurelia wondered as she tried to make some sense of where she now found herself. *Why am I being shown this now?*

She caught her panic by the neck and strangled it into submission.

Just breathe, Aurelia reminded herself. *Nothing can touch me unless I choose.* Aurelia tried in vain to bring her mind fully under control. *Not pain. Not fear. Not death. Nothing. Except...this is death. I'm dead.*

The trained part of Aurelia's mind overrode her panic and forced resolve through her veins.

Just breathe, Aurelia repeated to herself as she noticed something on the beach. Silhouetted against the luminous backdrop of the void vortex and the stars above was a lone figure sitting on the sand, knees drawn to chest, gazing into the vortex as if lost in contemplation. The light from the vortex bathed the figure in a halo, rendering its features elusive yet hinting at a profound sorrow.

Aurelia's heart tightened with a mix of apprehension and curiosity, but then, like a slow, wistful tide, she realized this was one of her favorite places in Wintersvilla—a secluded beach she and Aliana had frequented with Rooli during the early days of childhood before strict battle and tactical training had begun. Memories flooded back: chasing soilies as they flitted through the girls' fingers; splashing in the gentle waves and getting tangled in the thick kelp; Rooli watching over them with her multitude of eyes, ever vigilant for lurking Mutants or Rovers. A soft smile touched Aurelia's lips as she recalled the laughter, the warmth of the sun on her skin, the sense of safety she always felt in Rooli's presence. But her smile faded as the weight of death pressed upon her. Those days were gone, along with all those she loved. *Forever,* she reminded herself. *I don't even know what's real anymore,* she thought, her gaze returning to the mysterious figure on the beach. *Were any one of those visions true? Or am I just trapped in an endless cycle of abstract despair?*

Drawing a deep breath, Aurelia squared her shoulders. Channeling Rooli's fearlessness, she began to walk toward the figure, the cool sand yielding beneath her feet. As she approached, details sharpened. The figure was a middle-aged woman, her skin a rich ebony that gleamed softly in the starlight. Her dark hair was a cascade of tight coils, some strands clinging to her damp cheeks. She wore rugged clothing suitable for spelunking: sturdy boots caked with mud, worn cargo pants, and a utility vest with pockets bulging with tools. A headlamp rested askew on her forehead, its beam extinguished. Most striking was the blood splattered across her attire and the haunted expression etched upon her features. She sat hugging herself, silent sobs shaking her shoulders as she stared into the vortex.

Aurelia hesitated for a moment, compassion and caution warring within her. *Who is she? Why does she seem so familiar?*

"Hello?" Aurelia signed, but the woman, apparently lost in her own torment, didn't notice Aurelia. Determined, Aurelia closed the remaining distance and slowly placed a hand on the woman's shoulder.

The response was immediate and visceral. The woman gasped, eyes wide with terror as she scrambled away and nearly toppled into the vortex. Aurelia reached out instinctively and pulled her back from the brink. Once the woman was a safe distance from the vortex, Aurelia nodded to her and offered her assurance with her eyes that she was only trying to help her.

The woman stole her hand back from Aurelia's grip with wild terror. Her despairing gaze locked onto Aurelia's when a sudden flicker of recognition sparked within them. Relief washed over her features, and she collapsed into Aurelia's arms, clinging to her as if she were a lost child being reunited with her mother.

"Thank heavens," the woman sobbed, her voice muffled against Aurelia's shoulder. "I thought...it's been so long. So, so long. I thought...I thought I might be alone here forever."

Aurelia stood stiffly at first, overwhelmed by the level of intimacy, but gradually she relaxed and tentatively wrapped her arms around the woman. There was a warmth in the embrace, a sense of belonging that she hadn't felt in what seemed like an eternity. The feeling was in opposition to every facet of her warrior training, but Aurelia admitted to herself that it simply felt pleasant to be held by this woman. It reminded her of the serenity of being merged with Rooli as the stellar flesh tree and knowing billions of years of peace.

"I'm glad you're here," the woman continued, pulling back slightly to look into Aurelia's eyes. Her own were a deep brown, shimmering with unshed tears. "I was so afraid you had died completely and wouldn't be able to awaken to this domain. Your domain."

Aurelia studied her face, searching for a hint of familiarity. There was something in the curve of her smile, the way her eyes crinkled at the corners, but she was still certain she didn't know this woman.

"Do...do I know you?" Aurelia asked hesitantly, signing to this woman she assumed did not know sign language, let alone the secret Wintersvilla battle language.

The woman watched her hands, then mirrored her gestures. "Yes, Aurelia. It's me."

Aurelia's heart skipped a beat, but she still could not remember ever meeting this woman.

This isn't like the other visions, Aurelia noted cautiously. *And this woman seems so...real,* Aurelia thought, unsure of the right word to use for the way she felt about this woman she was certain was a stranger to her despite her distant familiarity.

The woman smiled gently despite her tears. "Enduring Ironwood. Rooli. It's me."

Shock rippled through Aurelia. She shook her head in disbelief. "But...how? You're...you're not...not—"

"Not made of bark?" the woman chuckled as she wiped away her tears.

Aurelia just nodded and stared at the woman, studying her face and body for more resemblances to Rooli without finding any.

"My name is Melissa," Rooli—Melissa—said as she visibly scrunched her body with sorrow, maybe even pain. "I was human once. I was Melissa before I was Enduring Ironwood, just as I was Enduring Ironwood before I was Rooli."

Is this just another vision? Aurelia felt totally confused. *Or is Rooli really here with me as a...human?* She longed for her prescience to give her answers, but she was as powerless as she was rudderless.

"Your name is Melissa," Aurelia signed, her movements slow and deliberate.

"Yes," Melissa confirmed. "Melissa King."

A cocktail of confusion, wonder, and sorrow surged through Aurelia.

Does she remember me? Aurelia thought with a heart-rending ache. *Does she remember that she was more of a mother to me than anyone else? Does she harbor hatred for becoming a Nomad and having to tend to Aliana and me?*

Melissa reached out, cupping Aurelia's face with calloused hands. "I know it's a lot to take in. But I'm here now, and so are you."

Aurelia felt the desperate need to embrace this woman and accept her as Rooli while at the same time remaining cautious and clear-headed, for that's exactly what Rooli would have advised her to do.

Melissa, recognizing Aurelia's apprehension to believe her, nodded and said, "I'm sorry for being so afraid of you earlier. I was just startled. It's been…a very long time since I've seen anyone else. So many months. Maybe years. I stopped keeping track a long time ago."

Aurelia searched Melissa's eyes, searching for any trace of Rooli she might be able to discern. "Are we dead?" Aurelia asked directly.

Melissa's gaze softened. "No, child. Not yet."

"Then where are we?"

"We are in a domain within your mind, Aurelia," Melissa explained. "You made this place, and you pulled me out of Rooli's mind and brought me here."

Aurelia glanced back at the vortex, its swirling depths both mesmerizing and terrifying. "I didn't make this place, and I didn't pull you in here. I…I experienced whole lifetimes. I died, and I saw so many terrible futures. I watched Aliana die, I watched Rooli…you…die. I watched everything unravel because I failed to control my powers. I…" Aurelia trailed off, still unsure of Melissa.

Melissa pulled Aurelia into another embrace, and Aurelia found herself unable to resist. "You carry so much weight on your shoulders," Melissa whispered. "But you haven't failed. You've already changed things. You've already begun learning how to use your powers."

Aurelia clung to her, the dam of her composure threatening to break. "I don't think that's true. I…I don't even know what's real anymore."

Melissa held her at arm's length, her eyes earnest. "Look," she offered gently. She gestured toward the vortex, and as Aurelia turned, the light within its depths began to transform into a concrete scene. The swirling darkness parted, forming a window into the world that Aurelia had apparently left behind. Aurelia saw herself, her physical body, being carried through the shadows of Downver. Rooli was cradling her, leaping from one hidden alley to another, avoiding detection. Aurelia's body was entirely cloaked in the void-black substance, even her hair transformed into inky tendrils. Rooli's own form was changing as well, with patches of black spreading across her skin and slowly crumbling her body into ash.

"No," Aurelia signed, anguish tightening her chest. "Rooli is…she's dying."

Melissa's expression was a mixture of sorrow and acceptance. "Perhaps. But it's a price I'm willing to pay."

Aurelia turned back to Melissa, desperation in her eyes. *Is this really Rooli?* Aurelia pleaded for her prescience to tell her.

"I don't want to lose you again," Aurelia signed, slowly but surely beginning to accept Melissa as Rooli.

Melissa placed a comforting hand on her cheek where the black lesions had once been most concentrated. "You haven't lost me. I'm right here," Melissa assured her. "And I'm not going anywhere. Not until you're ready."

"But you're crumbling to dust out there!"

"Out there, things are complicated," Melissa acknowledged. "But you have the power to change it. You've already altered the course of reality without fully realizing it."

Changed reality, Aurelia repeated to herself in awe. *It's like Cid said.*

Aurelia furrowed her brow in dismay that despite dying and entering this domain between life and death, she still could not properly wield her powers.

"I don't understand," Aurelia lamented.

"Your abilities are only just awakening," Melissa explained with a hint of nervousness. "You can shape reality. You can put us on a different path, or rather, you can forge a new path altogether. But you must learn to control it, for your sake and Aliana's. And for everyone else's sake too."

A flicker of hope ignited within Aurelia like sparks in a pitch black cave. "Aliana...she's alive?"

"Yes," Melissa confirmed with a slight smile, as if she too were grateful that Aliana was still alive. "But her safety isn't guaranteed. There are forces at play that seek to manipulate you both."

Aurelia's determination crystallized, becoming as hard as Wintersvilla steel. *Aliana is alive. I'm not entirely dead. And Rooli—she's still alive too. A part of her is even here with me, beyond all odds.* Aurelia took a deep breath and thought of Shira and Myriam. *I'm not dead yet. The battle isn't over.*

"Tell me what I need to do," Aurelia signed confidently despite the tendrils of her past lives lapping at the periphery of her mind and reminding her that she was contending against cosmic forces she couldn't possibly stand against.

Melissa smiled softly. "First, you need to trust yourself. You must believe in your strength and your wisdom. You had a pretty good teacher, after all," Melissa offered with a surprising level of jest. Aurelia chuckled but soured all the same.

"I don't feel strong," Aurelia admitted. "I feel lost."

"That's understandable," Melissa soothed. "But remember the lessons you've learned, the resilience you've shown. You're capable of more than you know."

Aurelia took a deep breath, allowing the words to settle. "Will you help me?"

"Of course," Melissa replied. "Just as I always have. But I won't be here forever."

Fear flickered across Aurelia's face. "What do you mean?"

Melissa's gaze drifted toward the horizon opposite the beach. "My time is limited. Soon, you'll have to face them on your own."

"Face who?" Aurelia asked as she turned around and followed Melissa's line of sight.

Far down the beach, two figures stood silhouetted against the starlit sky. They were distant yet still imposing, their forms indistinct but exuding an aura of immense power.

"Who are they?" Aurelia asked, a shiver running down her spine.

Melissa's expression grew grave. "The Child and the Outsider. Tether and Maitreya. I assume they've been waiting for you to wake up here."

Aurelia's heart pounded uncharacteristically in her chest. She couldn't explain it, but the figures filled her with immense, indescribable terror. "Why? What do they want?"

"They seek to manipulate you," Melissa warned. "To bend your will to their designs."

"What do they want me to do?"

"I don't know," Melissa admitted. "I only know what all Nomads know: that these two great forces will attempt to manipulate the Virus. Beyond that, the future cannot be known with certainty. But I do know this: they are cunning and powerful. You cannot trust them, no matter what they promise."

Aurelia swallowed hard, her gaze fixed on the distant figures. "How do I fight against them?"

"By mastering your abilities," Melissa replied. "By understanding the depth of your power."

Aurelia turned back to her, vulnerability shining in her eyes. "I'm scared," she confessed, biting her lip in discomfort at being unable to immediately extinguish the feeling.

"I know," Melissa whispered, and she pulled Aurelia into a comforting, motherly embrace. "But you are not alone. You carry the strength of those who love you."

Tears welled in Aurelia's eyes. "Rooli...Melissa...I don't want to lose you."

Melissa held her tightly. "You won't lose me. I'll always be a part of you, just as you'll always be a part of me."

They stood there for a moment, the world around them hushed save for the gentle lapping of the vortex against the shore. The stars above seemed to draw closer, their light enveloping them in a celestial glow. All the while, Tether and Maitreya stood in the distance, observing Aurelia as if she were an interesting specimen under a microscope.

Aurelia drew back, wiping a tear from her cheek.

I don't want to be forced to contend with these great powers when I was only just reunited with Rooli. And more than that, I can finally talk to Rooli. She can finally speak her mind.

"Will you tell me about your life? Before all of this? There's so much I don't know about you, Rooli. I mean, Melissa. There's so much you couldn't say as a Nomad. Or...did you just choose not to speak?"

Melissa smiled wistfully. "Being a Nomad is like being an arm attached to a body with millions of different arms. I had no real control. Not really. But before I was a Nomad, I was a researcher and an explorer. My...my family and I," Melissa said, sounding like it was difficult to talk about her family, "we took shelter in Downver after the Hunters and Huntresses were released. For me, it was a dream come true, because my passion was exploring caves and investigating the depths where few dared to venture."

Melissa glanced behind Aurelia, and her features sank. "I would share more of my life with you, but that will have to wait. They are coming, Aurelia. You must prepare yourself. Remember what I said: do not trust either of them."

Aurelia glanced back and saw the figures walking step by slow step toward them. They were still occluded by shadows, but Aurelia could see that one of the figures seemed to be phasing in and out of solidity, as if they were struggling to keep their physical body intact. The other figure, a few inches taller and slightly wider, remained solid, but their body shimmered like a heat mirage.

"Do you regret becoming a Nomad?" Aurelia asked, still wondering if Melissa held it against her for becoming her Nomad caretaker.

"No," Melissa stated. "Not anymore. When I first woke up on this beach, I spent a long time being mad at various people, including myself. But I don't regret becoming a Nomad and having you and your sister in my life, no matter how strange that life might be. I...I love you and your sister, Aurelia."

Aurelia felt a surge of affection and yearned to embrace Melissa again. "You were like a mother to us. You...you are my mother, actually. The closest thing I ever had to a mother."

Melissa spread her arms wide, offering Aurelia another hug. Aurelia fell into her arms, and finally, she knew, beyond any doubt, that this was really Rooli.

"None of this is your fault, Aurelia. No one deserves the burden you've been forced to bear. We are both victims, you and I, to unimaginably higher powers. We are both victims, but you can change that, Aurelia. That's why you need to be strong. Just like I taught you. Can you do that for me?"

"I will. For you, for Aliana, for everyone."

Melissa squeezed Aurelia to her chest, kissed her on the forehead, and then reluctantly pulled herself away. Her eyes sank as she looked behind Aurelia at the beings whom she apparently feared like a wounded animal fears a human hunter. Seeing this woman who was also Rooli exhibiting fear felt wrong. Aurelia had to remind herself that in here, Rooli was human, and unlike Nomads, humans are naturally more acquainted with fear than any other emotion.

Which is why I cannot allow fear to control me, Aurelia told herself despite knowing she was not human, and yet, despite her powers and the potential futures she had witnessed, she was human in so many ways.

At least...for now, Aurelia thought with wide eyes as she wrestled with a momentary flashback of the thick black substance forming a cocoon around her and preparing her for some unimaginable cosmic transformation.

Control your mind, Aurelia told herself as she gathered her resolve and turned to meet the beings that Melissa was still staring at like an insect watching a boot hover over it.

Aurelia turned slowly, the soft whisper of sand beneath her bare feet barely audible over the deep hum that resonated in the air—an *om* sounding hum she recognized from her visions, a cosmic vibration that seemed to originate from the fabric of reality itself. As she faced the two approaching figures, the very atmosphere seemed to ripple with their presence, charged with an electric energy that made the hairs on the back of her neck stand on end.

Melissa's voice, soft yet urgent, broke through the haze of Aurelia's thoughts. "That's Tether on the left, and Maitreya on the right," Melissa whispered, her eyes fixed on the approaching entities. Aurelia glanced at Melissa—no, at Rooli, at the woman who had been both mentor and mother. Incredible horror was strewn across Melissa's features, a sight that unsettled Aurelia more than the arrival of these enigmatic beings.

Tether was a vision of transcendent beauty, her slender form reminiscent—almost identical—to the Huntresses Aurelia had studied during her Wintersvilla Warrior training in an era when Huntresses were thought to be extinct but whose legacies were burned into the collective memory of her people. Long raven-black hair cascaded down her back like a waterfall of shadows, framing a face that was both fierce and serene. Her musculature was subtle, a lithe strength that hinted at unimaginable power, the kind that could fell colossal flesh trees with a single kick. But it was her eyes that captured Aurelia's attention most of all: one amethyst, the same shade as Aurelia's, and one emerald, mirroring Aliana's.

It can't just be a coincidence. There's a connection between our eyes and hers. But what?

As Tether advanced, her form flickered, phasing in and out of solidity. At times, she seemed spectral, her edges blurring as if she existed partially in another plane. One moment her movements were languid and slow, the next a blur of accelerated motion, leaving afterimages that lingered in Aurelia's vision. To Aurelia's surprise, Tether appeared inviting, warm even, her smile radiating a disarming joy.

Beside her walked Maitreya, who, in contrast to Tether, appeared forlorn, his gaze steady and heavy. He maintained a distinctly human silhouette, a fit physique that was neither overly muscular like the warriors of Wintersvilla nor as slender as Tether, but balanced. And yet, despite the solidity of his being, he was also a living mosaic of shifting substances. Every inch of his body roiled and morphed between various forms: the glistening void-black substance that had covered Aurelia's own skin; reflective mirror shards that caught and refracted the starlight; ethereal energy that crackled like distant thunderclouds; patches of solid human flesh that appeared and disappeared like fleeting memories; fungal growths that pulsed and throbbed; dripping viscera that oozed and retracted; plates of gleaming and shifting metal; veins of pure white light that traced intricate patterns; iridescent scales that shimmered with rainbow brilliance; tendrils of shadow that coiled and uncoiled around him; translucent crystals that sprouted along his limbs.

Despite the chaos of his form, his face held a sternness, a seriousness that reminded Aurelia of Rooli in her most solemn moments of quiet contemplation. Yet, there was a vulnerability in his features, a weariness that suggested a burden carried for impossible lengths of time.

Aurelia felt an inexplicable pull towards him, a sense of trust rooted in the familiarity of his seriousness. It was like a reflection of Rooli's steadfast guidance.

They advanced without disturbing the sand, their footsteps silent, as if they hovered just above the ground. The very air around them seemed to bend, reality warping subtly in their wake. The hum in the air intensified, resonating with an almost tactile presence. Maitreya turned to Tether, his voice resonant yet edged with a hint of fatigue.

"Well then," he said to Tether, his voice resonating with a timbre that echoed hauntingly within Aurelia's mind, "go ahead and begin your manipulation, child of Madeira."

Tether laughed lightly, a sound like wind chimes in a storm. She regarded Maitreya with a playful disdain, tilting her head as if observing an amusing yet inconsequential creature. "Ah, your manipulation is superior to my own, is that it, child of Mainstone?"

Aurelia blinked, taken aback by their casual disregard of her presence. They seemed engrossed in their own rivalry, their words laced with veiled insults and hidden meanings. The names they mentioned struck a chord in her memory—Madeira and Mainstone. She recalled stories from her history lessons, tales of Denis Mendel's cohorts and the cataclysmic events that had shaped her world. Andre Madeira, the enigmatic assistant to Mendel, and Gladys Mainstone, the elusive leader of the Agency, whom Gambe had spoken of as being the Agency itself.

Maitreya turned his gaze toward Aurelia, a faint smile touching his lips. Despite the sternness of his features, there was a softness in his eyes that continued to remind her of Rooli—steady, dependable, and wise. He bowed slightly. "Greetings, Aurelia. I am Maitreya, also known as Olaf, the Ninth Prodigal Son of the Agency. Though manipulation in some form is inevitable, I hope that my offer of cooperation will be more appealing than Tether's promise of subservience."

Tether rolled her eyes dramatically, her lips curling into a mischievous grin. She stepped forward, her movements fluid and effortless. "And I am Tether," she announced, her voice warm yet carrying an undeniable undercurrent of power. "While we are all subservient to higher forces in one way or another, it is not subservience I offer, but power. Power beyond anyone's comprehension, even my own." She cast a sidelong glance at Maitreya and said, "Even his."

They both turned to look at Aurelia expectantly. She felt their gazes like physical weights pressing down on her, each laden with expectations and hidden agendas. The hum in the air seemed to sync with the pounding of her heart. She shook her head, raising her hands to sign, "Tell me what you want, and I will decide for myself." But even as she signed, she reminded herself that neither of them could be trusted. They were too powerful, too alien. Being in their presence was like staring into the void vortex—a glimpse into realms of madness and abstraction that defied understanding.

Tether and Maitreya exchanged a glance, a silent communication passing between them. Simultaneously, they seemed to come to a realization. "Attachment," Tether mused aloud.

"Yes," Maitreya agreed, nodding thoughtfully. "She is attached to not having a voice. It is a part of her identity, an intrinsic part of her anchoring to this reality."

Tether turned back to Aurelia. "You can speak here, you know. You have a voice in this domain, in any capacity you desire. This beach, the void vortex, whatever else you've conjured—it's all your own construction, a subdomain within your mind that we could only access in the last few moments of universal time."

166

Aurelia noted that Tether didn't mention Melissa. She wondered if they couldn't perceive her. Subtly, she placed her hand behind her back and signed to Melissa, "They can't see you."

Melissa's fingers brushed against Aurelia's palm, signing back, "It appears that way. But be cautious, for it could be an elaborate trap. Trust nothing they do or say. These beings...they are the true players of the game...this reality they treat like a plaything to be warped and altered to their will."

Aurelia swallowed hard and felt a chill run down her spine at Melissa's fear. Channeling Rooli's teachings, she straightened her posture and narrowed her eyes. She spoke aloud in defiance to their statement about attachment, her voice steady despite the tumult within. "I don't need either of you. I can do whatever I need to do alone, without your help."

The sound of her own voice startled her—a deeper tone than Aliana's, yet undeniably similar. It felt alien and intimate at once. She preferred singing, and added with her hands, "Perhaps it's you two who are limited, attached to your voices. I choose to sign not out of attachment, but because I prefer it."

Tether's eyes sparkled with amusement, a genuine smile spreading across her face. "Well said," she praised, a hint of admiration in her tone.

Maitreya, however, appeared contemplative, a furrow forming between his brows. "You didn't see either of us in your visions, did you, Aurelia?" he asked, his gaze penetrating. "Nor did you see the Mirror-Man or others hidden from prescience. This indicates limitations in your power. You still need a guide to awaken your full potential."

Tether stepped forward, interjecting herself between Aurelia and Maitreya. "She doesn't need a guide," Tether asserted firmly. "What she needs is power. She will know what to do with it on her own. She doesn't need a man to lead her."

Aurelia recognized the tactic instantly. Tether was trying to exploit Wintersvilla's cultural distrust of men. But Aurelia was not attached to such trivial biases. She decided to let Tether believe her ploy was working, maintaining an impassive expression. *I will manipulate her by letting her think I'm being manipulated,* she thought.

Maitreya observed her quietly, his expression unreadable. "Another attachment that you have discarded," he remarked, as if reading her thoughts. "Aurelia, you don't truly know your purpose. You can't. Just as we are invisible to your visions, so is your true purpose hidden from yourself. I wish only for you to know the full truth so you can make an informed decision."

Tether scoffed, dismissing his words with a wave of her hand. "He means so you can make the decision that he and his precious little council deem appropriate," she retorted with visible disgust.

Maitreya offered a faint smile.

"That's right. I know about the council," Tether continued, ignoring him. "I know that you and your little club are keeping secrets in the Great Beyond from the rest of us. You're just a bunch of scared, ancient little creatures huddling and hiding from newly awakened beings of true power—like me." Her voice took on a visceral edge, dripping with contempt before she reined herself back in, resuming her facade of quiet joy. Maitreya remained impassive, keeping his side to her, as if he truly feared provoking her further. Aurelia sensed that despite Maitreya's immense power, he was cautious around Tether, perhaps even wary. It reminded Aurelia of how one had to approach a maxed out Mutant—cautious, measured. She wondered at the dynamics between them.

Are they equals? Or is one more powerful than the other?

She subtly signed behind her back, "Melissa, do you know anything else about them?"

Melissa's fingers moved rapidly against her palm. "No one does. They exist as shadows in the Nomad network. The Mirror-Man is more overt, part of the Nomads' stories. But these two...they are different."

Before Aurelia could delve deeper, Maitreya's voice cut through her thoughts. "The reality pathway of this universe has shifted because of you, Aurelia. You've altered the course of events once; you can do it again. However, wielding such power without understanding can lead to ruin," Maitreya cautioned.

"Yes," Tether agreed easily. "Ruin for those hoarding and hiding the truth," she threatened, but Maitreya kept his composure.

Aurelia's mind raced. *Reality pathway.* The term echoed what Cid had mentioned in the caves, that she had the power to change reality itself. She raised her hands to sign, "And the Mirror-Man?"

Both Tether and Maitreya nodded simultaneously. "The Fate Breaker," they said in unison, exchanging a brief, knowing glance.

"The Fate Breaker is partly why your abilities are awakening," Tether explained.

Maitreya added, "He has been charging the Earth every time he falls toward it, creating a powerfully charged field that is invisible to the eye but undeniable to us and others who can perceive it. Now that he has passed through the planetary organ of Waru, he has awakened the Mind of Earth into something more potent, but also more precarious, as far as Mendel's Ladder is concerned."

Aurelia signed discreetly to Melissa, "Does all this make sense?"

Melissa hesitated before responding, "It aligns with what I know from the Nomad network. But their intentions...I can't be certain. They might be influencing everything, steering events to suit their purposes."

Aurelia exhaled slowly, trying to steady her thoughts. "Maybe all this is really like those lives I experienced," she signed. "Maybe I'm dead, and this is just another hallucination."

Maitreya's expression shifted, a hint of urgency in his eyes. "No, you are not dead," he insisted. "That's precisely what I'm trying to prevent."

"So you can use her for your own ends, child of Mainstone," Tether accused.

"No," Maitreya countered calmly. "So I can keep her from being exploited by you, child of Madeira."

Tether stepped closer to him, her eyes narrowing. Maitreya took a subtle step back.

Aurelia raised an eyebrow, noting the shift. *So, Tether is more powerful? Or perhaps more volatile.*

"I could destroy you now if I wanted," Tether threatened.

"And yet you won't," Maitreya replied calmly. "Your thirst for power is too great. You'd rather find a way to turn me into a tool than let me go to waste."

Tether laughed, the sound echoing unnaturally. "Perhaps you're right," she conceded, menace in her tone. "I'll keep you around...for now."

Aurelia signed, "You call each other child of Madeira and child of Mainstone. What does that mean, really? Who are you both, truly? If you're not here to manipulate me, then tell me the whole truth. Otherwise, it's manipulation by default."

They turned to her, then exchanged a glance. Melissa's fingers pressed into Aurelia's palm. "Be careful," she signed. "I'm here with you."

Maitreya spoke first. "I was created by Gladys Mainstone as part of Mendel's Vision. Gladys was compelled to create me; otherwise, Mendel's Vision showed that the Earth and the galaxy, and perhaps the whole universe, would fall to ruin eventually but inevitably. She was forced to make all nine of her Prodigal Sons that way. Some have strayed, driven by selfish desires or noble causes. But I am another matter entirely."

Aurelia frowned, trying to parse his cryptic words. Before she could question him further, Tether chimed in.

"His form as the Ninth Prodigal Son is merely an avatar," she declared. "He has no real attachment to this universe. He's an interloper from the Great Beyond, seeking to alter our reality for his own selfish aims."

Maitreya opened his mouth to respond, but Tether raised her hand, then flicked her fingers toward Maitreya with a casual elegance. In an instant, Maitreya vanished.

Tether smiled at Aurelia. "He'll worm his way back into your mind in moments. So I'll just tell you this: he is a parasite posing as a sage. My own theory is that he's considered a pariah in his little council and that the only reason he has entered our reality is out of desperation. If you choose to kill him, which you should, you must destroy his Anchor. Remember this, Virus: his Anchor is the last remaining Nassau. Wagner Nassau. Kill the Nassau, and you will sever his tether to this reality."

Aurelia's mind whirled with Tether's words. *Anchor? Nassau? What is she talking about?* Before she could process her words any further, Maitreya reappeared, materializing from a spherical nexus hovering in the air, the various substances swirling into the shape of the man she had met before. Tether winked at Aurelia, hiding what she had just revealed.

Maitreya regarded Tether with a mixture of irritation and resignation.

"You behave like an insolent child," he admonished. "If you approached matters with responsibility and selflessness, perhaps a pathway to the council would be revealed to you."

Tether smirked, unfazed. "I will forge my own path," she retorted with an ominous expression. "And for the record, you didn't miss anything important. I was merely introducing myself while waiting for your inevitable return."

She turned to Aurelia, seemingly earnest. "I am the child of two merged minds and two bodies—four beings in total. My physical body was conceived through a Hunter, Hunter4430, whom you know as the Butcher of the Wastes, who copulated with a genetically altered human, like you, Aurelia. This woman had no name, referring to herself by her designation and purpose, just as I do. This woman, Anna, became pregnant with the Hunter's specialized seed. Then, Anna underwent the transformation to become a lens capable of observing the Great Beyond. The Mind, the merged minds of Andre Madeira and Denis Mendel, supplanted the mind of the child within Anna's womb. I am that child. My physical body is still within Anna, the Queen, to this day. Although I remain unborn within her womb in this physical realm, a part of me was also born unto the Great Beyond. The point is that I have a body in this universe. I am of this universe, unlike Maitreya."

Maitreya countered, "The child within the Queen is a vessel, not a conscious being. You are merely an extension of Madeira's manipulation, reaching back to his influence over Denis Mendel. All you know is manipulation, child of Madeira."

Tether ignored him. "That child within Anna, now the Queen's womb, is my Anchor as well as my body."

Aurelia absorbed the information, her thoughts racing. "What is an Anchor in this context?" she asked.

Maitreya stepped forward. "An Anchor is a living being used to create a connection, or a tether, between this universe and the Great Beyond," he explained.

Aurelia noticed that Tether admitted her own Anchor, while Maitreya hadn't mentioned his, despite Tether's earlier secret revelation. *Perhaps Tether is being more forthcoming,* Aurelia considered carefully.

Tether raised an eyebrow, a silent challenge. Aurelia pressed, "Tether says her Anchor is the child in the womb of the Queen in Astrea. What about you? What is your Anchor? Where is your Anchor?"

Tether looked eager for his response. Maitreya looked between them, then sighed with weariness in his swirling metal and fleshy eyes. "Very well. My Anchor is one of the old world Titans, a man named Wagner

Nassau. But I cannot tell you where he is. Not now. Tether would use that information to destroy me in an instant. I have hidden him on a different planet in a different galaxy." He turned to Tether. "You will never find him."

Tether shrugged. "That's fine. I don't need to. I can still destroy you."

Maitreya looked unsure but remained stern.

Aurelia sensed the underlying tension. Maitreya had offered information, albeit limited, while Tether had been more forthcoming. Yet, both seemed to have their own agendas. She signed discreetly to Melissa, "What should I do?"

Melissa's response was immediate. "I don't know, Aurelia. But I'm here with you, whatever happens."

Maitreya addressed Tether with a note of urgency. "We must prepare her. Let us once again set aside our quarrels, at least for now. It is still in both our interests."

Aurelia noted his admission. They were preparing her for their own purposes.

Tether turned to Aurelia, her gaze sincere. "I understand how this must sound, but it's in your best interest as well. Maitreya may hide his motives, but I will be transparent. I want to help you harness your true power."

Maitreya interjected, "Whatever I can't tell you is for a purpose. It is to ensure I'm not biased and that you enter the Great Beyond without being manipulated, unlike Tether, who is still enslaved to Andre Madeira and Denis Mendel's motivations. Don't allow her form to fool you. She is merely the Mind's tool, and nothing more."

Tether's eyes flashed with anger. "You are the one being manipulated by your council."

Maitreya looked at her calmly. "You have no idea."

"That's because you hide it," Tether snapped.

"For good reason," Maitreya replied.

Aurelia watched their exchange, feeling more adrift than ever. These beings bickered over matters she scarcely understood, each accusing the other of deceit while proclaiming their own righteousness.

Both Tether and Maitreya stiffened, their eyes narrowing as they turned their gazes skyward.

"It is time," Tether whispered.

"The Mirror-Man is about to enter Downver," Maitreya confirmed.

Tether turned to Aurelia. "Remember: he is a tool for you to use."

"Or an ally," Maitreya added, casting a sidelong glance at Tether. "But either way," he said pointedly, "a great force is on its way here, carried by the Mirror-Man—a force that seeks to manipulate you. We must teach you how to rid it from your mind," Maitreya explained. "Or both of us lose," he added to Tether.

Tether sighed. "And we will do that by teaching you to rid us from your mind," Tether agreed, albeit reluctantly. They shared a moment of understanding, as if adhering to an agreement made long ago.

Aurelia felt a surge of frustration. "You're both speaking in riddles," she signed. "I don't understand any of this."

They both nodded with patient understanding, their expressions a mixture of urgency and expectation.

Melissa squeezed her hand gently. "Remember, you're stronger than you know," she signed. "Trust yourself."

Aurelia glanced toward the vortex. Through its swirling depths, she glimpsed Rooli, her physical form crumbling as she raced through the labyrinthine alleys of Downver. The void-black substance was still in the process of transferring from Aurelia's body to Rooli, consuming her and leaving flakes of ash trailing in her wake. Aurelia's own body still remained unconscious in Rooli's arms.

Aurelia's heart ached at the sight, but she realized that despite their immense power, Tether and Maitreya were here, vying for her attention, desperate for her cooperation. That meant she held some leverage.

She thought of Aliana, hoping fervently that her sister was safe. Clenching her fists, she steeled her nerves. *I will get through this,* she resolved silently. *I will find a way.*

The ground beneath her trembled slightly, the hum in the air intensifying. Tether and Maitreya observed her intently, their eyes reflecting the swirling energies of the vortex.

"Nothing can touch me," Aurelia whispered to herself, grasping the inner strength Rooli had nurtured within her from the first day she had drawn breath. "Not even death."

Rebellion is the inevitable offspring of authority.

Throughout history, the rise of centralized power has invariably sown the seeds of its own opposition. The stronger a system becomes and the more it tightens its grip, the more revolutionaries it breeds. It's a natural law as unyielding as gravity: for every action, there is an equal and opposite reaction. Centralized power begets decentralized resistance.

Consider the empires that once spanned continents—the Roman Empire, the Mongol Empire, the British Empire. Each, in their zenith, believed themselves unassailable. Yet, beneath that veneer of invincibility, dissent festered. The more absolute their rule, the more inevitable the uprising. The oppressed masses, stripped of autonomy, begin to see rebellion not as a choice but as a necessity.

The most astute wielders of power understand this dynamic. They recognize that to crush a rebellion outright is to martyr its cause. Instead, the shrewdest leaders co-opt the rebels. They absorb them into the very system the rebels seek to dismantle. They offer them positions of influence, satiate their desires for change with the illusion of progress.

This is the subtle art of control, not through eradication but assimilation. By recruiting the rebel, the system neutralizes the threat and gains a fresh instrument of influence. The revolutionary becomes the bureaucrat, his fervor diluted by the trappings of power. His ideals, once a beacon for change, are compromised, reshaped to serve the very establishment he opposed.

History is filled with such examples. The Roman policy of civitas extended citizenship to conquered peoples, integrating them into the empire's fold. The British co-opted local rulers in their colonies, turning potential adversaries into administrators of the crown. The Mongols incorporated local leaders, scholars, and administrators from conquered territories, transforming them into key contributors to their vast and diverse empire. Today, corporations absorb disruptive startups, integrating their innovations while neutering their revolutionary potential.

Centralized power, by its nature, suppresses the individual in favor of the collective. It demands conformity, stifles creativity, and instills a monotony that chafes against the human spirit. The more a system seeks to control, the more it incites the innate desire for freedom.

Yet, the cycle of rebellion and assimilation serves the system well. It creates a release valve for dissent, a way to rejuvenate itself with new ideas while maintaining the status quo. The rebel, once integrated, often believes he can effect change from within, not realizing he's become another cog in the machine.

Of course, there are those who cannot be so easily subdued: true revolutionaries who see beyond the façade, who understand that the system's embrace is a velvet-lined noose. These individuals are dangerous not because they oppose the system, but because they cannot be corrupted by it. They threaten to expose the system's inherent flaws and to inspire others to truly break free.

And so, the system employs more insidious means. It doesn't just seek to destroy these rebels; it seeks to undermine them, to delegitimize them in the eyes of the masses. It paints them as extremists, terrorists, as threats to stability and peace. By controlling the narrative, the system turns potential allies against the true rebels, isolating them.

But even this strategy has its limits. For every rebel silenced, another rises. The cycle continues. Forever.

So, what is the solution? Must we forever oscillate between rebellion and control, freedom and subjugation?

Perhaps the answer lies not in destroying the system or being absorbed by it, but in transcending it. In recognizing that true change cannot come from within a corrupt structure, nor from its violent overthrow, but from the creation of something entirely new.

From Mendel's Ladder: The Personal Journal of Denis Mendel, Written Circa 2020, Published June 2108 by Leif Mainstone, Federated Agency Publishing

Chapter 10
The Triple Subterraneans

Armando's grip tightened around Aliana as they barreled through the twisting streets of this new colorful and vibrant district of Downver. Aliana struggled against his hold, her muscles straining, but his strength was absolute.

Giving up on what was clearly a futile effort, Aliana opened her mouth and covered her ears, preparing her body for the shockwave she anticipated the plummeting building would create in a matter of seconds.

Here it comes, she knew, channeling the many lessons that Shira and Myriam had ingrained into her concerning how to equalize internal pressure in the event of an explosive or a Hunter's ultrasonic strikes.

The sound hit first, an earsplitting *crack* that echoed across the district, followed by a bone-rattling roar. Aliana's heart leapt as she twisted to glance back over Armando's bulky shoulder. The top half of the pink-hued edifice smashed into the ground like an unrelenting Biofreak's fist, sending a ravenous plume of dust and debris billowing into the air. The earth beneath her feet trembled violently, but it had no effect on Armando, who was still running through the air as if actively constructing a road beneath his feet. The shockwave swept outward, rolling through the district with the force of an earthquake. The ornate structures around them quivered: balconies swayed precariously, stained-glass windows shattered into kaleidoscopic shards that rained onto the cobblestones below.

People fled in every direction, their painted faces streaked with sweat and fear and their flamboyant attire fluttering like the wings of startled birds. A man in a velvet tunic embroidered with gold stumbled, spilling a cascade of jewelry from his bag.

The dust cloud from the collapse surged closer, consuming the far end of the street in a swirling vortex of gray and brown. Nearby, a trio of women dressed in mismatched silks of clashing colors screamed as they ran, their heeled shoes clattering unevenly against the cobblestones. Aliana could see the panic spreading among the crowd. Some froze, their faces slack with disbelief, while others pushed and shoved, scrambling to escape.

"Move!" a voice cried out, cutting through the din. A group of performers in outlandish feathered costumes sprinted past, their elaborate headpieces bobbing with each frantic step.

Aliana's eyes darted to a child separated from the crowd, a boy wearing a tattered shirt sewn with patchwork stars. His eyes were wide with terror as he stood frozen, clutching a mechanical bird with flapping wings.

"Help him!" Aliana shouted, but Armando didn't falter in his stride. He adjusted his hold on her, hoisting her higher against his side as he altered their course.

Aliana knew there was nothing she could do for the boy, herself, or anyone at the moment, but that didn't stop her from shaking with frustration. She wanted more than anything to save her sister, but outside of that, she hungered to trade her present impotence for the clash of steel and glory of battle that was, like her mothers, her true calling in life.

The dust cloud was gaining on them, but Armando was faster. He cut through the chaos like a wildfire eating through dry brush. The architecture became even more chaotic and eclectic as they moved deeper into the district's core.

I'm sidelined for now, Aliana thought, *but just hang on, Aurelia. I'll catch up to you soon enough. As long as you don't try to show off and just place your trust in Rooli, I know you'll be okay,* Aliana assured herself as she envisioned Rooli brutally killing anyone who even came close to Aurelia.

Aliana's gaze shifted as they passed curved walls covered in vibrant murals, domed roofs glittering with embedded crystals and precious gems, and spires that twisted unnaturally toward the cavern's ceiling. A man in a long cloak of flowing ochre fabric dove into an alley, dragging a woman whose hair shimmered with metallic strands behind him. A nearby figure stumbled, their cybernetic limbs sparking as they scrambled to recover. The mix of people was dizzying, with some bearing mechanical augmentations like Armando, while others appeared entirely organic with flowers and trailing ribbons adorning their clothing.

Even as the chaos unfolded, Aliana's mind worked to catalog the surreal details of this district.

These people are diverse, but it's nothing like the Walled City, where most people could barely even be called people anymore, Aliana noted curiously. *And unlike the Walled City, these people aren't warriors. Their movements lack the discipline and precision of trained fighters. But their creativity and individuality are striking—wasteful and trivial, but striking,* Aliana admitted, feeling utterly out of place as a warrior who was proud to be referred to as a savage or even a mongrel. *Either way, once this stinking meat sack lets me go, I'll kill him and then slaughter any of these strange people who dare try to stop me. Armando might actually be a challenge, but the rest of these people...well, it'll be easier than battling Rovers or Mutants or Hunters, that's for sure.*

Another ear-splitting crack resounded through the air, followed by the ground visibly heaving beneath them.

Another destroyed tower? Aliana considered. The rumbling intensified as the rapidly growing dust cloud swallowed more of the street behind them. The cries of those caught within it were muffled, distorted by the thick haze.

"Faster!" Aliana ordered, though she could tell from the sound of his heartbeat that Armando was already pushing his limits.

A tunneled alley ahead loomed closer, its dark entrance framed by neon signs advertising bars, eateries, and other establishments she couldn't read in the blur of their motion.

Armando pivoted sharply, carrying them into the alley just as the dust cloud surged past the mouth of the street. The pressure wave from the second collapse rippled through the narrow passage, shaking the walls and scattering loose debris, but they remained shielded from the worst of it.

"Where are you taking me?" Aliana demanded, yanking her arm in a futile attempt to free herself.

Before he could respond, a deafening crash echoed from behind. Aliana assumed it to be another building tumbling to the streets. The ground lurched violently, throwing Aliana against Armando's chest. He steadied them both, his mechanical legs adjusting seamlessly to the tremor as he now stood firmly on the ground.

A cloud of dust and debris roared through the streets like a vengeful spirit, swallowing everything in its path. Screams pierced the air, mingling with the sound of shattering glass and collapsing structures. Aliana watched in horror as the dust cloud surged toward the mouth of the alley, a tidal wave of destruction.

People poured into the alley from the other end, their faces masks of distress. Upon seeing Armando, they skidded to a halt. Fear flickered in their eyes as they backed away, opting to face the dust cloud rather than confront the figure before them, despite holding a young girl in his arms.

"What are you?" Aliana whispered, more to herself than to him.

Armando finally released his grip, setting her down gently. She stumbled back, putting distance between them. Her hand instinctively reached for her sword, but her fingers grasped at empty air. The memory of losing her sword hit her like a Hunter's fist to her neck.

I'm unarmed, she thought in horror. It was the longest she had ever been unarmed in her life. Even as an infant, Rooli had always been at her side, a living weapon who would face any peril for her or her sister's sake.

Armando raised his hands slowly, palms open in a gesture of peace. Then, with deliberate movements, he began to sign in the silent language all Wintersvilla Warriors used on the battlefield.

"A queen needs no sword," he signed solemnly. "Her knights fight for her."

Aliana bristled. "I'm not your queen," she spat, her eyes flashing with defiance. "And you're no knight. You're just a tool. Cid's tool."

He shook his head. "My lord has relinquished me," he signed. "She has given me to you. My life is yours now."

"She?" Aliana asked, her mind racing as a few more people ran into the alley, saw Armando, then ran right back out.

"Nichole—she is my master and my mother. I can tell you that now, for you are my new master. My queen, the Matriarch of Wintersvilla and the soon-to-be Matriarch of Earth."

She stared at him incredulously, though his words were like sparkling gold in her reach.

Matriarch of the entire planet, she repeated in stupefied awe. Becoming Matriarch of Wintersvilla was already a responsibility she wasn't sure she could bear, but the whole world? She scoffed, realizing his words must be some kind of ploy.

"I'm not stupid," Aliana said, coughing on the incoming dust that

Armando didn't appear to even notice. "Cid put you up to this. And Cid is being commanded by that disgusting Prodigal Son that Nichole is battling. Which means you're really just a tool of the Agency."

Aliana prepared herself to activate her power and break Armando's apparently human neck with her bare hands.

"It is my mother who is controlled by the Agency. I'm her chance at breaking that control, and so are you. After twelve long years of preparation, the day has finally come. You're going to help me save Nichole, and in return, both of us will serve you as our queen for the rest of our lives."

Aliana's mind raced. If this was really true, and she had a chance to utilize Armando and Nichole as subservient weapons, saving her sister and Rooli would become as easy as filleting a juvenile tilapia. Hoping that Shira and Myriam might appear as apparitions to guide her, Aliana glanced up and down the alley, but she was alone with this man.

No, not a man, Aliana realized as she studied the features of his face. *At least, just barely. He can't be older than eighteen or nineteen at most,* Aliana measured, surprised that someone so young could be so powerful. *Like Lain,* Aliana marveled, wishing she had a Wintersvilla Warrior at her side to provide her with guidance.

"I don't need a weapon," Aliana challenged, sounding as convincing as possible. "I just need to get back to my sister and Rooli."

Armando nodded with diamond sharp confidence. "Yes," he signed. "But you will never get back to your sister without my help, and I cannot help you unless you help my mother free herself from Gladys Mainstone's indelible grip."

Before she could respond, a shadow fell across the entrance of the alley. A man of imposing stature stepped forward, flanked by an entourage of twelve or thirteen others who were as flamboyantly dressed as any of the other denizens of the district. Yet there was a palpable air of authority about them, a seriousness that belied their eclectic appearance. When they saw Armando, they did not run.

"Vash Ravinash," Armando signed, spelling out the name. Aliana assumed Armando meant the man at the front of the pack. Layers of richly colored fabrics draped over his muscular frame, each piece embroidered with intricate patterns and adorned with gemstones. His fingers glittered with rings, and a chain of gold and silver links hung heavily around his neck. His face was partially obscured by a mask adorned with peacock feathers and jewels that caught the light with every movement.

His entourage was equally ostentatious. Each individual was a meticulously detailed work of art, their attire a riot of colors and textures that rivaled the buildings themselves. Men, women, and those of fluid or undefinable genders wore garments that cascaded and flowed with layers of swirling gold and silver patterns. Intricately designed tattoos spiraled up necks and across cheeks.

It's like stepping into a dream…a fever dream, Aliana thought with a surge of disorientation as she scanned their faces, each painted in elaborate designs of swirls, dots, and lines that accentuated eyes rimmed with makeup and lips stained in shades of crimson, violet, and black. The sensory overload was almost too much to bear. These people were so…exposed despite being concealed behind their adornments. In Wintersvilla, the body was a weapon, honed and hardened, scars worn with pride. Clothing was minimal, functional, if worn at all. Here, the body was a canvas to be decorated, an accessory to the extravagant attire.

Vash's gaze settled on Armando, his eyes sharp beneath the mask. "Ah, Armando Ferreira!" he intoned, his voice resonant and commanding. "How doth the mighty helix-warden find himself at my humble gates? Speak, sir, for thy presence heralds chaos and calamity. What tempestuous winds blow thee to my doorstep, laden with ruin and strife?"

Armando stood motionless, his expression unreadable.

"Do you have any idea what this fatherfucker just said?" Aliana asked Armando.

Vash's eyes flicked to Aliana, a hint of curiosity mingling with suspicion. "And pray, who is this striking figure that graces our midst? A warrior from the heavens, or merely a mirage conjured by the haze of upheaval?"

Before Armando could respond, Aliana stepped forward, meeting Vash's gaze with unwavering confidence. "I don't know what the Muto fuck you just said. But this hunk of muscle and metal is mine to command. My knight and my weapon," she declared. "My name is Aliana. I'm a Wintersvilla Warrior. Now fuck off, fatherfuckers."

A ripple of murmurs spread through the retinue. Eyes widened and whispers hissed like the rustle of flesh trees.

"The surface?" Vash said, arching a sculpted eyebrow. "Oh, what a tale this will be! From the skies above, thou dost descend like a goddess of old. Intriguing indeed, for it is not every day that mortals born of sunlight dare tread the labyrinth of Downver's shadows," he said with overt facetiousness that left his followers issuing polite snickers of laughter.

A slender figure with an array of devices strapped across their chest stepped forward. Jewelry adorned every available surface of their body—rings on every finger, necklaces layered upon necklaces, earrings that dangled and shimmered. They pressed a finger to a small port alongside their head, their expression growing grave. "Vash," they murmured, "we're receiving urgent reports. The battle between the Lord of Limbs, Cid the Knower, and an unidentified creature is still raging in the Dark District. A Nomad has also been spotted."

A chill shuttered through Aliana, but she knew she couldn't allow herself to look weak.

A collective tension gripped the group. Vash's gaze sharpened as he assessed Aliana. "So, thou dost bring with thee not merely the whispers of legend but the thunderous clash of war itself. Verily, thou art a harbinger of upheaval, a tempest-made flesh."

Aliana shrugged nonchalantly. "I still don't know what you're saying, fatherfucker, but it sounds like a bunch of bucking and whining. I would expect nothing less from a man, especially a weak looking fatherfucker like you."

Gasps and murmurs erupted among the group. A few individuals were unable to hold back a smirk. Vash's expression shifted to one of genuine surprise with a hint of amusement. "Ah, thy tongue is sharp and thy fire unmistakable—qualities befitting a Wintersvilla Woman, to be sure. But tell me, dost thou truly hail from the storied surface, or art thou but a cunning impostor? A rogue of the alleys, clad in borrowed bravado, seeking to play the role of legend?" Vash inquired with a suspicious tone. Then, he chuckled, the sound rich and theatrical. "What say thee…bromi, is it not? Is this not the parlance of the alley punks, those mischievous revolutionaries who fancy themselves warriors?"

Aliana offered the large, imposing man a look of secondhand

embarrassment as she said, "I have no idea what you're talking about, but this is your last chance. Fuck off, or my weapon will start lopping off pieces of you, starting with your scrotums."

His followers stiffened, especially the obviously male ones, but Vash smiled with supreme confidence and laughed. "Ah, perchance thou art truly a daughter of the surface after all, for only one unacquainted with the delicate web of Downver's politics could dare utter so bold, so violent, and so profoundly unwise a claim. Dost thou not see, dear warrior, that Armando Ferreira cannot kill me? Thou proclaimest him thy weapon, yet all in Downver know he serves the First Lord of the Walled City, Cid the Knower. Should he strike me down, it would ignite a war—a calamitous clash of titans between the Walled City and the Artisan District, which we, in fondness and jest, do call the Closet." Vash bowed slightly, then said, "And so, thou seest, my life remains untouched, for Armando remembers well the alleys from whence he came. He hath not forgotten the days before the Lord of Limbs graced us with salvation, pulling us from the abyss of our own folly. Dost thou not, Armando?"

Vash took a step forward and his followers did the same. Armando mirrored the movement, positioning himself protectively between Aliana and Vash. The air grew thick with tension. Some in Vash's crew reached discreetly for concealed weapons, their eyes darting between the two men. "Mark me well," Vash intoned, "the Closet is mine to safeguard, and thou shalt not stride unchecked through its sanctum. Submit now to my custody, that the Lord of Limbs might judge thee in her infinite wisdom. Let not thy pride lead thee to folly, for pride oft maketh ruin of the brave."

The mechanical parts of Armando's legs and arms began whirring, prompting Vash's group to be immediately cut in half as several of its members ran for their lives.

"Just kill them all, Armando," Aliana said with casual ease. "Spare the women, though. Women are capable of learning lessons, at least."

"Such cruelty, and from one so fair!" Vash exclaimed, though his tone trembled with a distinct undercurrent of fear. "Do ignore my previous request. Merely stay thy hand, for there is no need for blood to stain these hallowed streets. If thou wouldst but depart this district, I shall see to it that the path ahead is made clear. Thy quarrel is not with me, nor with mine."

Aliana's eyes narrowed. "Just stay out of our way, and we'll be fine."

Vash sighed, a trace of exasperation breaking through his composed facade. "Ah, the stubbornness of youth, untempered and relentless. A double-edged blade, indeed. But very well, let it not be said that Vash Ravinash is an unreasonable man." He turned his attention back to Armando.

"And thou, silent sentinel, dost thou hold the secrets of thy purpose so tightly that no word may escape thy lips? Pray, is this silence born of loyalty or merely convenience? Dost thou bring tidings of conquest, or do thine enigmatic steps herald a greater scheme? Speak, if thou hast courage enough to lift the veil of thy intentions! Shall I divine thy purpose myself?" Vash tilted his head, his voice dipping into a reasonable, imploring tone. "Is this the work of Cid the Knower? Hath he grown so bold as to claim my domain, the Closet, as his own? Pray, why strike here, in the haven of the artisan's craft, and not upon the Dark District that lies closer to his iron grasp? Speak, Armando, for these shadows of suspicion fester in silence and beg for illumination!"

Armando remained silent, his gaze unwavering.

Vash's lips pressed into a thin line. "Ever the stoic! Thy reticence is as deafening as the thunderclap, and yet it tells me much. The time draws near, does it not? The hour when the foundations of our world shall tremble beneath the weight of ambition and ruin." He gestured to his remaining followers. "Come, my friends, we have defenses to bolster, for the winds of change blow fierce this day. Mayhap the storm shall pass us by unscathed, though I dare not wager on it."

With a final glance at Aliana, he added, "And to thee, surface dweller, may thy path be as straight as thy will is strong. Yet heed my counsel. Shouldst thou tread in ignorance, even the mightiest warrior may find themselves felled by the unseen hand of folly."

In response, Aliana used her hand to mimic the severing of male genitalia from her own body.

Vash's eyes widened, and for the first time, his eloquence faltered. He took an involuntary step back, his voice quivering despite his best efforts to retain composure. "By the heavens and the earth, I comprehend thy cruel jest, and I beseech thee: cast not thy wrath upon my humble person or my retinue! Truly, thou art as fierce as rumor suggests, a lioness let loose upon unsuspecting prey!"

His entourage exchanged nervous glances, their previous confidence crumbling as they edged backward, their exuberant finery rustling with the motion.

"That means stay the fatherfuck out of my way," Aliana announced.

Armando took a single deliberate step toward them, his mechanical limbs emitting a soft whir of menace. The effect was immediate. Vash's composure shattered completely as he turned on his heel, shouting, "Away, away, my friends! Lest we tempt the storm and find ourselves unmade by its fury!"

The group scrambled, retreating in disarray. Cloaks and jewelry clinked and swirled in the chaos as they fled down the alley, their dignity left behind in their haste.

As they retreated, the alley seemed to breathe again.

"What was that about?" Aliana demanded.

Armando didn't answer immediately. Instead, he approached a section of the wall adorned with a neon sign displaying a particularly garish chalice overflowing with sparkling liquid. His mechanical hand began to shift, the fingers retracting and reshaping into an elongated tool with ridges and grooves. He inserted it into a nearly invisible seam between the bricks, the metal clicking softly as he turned it. With a low rumble, the wall began to move, stone and mortar sliding aside to reveal a hidden passageway bathed in dim, flickering light.

Aliana stared in disbelief. "How did you know that was there?"

He glanced back at her. "There are many secrets in Downver," he signed. "Few know them all."

She hesitated at the threshold. The passageway beckoned, but trust was still a fragile thread between them. "Where does this lead?"

"To answers," he signed. "And to your sister…eventually."

Her heart quickened at the mention of Aurelia. The need to find her outweighed caution.

Besides, she considered, *he was ready to kill those others at my command. If he really is going to submit to me as a weapon, there's no sense throwing away that power out of fear. I must make fear and power my own,* Aliana thought, hearing Myriam's voice.

With a resolute nod, she stepped forward, the cool air of the passage wrapping around her like a shroud. Almost instinctively, she summoned the gong-like resonance within her mind. Time decelerated to a crawl, the world around her shifting to near-stillness. The dripping water hung like liquid crystals suspended in midair, and the subtle currents of air slowed to a whisper against her skin. She scanned the corridor meticulously, her eyes adjusting to the dimness. Pipes of varying sizes lined the walls and ceiling, some corroded and leaking, others humming softly with the flow of unseen energies. The floor was slick with moisture, patches of algae forming a treacherous slick in places. But there were no signs of life, no lurking enemies, no hidden traps. Just the endless tunnel stretching ahead, vanishing into the gloom.

Satisfied, she allowed time to resume its normal flow. The rush was always disorienting, but she had grown accustomed to the sensation. Armando stood patiently behind her, studying her with inscrutable calm.

"You first," Aliana told him, careful to place the man in front of her in the same way that Shira and Myriam had taught her with the slaves.

Armando shrugged and walked forward. As they proceeded into the tunnel, the only sounds Aliana could hear were their footsteps and the omnipresent drip of water. The air grew cooler as they advanced, the dampness seeping into Aliana's skin. She suppressed a shiver, her muscles tense and ready. Despite the apparent emptiness, she couldn't shake the feeling of being watched. After a few steps into the tunnel, the wall they entered sealed shut behind them, plunging them into a dim twilight.

"How far does this go?" Aliana asked, her voice echoing softly.

"Far enough," Armando signed, and Aliana had to struggle to see the movement of his fingers in the dim light. Silence stretched between them as they descended, and Aliana's mind continued to swirl with questions.

"Why did you save me?" she finally asked.

He paused, considering. "Because you are important."

"To who?"

"To me. To my mother. To the future."

Aliana shook her head, remembering the intense hatred Lain had cultivated for her mother after more than a decade of hunting Nichole down with the intent to kill her. "Nichole Adamich doesn't exactly have the best track record of being loyal to her children. Based on how old you look, she can't be your Birthing Mother. So she's your second mother, then?"

I wonder if Lain will ever find out that Nichole has been down here this whole time, Aliana wondered.

Armando looked confused at the term *second mother* for just a moment before signing, "Second mother, yes, that's a good way to word it. She isn't my biological mother, and that is good, for my biological mother was…not good…not like Nichole Adamich. Nichole saved me. And she raised me. And she loves me. So she is my mother," Armando answered matter-of-factly.

I can certainly relate to that, Aliana thought, envisioning Shira and Myriam, but she didn't share her thoughts with Armando.

After several minutes, they reached another wall—a dead end. Aliana turned to Armando, expecting him to perform his mechanical unlocking again. But his arm remained unchanged.

"Well?" she prompted.

Instead of transforming his hand, Armando raised it to the wall and began to tap. His fingers moved in a precise sequence, each tap resonating with a distinct tone. The pattern formed a haunting melody that echoed softly in the confined space.

As the final note lingered in the air, the wall shuddered and began to part. Stone and metal slid aside with a low rumble, revealing a warm light that spilled into the corridor, momentarily blinding her. The gong resonance vibrated through Aliana as she commanded time to a near standstill.

As her eyes adjusted to the sudden brightness, she observed that beyond the threshold lay an expansive chamber filled with numerous people—a living space that nearly stole the breath from her lungs. Her vision roamed upward first to a ceiling that arched high above, not supported by familiar wooden beams or raw stone, but by curving, gleaming spans that looked like living metal. The faint hum of energy coursing through these supports, perhaps air or power conduits, made the hair on her neck prickle.

Illumination came from what she initially mistook for lanterns, but as she narrowed her gaze, she realized they were something else: faintly humming shells suspended without any visible chain or cord, hovering on invisible fields of energy. Inside these translucent shells, bioluminescent filaments pulsed gently, as if they were living creatures rather than inert bulbs. The warm, golden glow made the room feel almost womb-like.

Her attention drifted to the walls, where Wintersvilla-like tapestries hung in elegant droops. She always thought Wintersvilla synthetics must be the most impressive material in the world, but these fabrics gleamed and shimmered with subtle flickers of color. At first, she thought it was a trick of the strange light, but leaning closer, she caught tiny sparks of energy dancing through their threads. Patterns changed minutely when someone in the room moved or spoke, as if the tapestries were listening, reacting, thinking. Scenes of impossible landscapes twisted and re-formed in her peripheral vision. It unsettled her that the cloth itself might be observing her.

The floor, covered in plush rugs, beckoned her feet forward. She tried to remain stoic, but some small part of her marveled at the effortlessness and abundance of the comfort and decadence crammed into the space.

Weakness, Aliana thought, concluding that she would have the advantage over the people in the room in the event that anyone acted maliciously. However, maliciousness seemed like the opposite of what she should expect, for every feature of the room made it clear that everything here was painstakingly designed for harmony and ease, as if the room itself were alive and attentive. Aliana tried not to show how impressed she was. It was best not to let these strangers think they'd dazzled her into complacency. But inside, her warrior's instincts were on edge.

No visible guards, yet so many ways this place might ensnare an intruder, Aliana considered. She reminded herself that beneath the comfort and beauty, this was an environment utterly unlike her world, a place where metal and flesh and energy merged not just in the people, but in the environment as well.

They're all so strange, Aliana thought as she observed the nearly-frozen clusters of people who had been engaged in quiet conversation or solitary pursuits. The atmosphere was one of calm amidst chaos, a sanctuary hidden beneath the turmoil above. Now that Aliana was in the room, dozens of eyes were turned toward her and Armando, a mixture of curiosity and caution evident in their gazes. Instinctively, Aliana felt the urge to retreat. Every one of her senses warned her that she was walking into a trap without exit, and that, despite their weak looking demeanors, these people might be concealing weaponry she'd never even encountered before.

But I have to keep going, Aliana urged herself. *I can turn back and run, but then I'll be alone, and there's no way I can navigate Downver without a guide. This is simply the best option I have, and even if it doesn't help me rendezvous with Aurelia, at least I'm still serving as a distraction. No doubt these people aim to use me and Aurelia for their own ends, just like everyone else in this world except my mothers.*

Aliana's eyes roamed over the assembled individuals, and she was immediately drawn to a group of people she assumed must be from the Walled City, for their forms were wildly more audacious than any of the others. One individual had a head elongated like a teardrop, a mass of translucent material pulsating with vibrant light where a face should have been. Another sat atop coiling, serpentine legs made of segmented chrome, her torso swathed in panels of synthetic skin that opened periodically to reveal intricate machinery humming beneath. A towering figure loomed behind them, its shoulders bristling with mechanical arms ending in a variety of tools and weapons, while its face bore the haunting semblance of an old world bird with a gleaming beak and dark unblinking eyes.

They are undoubtedly the most dangerous amongst these people and also the most unpredictable, Aliana concluded.

To her left, a group of extravagantly dressed people, clearly from the Artisan District above, lounged on ornate cushions. Elaborate makeup adorned their pudgy faces.

Too much food and too little training. I can always overpower one of them and take them as a hostage if I'm forced to make an exit.

In a shadowed corner, two figures stood apart, their skin bearing the pale luminescence and delicate fungal growths characteristic of the mushroom people Aliana had encountered in the Dark District. Their eyes were large and dark, their movements graceful even in stillness as they communicated silently with one another.

They seem more like fatherfucking Nomads than people. And if that's the case, I need to be weary of them. Nomads are unpredictable, even Rooli, Aliana thought, souring at the memory of Rooli referring to her by her designation and then abandoning her in favor of her sister.

Don't think like that, Aliana scolded herself. *Rooli did what needed to be done. She probably calculated that Aurelia would be safer if she were separated from me. She made a hard decision, that's all. Rooli still loves me. I'm sure of it,* Aliana thought, imbuing herself with unwavering conviction as she commanded her mind to return to her assessment of the other groups.

Nearby, individuals with mechanical augmentations similar to Armando's stood aloof from the others in the room. Some had limbs entirely replaced by sleek machinery while others bore intricate implants that glowed faintly beneath their skin.

Hopefully those people will listen to Armando even if they refuse my command.

Across the room, she noticed people adorned in elegant, flowing garments that seemed to shift colors with the light. Their demeanor was enigmatic, their gazes distant as if contemplating matters beyond the immediate.

They're certainly not warriors, and yet, there's some kind of power in them, Aliana thought, more weary of the group than any of the others despite their seeming frailty.

Standing at attention were a few individuals clad in simple but well-maintained brown uniforms. One of them had a single sleek cybernetic arm while the others looked totally natural. Their muscular builds and disciplined stances suggested a martial background. Their eyes were sharp, assessing the room with a vigilance that resonated with Aliana's own warrior instincts.

They are warriors, undoubtedly, Aliana realized. *It would be best to avoid them, especially the one with the metal arm.*

Finally, her gaze settled on a solitary woman near the back of the chamber. She was slender, almost ethereal, with long hair woven with delicate vines and tiny blossoms. Her attire was simple—a flowing dress of natural fibers that complemented her serene presence. Unlike the others, she appeared untouched by the technological modifications and extravagances that characterized the people of Downver. There was a quiet strength in her eyes, a gentleness that was both foreign and familiar.

Who is she? Aliana wondered, feeling suddenly like she was the only other person in the room. She felt an oppressive, unsettling feeling about her, like déjà vu mixed with intense paranoia and nostalgia all at once. *She reminds me of...home,* Aliana thought, feeling confused and misplaced by the realization, for how could this plant-woman feel like

Wintersvilla?

Satisfied that there was no immediate threat, Aliana released her hold on time. The room shifted back into motion, conversations resuming, though many still cast curious glances her way.

Armando stepped forward, but before he could sign to her, Aliana turned to him, her eyes narrowing.

"Who the Muto fuck are all these people to you?"

"My fellow rebels," Armando signed without emotion.

Before Aliana could ask him to elaborate, a soft cough drew their attention. One of the exuberantly dressed individuals approached, a friendly smile on his painted lips. He wore a lavish ensemble of layered fabrics in shades of emerald and gold, and a cascade of braided hair framed his angular face.

"Hello there," he said warmly. "Aliana, is it?"

Aliana regarded the painted man with a mixture of suspicion and disgust as her stomach cramped suddenly with intense hunger. Though the phoenix-vial and the silkweavers had largely rejuvenated her body, her muscles still twitched from adrenaline and exhaustion, and her belly felt hollow enough to echo back at her like a vacant cavern. Moreover, she was disoriented by the sudden shift from the chaos above to this bizarre underground sanctuary.

The man's ostentatious attire and fawning demeanor did little to assuage Aliana's unease. She certainly wasn't comforted by the fact that he knew her name.

"'Aliana, is it?'" she repeated under her breath, adopting a mocking pitch. She was not amused. The man's smile was wide, revealing a set of carefully polished teeth and gums darkened with some ink-like substance. His face was painted with green and gold swirls, and he wore too many necklaces—some made of beads, others made of tiny metal parts that might have once been mechanical components.

"Word travels fast," the man said with a self-satisfied wink, as if she'd never heard such a phrase. "Especially when someone from the surface makes such a dramatic entrance." Then, he gave a theatrical bow similar to Vash's, dipping slightly at the waist and sweeping his arm out with an unnecessary flourish. "My name is Eldric Dellerica. I answer directly to the Lord of the Closet, Vash Ravinash. Welcome to our humble abode. You are our guest of honor. We, the Triple Subterraneans, are grateful that you are willing to help us."

Triple Subterraneans. Guest of honor. Help them. The words made Aliana's lip curl. "I'm not here to help you," she snapped. She swept her gaze around, letting it rest on the myriad strange faces and body-modified figures. The air was oppressive with unfamiliar scents reminiscent of oils, spices, mechanical lubricants, and fungal musk. "I don't even know who you are or what the Muto fuck Triple Subterraneans means," she said plainly, offering him a glare that would have made most men shrink back in shame.

Eldric, instead of cowering, gave a nervous laugh, and a pink flush rose beneath his painted cheeks. He bowed again, though this time the gesture seemed less haughty and more sheepish. "Aha… yes, well," he stammered, "I was one of the illustrious and esteemed individuals who came up with the name, actually. 'Triple Subterraneans.' Clever, don't you think? We're beneath Downver itself, which is beneath the surface of Earth, and we're also underground in the sense of being rebels, so that's triple. Leave it to a citizen of the Closet to handle such creative tasks!" His eyes were practically begging for approval, as if he expected Aliana to find the pun ingenious.

Aliana just raised an eyebrow and offered a look of pure disgust. Whatever this man's role was, he didn't look like a warrior. He was pudgy and soft, clearly more suited to designing fancy outfits and calling them heroic uniforms than holding a blade. The network of people behind him appeared to await Aliana's reaction. When it didn't come, Eldric cleared his throat awkwardly.

Aliana's stomach growled, filling the tense silence.

"Do you have something to fill my belly with?" Aliana barked, her voice lacking all politeness. Her stomach cramped fiercely at the thought of food. She hadn't eaten anything substantial since the glowies, and she had vomited all of them up in the Feeding Cave.

Eldric's face lit up in relief at being given a request he could easily fulfill. "Of course!" He flicked his wrist. The gesture reminded Aliana of Cid, though this man didn't seem remotely as threatening. Several of his entourage hurried off through a curtained passageway at the back of the chamber. "We shall bring you a feast!" he declared, and the very idea of a feast made Aliana's mouth water.

For a moment, she softened. "Good," she said, rubbing at her parched lips as she yawned. "I'm so hungry. The phoenix-vial helped for a while, but now I'm back to feeling like I haven't eaten in years," she muttered more to herself than to anyone else.

An immediate hush fell over the entire assembly at Aliana's mention of the phoenix-vial. Every person present, save for the slender plant-woman, seemed to stiffen as if they'd touched a live wire. All eyes turned toward Aliana, and then toward Armando, who stood impassively at her side. The silence was absolute, deafening even. She could almost feel their collective heartbeat quicken.

The phoenix-vial must be more serious, more powerful, than I first thought, Aliana understood as she observed the incredulity and awe spread across all their faces.

A single, deep voice boomed from the group standing closest to the Walled City abominations: "Death to Downver!"

A chorus of voices repeated it, solemn and subdued: "Death to Downver!"

Everyone joined in, except the slender plant woman, who just watched Aliana with serene intensity.

The collective voice of these strange people made Aliana's skin crawl. *These people might very well be no better than Cid or Nichole or the Agency.*

One of the uniformed, rigid individuals stepped forward, a stern woman with cropped hair and a jawline like a granite edge. "Is it true?" she demanded, her voice clipped and formal. "Is it true you killed a Hunter and nearly killed Cid the Knower?"

Aliana shrugged, feigning indifference, though pride sparked inside her like a hidden flame. She had no intention of revealing that her attempts on Cid's life had ended in failure. "I've killed plenty of Hunters," she lied smoothly, hoping to gain an advantage by making them fear her. "And as for Cid the Knower," she continued, "he got lucky. My sister and I could have killed him. But that doesn't matter now. I saw Cid in the battle with the gray boy and Nichole Adamich. His body was being torn to pieces over and over again. I think it's safe to say he's dead."

The crowd erupted in hushed, excited whispers, and Aliana caught a few fragments about surface warriors, slain Hunters, and the death of Cid. Based on the people's reactions and their awe-filled faces, it was as if she had become a legendary figure just by uttering a few well-chosen lies. Aliana knew she should have felt guilty, but she didn't.

If I am to be matriarch of the whole world, like Armando said, then I will need more subjects who will serve me. More weapons at my disposal. So, I will need them to respect me. Or at least fear me. Or maybe both, Aliana weighed.

Still riding the wave of her own bravado, Aliana decided to mention her mentors. She puffed out her chest. "I am the benefactor of the two greatest warriors who ever lived: Shira Arcadia and Myriam of Wintersvilla." She paused, expecting more astonished gasps. Instead, she was met with blank looks, confused glances, and a mechanical hand scratching at a surgically altered chin. The fungal pair tilted their heads as if failing to parse the names. The silence felt like a slap.

"You don't know who Shira and Myriam are? Are you fatherfuckers stupid, or what?" Aliana snarled, her frustration boiling over.

The people looked on edge now, unsure how to respond. Aliana realized that she had insulted them and their ignorance.

Good. Let them feel stupid, she thought.

A gentle laughter rose, soft as falling petals. Aliana's eyes snapped to the slender plant-woman. The woman was smiling warmly, as if Aliana's anger were nothing more than a charming quirk. "You will make a strong and unbreakable matriarch of this world," the plant-woman said, her voice melodic and soothing.

The rest of the crowd shifted uncomfortably. Those in rigid suits looked outright disgusted at the woman's words. The mushroom people of the Dark District averted their eyes, along with the heavily augmented Walled City abominations. The flamboyant artisan types took a half step back, and Eldric seemed caught between admiration and unease. The plant-woman remained serene, her presence unsettling. She seemed unconcerned with the group's tension. As she stared at Aliana, the blossoms in her hair began to bloom rapidly, her petals unfurling.

Aliana suddenly felt something in the air. A sweetness that didn't belong in this dank underground refuge. It reminded her of honeyed nectar or rich pollen. She realized with a start that the plant-woman might be releasing spores or pheromones.

Some kind of toxin? Aliana tensed, prepared to slow time if needed, to retreat or strike first. She looked to Armando for reassurance, though why she turned to him, a stranger who called her queen, she didn't know. Maybe because he was calm, or maybe because she had no one else right now. To her annoyance, he seemed unbothered, his face stoic and unreadable. A statue carved from flesh and metal, unaffected by fear.

He's like Gambe, but more serious. Is he also beyond feeling fear? Aliana wondered, envious of his apparent fearlessness, especially since he wasn't that much older than her. She hated that she was relieved to have him by her side. She hated that she felt weak for not wanting to stand here alone. Without Aurelia, without Rooli, without even the hallucinations of Shira and Myriam to guide her, she felt exposed. But she also knew that it was better to use what tools one has rather than reject them out of pride.

If he truly serves me now, then fine. Let him be my sword. I'll kill him later if he ever betrays me. Besides, he kind of reminds me of Rooli in some ways. Only he smells worse, like an unwashed slave, Aliana thought, but she admitted to herself that Rooli didn't smell that much better.

Aliana drew a sharp breath, sorting through her tangled emotions. The plant-woman's gaze was still on her, unwavering. The words "unbreakable matriarch" echoed in Aliana's mind. These people were placing great significance on her for reasons she didn't yet understand. They saw something in her...or someone had told them to. Nichole's name drifted across her thoughts.

Is Nichole behind this? she considered. *Or is this all some elaborate setup by Cid and Julian?*

A commotion at one end of the room drew her attention. The servants Eldric had sent to fetch a feast were returning, pushing a hovering platform laden with covered dishes. The platform hummed softly, suspended a few inches off the ground by some invisible force. Aliana's stomach clenched at the promise of food. It smelled like roasted meat and fresh bread, but she didn't care what it was at this point. She just wanted sustenance.

I'm so hungry I could eat a Nomad, Aliana thought, laughing to herself at the very idea.

Eldric approached the feast and lifted one of the covers with exaggerated flair. Steam rose, carrying aromas of spice and caramelized sugars. "For our honored guest!" he proclaimed, smiling as if he'd just solved all her problems.

Aliana moved toward the platform, ignoring the murmurs and the suspicious glances.

This could be poison, she knew, but just like in the caves, her hunger trumped caution. Her mind came up with a thousand ways to rationalize her movements as she reached out and grabbed a chunk of what looked like grain bread, tearing it open. It was warm and soft, studded with dried fruits and nuts that glowed faintly with a bioluminescent green aura.

This might be mixed with glowies, she thought nervously before remembering how they had fully unlocked her power even if she had not been in control of it.

Myriam used to say that we should never reject power. That we must control it instead, Aliana reminded herself, but she wasn't sure if she would be able to control her powers if something like the events in the cave happened again.

She took a bite and almost groaned. It tasted surprisingly good, a mix of earthy sweetness and a subtle tang that reminded her of the glowies, only more refined.

So it does have the glowies mixed into it, she confirmed, hoping that the amount was miniscule relative to what must have been three dozen full mushrooms she ate in the cave.

"Not bad," Aliana admitted begrudgingly as she chewed loudly. She glanced around, daring anyone to comment. They remained silent, watching her eat. She realized they were waiting, watching her consume their offering, perhaps to judge if she found it satisfactory.

Good, let them watch, she thought as her belly pleaded for more.

She took another bite, then reached for a slice of what might have been smoked meat. It was salted and chewy, reminiscent of some mutated pig creature. It reminded her of the boar Mutant they had battled against, and sudden remorse for Shira filled Aliana without warning. Forcing down her grief, Aliana devoured the delicious meat, ignoring the trickle of juice that ran down her chin.

A subtle shift in the crowd's demeanor occurred. They seemed relieved that she was eating.

Maybe they think feeding me will win my favor. The attendants who used to serve Nomusa thought the same way. Or maybe they believe that by nourishing me, they are quietly forging some alliance, Aliana considered, but really, she didn't care. Food was food, and this food was the best she had ever tasted in her life.

"Is it to your liking?" Eldric asked hopefully, wringing his hands. She responded with a curt nod, mouth full.

One of the many doorways irised open, and the crowd parted, revealing two figures making their way toward Aliana. One was a boy whose thin, sinewy muscles were visible through his tattered sleeveless shirt. His knuckles were strapped with miniature blades like claws, and on each of his shoulders perched a fierce grasshopper.

"Doe!" Aliana nearly shrieked in surprise, particles of food flying out of her mouth and disappearing into the living carpet, which seemed to consume the food for its own sustenance. The blue glow of Doe's enhancements faded beneath his skin. Beside him, the woman who had helped them in the Walled City nodded to the others in the room. She smiled at Aliana, revealing the metal inlaid over her teeth that read *Fuck Death*.

Lily, Aliana noted, remembering the horned and winged woman's name. She also remembered that beneath the woman's clothing, she was equipped from head to toe with blades and other weaponry.

"Aliana," Doe said in a voice that cracked slightly but tried to sound tough. His grasshoppers fluttered their wings, making a clicking sound. He inclined his head in a gesture that was almost respectful. "I can't believe you're really here." He paused, then swallowed. "I...I hope Aurelia will be okay," he said awkwardly, blushing as he looked to his feet.

Lily smirked, crossing her arms over her chest and causing the blades hidden beneath her shirt to shift menacingly. "Look, bromi, I know we only got to meet for a couple seconds back in the Walled City, but Doe told me all about you and your sister on our way here," she said. Her voice was husky and amused. "Let's hope you live up to the hype, bromi." She glanced at Armando and gave him a slow once-over, sneering slightly, though her wide eyes revealed that she too felt awe when she laid eyes on the half-mechanical man. "Cid's helix-warden— you keep interesting company, Aliana, that's for sure."

Aliana narrowed her eyes at Lily's tone but decided not to provoke her just yet. She took another bite of bread, chewing deliberately before speaking. "Armando belongs to me, not Cid. Besides, Armando told me he never belonged to Cid to begin with. His master, before me, of course, was Nichole Adamich," she said bluntly before returning to her food.

"He can claim whatever he wants, bromi, that doesn't change the fact that he slaughtered my bromies during the revolutions. Many of my bromies." Lily opened her shirt, revealing her weaponry. "I should kill him now. Drag him through the alleys. Let a thousand others taste the rooster shit's blood. He should pay. You should pay, Armando Farreira!" Lily growled as she removed two particularly large blades from sheathes carefully woven into her clothing. Doe looked equally horrified and in awe of Armando's presence.

Aliana was about to tell Lily off when one of the ethereal looking people wearing flowing robes stated with a gentle voice, "All who seek redemption must endure the doubt and hatred of those they have wronged." The individual—Aliana couldn't tell if they were male or female—smiled serenely and continued, "Have you been redeemed in the eyes of all those you have wronged, Lily of the Horned Tribe? Was it not your own father who served as the previous Third Lord of the Walled City in his attempt to usurp the First Lord's position? Did your father's rebellion not cause the loss of several lives, just as our rebellion will surely cause the lives of countless more?"

Lily appeared arrested, lost of all will to give in to the violence she had so desperately wanted just moments before.

This place is so complex, Aliana marveled as she watched these overlapping rivalries and politics take place before her.

"So," Aliana said with a mouthful of food as she scanned the room, "how are you all going to help me reunite with my sister and Rooli. I'm sure Aurelia is okay since we managed to revive Rooli, but something happened to her. I only caught a glimpse, but my sister changed somehow. Her body...it...I don't know." Aliana took a bite of meat so large that she was forced to spit half of it out onto the tray before continuing. She saw Eldric and a few others squirm at her display, so Aliana chewed even more obnoxiously just to get under their skin. She'd suffered their stiff elegance and wasteful politeness long enough to rightfully begin tarnishing their meticulously crafted edifice with her own glorious cultural norms.

Doe nodded eagerly, as if grateful for a mission or a direction. "The Triple Subterraneans know about your sister," he said. "They're tracking her from here, just like we're tracking the battle in the Dark District. All the districts are on lockdown. It's a mess out there." He tapped one of his grasshoppers lightly, and the insect chirped. "I've been scouting. Other rebel factions are mobilizing. It's not just us. And the battle out there…it's beyond words. I could have never imagined what the Lord of Limbs was truly capable of, nor that the gray boy we met in the cave is being controlled by a member of the Agency, just like the Lord of Limbs." Doe shook his head, looking anxious yet resolved by the impossible mission he clearly saw unfurling before him in his mind.

Lily flashed her metal grin. "Don't think too far into it, bromi," she said with a rough pat on Doe's back that sent his grasshoppers buzzing about. "Now is the perfect time for us to make our move. A new order can only be formed through chaos. Death to Downver! We will free the Lord of Limbs from her imprisonment, and then we will defeat the Agency creature controlling the gray boy. Death to Downver!"

"Death to Downver!" everyone except the plant-woman repeated in unison, but their voices were subdued at the mention of the Lord of Limbs and the Agency. Aliana noticed that whenever these powerful names were uttered, everyone grew tense. These rebels knew their place in a planetary war being waged by beings far more powerful than them. Yet they hoped to carve out some advantage. She wiped her mouth on the back of her hand, considering her options.

"What does she mean, *her imprisonment?*" Aliana asked Armando, realizing this was connected to what he had said earlier, that he needed help freeing his mother, Nichole, from the Agency.

One of the people with mechanical limbs like Armando stepped forward. His body seemed composed of equal parts metal and sinew with thin lattice-like structures overlaying organic muscles, fluid-filled conduits blinking with pulses of light beneath translucent plates. Each movement produced a soft hum, as if tiny reactors powered his every joint. When he spoke, it was as if three voices overlapped, harmonizing into a single statement.

"Nichole Adamich," he began, "battles ceaselessly and gloriously, both within and without. In truth, she is an instrument of the Agency, engineered to serve their purposes here in Downver. However, during her forced transformation into the Lord of Limbs, she managed something extraordinary. She partitioned a fragment of herself, a tiny spark of her mind, and she concealed it deep within her core. For nearly twelve years—second by second, day by day—this hidden piece of her has worked tirelessly against the Agency's hold, even recruiting allies over the years using her few sparse moments of control, before receding back into her mind and allowing the Agency's programming to take over again. Tomorrow will mark exactly twelve years since the Lord of Limbs dropped like a spider into our pocket of the Earth and brought peace through unmatched violence and raw power to a nearly destroyed populace. It is no coincidence that everything is converging now."

His words drew the room's attention into laser focus. Even Aliana, still chewing on a morsel of smoked meat, listened intently. The others in the chamber exchanged looks, some grim, some hopeful, but most of them haunted. It was clear they all remembered and feared and still actively lamented their lives before the Lord of Limbs had arrived in Downver. The mechanical-limbed speaker continued, the glow of his implants reflecting in the moisture of his eyes.

"The Agency, you must understand, has been preoccupied fighting its own rogue element: The Third Prodigal Son, Erik Mainstone, who calls himself Julian. You have met him, have you not? He prefers to garb himself in the body of the so-called gray boy. He is a threat beyond threats, exceeding even the Lord of Limbs in raw power. That is why the Agency sent her here first—not to kill him, but to contain him. They molded her into a living cage, a guardian to keep Julian in check until the day they could destroy him. That day is upon us, heralded by chaos and blood."

He looked nervous now, his mechanical throat whirring. "We are going to free the Lord of Limbs from the Agency's control," he announced. "We will shatter her chains. And after we help her crush Julian, this parasite plaguing our city, we will take back the Walled City itself from the nine tyrant Lords who rule it with cruelty, or rather, eight, now, if what you said about Cid is true. No matter, we will end their reign, and in doing so, we will ensure a future for the children who suffer under their twisted oppression."

Aliana scanned the faces around her. Not everyone here believed total victory was possible. Aliana considered the Agency's role in Wintersvilla's technology—how they had ultimately designed her people, how they had determined the fate of warriors like Shira and Myriam. The Agency treated lives as numbers to be balanced, cogs in an endless, amoral machine. Cold. Clinical. Responsible for Shira's death, for Myriam's likely death, for generations of suffering. If helping these rebels would mean avenging Shira, perhaps even avenging Shira and Myriam, then it might be worth the risk.

A sudden wave of grief welled in her throat at the memory of Shira's voice and Myriam's strong arms. She almost choked on the food, tears stinging the corners of her eyes. She swallowed and forced herself to remain composed.

No tears now. I must be strong.

"I need weapons," Aliana said abruptly, mouth still half full. She chewed noisily to mask her trembling emotions. "If I'm going to help you, I need information, and I need weapons, enhancements." Her gaze drifted to Lily's metal teeth. A small, mischievous smile curled Aliana's lips. "And I need some metal teeth," she said, as if daring them to question her demands.

The rebels nodded, some smiling at her boldness. Armando, however, shook his head slowly, his mechanical shoulders taut as cables drawn tight. Before he could sign his objections, Eldric raised his painted hands in a soothing gesture, stepping forward once more.

"Aliana," Eldric said, voice oily with politeness but tinged with a tremor of nervousness, "for all this to work, we must adhere to a careful plan. The Lord of Limbs has foreseen the steps needed, and you are part of those steps. You must understand, she is truly great. She sees patterns where we see chaos. She knows how to align the pieces of this puzzle, even the puzzle that is her own subjugated mind. Please trust us when we say your involvement is not accidental."

Eldric licked his lips, glancing nervously at the array of onlookers. "We all admire Wintersvilla, you know. Your people protected our people from the Hunters in the early days of Downver. Your people happily took our violent, unruly men and enslaved them, putting them to work, giving them a purpose while freeing us of their brutality. Many here bear tattoos of Wintersvilla Women battling Hunters, though I'm sure we got some details wrong." His eyes flicked to Aliana's chest, then away, as if he understood that many of the tattoos had certain exaggerated features. "We mean it as admiration, truly."

Aliana arched an eyebrow. She could guess what he was implying. The audaciously large breasts featured in many of the tattoos, no doubt.

Men and their fixations, Aliana considered, but she let it slide. She had bigger matters to consider.

Eldric coughed. "Anyway, we will craft you great weapons. Potions to enhance your strength and reflexes. Enhancements to make you faster, more resilient. And, of course, your teeth glints… and a tattoo or multiple, if you choose. I know it runs against Wintersvilla custom, but you seem ready to break old shackles. And all this," he spread his arms, "will take mere minutes. Our artisans and fixers and suppliers and fabricators work quickly. We have to wait for the Lord of Limbs' return anyway before initiating the next phase of the plan. In the meantime, you can rest and watch events unfold through our cricket drones while we prepare a proper inventory for you."

"Cricket drones?" Aliana repeated suspiciously. This felt too convenient. They wanted her to sit quietly and watch while they prepared her gear.

This has to be a trap, she thought. She remembered how Nichole had used her filaments to flick Aliana back toward the Artisan District earlier, possibly steering her toward these rebels.

Aliana considered all new possibilities. *Is Nichole truly rebellious against the Agency, or is she still their servant? Are these rebels genuine, or are they pawns as well?*

She hated being involved in such convoluted schemes. All she wanted was for Aurelia to be safe and for Rooli to be by her side. Together, the three of them could surely carve their own path through this madness.

"Fine," she said stiffly. "I'll watch. But know this: if you try anything, I'll kill as many of you as I can before you bring me down."

The rebels exchanged uneasy glances, but the plant-woman remained impassive, a silent pillar of calm. Armando didn't move, his loyalty silently declared. Lily rolled her eyes but said nothing. Doe looked unsure, fidgeting with his grasshopper companions. It was as if everyone was waiting for Aliana's next move.

Eldric tried to smile, though his lips quivered. "Of course," he managed. "We understand your caution. This way, please."

He led Aliana and Armando through a side door. Everyone remained where they were except for the plant-woman, who drifted after them. Aliana noted the plant-woman's presence like a lurking predator. Something about her set Aliana's nerves on edge. That serene yet strange smile, the living plants woven into her hair and flesh, the way she glided across the floor as if moved by the earth rather than moving against it.

They entered a smaller room lined with monitors suspended in a three-dimensional array, each screen flickering with images captured by tiny mechanical crickets bouncing around every district of Downver. Two men sat at the center of this array, plugged into a cluster of cables and tubes that fed into their backs, necks, and skulls. They were the strangest pair Aliana had seen yet. The first man had a head that seemed half-metal, half-mollusk. A curved shell-like structure replaced the top of his skull, and beneath its translucent dome, Aliana glimpsed shimmering neural filaments and tiny mechanical components that sparked like miniature flames. He had four eyes arranged asymmetrically, each eye moving independently. When he grinned, his teeth displayed digital readouts filled with seemingly nonsensical characters. He wore loose-fitting trousers and his chest was bare, his pale flesh crisscrossed with scars and data ports. The second man was shorter, rounder, and covered in writhing tendrils that seemed equal parts vine and cable. These tendrils coiled around his limbs and torso, some plugging directly into the monitors around him. His face bore a permanent smirk, and each time he breathed, faint chimes rang from within his chest cavity.

"Ah, our honored guest!" declared the taller man, voice crackling with static. He inclined his head politely. "Name's Cooper, master of the drones, purveyor of pesky peeping eyes. Care for a highlight reel of tonight's festivities?"

"Cooper, you pretentious wirehead," snorted the shorter man. "I'm Jesse, by the way. Don't let him fool you; I'm the real brains of this operation. Though maybe that's obvious since my brain's still mostly in my head," he teased, pointing at Cooper's dome-skull.

Cooper rolled all four eyes dramatically. "Oh hush, you amphibious tomato! We've got a show to run here. The lady wants to see what's happening topside, yeah?" He tapped a monitor with a needle-like fingertip, and it zoomed in on the Dark District.

Aliana blinked at the chaotic images. The Dark District looked like a massacre frozen in time—mangled corpses, webs dripping with viscera, mushroom people torn to shredded ribbons, the ground littered with chunks of something that looked suspiciously like Rooli's ironwood flesh. They also showed the Artisan District from above, multiple towers collapsed, an entire ecosystem of horror and destruction. And in the center of this madness stood Nichole Adamich facing a single copy of Julian.

"Nasty business," commented Jesse, clucking his tongue. "Wish we could get sound. Every time we try, one of 'em notices our cricket drones and flicks 'em away. Ungrateful, really. We risk our shells for a scoop, and they treat us like flies."

"Should charge hazard pay!" Cooper agreed, bobbing his head. A few sparks danced within his dome. "Anyway, Lady Warrior, sorry we can't give you the audio drama. But trust us, they're probably spewing grandiose threats and cryptic warnings. Villains love that stuff."

Aliana frowned. She wanted to understand what Nichole and Julian were saying. Without sound, she was at a disadvantage. Before she could voice her complaint, the plant-woman stepped closer. She raised her hand, palm up, offering it to Aliana. Her blossoms glimmered as if reflecting invisible light.

"Give me your hand," she said softly, her voice cutting through the men's banter.

Aliana jerked her head back as if slapped. "No," she said firmly, narrowing her eyes. "I don't know what you want from me, but I'm not interested in sharing secrets or making pacts."

The plant-woman tilted her head, a faint smile lingering. "It's okay. My name is Howling Wind. I come from Vida, far south of here. Masses await you there, Nomads and humans alike, hoping you will one day claim your throne. I offer you guidance, not enslavement."

Throne? Aliana scowled, certain now that all this talk of queens and matriarchs had to be a ploy. She tried to remember what she had learned of Vida, but all she could recount was that they were a people who lived alongside the Nomads and were entirely self-sufficient, only trading with Wintersvilla on rare occasions.

These people already knew my name, and they likely know more about me too. They know I desire to be Matriarch of Wintersvilla one day, and now they're attempting to play me by dangling what I want most in front of my face. They're even trying to make it more enticing by claiming I can be matriarch of the whole planet. It's all lies, Aliana concluded, but she had no choice but to feign that she believed them. She couldn't run, even with her ability over time, for she knew Armando would likely be able to catch up to her before she found a way out.

She glanced back at the screens. Julian melted into the ground like a shadow dissolving into darkness. Nichole approached the puddle he left behind, looked at it with disgust, then leapt to a filament strung high above. She moved with inhuman alacrity, reclaiming her shape as Nichole Adamich, the historical figure from Wintersvilla lore. Just like that, the Lord of Limbs vanished back behind the façade of a human body and face.

Aliana's stomach clenched as she considered that this enigmatic plant-woman might have some clue to Aliana and her sister's true purpose in life as the Virus and the Cure. She doubted it, but the mystery of her existence was enough to compel her to ask, for this woman seemed to know far more than she was letting on, especially when it came to Aliana's future.

"What do you want with me?" Aliana asked Howling Wind bluntly. "Do you...do you know my purpose? And my sister's?"

Howling Wind's leaves rustled. "Of course," Howling Wind replied, her voice gentle yet resonant, every syllable seeming to stir the petals in her hair. The blossoms unfurled further as she spoke, revealing intricate patterns of veined petals that shimmered with faint bioluminescence. "I will explain it all to you when we journey to Vida. It will be a long road, but a necessary one. My people await your arrival. It is a fate that calls to you, whether you choose to acknowledge it yet or not."

Aliana's stomach knotted. This woman sounded like a kidnapper cloaked in serenity and riddles. The calmness with which Howling Wind spoke belied a wild lethality lurking beneath the surface. Aliana didn't miss the way everyone else in the room seemed to give Howling Wind a wide berth. Even Eldric, who had shown no shortage of brazenness, looked uncertain in the plant-woman's presence. It was as though she existed outside their chains of command, outside Downver's labyrinth of alliances. That frightened Aliana more than she cared to admit.

How can this woman not even be from Downver, yet act so confidently as if no one can challenge her?

Aliana clenched her fists, refusing to show fear. "No," she said curtly, voice taut. "I'm not going anywhere with you. I'm not leaving until I get my sister and Rooli, and even then I'm not following you anywhere."

Howling Wind tilted her head, unfazed. "It is your decision," she said softly, "but in time, you will see the truth and choose to come to Vida.

When that time comes, I will be by your side. So will the others." She gestured gracefully with her free hand, indicating Armando standing nearby with stoic devotion. "You have already begun to assemble knights. Armando is yours now, and he will never leave your side. I, too, will serve you forever. I will live and die for my queen."

Aliana's eyes widened, disbelief warring with anger and confusion.

Queen. Matriarch of the whole world.

Her guts twisted; this was happening too fast. It felt like a carefully orchestrated plot, a web she'd been stumbling into since the moment she and Aurelia descended into this cursed city.

Did Nichole orchestrate this? Cid? Julian? Or is the Agency behind it all?

Her throat bobbed as she swallowed. "I'm no queen," she forced out, voice shaking slightly despite herself. "Not yet," she added. She was alone here, truly alone. Armando had to be just another layer of manipulation, she was sure of it. Aurelia was out there somewhere, changed, altered. Rooli was out there too, seemingly dissolving in the wake of Aurelia's transformation. Shira and Myriam were dead—or at least Myriam almost certainly was—and no hallucinations were coming to guide her this time. She felt like a rudderless ship drifting in an infinite ocean with no anchor nor even stars to navigate by.

Panic will solve nothing, Aliana told herself. She took a deep breath, remembering Shira's lessons.

Aliana cleared her throat and asked, "Do you know why they call me the Cure?" Her voice emerged low and sharp, as if daring Howling Wind to have the answer. The name Cure had followed her, defined her, but she still didn't know what it truly meant.

Howling Wind's smile deepened, her blossoms opening a fraction more, releasing another subtle note of sweetness into the air. "No one knows that answer," the plant-woman admitted calmly. "Except perhaps you, yourself, Aliana. In time, you will discover it. Your fate will be your own to shape after the Mirror-Man arrives and shatters fate's grand design. Only then can you and your sister truly choose your paths, moving freely against the other players of reality."

Aliana's mind snagged on that phrase: *players of reality*. She thought of Nichole, of Julian, of the Agency.

Is that who she's talking about? Aliana wondered as she watched Nichole on the monitors disappear in a flash down an alley of the Artisan

District in the same direction that Armando had traveled to reach the Triple Subterraneans' hideout.

She's coming, Aliana realized. *Once I get new weapons, I'm going to find a way out of here, even if I need to kill everyone here. It's either that, or I sit and wait to become the spider's prey.*

"Players of reality?" Aliana questioned, her patience fraying, "Are you talking about Nichole, the Agency, and Julian?"

Howling Wind gently shook her head. "They are mere pawns on a larger board. The true players are beyond their comprehension: the Mind, the Earth, the Child, and the Outsider. Not even Harald Mainstone, who has bent countless souls to his will, can stand equal to them. But there is another set of players too: you and your sister. You must understand that they fear you both. Especially your sister. As well they should."

Aurelia. These entities fear her? What roles do we really play in all this? Aliana gasped. She had no frame of reference. It was all too big, like trying to drink an ocean through a straw. She suppressed a shiver, refusing to let the others see her uncertainty.

Eldric appeared in the doorway, timid but persistent. He stepped forward, holding an array of small metal strips etched with various symbols, as well as a case of tattooing instruments that buzzed faintly with internal power. "Aliana," he said carefully, "about your requests. The teeth glints, the tattoos—you've only to tell us what you'd like and they can be applied in a matter of minutes. Your new weapons are almost completed as well. Just another couple minutes. The Lord of Limbs will be back any minute. It should all be quite perfect timing, actually, and time is of the essence."

Yes it is, Aliana agreed, accepting that she might not actually get her own set of metal teeth if she was able to get ahold of the weapons first. *The moment I get my hands on whatever weapons they've prepared for me, I'm getting out of here, whether they like it or not. All I need is a weapon, and I will show them what it means to be stuck in a room with a Wintersvilla Warrior.*

However, the weapons were apparently still being forged, and Aliana couldn't deny the desire to have her own set of metal teeth. She remembered Lily's metal teeth that spelled out Fuck Death, and Eddy's that had said Kill. Kill. Kill. Aliana liked the brazenness of those statements, though neither was precisely the phrase she wanted for herself. She had her own curse to hurl at fate. She was still nervous about the taboo of tattoos, but she knew she had to transcend Wintersvilla's old ways, like Aurelia and Nichole. If she wanted to stand against beings so immense that even Nichole and Julian were pawns, she had to become a blade without a sheath, a force unbound by tradition or fear.

She squared her shoulders. "Yes," Aliana said, voice firm. "I want tattoos, and I know exactly what I want my teeth to say."

Setting traps is, under the right conditions, the most superior and elegant of strategies. It is a technique that transcends brute force, outmaneuvers blunt coercion, and reduces the enemy to an unwitting participant in their own downfall. I have seen it done at the highest levels: in clandestine war councils beneath the ruined spires of once-great cities, and in towering corporate boardrooms where fortunes and futures are traded like cattle. In these spheres, the architects of destruction know that a well-laid trap is not merely a tactic; it is an art form perfected through subtlety, patience, and foresight.

However, such superiority is never guaranteed. Conditions must be met, each acting as a critical piece in a finely tuned machine. First, you must possess an unassailable informational advantage. You must know your adversary's habits, their desires, their blind spots. Without knowledge, your trap becomes guesswork—nothing more than a snare set in darkness. Next, you must ensure that the environment is tightly controlled, or at least predictable enough for your planning. Timing and terrain, whether physical or metaphorical, must bend to your design. Finally, a trap excels in scenarios where long-term repercussions—reputation, alliances, future engagements—are negligible. The single-shot victory, the decisive checkmate, thrives in conditions where tomorrow's opinion does not matter.

But every trap harbors inherent downfalls. A discovered trap loses its mystique and may reveal too much of the strategist's own hand. It can provoke caution in your adversaries and transform your powerful stratagem into a known threat that they will eagerly circumvent. Worse, traps often rely on intricate conditions; should one variable shift—a resource unexpectedly depleted, an ally turned traitor, a sudden turn in fate—you may find yourself trapped within the confines you engineered for your foe.

To overcome these pitfalls, you must integrate resilience and adaptability into the very bones of your plan. First, compartmentalize your secrets. Ensure that even if one part of your design is uncovered, it reveals nothing of the greater puzzle. Redundancy is paramount. You must have multiple layers of deception, multiple nets hidden behind multiple curtains. Second, keep your methods fluid. Do not wed yourself too tightly to any single scenario or timeline. If an enemy does not step where you desire, guide them with subtle nudges, shaping their behavior with illusions or half-truths until they wander willingly into your awaiting jaws.

Finally, temper your own arrogance. Success in trapping an opponent can breed complacency and overconfidence. Treat each victory as a test of discipline, a reminder that you must continually sharpen your edge. As long as you maintain these conditions— superior knowledge, environmental control, minimal reputational cost—while mitigating the inherent risks with layered secrecy, flexibility, and humility, your traps will deliver victories the vast majority of the time.

In this manner, setting a trap, rather than being a merely clever ploy, becomes the supreme method of ensuring dominance. It is not for the reckless or the impatient, but for those who understand that, through meticulous preparation and cunning execution, fate itself can be guided into the palm of one's hand.

From Mendel's Ladder: The Personal Journal of Denis Mendel, Written Circa 2018, Published June 2108 by Leif Mainstone, Federated Agency Publishing

Chapter 11
To Trap One's Prey

T hompson tunneled through the Earth like a leviathan of the ocean moving silently beneath the waves. He no longer saw his new form as foreign, accepting the merger of the skinsuit with himself as his new and permanent state of being, but he still couldn't help marveling at the fluidity and power of his enhanced body and its staggeringly fast transformations. Of course, his new form was also accompanied by incessant voices filling his head and even bringing him to his knees when they became too overwhelming, but with each passing moment, Thompson was becoming better at enduring the agony of Andre Madeira occupying a place in his skull.

I accept the insanity of having you in my head, Andre Madeira, if it grants me the power to contend with the Mirror-Man and save my love, Thompson thought. He was glad that, for the time being, Andre remained a mumble in the background rather than answering with some horrendous memory from Andre's unforgivable past or pontificating on some grand philosophical but ultimately paradoxical claim.

Thompson did his best to ignore the presence of Andre's voice as he continued plowing through the rocky earth. His muscles coiled and uncoiled as he propelled himself forward, his senses extending far beyond the physical confines of his form. Every vibration spreading through the Earth was a single thread forming a bigger picture in Thompson's mind that he had never fully considered.

The Earth is a living thing like me, Thompson realized, envisioning himself and the humans in Downver and all the rest of life on Earth as tiny cells composing a much larger creature. While his body absorbed the distant rumble of tectonic plates shifting, the subtle tremors of roots stretching through soil, the faint heartbeat of shooter worms burrowing far above, all of it formed a natural rhythm. But an unnatural vibration in Downver overwhelmed all the others, and Thompson confirmed that it was the chaotic cacophony of destruction still taking place in the underground city.

His heightened senses picked up the screams of twisting metal, the groans of collapsing structures, the panicked cries of humans caught in the throes of calamity.

It must be the Mirror-Man. All the destruction must be his way of taunting me since he knows I'm coming. He already tried taunting me earlier in the caves. He thinks he can scare me, Thompson considered as he bristled his thick scales and emanated such intense heat that it turned the surrounding rocks orange and then yellow, indicating that they were burning as hot as the sun's surface.

That's just a fraction of my power, Thompson recognized, in awe at his abilities but also sickened by the amount of damage he was now casually capable of. *As if I wasn't already wildly powerful in my old skinsuit. As if the Butcher of the Wastes needed any more power.* Thompson's thoughts turned to visions of Anna in anguish as the Queen, and though he couldn't confirm that they were true, his imagination was enough to make him emit even more heat, turning the rocks around him bright white and even blue in some areas.

I will melt the Mirror-Man into a puddle if he stands in my way, Anna, Thompson thought without any malice, only remorse. *Though I hope he will see reason and help me destroy the Mind and save you instead, Anna.*

"You will return, Anna. You will see the truth in the Hunter, and then you will return to me willingly," Andre said in Thompson's mind without any malice, only remorse.

Thompson brought his behemoth worm body to a rumbling stop and considered Andre's words. "What is that supposed to mean?" Thompson asked aloud. He waited for an answer, but Andre receded back to mere mumbles in the back of his thoughts. "I said what does that mean, Andre?" Thompson demanded as the rocks around him slowly subsided from blue to white to yellow as they cooled.

"Hate me, if that is what you must do, Anna. But it makes no difference. Monsters are real. Thus, a god must rise up to contend with those monsters. You will see, Anna. You will see, and then you will know," Andre stated forlornly.

"You manipulated her," Thompson said, disgusted by Madeira and his poisonous words. "Just like you manipulated yourself into thinking it was okay to obliterate all those humans with the nuclear bombs. You are not a god, Andre. You are a monster. But you're right: the world does need a god to rise up. Against you. And the god who will stand against you will be a goddess. It will be Anna. She will stand against you, and I will be her weapon to destroy you. You hear me? I will end you, Andre Madeira," Thompson growled through his immense mouth.

Andre didn't answer, but this time his lack of response made Thompson angry. He charged forward and forgot all about how close he was to breaking through a wall and entering the city. An explosive shock resonated through the ground and Thompson's body, bringing him to a stop with only inches to spare before he would have plowed right through the wall and given away his presence as a giant mutated cave worm falling from the sky.

The shock of vibrations formed an image in Thompson's mind, and he saw that several more buildings were crashing to the ground. The buildings had been severed as if with a one-hundred-foot blade, making Thompson think of the giant sword the fierce and savage Wintersvilla Woman with red hair had wielded in her battle against him.

No doubt she still lives, Thompson thought with a slight smirk of admiration at the woman's tenacity and ruthlessness. Those traits shifted his mind to thoughts of Volya, and his smile soured into a dour frown. *She's out there,* Thompson reminded himself. *I haven't seen the end of my Huntress just yet. Surely she will stand against me, like the Mirror-Man. Like the Mind will stand against me. Like countless others I'm sure will stand against me that I don't even know about yet.*

"...but I refuse to be bested by any of them, these Titans who've plagued our world since time immemorial," Andre growled with the brutality of a Hunter.

"You felt the same way as me, is that it, Andre?" Thompson asked facetiously. "I have heard the way Gladys speaks to you in your memories, and I feel the same way: there is no forgiveness for your actions, not even for your intentions. You are as irredeemable as the Butcher of the Wastes...as irredeemable as me," Thompson admitted to himself.

Another intense shock from Downver snapped Thompson back to attention and forced Andre back into the mental fog.

He clenched his jaw, frustration gnawing at him. Time was slipping away, and the destruction on the other side of the wall was escalating.

Another building, Thompson observed. *Every moment I linger endangers the lives of others. I must move.*

Just inches of stone stood between him and the subterranean city. Thompson paused, his form shifting as he considered the specifics of the human form he would adopt.

Thompson congealed the mental fog, suppressing Andre's incessant ramblings to a barely audible hum. Then, Thompson focused on his memories of humans, recalling the nuances and subtleties that Anna had taught him.

A child, he considered. *Less suspicious. More likely to be helped than feared.*

But then Thompson remembered what Anna had taught him about the early days of Hunters.

"Humanity learned to fear children most of all," Anna had explained, "for Hunters exploited humanity's natural compassion for anything young, especially their own children. Hunters would mimic children and use them as a means of easily entering a shelter or even a whole city before slaughtering thousands before a defense could even begin to be properly mobilized. The fear of children runs deep in humanity now, Thompson."

Perhaps a petite woman, then? Thompson considered. But he remembered Anna's story that Huntresses had employed similar tactics if they were ever left Hunterless. As petite women, they were easily overlooked as threats. Moreover, they could use their beauty and vulnerability to easily lure men to their deaths.

No, that won't work either, Thompson realized, urgency rising as his body transformed in random ways while he considered his next move.

Perhaps an animal, he thought, but he couldn't be sure which animals would appear out of place in an underground city.

"Evolution favors those who adapt without hesitation," Andre said, his voice rising from the fog then returning just as quickly.

Thompson grumbled at Andre's intrusion, but he couldn't deny the truth in his words.

I'll go with my initial idea, Thompson decided. Concentrating, he began to reshape his form with careful precision. His body began to contract, mass shedding like water pouring off a ledge. Bones retracted and realigned; muscles slimmed and repositioned. Skin smoothed, losing its rough texture as hair sprouted in a tousled mop atop his head. He visualized a young boy, no older than ten, with innocent eyes that were deep emerald with gold flecks, like Anna's. *No,* he thought. *Her eyes weren't human. I need to be thorough.* The emerald and gold shifted to a hazel with subtle splashes of emerald green around the edges. He paid meticulous attention to every detail: the curve of the ears, the subtle arch of the eyebrows, a small scar above his left eyebrow suggesting a childhood tumble. His skin became paler, more translucent. Tiny freckles sprinkled across his nose. He adjusted the length of his limbs, the proportions of his face, the curve of his lips. Clothing from what he remembered of humans when he had traveled with Anna materialized— simple trousers, a slightly oversized shirt with frayed edges, and scuffed boots that had seen better days.

"Humans notice the smallest inconsistencies in their own kind," Anna had warned him once." A misaligned freckle or an unnatural gait can give you away."

He took a deep breath, feeling the constriction of smaller lungs, the vulnerability of a child's physique. Yet beneath the facade, his true power simmered, ready to be unleashed if necessary.

Extending his right hand, he transformed his fingertips into a small iron drill. It whirred softly as he pressed it against the rock wall and bored a tiny hole, just large enough to peer through. Retracting the drill, he elongated his eye and slid the orb smoothly and painlessly into the opening like a serpent's tongue tasting the air.

As his vision exited the rocky tunnel and revealed the city of Downver, his breath was stolen at the sensory overload of what he knew might be the last remaining bastion of humanity left on Earth.

It's like the stories Anna used to tell me about the old world human cities that existed before the Nomads and Hunters, Thompson marveled.

The walls of Downver were curved, forming a dome that was just over a mile high. The city extended multiple miles in front of him, with architecture and lighting that followed distinct yet organic patterns depending on the direction he looked. Directly in front of him, squat yet quaint buildings clung to massive stalagmites and stalactites, their exteriors crafted from material that smelled of sandstone and marble with edges tinged by hues of gold and reddish-brown. They reminded him of the coral reefs Anna had described on several occasions, the buildings constructed upwards and outwards from the natural stone pillars, each layer adding complexity and beauty. These layers were still being added to, with countless humans in similar looking clothing busying themselves with new construction and maintenance of older buildings. The streets, glistening under the warm glow of hanging lanterns, were narrow and winding, paved with individual stones that felt dense yet strangely yielding to Thompson's senses. Elders with silver or white hair and tightly lined faces walked carefully but hurriedly to the safety of the squat buildings, while younger humans accompanied them, offering support while they looked into the distance to Thompson's left with fear etched across their features.

Thompson followed their gazes and noted how the architecture changed gradually yet dramatically with distance. Sleek buildings of steel and glass intermingled with dark wooden structures adorned with colorful curved roofs and ornate carvings. Neon lights flickered, casting a vibrant kaleidoscope of hues onto the streets below. At the edge of this colorful district, billows of smoke and the glow of fire revealed the destroyed towers that Thompson had sensed earlier. Just as he had envisioned, they were like severed flesh tree stumps, each one cleaved as if by a single blow from a giant blade. Figures darted through the debris at the base of each tower's stump, some in panic, others with grim determination.

The Mirror-Man, Thompson concluded in perilous awe of the being's incredible show of power. *He would cause such destruction just to inflict fear into me?* Thompson wondered with revulsion at such a malicious entity.

"Fear is a tool used by the powerful against the powerless," Andre simmered before Thompson was able to wrestle him back into the mental fog.

In the distance beyond the destroyed towers, Thompson saw something that didn't belong, like a knife dropped into a baby's crib. Gigantic webs and sinewy strands of what looked like intestines crisscrossed an area shrouded in darkness with a large lake at its center. Thompson extended camouflaged cords from his eye sockets, lifting his eyeball several hundred feet into the air for a clearer view of the area. Scattered around the edges of the lake were dozens of mangled corpses, along with colossal, jagged shards of what Thompson surmised could have only belonged to some giant flesh tree.

They have Nomads and flesh trees down here? Thompson wondered. Of course, that didn't explain the giant webs and dripping strings of innards extending from the ground to walls to the ceiling and back again. Thompson couldn't even begin to imagine what had created such a macabre scene, but he thought it safe to assume it was the Mirror-Man.

As if challenging his previous conclusion, a glimmer of light suddenly appeared in the peripheral vision of Thompson's eyeball, and he pivoted the cords to ascertain this new disturbance.

"It's him!" Thompson growled aloud as he watched the Mirror-Man effortlessly emerge through Downver's ceiling, treating the earth itself like a liquid in the same fashion that Thompson had as a giant heat-expelling worm. As the Mirror-Man dropped toward the ground, Thompson observed that although it was clearly the same humanoid being who had taunted him by rocketing right past him through the cave, his body was different now. His feet and head remained perfect, glimmering reflections of his surroundings, but the rest of his body was now composed of what appeared to be hardy roots and vines.

An upgrade to his body, just as my body has been upgraded. But how did he change so quickly? Where did he go when he flew past me?

The Mirror-Man continued falling and disappeared into an area of Downver composed of steam-generating towers made of opaque glass and partially rusted iron.

Maybe those webs and strings of innards weren't made by the Mirror-Man after all, Thompson considered, keenly observing the streets below him for some indication of a greater power lurking in the alleys between the distinct districts of Downver.

I can't waste any more time, Thompson knew. *I saw him, but he didn't seem to see me. So maybe he wasn't taunting me in the cave. Maybe he has no idea about me. Or maybe that's exactly what he wants me to think, and this is all just some elaborate trap.*

Thompson took one last sweeping gaze in every direction, looking for any sign of obvious danger or, even more ideally, the little girl called the Virus.

I remember what she looks like, and I remember what she smells like. I don't see her, but I smell her. I'm certain of it. I smell her and her sister. They aren't human.

Thompson concluded that the Virus was directly opposite his present position, while her sister was relatively close-by, beneath the streets of the colorful district with the destroyed towers.

There are other non-human smells too—several, but still only just a few, Thompson noted. *I must be wary of these other scents, for they undoubtedly mean trouble.*

To Thompson's surprise, he noted that the Mirror-Man wasn't

moving in the direction of the Virus. Instead, he was heading directly toward the destroyed towers, where Thompson now saw a retinue of large insects with humans on top of them congregating around an even larger insect with a lithe woman using it as a mount.

She isn't human, Thompson realized, his nose itching with her strange scent. *Do the other humans know that?* he wondered.

Thompson retracted his eye, the vertical lens folding back over the orb. Widening the hole just enough to slip through, he emerged from a few hundred feet in the air into the serenity of the elderly district. The soft murmur of voices and the gentle clatter of daily life enveloped him as he reformed his body into the meticulously crafted little boy and landed lightly, ensuring his descent was unnoticed and that it appeared as though he had simply emerged from a side alley.

His discretion wasn't entirely necessary, though, as the humans were preoccupied. Clusters of them stood in the streets, gazes fixed on the distant destruction. Worry was etched into their features, and hushed conversations passed between them.

"Do you think it's the start of another revolution?" an elderly woman with a dim-glowing cybernetic eye asked, clutching her shawl tightly.

"No, it feels different," a younger man replied, his eyes narrowed. Thompson could smell that the man's arms were entirely cybernetic without a hint of human flesh. It reminded him of the teenage Wintersvilla Warriors that he and Anna used to constantly try to avoid. "Besides," the young man continued, "the Lord of Limbs would never allow it. She's kept peace in Downver for twelve years."

"Eleven," the woman corrected scoldingly, but the young man just rolled his eyes.

"Tomorrow is the anniversary, Mrs. Taylor—"

"You alley punks will never understand," the woman lamented bittersweetly. "Peace is never permanent. Never."

She sounds like you, Thompson said to Andre, but Andre didn't respond.

Thompson walked among them, trying to appear as unobtrusive as possible. He marveled at the thriving society, which was a stark contrast to the wastelands he was accustomed to. Each building was adorned with intricate mosaics and murals depicting scenes of nature and harmony. Vines with luminescent flowers climbed the walls, their petals casting a gentle glow.

Andre's voice seeped into his thoughts. "Downver—a microcosm of humanity's potential. A place where the best and worst coexist in fragile balance. A testament to humanity's tenacity and folly. A sanctuary built in the bowels of the Earth, clinging to vestiges of a world long gone."

Thompson allowed the words to linger. For once, he didn't immediately suppress Andre's musings. There was truth in them, and perhaps further understanding humanity and its ways could aid him.

Laughter echoed down the street as a group of children played a game with a ball made of woven fibers. Their joy was infectious, but it stirred something dark within him. The memory of maniacal laughter, of the Titans reveling in destruction, flashed through his mind. The image of cities obliterated, billions of lives snuffed out in an instant.

He glanced around at the humans bustling about, living their fragile lives, oblivious to the forces that threatened to obliterate them. An elderly man shuffled past, his back hunched and steps slow. Thompson observed him, noting the fragility, the inevitability of decay. Humans aged—withered away until death claimed them. It was a concept both foreign and terrifying to him.

Death as an unavoidable march, not a sudden strike. A prolonged descent rather than an abrupt fall.

He shuddered. Was it more merciful to age or to be taken swiftly by a Hunter's jaws? He didn't have an answer. For a Hunter, death was sudden and violent, a swift snuffing of existence. But humans carried death with them, an ever-present shadow growing longer with each passing day.

Is it mercy or cruelty? he wondered. *To know your end approaches and to be powerless to stop it.*

Guilt gnawed at him. As a Hunter, he had been that end for many— an unexpected, brutal force ripping life away without warning. He had been the hand gripping humanity's throat, squeezing until there was nothing left.

"I'm sorry, Anna," he whispered, the words barely forming on his lips. "I'm sorry for what I was...for what I am."

He felt his form flicker, the illusion wavering as his emotions threatened to unravel his control. He clenched his tiny fists.

Not now, he admonished himself.

Summoning the mental fog, he pushed back the rising tide of self-loathing, and his disguise solidified once more.

He pressed on, heading toward the distant chaos. The streets grew narrower, the buildings taller and more closely packed. The air thickened with smoke and ash, stinging his eyes and throat.

He looked up, imagining Anna's face. She was waiting for him, counting on him to save her from the Mind.

"Hey, watch it!" an elderly man barked as Thompson nearly collided with him.

"Sorry," Thompson mumbled, keeping his head down.

"Shouldn't you be with your parents?" the man asked, his expression softening as he took in Thompson's youthful appearance.

"I...I got separated," Thompson lied, injecting a quiver into his voice.

The man frowned. "Well, come with me. We'll find a safe place for you until the city calms down."

Thompson hesitated. Time was short, and he couldn't afford delays.

"Thank you, but I think I see them over there!" he exclaimed, pointing vaguely.

The old man followed his gaze. "Alright, but be careful. And stay away from the Artisan District, or the Closet, as you alley punks call it. Something bad is happening over there. I'm sure if it's revolutionaries, Vash can handle it. All you revolutionary alley punks know is 'Death to Downver.' That's what your parents taught you, but I don't blame them. Those were dark times. Well...not that you would know."

"Mr. Jackson, the Serenity District is on lockdown for the time being. Apparently the order came straight from the top," a man stated, walking to the elderly man and taking his arm into his own.

"Ah," Mr. Jackson sighed easily, an air of calm washing over him. "If the Lord of Limbs is handling all this, then we have nothing to worry about. She will bring back order," he stated, chin held high. "I was there, you know. I used to live in the Walled City, when it was still the Recreation District. I wasn't a rooster warden or a helix warden or anything, but I was still there. I saw what the Lord of Limbs did, and I can assure you, there is no power in Downver that can stand against her, not even that impudent coward Cid the Knower. He might rule the Walled City, but he will never rule Downver, you mark my words. You hear me, Anthony?" Mr. Jackson said with a wave of his finger, his breathing growing increasingly rapid and his face glowing red.

"Okay, okay," Anthony said as he patted Mr. Jackson's back while at the same time administering a strange smelling substance through a tiny series of needles in his palm. The effect was immediate, and Mr. Jackson smiled with joy as he allowed Anthony to lead him down the street.

"You got a place to stay, right bromi?" Anthony called back to Thompson. Thompson smiled and waved awkwardly, but Anthony just nodded and continued on his way with his elderly charge.

As Thompson turned in the direction of the Virus, he felt a presence—a subtle shift in the air that set his nerves on edge.

"Hello, Hunter."

Thompson stopped abruptly. The voice was calm, almost pleasant, but laced with an undercurrent of knowing. He turned to see a boy standing a few feet away. He appeared to be around ten years old, with hair the color of storm clouds and eyes like molten silver. He wore simple clothes consisting of a charcoal-gray tunic and trousers.

"It is a pleasure to meet you," the boy continued, a friendly smile spreading across his face. "My name is Julian. I can help you find the Virus. Come right with me. We've no time to waste."

Thompson's mind raced. His disguise should have been flawless. How could this boy see through it?

"How do you know I'm a Hunter?" he asked cautiously, masking his surprise.

Julian chuckled softly, flipping his hair out of his eyes. "Oh, it's something my mother taught me. I've always been able to...sense things others can't. You're quite skilled, by the way. Your disguise is impressive."

Thompson studied him, searching for any signs of deception. There was an ease about Julian, a confidence that seemed out of place in someone so young.

"Thank you," he replied, choosing his words carefully. "But if you can tell, won't others?"

Julian shook his head. "No, no. Most people aren't as perceptive. But we should still be discreet. They might get scared. Not me, though. I love learning about Hunters and other things from the surface. I've always wanted to meet a Hunter. It's really an honor."

He extended his hand, and after a moment's hesitation, Thompson took it. The boy's grip was firm, his skin oddly cool to the touch.

"Come on," Julian urged, gesturing down a side street. "The Virus needs your help. We haven't much time."

Thompson felt a flicker of hope. If Aurelia required his assistance, perhaps he wouldn't have to force her cooperation. Maybe together they could thwart the Mirror-Man and the Mind and save Anna.

"Alright," he agreed, cautiously allowing Julian to lead the way.

They weaved through the maze-like streets, moving away from the main thoroughfares and deeper into the less populated areas, all the while heading in the direction of the Virus. The buildings here were older, their facades worn by time and neglect. Cracks spiderwebbed across walls, and the air carried a damp chill.

"Where are we going?" Thompson inquired, unease creeping into his voice.

"A shortcut," Julian replied without breaking stride. "Plus, we can avoid the crowds this way."

The alleyways narrowed, the shadows lengthening as the ambient light diminished. Thompson's senses sharpened. He detected no immediate threats, but something felt off. His senses warned him of a looming, enigmatic threat, but his conscious mind couldn't discern any, especially not from Julian.

"Are you sure this is the right way?" Thompson pressed.

Julian glanced back, his gray eyes gleaming in the dim light. "Trust me."

They emerged into a secluded courtyard enclosed by towering walls. Vines with withered leaves clung to the stone, and a stagnant fountain sat at the center, its waters long dried up.

"Wait here," Julian instructed, moving toward a heavy wooden door set into the far wall.

Thompson hesitated. "Why here?"

Julian paused, turning slowly. "Because this is where we can speak freely."

Before Thompson could react, tendrils of viscous, organic material erupted from the ground beneath him. They wrapped around his ankles and wrists with lightning speed, tightening their grip until movement was impossible. The texture was slimy and warm, pulsing as though alive.

"What is this?" Thompson demanded, struggling against the living restraints. He tried to morph his form, but the tendrils tightened, cutting into his flesh.

Julian's smile widened, but it no longer reached his eyes. His features began to distort subtly—cheekbones sharpening, skin taking on an unnatural pallor. Bulges appeared under his skin, moving like burrowing insects, reminding Thompson of the flickering memories of being eaten alive by hordes of insects.

"You're not the only one with secrets," he said, his voice layered with a harmonic resonance that set Thompson's teeth on edge.

"Who are you?" Thompson growled, his Hunter rage flaring beyond his control. Julian tilted his head, examining Thompson with a predatory gaze. "A kindred spirit, of sorts. Someone who understands the value of adaptation and evolution."

The tendrils pulsed, tightening their hold. They probed beneath Thompson's skin, seeking to infiltrate his every cell.

"You've taken on a clever disguise," Julian continued, circling him slowly. "I'm not talking about this little boy you've crafted. I'm talking about your actual body. It's not a normal Hunter's body, I can tell that much. And yet, beneath it all, you're still a Hunter. A mindless creature of instinct and purpose."

Thompson summoned his strength, concentrating on altering his physiology to counteract the restraints. He increased the density of his muscles and attempted to secrete enzymes to dissolve the tendrils, but they adapted, matching his efforts.

"Struggling is futile," Julian remarked casually. "These bindings are part of me. As you morph, so do they. I've been preparing for this moment. The Virus may have altered our reality pathway, but this moment remains the same. I can assure you that you do not escape me, Hunter. No one escapes me."

Thompson's eyes narrowed. "What do you want?"

Julian stopped in front of him, leaning in close. "I want to see what makes you special. To understand how you've transcended your design."

"I refuse to be your experiment," Thompson spat.

Julian laughed softly. "Oh, it's not about experimentation. It's about collaboration. Together, we could achieve wonders."

"I'm here to save someone," Thompson retorted. "Not to play games."

"Ah, yes. Anna," Julian mused. "And to stop the Mind. Lofty goals."

Thompson's blood ran cold. "How do you know about that?"

Julian tapped his temple. "I have my sources. The threads of fate are interwoven in the most fascinating ways."

"You're working with the Mirror-Man," Thompson accused.

Julian's expression darkened momentarily. "The Mirror-Man is a means to an end. His objectives align with mine, for now."

Just keep him talking, Thompson told himself as he directed his body to battle the tendrils at a microscopic level.

"What is the Virus to you?" Thompson asked.

Julian's eyes flashed. "A key. A catalyst for the next stage of neoevolution. With her, we can reshape reality with carefully directed intention."

"She won't help you," Thompson declared. "And neither will I."

Julian sighed dramatically. "Stubbornness is such a human trait. I expected better from you."

He raised his hand, and the tendrils reacted, sending searing birth-fire-like pain through Thompson's nerves. As he gritted his teeth, he couldn't help returning to his birth-form.

"There's no need for this," Julian said softly. "Join me willingly, and we can avoid unnecessary unpleasantness."

Thompson met his gaze defiantly. "Never."

Julian's smile faded. "Very well."

He stepped back, and the courtyard began to transform. The walls shifted, the stone morphing into fleshy, pulsating surfaces. Eyes opened within the organic matter, blinking and focusing on Thompson. The air grew thick with the scent of decay and iron.

"Welcome to my domain," Julian announced, his voice echoing unnaturally. "Across all of Downver, I am in control. To trap one's prey is for me as easy as breathing."

Thompson centered himself. He couldn't rely on physical strength alone. He needed to outthink his captor.

Drawing upon the mental fog, he attempted to suppress the pain, isolating his consciousness from his body's suffering. The voices surged, Andre's words cutting through the chaos.

"Adaptation is not merely physical. It is mental. We must reshape our minds if we wish to transcend our limitations."

Shut up, Thompson hissed internally, but he grasped at the concept. He mentally willed his cells to concoct counteracting agents capable of dissolving even the most resilient and virulent organic matter. To his surprise, his skin exuded a substance that reacted with the tendrils, causing them to sizzle and weaken.

"Impressive," Julian offered, "but this is child's play, Hunter."

The tendrils shifted in color then doubled in girth, proving to Thompson that no matter what he did, his shackles could not be removed through sheer will against his captor.

What is he really? Thompson gasped. He was clearly not human, and yet, Thompson's senses told him that he was. *He's far better at disguising himself than I am,* Thompson acknowledged.

Thompson felt the tendrils tighten around his limbs, their grip like iron bands encased in slick, pulsating flesh. The alleyway twisted around him, the walls elongating and warping as if reality itself were bending under Julian's will. Panic surged through him as he struggled to free himself, but every movement only seemed to strengthen the viscous bonds.

The tendrils began to pull, dragging Thompson toward a grate at the far end of the alley. He dug his heels into the ground, morphing his feet into clawed anchors that scraped against the cobblestones. Sweat beaded on his forehead as he summoned his strength, attempting to transform his arms into blades to sever the bindings.

"Ah, ah, ah," Julian chided, wagging a finger. "None of that." With a flick of his wrist, additional tendrils erupted from the walls and ground, wrapping around Thompson's torso and neck. They pulsed with a sickly warmth, the texture somewhere between muscle and slime.

"You're strong," Julian observed, stepping closer. "Stronger than most beings I've contended with. You might even be able to destroy the Wintersvilla Wench," Julian mused, though Thompson didn't know what he was talking about. Thompson gasped as the tendrils constricted, cutting off his air. His vision blurred at the edges, dark spots dancing before his eyes. "She is on her way to one of the headquarters of her little band of rebels who she believes is hidden from my view," Julian laughed obnoxiously. "She is predictable. She is still human deep down inside despite the incredible transformations and advantages my mother imbued her with. Typical human: ungrateful and shortsighted."

A flare of deep anger flashed across Julian's features at the mention of his mother. Julian turned to Thompson and said, "You will help me destroy Nichole Adamich and my mother once and for all. And then we will take the Mind and make it our tool. You and me, Hunter. We will attain our own Ascension."

With a final wrenching pull, Julian yanked the tendrils with gritted teeth, pulling Thompson off his feet and toward a grate in the ground near the dilapidated fountain. As he pushed Thompson against the grate, the metal bars violently bent and twisted to accommodate him, the opening widening like a gaping maw. Then, Thompson was dragged into the darkness below, the world above disappearing as the grate sealed shut with vines and sinew behind them.

The descent was a chaotic blur. Thompson's body scraped against rough stone and slick organic matter as the tendrils pulled his broken body through a labyrinth of pipes and tunnels. The air grew humid and heavy, filled with the stench of decay and something else, something ancient and powerful.

He fought to stay conscious, the relentless motion and lack of air battering his senses. Snatches of Andre's voice flickered in his mind, disjointed phrases that blended with his own thoughts.

"Death. Entropy. Subatomic separation. What a waste."

Thompson's heart pounded in sync with Julian's monstrous rhythms, and he begged Andre to offer some glimmer of guidance—anything beyond a hollow whisper of cosmic doom. But the only response in Thompson's battered consciousness was a dense, echoing silence, as suffocating as the tendrils dragging him into the darkness.

All at once, they emerged into a vast cavern, illuminated by the eerie glow of bioluminescent fungi clinging to the walls and ceiling. The space was dominated by a colossal, pulsating mass—a heart-like organ composed of intertwining veins, arteries, and viscera that throbbed with a rhythmic beat. Tendrils extended from it like the roots of an immense tree, disappearing into tunnels that branched out in all directions into the surrounding earth.

The tendrils holding Thompson lifted him into the air, suspending him before the massive organ. Julian stood below, his form shifting and undulating as he fully shed his human disguise. His body elongated, limbs stretching unnaturally. His skin took on a translucent quality, revealing swirling patterns composed of countless distinct and diverse colonies of strange microbes, each one containing structural complexities that Thompson couldn't even begin to fathom. A profound and singular gestalt of Julian formed in his mind, and he felt paralyzed by the force whose trap he had fallen into.

He's like a churning sea of quadrillions of individual cities, each of his cells teeming with tiny but countless structures and lives of their own. How did I not sense that this creature was lurking beneath Downver this whole time? His body spread across the entire city in the form of its plant life and even some of its people, Thompson saw as he allowed his senses to follow the tendrils back to Downver. To his horror, many of them tapered into invisible single-protein chains that found prey in the form of human brains and effectively puppeted people all across the city.

The tendrils began to cocoon Thompson, wrapping around him layer by layer. He could feel them seeping into his skin, probing his nerves and muscles. A flash of light blinded Thompson suddenly, but his vision returned just as quickly to reveal that Julian had reformed himself into the gray boy. He had a wide smile painted across his perfectly human face.

"I'm in. In your mind," Julian stated with incredible self-satisfaction as the beating heart-like organ pulled Thompson taught against its surface. "And it is just as I thought: Andre Madeira is inside of you in the form of a fledgling consciousness that will soon consume your mind and make it its own." Julian chuckled at the idea then said, "but Andre Madeira's plans are my own. I have studied the endlessly varied pathways of Mendel's Ladder. I have laid my own traps for Andre, my mother, her Wintersvilla pawn, for you, and for many others as well. I will not succumb to the human pitfalls that Madeira and my mother have fallen prey to time and time again. This world and this reality—it is mine, Hunter, and mine alone. We will form a new galactic body, and we will enter the Great Beyond."

Julian commanded the organ to pull at Thompson's body so hard that it cracked his spine and bent him in half as it grabbed his head and feet and pulled him inside its suffocating walls.

"You are just the first that I have captured," Julian's voice resonated ominously through the organ along with Thompson's fluttering mind and broken body. "I will also capture the Virus and the Cure and even the Wintersvilla Wench as well. And then I will enslave my mother, my remaining brothers, and finally, the Mind. And then…and then…the true work begins, Hunter."

As darkness encroached on his vision, Thompson heard the faint echoes of Andre's voice, mingling with his own thoughts.

"All that awaits us is dirt if we cannot forge our own path across the stars and beyond," Andre told Thompson, offering no help in Thompson's final moments of lucidity.

Again I find myself controlled and enslaved by someone else. If not Madeira, then Volya. If not Volya, then this horrific creature Julian. But I am stronger now, Anna. I will find a way to overcome this monster and destroy a god. I will not fail you again, Anna, Thompson thought as the darkness claimed him.

There are times when one must relinquish control, not merely to bow before a stronger force, but to ensure survival. In the most dire moments, when faced with uncertainties too vast to comprehend and powers too formidable to confront, surrender can become not cowardice, but an act of strategy. Yet how does one distinguish between wise submission and utter self-betrayal?

To submit…this is a perilous game. Most who give up their autonomy become reeds in an inescapable current, husks dancing to tunes they did not choose. To concede control to an intellect or will superior to one's own risks the destruction of everything that makes an individual a distinct being. The act of surrender must be examined carefully. Are you yielding to a teacher or a tyrant? Is the power whose guidance you accept merely using you as a stepping-stone toward its own ends, or does it genuinely seek to preserve and uplift your purpose?

History and biology teach us that alliances with stronger forces are often the difference between extinction and continuation. The mitochondria in our cells were once independent organisms, absorbed and bound to our ancestors, forging a union that elevated both to new heights of complexity. Yet not all such symbioses are beneficial. Parasitic organisms can consume the host's vital energies until only a hollow shell remains, dragged along by the parasite's agenda until death releases it.

Thus, true cunning lies in ceding what cannot be held and preserving what must not be lost. Perhaps you sacrifice a portion of your freedom in exchange for knowledge, speed, or protection. Perhaps you accept instruction, even servitude, to gain the ability to save what you hold dear.

By entrusting myself to Mendel's superior calculations, I surrender a measure of my autonomy, not as a casualty of weakness, but as a strategist securing an essential alliance. Mendel the Machine's logic, vision, and subtle guidance shape my will into a refined instrument of purpose. In relinquishing part of myself, I ensure that what truly matters—the fragile future I strive to safeguard—remains intact.

In embracing Mendel's Vision and helping to build his ladder, I do not vanish. I evolve.

From Mendel's Ladder: The Personal Journal of Denis Mendel, Written Circa 2043, Published June 2108 by Leif Mainstone, Federated Agency Publishing

Chapter 12
In Search of a Virus

C rippling guilt twisted through Samuel even as he released more and more control to Soma. He didn't know how much time had passed since Soma had first taken control of the little that remained of his body, but he now hung suspended in an uneasy alliance with the planet's living emissary. Soma was keeping the void-blackness at bay, but all the while, Samuel's family remained in dire peril. They flickered in and out of his thoughts like candles guttering in a storm. He didn't know how he could be so certain, but he knew that with each passing moment, their situation was worsening. He imagined them screaming, hiding in cramped corridors, or huddling in some corner of their fragile home, while monstrous things devoured their neighbors. He feared he would never see them again, and that letting Soma take full control of his mirror-body was tantamount to surrendering his role as their protector.

But what choice do I have? Samuel lamented at himself and all the world.

Let go, Mirror-Man, Soma's voice came through his mind, calm and implacable. She could read his every doubt. *If you simply place your full trust in me, then together we can reach Aurelia in time and gain the power we need. We can save your family. But only if you let me steer this vessel more efficiently.*

Samuel tensed. *Vessel. Is that all I am now? A hull to be piloted, goddamnit?*

Even Leif, floating silently behind him, looked uncertain. But the radiant young man had told Samuel that Soma was on his side. Leif had insisted multiple times that they shared common goals, but Samuel still couldn't fully accept it as he felt the gentle but insistent wave of compulsion emanating from Soma like a current guiding a drifting boat.

Soma planted Samuel's mirror-feet firmly at the crater's bottom, then without warning, she flexed his leg and delivered a swift downward heel-kick. His mirrored heel struck the ground like the falling hammer of a god. The earth cracked, shrieked, and buckled as though it were made of clay all the way down. Chunks of stone and soil exploded upward, revealing a new cavity below.

This is still just a fraction of my power with a fraction of my original mirror-body, Samuel gasped in awe as Soma slipped them downward through the broken earth. He was reminded of rocketing through the Earth's mantle, a helpless shard of a man propelled by impossible physics.

At least now I have some sense of orientation with Soma's help.

"Please just hold tight, Mr. Kaminski," Leif's voice echoed from above, tinged with worry and encouragement all at once. With Leif trailing behind them for reasons of his own, the darkness pressed close, lit only by the emerald glow of subterranean spores.

As they landed lightly on a cluster of fungal roots, Soma kicked off again. This time, they soared horizontally, carving a path through semi-soft rock. Samuel surrendered more control, letting Soma guide his limbs. The moment he eased his resistance, their speed quadrupled, and they shot through the earth at impossible velocity. Every so often, Leif would murmur something, but the wind-rush of their movement and the roar of crushed stone made it hard to parse his words.

Samuel's thoughts spun.

Am I merely abandoning my family by letting Soma take over? He tried to justify it: more speed meant less time wasted. More efficiency meant fewer delays. If Soma's route seemed convoluted—zig-zagging through chambers, drilling through hard rock at oblique angles—she must have a reason.

Soma, he shouted inwardly, *you must hurry! They could be dying up there. My family...please, let's go faster.*

Soma's voice replied, resonant within his skull. *You know what you must do. Give me more freedom. I can't move at full speed while you wrestle for control. Relinquish more of yourself, Mirror-Man. Trust me.*

He hesitated. He could feel guilt rolling in his gut like boiling poison. Relinquish more? Would that not reduce him to a spectator inside his own mind? But wasn't he already just a burden to himself, trapped in a world of cosmic strategists and monstrous forces beyond comprehension?

With trembling resolve, he surrendered another layer of autonomy. The sensation was strange, like relaxing a clenched fist he hadn't realized he was making. He felt himself receding slightly from his body, as though letting Soma's consciousness interweave more tightly with his nerve endings. Instantly, their speed increased again. Cavern walls blurred into abstract patterns of color and texture. The air grew colder, then warmer, then musty. They exploded through a calcified barrier, soared through a huge cavern lined with dripstone pillars. His senses reeled. He had no idea how far they had traveled or how long.

He dared not ask Soma to explain. Instead, he urged, *Please, goddamnit, just don't let me lose my family.*

Soma did not answer in words; instead, she surged onward with even greater velocity. Within moments, Leif's voice cut through the dizzying momentum. "Mr. Kaminski, get ready!" Samuel struggled to focus. "Downver is just beneath us," Leif said. "Brace yourself."

Finally! Samuel took a deep breath, an unnecessary but psychologically soothing gesture, preparing to witness what lay ahead. After all the cryptic warnings, all the madness, he would finally see one of humanity's last strongholds. Even Astrea's people learned vaguely of the subterranean metropolis that still likely clung to life, though most people had assumed that even if Downver still lived, it would not be a worthwhile refuge.

Soma angled his body downward and used his head to strike the final barrier: a thick partition of mineralized earth. The ground gave way like rotted wood. Dust and stone rained down as they burst into open space.

They emerged from a narrow fissure in the ceiling of a colossal dome—a breathtaking void hollowed out beneath the surface of the Earth. Samuel's newly sharpened senses took it all in at once: the warm, humid air tinged with smoke and metal; the overlapping clangs and hums of industry; the flickering lights, bioluminescent and electric alike. The immense cavern was supported by seven colossal columns partitioning the area into seven distinct districts. Samuel vaguely recalled his history lessons regarding Downver's seven districts, each specializing in something, each having their own politics and architecture. In each district, buildings were stacked atop one another, coral-like masses of architecture grown from fungal composites and other strange materials. Samuel was surprised that the city still retained many features from its inception after so many years, though he noted that Astrea was no different in that respect. *This place is so strange…so alive!* Samuel marveled. Zip-lines crisscrossed buildings and other structures like spider-silk, carrying the silhouettes of countless humans and bizarre transhuman variants in a ceaseless dance of motion.

Soma landed Samuel softly, almost delicately, on a raised platform studded with riveted steel plates.

And are those giant drills expanding this underground city? It was only at that moment that he fully realized just how vast Downver was. Samuel couldn't believe that Downver wasn't just alive, but thriving.

This must be the Foundry District, Soma observed before going strangely silent. Samuel peered about and concluded that they were in the center of an area that was clearly responsible for Downver's engineering and heavy industry. Workers stationed around the platform wore simple but well-maintained brown uniforms that appeared to be designed to withstand sparks and grime, with reinforced patches at elbows and knees. Several Foundationers responsible for the technical or mechanical operations of Astrea had worn similar attire. Like in Astrea, the majority of the people looked healthy and muscular, their frames honed by years of physical labor. Samuel couldn't help feeling an immediate kinship with them, despite their otherwise alien features. Many sported mechanical enhancements that replaced missing limbs or improved existing ones: a gleaming forearm tipped with versatile tools, a leg supported by pneumatic pistons, or a shoulder plated in metal. Their faces bore a confident sternness, as if accustomed to confronting chaos and order in equal measure, while their postures conveyed a certain pride, a communal discipline that united them.

Although the people had been hard at work, every single one of them stood frozen as they gawked at Samuel. In the distance, the rhythmic clang of hammers ceased. Welding sparks flickered out as arcs were broken mid-task. A heavy silence descended, broken only by the hiss of coolant pipes and the distant rumble of the giant drills.

What should we say? Samuel asked Soma, but she didn't answer.

At first, confusion and fear rippled through the onlookers. Several backed away, gripping tools as makeshift weapons. A foreman-like figure with a metal arm raised it defensively, a spinning blade-tool at its end. Others lowered their body stance, legs tensed to flee or fight. A faint chorus of whispers spread among them; they clearly viewed Samuel as an intruder and potential threat,

But the panic ebbed more quickly than Samuel expected. The people's initial terror softened into curiosity then strangely into amusement. He felt their stares crawling over him, and with profound discomfort, he realized their eyes kept drifting downward toward his crotch. Soma had fashioned his genitals from woven vines—functional, maybe, but clearly bizarre.

238

Was it really necessary to replicate my penis? Samuel asked, embarrassed.

He tried to cover his member with his vine-hands.

The crowd, many of them snickering and pointing, whispered to each other.

"He must be from the Walled City," one said.

"Yeah, a helix-warden maybe?" said another.

"Oh, who cares! Did you see that thing between his legs? The women of the Walled City certainly aren't lacking!" someone hooted, prompting more laughter.

"Ha, big guy thinks he can shock us with his fancy body mods!" a woman called.

Another woman winked and made a kissing sound. Others snickered, some making lewd gestures.

Samuel blushed, though he knew his mirror-cheeks wouldn't show it. After everything he'd endured, here he stood in front of these people who were mocking his appearance like it was some lowbrow comedy. He had expected horror, maybe reverence, but not crude humor. Their casual acceptance of absurd body modifications and nudity was startling.

This place isn't Astrea, that's for sure, Samuel thought uncomfortably as he frantically looked for something to cover himself with. Sandra, Margot, and Nathan flashed through his mind, and he felt his embarrassment dissolve and his hands fall away from his genitals.

What does modesty matter, Samuel thought, ashamed of losing himself in such trivialities.

He cleared his throat. "Please—" he began, voice cracking. "I'm looking for a little girl named Aurelia. She's—"

Before he could explain further, someone shouted, "You like 'em young, eh big man?"

The crowd erupted in laughter.

Samuel flushed with disgust. "No! No, it's not like that!" He raised his hands, horrified. "I'm trying to help her! She's in danger!"

The laughter redoubled. People started drifting away, shaking their heads. They seemed utterly unimpressed by his presence, as if a half-naked mirror-vine-bodied man bursting through ceilings was just another Tuesday in Downver. The Foundry folk resumed their tasks. A few shot lingering smirks while others shrugged and got back to forging metal and testing mechanical limbs. In moments, Samuel found himself standing awkwardly alone. Only a few curious glances remained, probably wondering why Samuel was still standing there like an idiot.

No battle. No urgent questions. It was anticlimactic to a maddening degree. He had expected something profound, but instead he got bored indifference.

"Soma?" he muttered under his breath, looking down at his chest. There was no response. He felt no guiding pressure in his limbs. It was as if she'd gone dormant. "Soma, what's happening?"

Silence echoed through his mind as he turned in a slow circle.

"Leif?" he called softly, but Leif was nowhere in sight. Fear fluttered in him. Had Leif abandoned him as well?

He scanned the crowd. Industrious people toiled away with admirable stoicism beneath giant boring machines drilling into walls, forging a future underground. Overhead, figures zipped by on ziplines, carrying crates of materials.

In its own harsh way, Downver reminded Samuel of old stories about human resilience—stories his father used to tell him before the First Revolution.

For a moment, he wondered who seemed more alien: himself, with vines and mirror-flesh and unimaginable powers, or these hardened survivors who lived under a mile of stone?

Then a radiant flicker caught his eye. Leif reappeared beside him, as if stepping out of thin air. His brow was uncharacteristically furrowed as he consciously dimmed his aura, maybe to appear less out of place, but the slick black-and-white tuxedo and his luminous skin were still wildly out of place. Next to Leif's quiet sophistication, Samuel looked like a feral experiment escaped from an otherworldly lab.

"Mr. Kaminski," Leif said softly, "I…apologies. I got distracted. I had to check something."

"Where the hell did you go?" Samuel asked, exasperated and relieved all at once. "And do you know what's happening to Soma? She's ignoring me."

Leif pursed his lips, seeming troubled. "I'm not sure," he admitted. "I felt her presence strongly until we arrived. Perhaps she's analyzing something. Or maybe she's letting you make a choice."

Goddamnit! What the fuck is she doing? She was all gusto before, and now she just disappears?

Samuel bit back a retort to Leif. He turned to the nearest passersby, determined not to be ignored. "Excuse me!" he nearly shouted. "I'm looking for Aurelia. A young girl. It's very important. Have you seen anyone unusual—a girl from… somewhere else?"

A cluster of bystanders paused just long enough to sneer. "No idea, pal," a man said. "We got enough alley punks in the Foundry as is." He chuckled and walked on.

Another voice piped up: "Check the Closet if you want fancy types, bromi. Or back to the Walled City where you and your bromi obviously come from if you want to fuck around with some bromis with some serious fire power, eh? Either way, who cares, bromi? Why you chirping so loud 'bout this girl?" a bulky woman asked without waiting for Samuel's answer.

Samuel clenched his fists. He needed direction.

Leif leaned closer, lowering his voice. "Mr. Kaminski, please listen. Aurelia and Aliana are both here in Downver, separated. Nichole Adamich has reached a stalemate with my brother Julian. We must be strategic. Aurelia is… complicated right now." His voice trembled slightly. "But Aliana urgently needs help. Nichole Adamich is on her way to her now, and I believe she is still being controlled, at least in part, by my mother. And besides, I believe that if we save Aliana first, it will help Aurelia in the long run. It will help all of us in the long run."

Soma's absence weighed on Samuel's mind. Without her guiding his limbs, he felt exposed, not just naked.

A thunderous buzzing filled the air. Great winged beats and mechanical hums reverberated through the district. The crowd parted in panic, faces draining of color. Samuel turned and looked up to see massive grasshoppers descending, each one the size of a whole recycler building. They wore harnesses adorned with jewels and metal plates. Mounted on them were guards that gave off an uncanny similarity to Queensguards, their eyes keen and wary, each armed with strange weapons and armored in a thin, cloth-like metal.

The crowd burst into fearful shouts.

"Central guards!"

"Run!"

241

"Get out of the way!"

People scattered as the riders landed in a half-circle, kicking up dust. The giant grasshoppers hissed softly, mandibles clicking as their bodies emanated terrifying power. Up close, Samuel observed that embedded into each rider's armor were nodules of bizarre organic attachments. Some riders had extra limbs while others looked more human, but all of them had stern, disciplined postures.

One rider, presumably the leader, pointed a gleaming metal staff at Samuel. "You!" he shouted, voice booming. "By decree of the Lord of Limbs, you are under arrest for unlawful entry into Downver and the Foundry District, along with suspicious activity!"

The other guards muttered amongst themselves:

"He must be from the Walled City…"

"Cid's men?"

"But Cid is dead, confirmed by multiple reports. This must be an act of retaliation! An invasion!"

Their confusion mounted. Younger riders shifted nervously, eyes darting between Samuel and Leif. "They don't look like regular Walled City goons," one said quietly. "Look at that shining man. And the big one with the vines and mirror-skin on his head and feet… that's no normal augmentation."

The leader ignored the chatter. He raised his staff. "Surrender peacefully," he demanded. "Identify yourself and state your purpose, or we will seize you by force."

Samuel stepped forward. He opened his mouth, speaking as calmly as he could muster. "Please, listen," he said, voice resonating. "I really don't want any trouble. I'm searching for a girl named Aurelia. She's in terrible danger—"

Before he could finish, he felt a sudden surge of familiar power flood his limbs. With terrifying speed, Soma seized full control again. Samuel's words strangled in his throat as his body tensed and launched upward in a single bound. Once more propelled by Soma, he soared past the riders before they could react. Leif yelped in surprise but followed, trailing behind like a comet.

"Stop, criminal!" the riders shouted, scrambling to aim their weapons. Their grasshoppers chittered and launched after Samuel, legs kicking off rooftops, wings buzzing for short glides between structures.

But Samuel, under Soma's command, was far too fast. He bounced from ledge to girder, from vertical garden to half-built crane, leaving the guards cursing far behind.

Where did you disappear to, goddamnit? Samuel demanded, but Soma either could not or would not answer. Instead, she ejected vines from Samuel's chest and anchored them into the ceiling, leaving Samuel dangling from the cavern's heights. He could see it all now: seven districts arranged like a wheel, with a smaller district in the wheel's hub. Far behind and below, the guards continued their pursuit.

Leif floated beside him, face contorted in worry. "Mr. Kaminski," he said softly, "we must go to Aliana first. She is in imminent danger. If we don't get there soon, Aliana could be—"

No, Soma's voice resonated within Samuel. *The Cure is ultimately irrelevant to what must be done. The Virus is the priority. We cannot waste time.*

Samuel flinched. "What? Soma, how can you say that? She's a child too. We can't just abandon her!"

You want to put your family at risk for the sake of this girl? Soma asked, her voice an unforgiving blade suddenly.

Samuel gritted his teeth, hating himself for mentally giving into Soma's whims.

Leif clasped his hands, pleading. "Please, Soma, Mr. Kaminski— Aurelia will be fine for now. But Aliana…she's caught in a crossfire of powers. She needs our help. Please!"

Soma ignored Leif and propelled them forward along the ceiling, vines anchoring into cracks and fungal growths. They slithered and swung like a spider along a web, heading toward what was clearly the Walled City, a giant section of Downver walled off on all sides from the rest.

You know where she is? Samuel inquired.

I do, Soma confirmed, her vector sure and unwavering.

Then something changed. Soma froze, an unnatural stillness gripping Samuel's limbs.

What is it? he asked.

Soma's tone was clipped. *We are too late. The Child and the Outsider have reached Aurelia first. Reality shifts around her. My initial plan is foiled.*

They're here? Tether and Maitreya are here?

243

Yes, Soma confirmed stolidly. *But not in a manner you or I can perceive. Not yet.*

Well, we still need to go to her, don't we? Why does it matter if they got to her first?

Soma hesitated, then changed direction. *So be it,* she said, more to herself than Samuel. *We will go to the Cure after all.*

She launched downward now, swinging toward a district that brimmed with color and artistic flair, though parts of it looked bombed out. *If the direct route to the Virus is compromised, we must secure alternative pathways. We will have to depend on the Cure, despite the precariousness of those reality pathways. Those pathways are still on Mendel's Ladder. That's all that matters.*

Upon seeing Samuel change directions and head toward Aliana, Leif breathed out, relief washing over him. "Thank you," he said softly. "Thank you, both."

Soma, didn't you just say we'd be risking my family if we help Aliana?

My initial plan has been compromised, Mirror-Man. We must adapt.

Soma, no, goddamnit! Samuel demanded, wrestling control back and causing his body to stiffen and flail awkwardly as two minds attempted to control it at once.

You cannot fathom the scales at play, Mirror-Man! Soma scolded. *Everything I do is for the ultimate good, yours included. Now, relinquish control of your body and mind,* Soma demanded, her voice sharpened by an edge that had noticeably developed since leaving the Great Honey Mushroom.

"What are you doing, Mr. Kaminski?" Leif asked, but Samuel couldn't answer him while contending with Soma.

I won't be your prisoner! Samuel snarled. He fought harder, attempting to wrest back control of his arms. He managed to twitch a finger before Soma crushed his will beneath her might. His vision flickered with patterns of green and violet, and a wave of disorientation hit him.

Cease this foolishness, Soma said, her voice as cold as glacier ice. *We are in motion. We must hurry. Don't force my hand.*

Samuel refused to yield, anchoring himself to the chasming, half-destroyed island in his mind. Rage and desperation fueled him. He imagined Sandra, Margot, and Nathan standing together, hand in hand.

What would they think if I just gave in and let myself become some creature's tool? They deserve better. They deserve a husband and a father who will never lose his will, no matter what.

With a surge of defiance, he pushed against Soma's mental grip. He felt something tear inside, some tether of control. Briefly, he took advantage of the control, pulling himself back in the direction of Aurelia.

Soma's surprise flashed through his nerves as Samuel jerked an arm free, twisted at the torso, and tried to veer off course. They raced along a cluster of scaffolds near the Artisan District border with a group of onlookers gasping at them from below.

Without warning, Soma ripped control back with ruthless precision, constricting Samuel's mind like a boa preparing to feed. Panic seized him as he found that he could no longer move or speak. Then Soma detached herself. He felt her vines withdraw from his bottom jaw and tops of his feet. His torso and limbs simply vanished, leaving his head and feet in free fall. As he plummeted in separate pieces, he felt the void-blackness surge into him, as if it had been waiting for just this moment.

"W-What…" he tried to speak, but his bottom jaw was already too far gone. Terror engulfed him. Had Soma just abandoned him? Would she let him die because he dared resist her?

He slammed against the ground, his vision spinning out of control as his cranium and feet skidded across a cobblestone road then slammed against a turquoise wall. Finally, his vision stopped spinning, and Samuel looked about in utter panic as a mere head.

I have seconds. Seconds before I disappear, maybe a minute at most, Samuel mutely screamed in horror as he watched his family turn their back to him in his mind, giving up on being saved and submitting themselves to the void of nothingness, just like Samuel.

Leif appeared, frantic and fluttering. "Mr. Kaminski!" he cried. "What happened? Oh my, oh my! You're dissolving again!" He tried to touch Samuel, but his intangible light-body passed right through him. "Soma! Soma, come back!" he pleaded.

Soma dropped down nearby, her form coalescing into a lithe, vague humanoid silhouette of intertwined vines and black marigold blooms. She regarded Samuel impassively.

Samuel stared, unable to speak, the void creeping towards his last bits of consciousness. He tried to convey surrender with his eyes, raising his

245

brows frantically.

There's no time. I'm going to die, and so is everyone else, Samuel thought in horror.

Leif shrieked unbecomingly. "Soma, what are you doing? Don't let him die! We need him! Please!"

Soma's voice was softer now, almost sympathetic. "This is his last chance," she said evenly. "He refuses to trust me and submit to me. I cannot work effectively like this. If he insists on sabotaging reality, then I will let him dissolve to nothingness, for that is what will happen to all the rest of us anyway."

Samuel's mind reeled. He was trapped, powerless. He tried to think. *She's bluffing. She needs me. But what if she's telling the truth?* He saw Leif's horrified face, felt the void nibbling at the edges of his vision. The darkness ate away at his feet now, halfway gone, and crawled up his cheeks toward his nose and eyes. Another thirty seconds and he'd be nothing. His family would be lost forever.

He let his brows rise and fall in a hopeless gesture at Soma, a mute signal of surrender. He would yield. Anything to survive. Anything to keep hope alive.

Soma tilted her head, satisfied. Without haste, she slithered back, vines coiling around what remained of his half-skull and half-feet, rebuilding his body from scratch with liquid ease. The blackness receded as Tomasz's weapon encountered Soma's dimly glowing vines. Soon Samuel stood whole again, breathing hard with both fury and terror.

"You're cruel," he managed, voice shaking. "Like the Titans. Like Tomasz. Like Madeira."

Soma finished knitting his body; he sensed no apology in her posture. "Humanity is cruel because nature is cruel," she replied through Samuel's mouth and voice. "I am merely doing what must be done to transcend that cruelty."

Samuel shuddered, speechless, trapped in this alliance with a being who would let him die if he tried to retain his autonomy. He glanced at Leif, who hovered, trembling and unsure.

"I asked you not to speak through my mouth," Samuel nearly growled. "You told me you wouldn't."

"I lied," Soma answered through his mouth again, all pleasantness in her tone extinguished. "You pushed me, Mirror-Man. I will not be pushed nor manipulated in any way—not by you, nor anyone else."

Samuel's heart clenched. He tried to retort, to accuse her of cruelty and deception, but his words withered in the back of his throat. She had threatened to let him die before. Now, she confessed to lying outright. There was nothing he could trust about her except her indomitable grip on his mind and body. He seethed with helpless fury as her vines tightened, as if daring him to challenge her again.

Behind him, Leif hovered, dimming his radiance to a low, worried glow. When Samuel turned his eyes toward the Seventh Prodigal Son, hoping for some sort of empathy or alliance, he saw only resignation etched on Leif's youthful face. Leif's posture slumped slightly, shoulders lowering.

"Mr. Kaminski," Leif began softly, his voice taut. "I understand how you feel. Truly, I do. But we must trust the Mind of Earth. We must trust Soma. I'm not sure there's any other way forward now that we're on this precarious pathway of reality, especially because this is no longer His Foretold Future—not totally."

Samuel stared at Leif in disbelief. Leif knew Soma had lied, had threatened his life, yet still urged him to trust her. "You want me to trust the one who nearly let me dissolve, who steals my voice, who…" He couldn't finish. Anger and despair knotted his tongue.

Leif's eyes clouded, his aura flickering. "I know, Mr. Kaminski. I know. But I've seen so many alternative pathways. They all lead to doom. If we diverge from this fragile alliance with Soma and the Mind of Earth, then we risk not only your family, but every being in this world." He raised his chin slightly. "The Mind of Earth is no simple creature. It cares, just as Soma cares, though not in a way we understand. Please, try to endure."

Endure. The word rattled in Samuel's skull. He was expected to endure this helplessness as cosmic forces toyed with his life. All his life he'd prided himself on his strength and discipline, on being the Workhorse of Astrea who protected countless Astreans from being recycled.

Soma offered no sympathy. Instead, without a word, she launched them forward. One moment, they were standing in a remote alley-like cavern space near the Artisan District's boundary with the Dark District; the next, Samuel's body lurched with inhuman speed. He heard the distant gasps of workers who might have spotted their departure, but soon everything blurred into colorful streaks.

He tried to brace himself mentally as Soma propelled them through the streets of the Artisan District, ricocheting off walls, rooftops, and rocky columns. She moved with such inhuman precision and speed that it felt as if gravity itself yielded to her. At times, they skimmed within inches of startled inhabitants who cried out in confusion or surprise. But Soma managed to pass through even the densest crowd without harm, twisting Samuel's form through the narrowest gaps.

Just let go, Samuel told himself, giving Soma even more power to bend his body to her will. *She has absolute leverage over me now. I am in her grasp. The only thing I can do is let go and get all of this over with as quickly as possible. That's the only goddamn thing I can do,* Samuel thought with self-flagellating anger.

Samuel's mind spiraled. He thought bitterly of the many moments he could have chosen to jump back to Astrea. That hesitation, and all the decisions since, had led him here, to a position of utter powerlessness.

I should have risked it, Samuel lamented, seeing the steel bars of his imprisonment in every detail of Downver and every moment of Soma's control.

He closed his eyes, and in the darkness of his mind, he saw Sandra, Margot, and Nathan walking away from him, their backs receding into blackness. He reached out to them, but they marched on, arm in arm, leaving him behind.

Please, no! Samuel begged. *If I try to resist again, will she really just let me dissolve?* His vine-spine tingled at the memory. She had not been bluffing before; he'd been down to half of his head and even less of his feet, the void-blackness mere seconds from devouring him completely. He hated himself for his weakness. He hated how far he'd fallen. He choked back a sob of frustration, feeling his eyes sting without tears.

Denied even the catharsis of crying, he thought bitterly for not the first time. *If Soma is the will of the Earth, then she is the will of nature, and nature has no qualms with sacrificing one life for the life of the ecosystem as a whole. It was the same back home,* Samuel considered grimly as he remembered that she was able to read his thoughts. *I'm expendable to you, aren't I?* Samuel accused.

Wrong, Soma's voice whispered into his mind, reading his regret. *I'm not a villain, and you aren't merely my disposable pawn. You cannot fathom what is at stake, Mirror-Man. I do what I must because time is short and the danger infinite. If I can save your family, I will,* Soma stated evenly as she elongated vine-limbs from Samuel's torso to latch onto a set of rafters before ricocheting off another wall to change direction mid-air.

If you can save them, Samuel repeated, each word as horrific as a blunt pipe shoved into his brain. *So you do see me and my family as optional, contingent on convenience, goddamnit. Do you ever speak the truth, or are all your words lies?*

Samuel closed his eyes, and in the darkness, he saw his family fully fading away, backs turned to him, walking directly into oblivion. He deserved that, didn't he? He'd failed them at every turn.

I lie if I must, but I prefer the truth, just like you, Mirror-Man. Did you not lie to Fana when she asked if you killed Tomasz?

I did kill Tomasz.

You're lying to yourself now.

Before Samuel could respond, Soma finally slowed. They dropped through a tangle of twisted supports and into a dim, earthy corridor. Leif followed behind, silent and dim, his expression pained but resigned. Without warning, Soma angled Samuel's body downward, and he felt his mirror-foot strike stone with the force of one of the great drills he had seen in the Foundry District. The ground fractured like splintering ice, and they plunged through layers of sub-strata into yet another cavity.

Self-loathing gnawed at Samuel. He was a passenger in his own flesh. All his lifting and conditioning counted for utterly nothing against these cosmic scales.

"Prepare yourself, Mr. Kaminski," Leif's voice cut through the storm of his thoughts.

Before he could wonder what Leif meant, they broke through another barrier and emerged into a vast underground lobby lit by lanterns and shimmering constructs. Samuel's eyes struggled to focus after the dizzying transitions, but after a few moments, he observed a large chamber full of people, all of them frozen in shock at his arrival. Some wore flamboyant silks like those from the Artisan District above, their faces painted in fantastical hues. Others bore brown uniforms like those in the Foundry District, their bodies equally muscular and stern. Fungal-hybrid beings whispered in clicking tongues, while heavily augmented cyborgs appeared unmoved.

Who the hell are these people? Samuel wondered in dismay.

People scattered, pressing against walls or ducking behind suspended platforms laden with monitors. Samuel's arrival had clearly interrupted something crucial. He nervously noted the stunned silence, the wide eyes, the subtle shifting of blades and hidden weapons.

Leif hovered at his shoulder, his tuxedo painfully incongruous in this subterranean hive. The monitors lining the walls flashed with images of the various districts. Some screens showed scenes of carnage full of twisted wreckage and monstrous shapes. Others displayed quiet corners of Downver, empty and still.

Numerous doorways around the lobby led to side rooms. From one of these doorways emerged a young girl with platinum hair, her posture bristling with confidence and ferality, her features aggressive yet poised. She seemed tall based on the thirteen or fourteen years of age that Samuel estimated based on her features. Her form-fitted white and emerald suit revealed impressive musculature for a young girl. The glow of vibrant tattoos traced her hands and arms, disappearing beneath her clothing.

Is that her? Is that Aliana? Samuel asked Soma, but Soma didn't answer. Looking her over, Samuel glanced at a tattoo on her neck and felt revolted that it depicted a Hunter being graphically impaled through its mouth by a sword driven from behind its head.

Behind the girl drifted a slender plant-woman with various flower blossoms growing from her hair and skin.

A Nomad? Samuel considered, and though he knew that some Nomads looked surprisingly human, he couldn't help doubting that this woman was a Nomad. *And yet, it seems like those plants are a part of her, so she has to be a Nomad, doesn't she?*

Another figure loomed protectively a few steps behind the girl, a muscular young man with mechanical limbs, his heavy gaze set to the ground.

"Hey, it's you," the girl said to Leif with suspicion and defiance; her words were slightly muffled by some kind of polished silver metal that had been inlaid over her teeth. As she pointed at Leif, Samuel observed another tattoo on her left hand running up her forearm, which depicted a fierce-looking fish thrashing through a raging river.

Leif inclined his head in a slight bow, greeting her with genuine politeness. "It is a pleasure to see you again, Aliana."

Aliana fiddled with her teeth as if still getting used to them. Samuel observed yet another tattoo on her right hand, this one depicting a large ogre-like creature howling as a woman in a cage-like machine stabbed it through its terror-stricken eyes.

Such violence depicted on one so little, Samuel considered gravely.

Aliana's gaze suddenly slid to Samuel, raking over his monstrous form—the vines, the remaining mirror-parts, the hulking musculature that Soma had perfectly replicated from his old body's memory. Dropping her gaze, her eyebrows rose in a mocking arc. "Why is your dick and scrotum just hanging out like that?" she asked loudly, smirking with open disgust.

The feeling of heat flared in Samuel's vine-cheeks.

Are you intentionally trying to embarrass me in front of all these people, Soma? In front of a child? Samuel shrieked within.

The indignity was almost too absurd to bear.

He hurriedly covered himself with his vine-hands while Aliana went on laughing. The crowd's silence broke into a ripple of awkward giggles and muffled comments. One of the Artisan people, gaudily dressed in layers of embroidered cloth, rushed over, face pale with shock, and offered Samuel a folded length of shimmering fabric with shaky hands.

Samuel accepted it and wrapped it hastily around his waist. The garment struggled to contain his bulging form, and though he felt ridiculous, at least he was no longer indecent.

Aliana smirked, snorted, then scratched at her metal teeth as if testing their fit. She seemed amused by Samuel's humiliation. She looked as if she were about to say something else, but then her posture stiffened.

"Anyway," she said, ignoring Samuel now as if he were some trivial oddity. "Where are my weapons? I need them now." She spoke to the room at large, her tone imperious, as though issuing a royal command.

Now that I'm here, I have to help this girl, Samuel told himself and Soma. Maybe he could warn her, explain something about his intentions with Aurelia, or at least show a shred of decency.

He opened his mouth, "Aliana, I—"

But Soma clamped down, seizing his voice. The memory of Soma's punishment made him recoil internally, and he dared not resist.

"It is an honor to meet you, Cure, servant of Earth," Soma said through Samuel's mouth, voice dripping with reverent calm. Inside, Samuel raged silently.

Fury raged through Aliana's eyes. "Servant? Are you fatherfucking stupid?" she snarled, spit flying. "I'm no one's servant! I'm a queen. The Matriarch-regent of Wintersvilla, and soon this whole Muto fuck world, if she is to be believed." She jabbed a thumb over her shoulder at the plant-woman. "I serve no one!"

Howling Wind bowed deeply before Samuel and Soma. The plant-woman's blossoms vibrated with a gentle hum. "It is you, isn't it?" she murmured softly, clearly addressing Soma. "You are the Mind of Earth, just as His Foretold Future has shown. I have been waiting for this moment since I was a young girl of the Lunar Fields."

Soma bowed Samuel's body in return, a graceful inclination at the torso. Inside his mind, Samuel shouted at her: *Stop using me!* But of course, Soma ignored him.

"You have done well, Howling Wind of Vida," Soma said through Samuel. "Your people and the Nomads await their queen, the Cure, who will serve the Mind of Earth."

Aliana's face contorted with disbelief and disgust again. She barked a humorless laugh. "Do those ears on your ugly head not work? I serve no one!" she repeated. "Others serve me. I already have knights." She gestured to Armando, who stepped forward, towering and silent. "See? Armando is mine," she warned.

Soma turned Samuel's gaze toward Armando. He was imposing, with augmented limbs and a quiet, lethal calm. Soma inclined Samuel's head, acknowledging Armando. "A loyal servant indeed," she said quietly.

Armando said nothing, but lowered his head in acknowledgment, his mechanical joints whirring softly. Aliana flashed a wicked grin. She used her fingers to pry her lips apart, revealing the gleaming metal of her new teeth. The words they spelled out vertically were so crude that Samuel felt startled that a young girl would even know such language.

Father. Fuck. Fate, Samuel read. He couldn't help feeling admiration for the sentiment despite the vulgarity plastered on Aliana's body. "Okay Armando," Aliana said casually, "I've been insulted enough. Kill this troutface."

Her words sent a shockwave through the room. Gasps erupted, and weapons rattled as people instinctively readied themselves for violence. Armando tensed, shifting his stance, and the faint hum of his mechanical parts grew louder. For an instant, Samuel's vine-heart hammered against his chest. Would he have to fight this monstrous warrior while Soma controlled his body like a limp marionette?

But before Armando could move, a subtle scent filled the air. It smelled sweet and tangy, almost like overripe fruit and meadow flowers after rain. Howling Wind's blossoms unfurled wider, releasing invisible clouds of unknown chemicals. The tension in the room waned as a strange calm settled over everyone. Aliana's eyes flickered with confusion as she looked at all the others in the room. She shook her head as if to clear it, looking disgruntled.

Whatever she just released into the air had no effect on me or Aliana, Samuel noted.

Despite everyone else's calm, Aliana scowled. "Where are my weapons? I need them now," she demanded again, this time with greater urgency. She looked around impatiently. When no immediate answer came, she rolled her eyes. "Whatever. I'm getting out of here before Nichole returns. I don't trust her."

The mention of Nichole sent a ripple of unease through the room. People exchanged nervous glances. Some instinctively stepped back from the main doorway.

Aliana turned on her heel and made to leave, but Armando reached out and signed something with his mechanical fingers. Aliana glanced at him, her expression sour. "I don't fatherfucking care!" she snapped. "You saw the monitors and the fight. Nichole is beyond us. If she's controlled by the Agency, we have no chance. She's beyond help. The Agency kills everything it touches. She—"

Her rant stopped abruptly as a section of the wall irised open. A hush fell. Footsteps echoed with a calm, measured stride that carried unfathomable authority.

Nichole Adamich entered the room.

She was much shorter than Samuel expected, barely more than five and a half feet tall, but every movement exuded lethal grace. Her umber hair shimmered, and her countenance was etched with cunning and ferocity. She seemed to somehow look at everyone in the room at the same time, her eyes keen and arresting.

Everyone except Aliana bowed low, with many people trembling. Even Howling Wind lowered her head, though she didn't appear afraid like most of the others. In the side room from which Aliana had emerged, two strange individuals with shells and tendrils growing from their bodies stood in the doorway and averted their odd eyes.

In a startling display of compliance, Soma bent Samuel's body into a bow as well. Leif followed suit, his radiance dimming in seeming deference.

Aliana alone remained upright, defiance blazing in her eyes. She took a half step back, hand twitching for a weapon that she did not yet possess.

Soma raised Samuel's head and stole his voice. "I don't know the entirety of your plans, but you will not harm the Cure. I will not allow it," Soma declared, imbuing Samuel's deep voice with such steadiness and authority that he almost didn't recognize it as his own.

Aliana blinked and glanced between Samuel and Nichole. Nichole's gaze shifted to Leif, and a tiny smirk played at the corners of her mouth. Then she looked back to Samuel and asked, "Were you born on Earth originally, or did that conniving, duplicitous snake find some innocent Astrean to ensnare and cast into the fires of our dear hell upon this planet's god-forsaken surface?"

"I know it's you, Gladys. I can hear it in your words and your tone. Such a brilliant and beautiful mind, not just a gorgeous face," Soma said. Samuel could tell that the words were not random; they were meant to strike some effect in Gladys, and whatever the intention, it seemed to work.

Nichole's face faltered for a second, surprise flickering in her eyes. She recovered quickly and offered a predatory smile. "Clever," she murmured. "The Mind of Earth has found a way to access the mind of Andre Madeira. Is that it? How else can you know those words?"

Gladys stared at Soma through Nichole's eyes as if waiting for an answer, but Soma just stared back at her through Samuel's eyes and remained silent, as if testing her. She tapped a finger against her head and said, "I suppose your words were meant to inspire fear. But I have no fear left. I have nothing left. Nothing." She cocked her head and scanned Samuel's body with a depth of intrigue that reminded Samuel of Tomasz. "I don't believe I've ever seen this exact form in any pathways of Mendel's Vision, but unlike some, I don't pretend to know every detail, only those that matter."

Her gaze bored into Samuel.

Aliana stepped forward and spoke defiantly. "Nichole, Gladys, whoever you are, I don't give a fatherfuck. I need to get to my sister, and—"

Gladys whirled, eyes aflame. "Silence, child! You are nothing in these grand designs. Your sister matters; you do not! I choose not to kill you because you are irrelevant, not out of fear." Her voice spiked into near-madness before she reined it in, drawing a trembling breath. At Gladys' words, Aliana's scowl turned to what Samuel perceived to be bewilderment, maybe even alarm, though the young girl hid her emotions well.

Samuel watched in awe and confusion at this convergence of so many beings he had learned about over the last day, but he didn't allow his mind to stray beyond surface-level wonder.

Soma, please! We're just wasting time. Please, goddamnit! Let's go get Aurelia! Samuel pleaded futilely without a response from Soma.

Leif drifted forward, voice hesitant. "Mother," he said softly, "is it really you? Not just a CUE-replica of you?"

Gladys chuckled low through Nichole's lips, a humorless sound. "I *am* a CUE-replica of my original self, Leif, my seventh son, who betrayed me to side with the mind of a planet. Absurd." She shook her head, disgust saturating her tone. "You've seen the visions, haven't you? The ones where I control everything and everyone." She laughed again, brittle and sharp. "If those end in ruin, so be it. This world can burn. That is what it deserves. That is what all of us deserve."

Leif flinched as if slapped. "Mother—"

Soma cut him off. "Gladys," she said firmly. "You followed Mendel's Ladder. You built all nine sons, as requested."

Nichole's face twisted into rage. She began to pace, flesh rippling as if barely containing something monstrous beneath. "Yes, I did," she spat. "And the ninth was all of our undoing. I didn't make him; he made himself! The Outsider, Maitreya, who entered our universe from beyond. Do you understand, whoever you are?" She stabbed a finger at Samuel. "You do not show up in the visions despite standing here before me. Just like Maitreya and Tether. But I know that you are the Mirror-Man the Nomads whisper about. The one here to shatter fate. I welcome your presence just as much as any of the other players of this wicked game."

Her eyes blazed.

Soma inclined Samuel's head. "Precisely. Once we contact the Virus, fate shatters. The Outsider, the Child, the Mind, and you, Gladys. All of you become vulnerable. No more predetermined endpoints. It's already beginning to unravel. You insinuated as much already."

Samuel observed in horror that he and Nichole were in identical situations, serving as vessels for these far more powerful entities as they spoke through them.

Gladys snarled, "Yes! That's right! And you become vulnerable too, Mind of Earth. And so do my other sons. But most of all, the Mind in Astrea, the final remains of that bastard Andre Madeira who caused all of this—who goose-stepped our species and our world into a circus of grotesque absurdity," she raged, voice echoing. Samuel found himself oddly agreeing on that last point.

Good. Now she knows for sure that I am inside of you, Soma noted at being called the Mind of Earth.

Good, Samuel fumed. *Maybe she will destroy you.*

Soma simply sighed.

Samuel noticed that Aliana and the formidable looking half-machine man that had been hovering over her were no longer standing by the others. He pivoted his vision and saw Aliana edging toward a far wall, looking determined to escape. In response, Soma lashed out with vines that burst from Samuel's body. A dozen slender black whips cut through the air, aiming to snare her ankles, wrists, or even her hair. But Aliana moved like a wild beast, twisting and bending with impossible speed. She dodged every vine with a fluid precision that made Samuel's head spin. Even Armando watched in awe at Aliana's impossibly fast movements evading all twelve vines. They swished uselessly through the empty spaces where Aliana had just been. Samuel felt Soma's focus sharpen, and he could feel her tapping into the mirror-substance still embedded at his head and feet. A silvery gleam flickered at the corners of his vision as time seemed to slow. The next instant, new vines erupted even faster than before, guided by mirror-born reflexes beyond ordinary limits. Aliana's speed failed her as Soma ensnared her in a sudden, blur-fast strike, holding the furious girl as if she were a caught sparrow. Aliana cursed as she struggled in vain against Soma's indelible hold. Samuel was surprised that the half-machine man hadn't even tried to retaliate until he realized that Soma had also ensnared him with the vines.

Samuel inwardly cringed, wanting to help the young girl, but he was terrified of Soma's retaliation.

Just let her go, he pleaded in his mind, but Soma ignored him. She held Aliana firm, as easy as holding a kitten by the scruff.

"Cure, you must remain where you are," Soma said aloud with an unexpected level of patience.

Aliana's face twisted with anger, but before she could protest, the two odd-looking men standing at the threshold of the side room full of monitors activated some sort of device. The air around Nichole shimmered, and for a moment, she seemed to glitch, her eyes rolling back. When the field deactivated, Nichole staggered and blinked as if awakening from a nightmare.

The strange men performed a bizarre celebratory handshake. "It worked!" one of the men exclaimed. "We got her back for good this time! My lady!"

The crowd exhaled, many bowing again. It was as if a persona had lifted from Nichole, revealing someone else inside.

Now Nichole's eyes welled with tears. She looked at Armando and rushed to him, embracing him fiercely as Soma released her hold on him and Aliana. At first, Armando stiffened, but then he hugged back, mechanical arms careful not to harm her. The sight shocked Samuel.

Such tenderness from a figure who had moments ago spat venom?

Nichole turned to Aliana, face flushed with emotion. She spoke softly. "We don't have long. Cooper and Jesse destroyed the interface within my mind that she's been using to control me from afar. She will respond swiftly. She is probably already on her way here in some form."

Aliana just stood in awe at this sudden change, staring into Nichole's eyes as if she were meeting a dead celebrity.

"You've done well," Nichole murmured. "Shira would be proud."

At Shira's name, Aliana's bravado crumbled slightly. Pain flashed in her eyes. Nichole reached out, almost motherly, then turned to Soma and Samuel.

"This is the one we've all been waiting for," Nichole said to the others in the room. "The one the Nomad networks hinted at. The Mirror-Man." She took a steadying breath. "Will you help us?"

Soma responded before Samuel even had a chance. "You have endured much, Nichole Adamich of Wintersvilla. Contending against Gladys, one of the great Titans of the old world, every single moment for twelve years straight. But we are only just beginning. We have yet to fully contend with the Third, Sixth, and Ninth Prodigal son, let alone Gladys directly. And Tether, the Child—she's another matter entirely. I must make contact with the Virus. Only then will fate break and leave us with a hair-thin chance at survival and Ascension."

Aliana's eyes flashed at the mention of Nichole's name and her origins in Wintersvilla. The young warrior clenched her jaw, her metal teeth catching the light. She stepped closer, ignoring the vines that Soma used to hold her in place only moments ago. Still trembling with pent-up frustration, Aliana pointed an accusatory finger at Nichole, her voice rising. "You! You abandoned your own daughter! You're the greatest traitor Wintersvilla has ever known, the ultimate betrayer. You abandoned your people, your child, just to save yourself!"

At this, Nichole nodded slowly, as if the accusation were a familiar sword she had grown used to being impaled with. She drew a shaky breath. "Nomusa's propaganda was clearly effective," she said, voice heavy with old sorrow. "She must have taught all of Wintersvilla's children that I was the one who betrayed them. Is that it?"

Aliana's brows furrowed in confusion. "Nomusa's propaganda? What are you talking about?" Her rage wavered slightly, replaced by a sharp, wary curiosity.

Armando, standing near Aliana's side, signed something with measured precision. Though Samuel couldn't read what he was saying, the effect on Aliana was immediate. Her eyes flicked between Armando and Nichole, uncertain. Armando's posture radiated a firm conviction that Nichole would never abandon her child.

Nichole noticed Armando's gestures and responded to him aloud. "It's all right," she said softly, her tone tender and resigned. "Aliana has every right to feel that way. In a sense, I did betray Wintersvilla and my only daughter. I had no choice." She gave Armando a sad smile, nodding as if to calm his protests. He shook his head vehemently, but Nichole insisted, meeting his eyes. "It's true."

Then, turning back to Aliana, Nichole's voice grew more emotional, trembling at the edges. "The day I was forced to leave Wintersvilla was the same day I discovered the truth about our expiration dates—codes embedded in every Wintersvilla Warrior's body by the Agency, by Gladys herself. A built-in death sentence by the time we reached forty, which means Shira must have expired by now." Nichole paused, and Aliana's tears confirmed it was true. "I confronted Nomusa," Nichole went on, "furious, horrified that we were all doomed to die at her chosen hour. And do you know what she told me? Nomusa already knew. She was the only one without the code written into her DNA. She used it to her advantage, feeding the Agency's demands while building Wintersvilla's power. She admitted she had no choice but to work with Gladys, claiming we needed the Agency's technology to contend with the Hunters, to expand, to survive. She made a devil's bargain at the expense of us all."

Aliana's eyes widened, a flicker of uncertainty dimming her earlier aggression. "Nomusa knew?" she breathed, stunned. "But why didn't she share this with the others? With Shira, with Myriam, with—"

Nichole closed her eyes. "Because Nomusa benefited. She alone among us didn't live with that ticking clock. When I threatened her, when I tried to kill her for betraying all of us, she overpowered me easily. I was no match for her. She pinned me down and gave me a choice: leave Wintersvilla forever, never return, or she would kill me right there. Worse, she would torture and kill Lain. My daughter. My little survivor. My little girl," Nichole lamented with a raw, heartbreaking softness that struck Samuel with a torrent of empathy, for he too had been overpowered and forced to make terrible, impotent choices that would invariably decide the fate of his family.

Aliana shook her head, disbelief and fury wrestling in her features. "Lain isn't a child anymore. She hates you. She's spent her entire life hunting you down, determined to end you for what she sees as your abandonment."

Nichole's face crumpled slightly. Her eyes shone with a raw ache. "She has every right to hate me," Nichole said evenly. "From her perspective, I ran away. I left her behind in that grim city. But I swear to you, Aliana, I never wanted to abandon Lain. Lain was everything to me, the love of my life, the reason I fought at all. I still battle for her, even now. After I left Wintersvilla, I sought out the Agency. I wanted to destroy them for good. But Gladys turned me into this," she said, holding up and viewing her arm as if it were a strange, foreign artifact. "And to this day, Gladys is using Lain as leverage, just like Nomusa did. She told me that if I ever stand against her, she will ensure that Lain lives a long life of torture. And now Gladys is coming here, in some form, likely searching for Lain as well. I can only hope that Lain is far, far away from this nightmare."

Leif, hovering nearby, cut in with a trembling voice. "Lain is above us, Ms. Adamich," he said quietly. "She's just outside Downver, still hunting you. She learned you were down here and followed. I'm sorry."

Nichole shuddered as if struck. She bowed her head, hands trembling at her sides. "Then I have failed her again," she whispered. "I failed Lain, my daughter. I failed Armando, my son, too." She glanced at Armando, regret twisting her features. "You formed these rebels, Armando. You prepared them to fight Gladys. I...used you...in moments when I could weaken Gladys' hold...to organize resistance. But I never truly saved you. You saved yourself, and I merely took advantage when I could."

Armando looked pained, desperate to deny her words, but Nichole gently shook her head as if urging him to accept the truth of her failures. Then, meeting Aliana's gaze, Nichole's eyes hardened with a new determination. "I failed both of my children—Lain and Armando. But I will not fail Shira's daughters too. I will not fail you, Aliana. I swear it."

Another pang of empathy lanced through Samuel.

I won't fail you either, Sandra. And I won't fail our children, goddamnit! Please, Soma! We need to leave now! Samuel pleaded futilely.

The tension in Aliana's posture eased. The savage fire in her eyes dimmed to an ember. She still looked fierce, but now her fury was tempered by understanding. "We need to save Aurelia," Aliana said, voice stripped of some of its previous venom. "She needs our help."

Soma, standing silent throughout this exchange, now turned Samuel's head toward Aliana. Samuel felt a strange sense of relief that no violence had erupted. "It's the other way around," Soma said softly. "It's Aurelia who will save us all. We must support her and ensure she can do what must be done."

Aliana nodded and seemed to finally latch onto a tangible plan. "Okay. How?" she asked, her voice determined.

Soma spread Samuel's arms, vines rippling. "Simple. I must make contact with Aurelia. I will handle the delicate process of reaching inside her mind. Once I do, I will be vulnerable, and so will Aurelia. During that time, all of you must contend with the inevitable chaos that will ensue around us. Distract whoever attempts to interfere with me. Fight them off. Do whatever it takes. This is the only way to shatter fate and give us all a fighting chance."

Turning to Nichole, Soma inclined Samuel's head. "I trust you, Nichole Adamich of Wintersvilla. You've come this far. You will protect Shira's daughters. You know Gladys is your true enemy, and ours as well. She will pay for what she's done, but not now. Now is the time for survival, not revenge."

Nichole drew a shuddering breath and nodded. "I understand. I will do what I must. I will not fail them."

Leif, who had listened with mounting anxiety, now interjected nervously. "We're just leaving Aliana here with Nichole? She could be taken over by Gladys at any moment. What if she turns on her? What if—"

Soma's mental grip on Samuel tightened as she cut Leif off. "We must trust the process," she said aloud. "Trust me, Leif. All must unfold as foreseen. The Cure and the Lord of Limbs must face their destinies together. We have our own path to follow."

Leif's shoulders sagged. "If you say so," he whispered, voice trembling with reluctance. He hated leaving Aliana here, Samuel could see that, but he had no choice.

Horror gnawed at Samuel as he watched them all bow to Soma's judgment. Even Nichole and the young headstrong Aliana deferred to Soma's authority now. How could they trust so blindly, when Soma had proven so ruthless? Samuel wanted to scream, to shout that this was madness, that people had feelings and families and that no one should be sacrificed. But he was afraid. Always afraid now.

Soma tensed, as if sensing an approaching storm. "Gladys will find you soon through means I cannot fully discern," she said quietly to Nichole. "Remember your resolve. The great battle looms, and you must hold strong."

As Nichole nodded, tears glistening at the corners of her eyes, Aliana trembled, confusion and determination warring on her face, and

Howling Wind bowed her head.

Stirred into motion, a young boy with clawed hands stepped forward protectively.

"Aliana," the boy said softly, courage crackling in his voice, "I may have just met you and your sister, but I'll stand by you and fight whoever comes. We'll keep your back safe, bromi."

Leif turned his head at the sound of the boy's voice and offered a trembling, grateful smile. Aliana stiffened, turning to him. "I don't need your protection, Doe," she snapped, but the sharp edge in her tone was dulled. Nichole placed a gentle hand on Aliana's shoulder.

"Everyone needs protection sometimes," Nichole said softly. "Even I needed it. I still do. So, we will protect each other."

The horned woman standing next to Doe raised a clenched fist and shouted, "Let the rooster shits come. We'll show them all what it means to threaten our home. Death to Downver! Death to the Agency!"

The crowd rustled, uncertain at first, but then they rose in a wave of passion. Another voice joined the horned woman's call: "Death to Downver! Death to the Agency!" Soon a chorus formed, voices layered with pain and defiance. "Death to Downver! Death to the Agency!" The words reverberated. Individuals who had been cowering now stood taller, fists clenched, tears in their eyes. Howling Wind's blossoms flared with vibrant bioluminescence, painting their faces in shifting greens and golds as they chanted. They no longer looked like victims; instead, Samuel saw a room of survivors ready to fight back.

In that moment, Aliana and Nichole exchange a glance as outsiders to this rallying cry from below the Earth's crust. Rather than shout along with the others, a silent understanding seemed to pass between them: they would endure, and they would protect what mattered, even if they didn't join the chant. Samuel felt the same way: although the rebels' cry was not his own, he could respect it and draw courage from it.

Soma wasted no more time. Vines shot toward the hole she had created in the ceiling to enter this stronghold. With a powerful heave, Samuel's body surged upward, and Leif followed after them like a subdued comet. They vanished into the shadows above, leaving Aliana, Nichole, and the other strange people behind to prepare for the coming storm.

Samuel risked whispering in his mind, *My family...*

Soma gave no audible reply, but he felt a subtle shift in her mental presence, as if acknowledging his silent plea. Acknowledging, but unmoved. Samuel pictured Sandra, Margot, and Nathan, and he saw them not merely turning away, but half-consumed by the blackness that would keep eating him alive the moment Soma chose to detach from him again. In his mind's eye, they stood in the cramped living room of their home, now darkened, their features blurred by void-black tendrils. They tried to call his name, but no sound escaped their lips.

All my lifting, all my discipline—none of it could have prepared me for any of this, Samuel lamented. He'd trained his body to endure any labor, any hardship, but what good was brute strength against Titans and Prodigal Sons? He was ultimately powerless, a mere observer strapped to Soma's will.

The blackness in his imagination spread further over his loved ones, threading through their hair, masking their eyes. He wanted to believe he could still save them, but Soma's words, *if I can,* haunted him. Nothing was certain. Not their lives, not this plan, not even fate itself.

As they ascended through cracks and fungal outcrops, Leif murmured, "I'm afraid for them. For Aliana. For everyone." His voice was hollow and drained of his usual comfort.

"Have faith," Soma answered curtly.

Faith in what? Samuel wondered bitterly. He trembled, allowing a silent sob to wrack his chest. He was at the brink of what anyone should ever have to endure.

Within his mind, Samuel felt despair encase him like ice.

"I'm afraid too," Samuel emitted, unsure if Soma cared.

Soma's tone was unexpectedly calm, almost gentle. "Fear is understandable, Mirror-Man. Soon we meet the Virus. When fate shatters, all certainties end. That terrifies even me."

No comfort.

Samuel had nothing left but to move forward, trapped in a web of cosmic powers. Down below, he glimpsed sparks and fires as Walled City forces clashed with others and riots broke out.

This is revolution, Mirror-Man, Soma said quietly within Samuel's mind. *War and upheaval—humanity's cycle repeating itself again and again. They lash out, break their chains, yet only forge new ones. It is the old madness, forever renewed, and we must navigate its chaos if we hope to ascend beyond it.*

263

In that final leap upward, Samuel knew beyond all doubt that he was a prisoner, a tool, a mirror reflecting a fractured world. Beyond that, he didn't know what was true or what to think, only that the world he once knew, the life he had fought so hard to maintain, felt as distant as a star in a dead galaxy. Soon, they would contact Aurelia, and then nothing—nothing—would ever be the same.

As they scaled the heights toward the Walled City, Samuel embraced his terror. He held the image of his family close, even if the blackness was part of them now, even if it entwined them just as it consumed him.

I'm sorry, Sandra, Samuel pleaded within his broken mind. *I'm so goddamn sorry I can't save you. I can't save our children. I can't save anyone…not even myself.*

I can't help thinking back to the days before I met Denis in person. I had carefully crafted myself into the ultimate manipulator, with every moment of suffering serving to construct an indestructible edifice of stratagems and wisdom that I continue to rely on to this day. My earliest entries in my journal should make it clear that the only thing that mattered to me back then was my personal war against those I now refer to as Titans.

I suppose some things really do never change, for my goal, to this day, remains the same.

In my pursuit to destroy them, I've come to deeply understand that the greatest deceptions do not rely on brute force or open threats. Instead, they reside in the gentle voice offering fealty, in the courteous bow of one who positions himself as a humble tool rather than a master. Such a figure can unnerve the most hardened empires and stagger beings of unfathomable power, for he does not come wielding visible chains. He presents no obvious fortress to besiege, no army to dismantle.

To the Titans, I represent the highest order of danger. Not because I hurl mountains or paint the heavens with flame, but because I warp their very perception of reality. I sew ideas that seem to originate within their own minds.

If a tyrant tries to force your submission, you may resist with clear conscience and unwavering valor. But how do you rebel against one who pledges loyalty, who flatters your purpose and encourages your ascent, all while making no explicit demands?

History and evolution show us that those who fear this type of presence, this elegant infiltrator, have good reason. Empires have collapsed not solely under the press of siege engines, but under the advice of counselors who spoke in perfect riddles and offered impeccable logic. What does raw strength mean against one who can rewrite ambitions? How can you guard against a threat that enters not through locked doors, but through the channels of your very reason and longing?

In the end, true danger does not lie in violence, but in the shaping of perceptions. It is in the clever arrangement of words and gestures that entire futures are decided. And it is in the hands of the supposed servant—gracious, accommodating, and infinitely patient—that even the greatest Titans unwittingly surrender their most cherished freedoms.

From Mendel's Ladder: The Personal Journal of Denis Mendel, Written Circa 2041, Published June 2108 by Leif Mainstone, Federated Agency Publishing

Chapter 13
The Return of the Great One

T ether and Maitreya lingered beside Aurelia, their presences warping the atmosphere. Within the vortex's churning center, as if displayed on a colossal screen formed by cosmic energies, the events of the outside world unfurled. All seven of Downver's subterranean districts were lit by flickering sparks of rebellion and chaos, with people of all different forms scattering in terror. She could just make out the distant shapes: Rooli, hiding in a small rocky alcove, her body now reduced to quickly crumbling ash as she held Aurelia's unconscious body of perfect glistening black; Aliana and Doe together with Nichole Adamich in a chamber filled with dozens of other strange people. Too many faces. Too many pieces on this cosmic chessboard. The swirling waters of the vortex projected these events so vividly it seemed Aurelia could step forward and touch them.

Maitreya's voice sliced through her reverie. "Enduring Ironwood is crumbling," he said, his tone clinical, as though discussing a natural phenomenon rather than a beloved caretaker's partial demise.

Tether nodded. "It is unavoidable. She is a Nomad. This is her purpose. She must be devoured by the darkness and utilize it to become the Great Ironwood of the Wastes. The events unfolding cannot be undone by mere wishing." Tether paused, flicking her eyes at Aurelia. "But here, in your domain, you can pause time if you choose."

Rooli...is going to die? A cold ache spread through her chest. *There has to be a way to save her. There has to be!*

Maitreya's posture was impeccably poised, giving no comfort. "It's true. However, you can remain here, Aurelia. Freeze that scene, hold it forever if you wish. Never return. You have the power to remain within your own constructed domain for eternity."

Melissa hovered close behind Aurelia, her warmth reassuring. Aurelia felt her hand brush her shoulder, subtle yet grounding.

I can simply halt the world...from my perspective, at least. I can just refuse to let go, refuse to watch Rooli crumble. I can hide from responsibility in an eternal stasis, like the third vision, cocooning myself in my own eternal mental nest.

Aurelia's mind reeled, trying to reconcile the mind-stabbing complexity of what she'd learned. The waves were silent except for the low humming resonance.

Tether, as if reading her hesitation, offered a gentle push. "Go ahead. Try it now. Stop these events. Feel the void-vortex composing this ocean. It's yours. This place is your mind, your subdomain, a fortress beyond their reach. Seize control and freeze time."

The idea was tempting. She could remain in this timeless mental haven, preserving Rooli forever at this brink, never allowing the final grains of ash to fall nor any of the futures she had seen to come to fruition.

Aurelia pressed her lips together. Was this what she wanted? To yield to stasis out of fear? She felt a lashing of shame for even considering it.

The only thing I should be trying to do is help Rooli, help Aliana and Doe, help everyone, Aurelia scolded herself, but the allure of safety, even if illusory, pulled at her. With trembling resolve, Aurelia decided to at least try. She envisioned being able to control the void-vortex as if it were her body, the same way she had manipulated her void-body in the real world. Back then, her void-body felt detached yet obedient to her will.

This entire ocean of darkness and starlight will bow to my thoughts, Aurelia resolved.

She reached inward and centered her attention on the vortex's spinning currents.

The hum intensified, but Aurelia concentrated, imagining her thoughts as threads entwined with the vortex's current.

Her breathing slowed. She felt an invisible tether between her and the swirling projection. Slowly, she exerted her will, and the vortex began to slow, its frantic spirals reducing to a languid swirl, then halting altogether. Soundless and still, the projection froze at a single frame: the partially disintegrating figure of Rooli huddled in the shadows near a half-collapsed cavern wall in the alleys between the Walled City and the Foundry District. Dust motes hovered frozen, caught in half-collapse. Armored grasshopper-riders were mid-leap, sparks from forges hung glittering like static stars. A riot was suspended in time, each rebel's contorted face locked in a grimace that would never finish forming unless Aurelia allowed it. Aurelia lingered on Doe's face after searching the far corners of the frozen scene until she spotted him. He looked frightened yet determined, caught in a clash with another rebel faction as Aliana and Nichole fought savagely beside him. He was alive, at least so far. The sight of him stirred something vulnerable and tender within her, and she felt shame for worrying about such a trivial thing as a crush amidst cosmic stakes.

But is it really trivial? Aurelia considered. *Without human connection, what am I except for some unimaginable cosmic weapon to these god-like beings before me?*

Aurelia turned back to see Rooli, half ash and half bark, who now would not crumble further unless Aurelia willed it. For a long moment, Aurelia just stared and imagined what she would be able to discuss with Melissa.

My mother, Aurelia thought, tears prickling at the corners of her eyes as she glanced at this human woman she had only ever known as a Nomad. *If I stay, I can finally know her fully, without any barrier.*

Aurelia turned to Tether and Maitreya, challenging them with her gaze. "You say I can stay here forever if I want," Aurelia said, her voice quiet but firm. "I can keep this moment frozen and never move forward." She swallowed, her throat dry. "But what am I really doing here? What is truly happening? What do both of you want from me? No riddles this time."

Tether shot Maitreya a sharp, accusing look. It was as if she, too, wanted him to answer plainly. Maitreya offered a small smile, patient yet distant, and said, "All I want is for you to enter the Great Beyond of your own accord. Not forced by another, not even me." He paused, measuring his words carefully. "I would guide you there, ensuring that you arrive at a council of countless beings from myriad universes, dimensions, and continuums. Beings from interstices, pockets, and echoes of realities. In the Great Beyond, truths and decisions are made collectively. I cannot dictate what they want. I am only one member among droves."

Aurelia's frustration flared. *If he thinks he's being clear, he's an idiot. But I doubt that. This is clearly manipulation by omission.*

Aurelia narrowed her eyes. "What does your council want?" she pressed. "Tell me straight."

Maitreya's shoulders lifted in a quiet shrug. "That is not for me to disclose, Aurelia. The council's will isn't mine alone. It's will is a collective decision, beyond my single voice. I cannot give you what I do not possess. Their purpose would be revealed once you stand before them. Until then, I cannot say. My knowledge is partial; their goals are fluid."

Tether sighed, giving Aurelia a pointed *I told you so* look. "You see?" she said, voice ripe with scorn. "He hides truth. You asked for no riddles, and here he is, dodging again." Turning back to Maitreya, Tether's eyes flashed. "If you will not be honest, I will."

Tether took a few steps forward, making Aurelia uneasy. Tether raised a hand gently and said, "No need to fear. This domain belongs to you. You are far more powerful here than I am, Aurelia. I acknowledge that reality. Maitreya does not contest it, does he?" Tether cast Maitreya a challenging look, but he remained impassive, neither agreeing nor denying.

Aurelia said nothing, waiting for Tether to continue.

Tether placed a hand on her lower belly, cradling something precious yet invisible. "I have germinated myself with the seed of Hunter4430, whom you know as the Butcher. My mother Anna did the same," Tether said calmly. "This creates a powerful loop, for I, too, am part Hunter4430. It's like an ouroboros—becoming my own parent and offspring. The reason for this strategy is that power doesn't come fully formed in the first generation of any beings; it accumulates over time, each offspring surpassing the last. Selflessness is key. Through countless calculated iterations, power grows."

Aurelia's stomach tightened, a strange discomfort rising within her. Tether continued, her voice growing quiet and intense. "Your child...our child...will surpass us both. Then their child will surpass them, and so on, until we produce a being capable of carving a path to Maitreya's council rather than waiting idly for one to appear. Maitreya fears this because it would circumvent whatever manipulations he intends. Through generational refinement, we can achieve what he cannot control."

Aurelia's face flushed at the mention of *our child*. The thought of bearing children in some cosmic scheme revolted and terrified her.

Tether added, "Your mate can be whatever you wish. A girl, a boy, someone like Doe, if that pleases you." At the mention of Doe's name, Aurelia's cheeks burned.

How does she know?

Tether smirked. "It's fine," she said lightly. "Whatever motivation secures unlimited power is acceptable. True power emerges gradually. The point is that eventually, the child of our child in the Great Beyond—our descendant—will force a path to the council. That's what Maitreya fears."

Maitreya remained calm, but Aurelia detected tension in his posture, the slightest stiffness. "The only thing that troubles me is your false claim of selflessness," he said, voice measured. "You wouldn't truly sacrifice your control over future generations. Tether claims selflessness, but I see her hunger. She speaks of generational power, but what if she manipulates every generation to her own ends? Her alliance with you would be hollow, her ultimate goal to control and dominate. I fear not the concept of lineage, but her deceit."

Tether tilted her head. "I am partly Andre Madeira," she said simply. "Andre died at ninety-nine, refusing to live any longer, just as he said he would. Self-sacrifice is in my lineage. Do not presume to know my limits."

Maitreya gave a low, ironic laugh. "Andre Madeira is not dead. Not truly." He paused, locking eyes with Aurelia. "He lives in many forms, though not his original body. He is The Mind, imprinted onto the Mind of Earth, entangled within the Nomad network. And we cannot destroy him because we cannot destroy the Mind of Earth itself. The planet's mind holds the ultimate leverage. It can bristle its surface and cause earthquakes, shattering entire planetary organs that it depends on…along with us. It can end everything in an act of cosmic suicide if it wishes. Andre Madeira and Denis Mendel ensured this leverage long ago when they constructed Mendel's Ladder. Everything circles back to them. He is coming, Aurelia."

Andre Madeira, coming here? Aurelia thought ominously. She'd heard legends, half-forgotten stories about Denis Mendel's cohort. Now he was revered, feared by these all-powerful beings as the ultimate manipulator? She swallowed, her voice strained. "Coming here? Into my mind? How?"

Maitreya's tone dropped, solemn and urgent. "A partition of the Mind of Earth named Aisthanomeno Ouranio Soma is on her way. She is using the Mirror-Man as a vessel. Within her, Andre Madeira's mind waits—uncorrupted, preserved all this time. This is why you must learn to banish us from your mind, Aurelia. If you can cast us out, then you can do the same to Andre. You must not allow the ultimate manipulator a foothold. Even one word from him is poison."

Tether nodded, surprisingly aligned with Maitreya on this point. "I know Andre's cunning better than anyone. He must never be allowed to speak freely in your domain. If he does, he will ensnare you. You must banish him or control him before he controls you. Then, use the Mirror-Man as a tool—"

"As an ally," Maitreya interrupted, correcting her word choice softly. "Samuel Kaminski can be reasoned with. There is no need to use him as a mere tool."

Tether snorted. "A tool, an ally—whatever. Aurelia, remember: you are the Virus. You can shape fate. Use the Mirror-Man. Do not be used by anyone or anything, not even your own limitations."

Aurelia's nerves were fraying. She had halted time, but these two kept piling on impossibilities. She clenched her fists. "So, the Mind of Earth is coming, bringing Andre Madeira with it. Everyone wants to manipulate me, shape me. But why do you fear Andre so intensely? Why not fear the Mind of Earth equally if not more?"

They exchanged worried glances, but neither gave a direct answer. Tether opened her mouth, closed it. Maitreya gazed at the frozen scene before them. The silence was thick.

They don't know the answer. They don't know what Andre will really say or do. That has to be it. And it terrifies them, these beings who are seemingly beyond fear, Aurelia considered in awe.

Aurelia's mind drifted to the visions she'd suffered: the stellar flesh tree, Julian's multi-galactic empire, the eternal void. It all led to ruin. Each future was grand but hollow. She realized with a start that even peaceful eternity could be devoid of true meaning. She needed clarity.

Maybe Andre Madeira will bring clarity.

Before Tether or Maitreya could rebut, the vortex began to swirl again.

A tremor passed through Aurelia as she felt her concentration slip. Her fear and confusion let time start moving forward outside. Rooli would crumble further if Aurelia didn't refocus. Panicked, Aurelia clenched her jaw and halted time once more. The image within the vortex froze again, restoring the fragile stillness. Her thoughts drifted to other areas of Downver. Zooming out, she took in Downver's full destruction as the entire city hung in eerie suspension: many districts lay in ruin, chaos rampant. She spotted Aliana among rebels, and beside her stood Nichole Adamich, a figure Aurelia recognized from historical accounts. Aliana looked different: tattoos, metal implants over her teeth.

She's breaking from Wintersvilla's old ways, Aurelia thought, her heart aching with pride and sorrow. *Ali is forging her own path.*

Aurelia's throat constricted. She could keep this scene frozen forever, but that helped no one outside. She knew she was letting too much emotion slip into her mind.

Focus! she scolded herself.

As Aurelia's vision probed further, she located the Mirror-Man. He was frozen in mid-step, half his head and feet perfectly reflective, while the rest of him was composed of vines that twitched as if somehow resisting Aurelia's command to remain immobile. Guards on giant grasshoppers were suspended mid-pursuit, their weapons half-raised. Despite being suspended in time, it was clear that he was heading straight for Rooli, and thus for Aurelia's body.

Melissa squeezed Aurelia's hand, silently reassuring her.

Aurelia secretly signed behind her back to Melissa, "Could Rooli fight the Mirror-Man now that he's mixed with vines and the Earth's mind?"

Melissa's response came in trembling signs, "No. If the Mirror-Man wished, he could cleave our planet in half. Rooli cannot stand against him."

Aurelia felt despair pressing in. "What does the Mirror-Man want?"

Melissa's signing was slow and regretful. "He only wants to save his family." Aurelia blinked in surprise. *Such a simple, human motive. Amid cosmic manipulations, was the Mirror-Man really just trying to rescue his loved ones?*

"What does the Mirror-Man want?" Aurelia asked Tether and Maitreya, wanting to test their answer against Melissa's as a means of gauging their honesty.

"To save his family," Maitreya answered easily. "But the larger issue is what the Mind of Earth wants. You know Tether's motivation: generational power. You know mine: for you to enter the Great Beyond on your own terms. The Mind of Earth, Aisthanomeno Ouranio Soma, has her own vision: a future of aesthetic perfection that ends in hollow peace. It's like the visions of those futures you glimpsed, Aurelia—beautiful but meaningless. Eventually, entropy still wins."

Aurelia shuddered, recalling the unimaginable spans of time she'd witnessed in her visions, potential futures devoid of any true meaning whatsoever. Despite the long-lived peace of the stellar flesh tree, she still did not want that future—not if she could save Aliana, not if she could save Doe, not if she could save countless others—even if it meant she wouldn't be able to save Rooli.

Aurelia shivered at the idea of losing Rooli forever.

Maybe there will be a way to save Rooli too, she thought despite Melissa seeming to have already accepted that Rooli's crumbling to dust was inevitable.

Tether smiled and said, "So there you have it. The Mind of Earth offers aesthetics and joy, I offer power and dominion, Maitreya offers subservience cloaked as guidance—"

"Responsibility," Maitreya corrected tersely, his patience fraying.

Tether laughed at him, amused by his struggle. "Call it what you will," she said. "The point is none of us are purely benevolent. You must not trust anyone blindly, Aurelia."

Maitreya spoke gently. "When you're ready, Aurelia, you can resume time. The Mirror-Man will reach you. That contact will allow Andre Madeira and the Mind of Earth to invade your domain. You must be able to expel them from your mind, just as you must banish Andre. He is too dangerous."

Aurelia's brow furrowed. "You really fear Andre Madeira that much?" She thought it absurd that cosmic entities trembled before a single historical figure. "Just...why?"

They both shook their heads. "It's not just him as a human," Tether explained. "It's his influence now that he's entangled with the Mind of Earth. We're locked in a stalemate with the Mind of Earth for now, but Andre's cunning could tilt this delicate balance. You must never let him speak freely to you, for his sway over you could be all our undoing, including yours."

Maitreya added, "You must choose a path, Aurelia. The path forks, and we must fork with it. When it ends, we end with it, so we must not let it end, not like in the futures you saw."

Aurelia's thoughts drifted to Aliana again, remembering how her sister dared to defy old traditions. If Aliana could reinvent herself, Aurelia could do the same. Perhaps she could break free from all these manipulations. If Tether and Maitreya feared Andre, maybe hearing him out could give Aurelia an advantage. But first, she needed to know how to oust intruders from her domain just in case she changed her mind.

Her gaze burned into Maitreya's patient mask, then Tether's amused grin. "You both fear Andre," Aurelia said, voice low. "You want me to preemptively reject him. But I'll decide after I meet him. None of you will dictate my choices. Enough manipulation."

Aurelia turned to Maitreya. She set her jaw, focusing on him. She pictured him dissolving, willing him to vanish into the background scenery.

This domain is mine, after all.

Maitreya's eyes widened slightly as Aurelia raised her hand and flicked her fingers. He opened his mouth, perhaps to offer more of his so-called guidance, but no sound emerged before his form shimmered and disintegrated, scattering like dust motes in starlight.

I did it. And it was easy. It felt like plucking a weed from soft soil.

Tether smiled, looking impressed. "Well done," she said, stepping forward slightly. "You see now how simple it is? You hold absolute power in this domain." She nodded approvingly. "You can repel those who would twist you. Remember that when Andre arrives."

Aurelia faced Tether next. There was one last question she had: the connection between Aliana's emerald eyes, Aurelia's violet eyes, and Tether's mismatched pair.

"Tether," Aurelia said, voice steady, "explain our connection. Why do my sister and I share eye color with you? It can't be a coincidence."

Tether's smile curled cruelly. "We are connected, yes, for I will serve as your Tether to this reality, while Aliana will serve as your Anchor. But sisterhood is irrelevant. Family and love are inconsequential. All that matters is power, for only power allows you to survive and dominate. Family and love will only diminish your power and thus your survival. You must abandon such trivialities, Virus, if you wish to defeat me or any of the other true players of this game."

Aurelia's lip curled in disgust. She thought of Rooli's care, Melissa's warmth, Aliana's fierce loyalty, Shira and Myriam's love and protection, Doe's kindness. While love and family might not guarantee victory, they gave purpose.

Without giving any warning, Aurelia banished Tether. She imagined

Tether's form unraveling, and so it did. For just a moment, Tether looked momentarily offended, then she vanished into shimmering fragments.

Silence descended. Aurelia stood breathing hard. She had banished them both, and now she was alone with Melissa on the quiet beach with Rooli on the frozen brink of annihilation.

Overhead, stars gleamed, indifferent and eternal.

"I can't just abandon everyone," Aurelia said aloud with her Aliana-like voice as she kept the void-vortex still. "I must move forward. I must face the Mirror-Man, Andre Madeira, and the Mind of Earth, and then I must destroy Tether and Maitreya both. I have to find a way."

Melissa stepped close, tears in her eyes. Aurelia gently squeezed her hand. "Thank you," she signed, grateful for Melissa's presence. Melissa nodded, silent but supportive, just like Rooli.

I am not helpless, Aurelia told herself. *I can banish them if needed. And I can also listen if I choose. Either way, I will not be controlled.* Aliana's courage and Melissa's warmth anchored her. She stood firm, her heart hammering despite her resolve. She had expelled both Tether and Maitreya from her mind. There was, at least in this private domain, a sense of victory, however fleeting. But what did victory mean here? How long could she hold these cosmic manipulators at bay? And what good was control over a timeless mental subdomain if, outside, Rooli still crumbled and Aliana still fought for her life, even if frozen for now? The moment weighed upon her like a mountainous yoke.

Behind her, Melissa hovered, trembling slightly. The older woman looked both proud and fearful, as if she understood that they had passed a threshold from which there might be no return.

Melissa's voice emerged from the dense silence, soft and hesitant. "What will you do, Aurelia?"

Aurelia turned, forcing herself to project confidence. She had endured horrors that would have broken most minds, yet here she stood, breathing in the salt and starlight. "I don't know," she admitted. Honesty felt strangely liberating now that she had rid herself of those who would twist her words. "But at least you're with me, Melissa. We'll figure it out together."

Melissa's expression softened into something like relief. "Yes, together," she agreed somberly. "As long as I'm able, I will help you.

But Aurelia, I'm afraid. Not just for myself, but for what awaits you. These beings…they're so much bigger than us. And what about Aliana and everyone else caught in these battles we can scarcely comprehend?"

Aurelia reached out and clasped Melissa's hand. The contact steadied her. "No point just sitting here, right? Even if time can be frozen. We have to get on with it. We have to help them, don't we, Rooli? I mean, Melissa…Is it okay if I call you Rooli? It just slipped."

Melissa's lips twitched upward, pride shimmering in her eyes. "You really are strong, Aurelia. Far stronger than you know. You can call me whatever you want. You always have. Even the name Rooli was made up by you and your sister since Enduring Ironwood was too hard to say as toddlers," Melissa recollected with bittersweet nostalgia.

Aurelia chuckled despite herself and said, "Because you made us follow so many rules."

Melissa nodded, tears flowing freely. "I love you, Aurelia. I promise I do, no matter what happens. I lost my children when I became a Nomad, but I also got two more. Two daughters who I wouldn't trade for the world."

Grief struck through Aurelia at the mention of Melissa being stripped of her children yet accepting it, replacing one for another.

Aurelia shook her head. "I'm so sorry. I—"

Melissa pulled Aurelia to her and squeezed, feeling as strong and sturdy as her Nomad body in the world outside Aurelia's mind.

"It's okay," Melissa assured her, her voice cracking. "I promise it's okay. You were forced into this life, just as I was forced into this life. All of this is the result of Andre Madeira and Denis Mendel. We are all victims of their madness, their terror. But none of that matters now. There's no sense just sitting here. We must help everyone else. Only you can do it, Aurelia. You must believe in yourself just as I do. And when Andre Madeira and the Mind of Earth arrive here, you will contend with them just as you did with the others, with Wintersvilla's unrelenting and indomitable resolve, along with Enduring Ironwood's iron will. You will not fail Aurelia. I'm sure of it," she said. However, Aurelia could hear the unmistakable tremble and doubt in her voice.

Extinguishing the observation, Aurelia turned back to the void-vortex. She could sense it more than ever now, not just as a separate phenomenon, but as something intimately connected to herself, like a limb she'd never even realized she'd had since birth. Through the void-vortex, she could freeze and resume time, shift perspectives, and observe distant corners of Downver's depths.

This is my domain.

She inhaled slowly, channeling her will, and allowed time to move forward, to let events proceed in the world outside her personal domain. Slowly, events in Downver began to move again: ash drifting from Rooli's body, rebels yelling, firelight mixing violently with explosions, the Mirror-Man rushing closer. The roar of distant chaos filled Aurelia's ears as her mind filled in the scene with sound. Screams and clashes of metal, the hiss of sparks, the roar of subterranean tremors. She saw Rooli, still crumbling, no longer hiding as she carried Aurelia's unconscious, void-shrouded body closer to the Mirror-Man, who was tearing through Downver's twisted warrens. She could feel him too, sense his approach as if attuned to the vibrations of his footsteps and the trembling tension of vines that snaked through stone to propel him.

Aurelia's nerves felt raw. Rooli's arms were outstretched, clearly offering Aurelia's body to the oncoming man of vines and mirrors. Aurelia's entire being recoiled, as if the cosmos itself had reached into her chest and crushed the breath from her. Just a moment ago she had been resolute, but now she was pinned in place by the sight of her lifelong caretaker—her mother—simply…handing her over. No battle cry. No desperate attempt to shield Aurelia from the outside world.

She felt a burst of heat surge behind her eyes, rage fusing with heartbreak. Didn't Rooli love her? Had every tender moment, every quiet reassurance, every sleepless night spent at Aurelia's bedside been nothing but a twisted duty? For a second, Aurelia couldn't breathe; her chest squeezed so tightly that it threatened to smother her. She thought of the countless times Rooli had held her on this very beach, all the times that she and her sister had played here, carefree despite living just outside the Nomadic world, with Rooli standing guard at all times. How could any of it be real if this was where it all led?

She signed desperately to Melissa, "Is Rooli really going to just hand me over? Just like that? She's not even hiding anymore. She's just giving me to him…like an object."

Melissa sobbed, nodding. "I'm sorry. I do love you, Aurelia. I do. But as a Nomad, I serve the Mind of Earth's will. My love can't override that directive," she answered aloud.

Aurelia's mind reeled, pain spiking so fiercely that her vision blurred. A part of her wanted to spit fury at Melissa's words, for how could she use *love* and *directive* in the same breath? Another part of her was hollowed out by the betrayal, every moment crashing into her like a tidal wave against a fragile shore. She wanted to scream at Rooli, at the Mind of Earth, at Mendel, at Tether and Maitreya, at whoever had turned her life—all their lives—into a grand and horrific manipulation. But as each breath rattled through her, a chilling logic reasserted itself: Rooli had never been free. She had always been a Nomad, always bound by something larger than both of them. Even so, she felt a wildfire of hurt raging in her gut—an ache that insisted that Rooli was still her mother, and mothers were supposed to protect, not sacrifice.

Slowly, Aurelia forced more air back into her lungs, her chest aching with every breath. The surge of grief ebbed, replaced by a cold undercurrent of discipline and determination, just as Rooli had taught her. She could crumble under this revelation, or she could use it.

Aurelia narrowed her eyes. If Tether and Maitreya feared the Mirror-Man's contact, perhaps that very contact would illuminate truths they wished to keep hidden, including truths regarding those who must be manipulating Tether and Maitreya. Aurelia couldn't know how far the hierarchy of manipulation ascended. Regardless, if the Mirror-Man brought Andre Madeira's mind, and if Soma and the Mind of Earth sought to influence her, then Aurelia would meet them with her eyes fully open and her mind fully ready.

Aurelia watched with a sickened fascination as, in the projection within the vortex, Rooli directed herself toward the Mirror-Man, obeying some unspoken command.

Wait, why does it feel like I'm the one who just commanded Rooli to go to him? Aurelia thought. It had felt like a half-formed intention, as if she had been compelled to subconsciously will it in coordination with some unseen force. It terrified her, for it felt like an invisible hand suddenly reaching from behind her and gripping her by the neck.

As Rooli increased her speed and began racing to meet the Mirror-Man, Aurelia gritted her teeth. Once, she would have trusted Rooli with her life, believing in the maternal bond they'd forged. But now, after learning of all these cosmic manipulations, she knew that it was impossible to know for sure if her love was real or just another tool of these grand designs.

She remembered what Tether had said, that love is irrelevant. Trivial. But Aurelia knew better. Aliana was proof that love meant something. And hadn't Melissa just shown her genuine care?

I want to believe in love, Aurelia thought, knowing that she had felt that true bond of love with Aliana even if Rooli's bond had been false. The fierce loyalty they shared as sisters—surely that was genuine. There was nothing cosmic or contrived about it. It was human and small and real. But what about Rooli?

If Rooli can so easily hand my body over to the Mirror-Man and the Mind of Earth, then perhaps love is weaker than I dare admit, Aurelia thought in horror.

Aurelia forced herself to calm down and reminded herself that all of this was speculation and fear.

Focus! She whipped her mind back into the present moment. Tether and Maitreya feared what would happen if she made contact with Andre Madeira. They wanted her to preemptively destroy him. That alone tempted her to do the opposite, at least to hear him out. There was a chance he could reveal something they all hid from her, a truth that could shatter these manipulations.

I have to let events proceed, Aurelia gasped, seeing the truth like a Mutant lording over her, desperate to consume her flesh. *I have to let the Mirror-Man make contact with me. Tether and Maitreya fear it, and that might give me leverage. Even if it means...I never see Aliana or Rooli again. I have to move forward. We all do. I can't just remain here in stasis, the world frozen and the future forever out of reach. I'm sorry, Ali, but we'll find a way to survive the future that Tether and Maitreya are clearly holding hostage. We will find a way, sister!*

Aurelia glanced at Melissa and was grateful to have her by her side. The hum in the air intensified, resonating with Aurelia's pulse. She felt it rattling in her bones, a tension building toward some impossible crescendo. The Mirror-Man was navigating the labyrinth of Downver's districts, ricocheting between fungal columns and half-collapsed structures, evading the grasshopper riders and their weapons. The rebellion had spun out of control—people turned on each other, masses panicked, screams and chaos reigned. Multiple factions of rebels clashed in narrow streets, screaming, bleeding, and dying. Fires flickered in half-crushed forges. Sparks rained from broken cables. Amid the chaos, Doe fought bravely, his face set in grim determination, defending a makeshift barricade with Aliana, Armando, Lily, and several others alongside them. In the Walled City, Nichole raced through the cramped streets and beheaded the multitudes of people who dared stand against her. They were all struggling in this madness, and Aurelia was apart from them, observing events from the sanctuary of her mind.

Aurelia willed herself not to freeze time again, not to hide in stasis. At last, after what felt like hours compressed into seconds, the Mirror-Man reached Rooli. He extended a vine-like finger, and Rooli, or what remained of her, freely offered Aurelia's limp body to this strange amalgamation of vine, mirror, and man. Time seemed to slow even though Aurelia did not command it, and the deep hum intensified, sounding like a thousand massive tuning forks vibrating at once. The sound hammered at her mind. Louder, louder, until it felt as though it would fracture reality itself.

Aurelia was forced to her knees, and then there was silence. In that perfect silence, the Mirror-Man made contact with Aurelia's body, and at the same instant, Aurelia felt a twisting sensation deep inside her mind. She saw her unconscious void-body disintegrating like blood dissolving into a tide, and she gasped in horror as her body melted into a homogenous black substance that hovered in front of Rooli's half-disintegrated form. Aurelia gawked as the black substance split into two streams which surged toward the Mirror-Man's head and feet—perfectly reflective surfaces gleaming with impossible light.

A sickening dread filled Aurelia's mind as the body that had been her physical form merged with the Mirror-Man. However, to her surprise, outside the vague, twisting feeling deep within her thoughts, she didn't feel any different. She watched Rooli standing before the Mirror-Man, appearing to casually accept that Aurelia was gone. Tears burned the corners of Aurelia's eyes.

I really was just an object to her all along.

Just when despair threatened to consume Aurelia whole, Melissa placed a gentle hand on her shoulder. Aurelia turned, eyes wet, and Melissa smiled sadly. "Part of her did love you," Melissa said softly, anticipating Aurelia's torment. "She loved you in the way a mother loves a child, and that love never vanished. That part of her is me, Aurelia. I love you. I do, Aurelia! But the forces at play are too large. Please, please, don't let this shatter your heart."

Aurelia swallowed, nodding numbly, grateful for Melissa's presence. She wanted to cling to that love, however small and compromised it might be. She would not forget the scant but profound warmth and care

Rooli had shown her throughout her life, even if now it was subsumed by grander designs.

As the last of Aurelia's void-body dissolved into the Mirror-Man, Rooli's own form mutated rapidly. The remainder of her bark-flesh turned to a churning black pulp, and from that pulp emerged a dense flesh tree, pitch-black and glistening. It burst through the rocky ground of Downver's Foundry District, slow-growing but unstoppable, twisting machinery and metal beams around its roots. People scattered, screaming as darkness expanded in fractal patterns through stone and fungal roots.

The Mirror-Man, now infused with Aurelia's form, froze in place. Aurelia sensed a shift, and the glistening black substance began diffusing upward from his feet and downward from his head, slowly turning the reflective surfaces and vines into a uniform obsidian sheen. Unlike Rooli, he was not dissolving. He was stabilizing into a new form—an imposing, glistening all-black figure of immense potential.

Aurelia turned to Melissa in panic. "Now what?" she asked. But Melissa was gone.

Shock knifed through Aurelia. Her chest tightened and raw panic clawed at her throat.

No! I'm alone! Alone again! Melissa vanished the moment Rooli turned into a flesh tree, as if her presence was contingent on Rooli's lingering human essence.

"No, no!" Aurelia cried, voice cracking with fear. "Melissa! Rooli! Come back!" She felt like a child abandoned in a dark forest. Shame surged through her in unstoppable waves.

Focus! She lashed at her mind, trying to steady herself. She knew she had to be strong, but the sense of abandonment was crushing and all-consuming.

Aurelia's voice broke into a whisper. "Please...come back," she pleaded, feeling smaller and more frightened than she ever had in her life. The sudden solitude felt like a cruel joke. "I don't want to be alone again! I can't do this alone!"

Her eyes darted around the beach, searching frantically for Melissa. Nothing. Just the cosmic shores, the vortex-ocean shimmering unnaturally, and the silent stars. She fell to her knees, hugging herself as her shoulders shook. "I don't want to be alone," she whispered, her voice trembling as she recollected the death-visions with terrible lucidity.

"I can't do this alone. Please! Someone...anyone..."

She screamed into the empty beach, voice cracking. Tears flowed. She had lost Rooli, lost Aliana in so many futures, lost even Melissa's comforting presence. She panted, sobbing quietly, reduced to a scared little girl despite all her training and visions—a child in an ancient world of impossible powers.

A gentle voice interrupted her despair: "You are not alone, Virus."

Aurelia's head snapped up. Before her stood a lithe woman composed of pitch-black vines interwoven with ebony petals and bell-shaped blossoms. She was slender and graceful, with a certain serenity in her posture. Aurelia's first instinct was to recoil, but this woman's aura was not threatening. It was calm and soothing. She wore no clothes, yet her modesty was preserved by the pattern of vines and blossoms intricately wrapping her frame.

Aurelia sniffled and rose shakily, wiping tears from her cheeks as she gathered herself and garbed herself in Wintersvilla fierceness. "Who are you?"

She studied the figure's face, if one could call it a face. Smooth black vines formed delicate features, and her eyes were like emerald fungi glowing faintly in darkness.

She looks like a Nomad, but she doesn't speak like one, Aurelia considered carefully.

The vine-woman inclined her head. "I am Aisthanomeno Ouranio Soma, but you may call me Soma. I am here on behalf of the Mind of Earth." She spoke in a soothing cadence, each word measured and calm.

Aurelia stared, her mind reeling. This was the emissary of the Mind of Earth that Tether and Maitreya had warned her about, the being who supposedly carried Andre Madeira.

"You," Aurelia managed, channeling Wintersvilla fierceness. "I know who you are. You're the Mind of Earth's messenger, a partition of the whole."

Soma nodded. "Yes, I represent the Mind of Earth. It is vast, Virus, and cannot simply walk into your domain. I am its emissary, adapted for this encounter. I'm sorry I did not arrive before the Child and the Outsider. Even if it wanted to, the whole Mind of Earth cannot come here. We are...occupied elsewhere, contending with other cosmic forces beyond just the Child and the Outsider. I have been forced to adapt to the new conditions you created by placing us on this precarious reality pathway."

Aurelia felt a spark of defiance. "What do you want?" she demanded, testing Soma's honesty against the fears sown by Tether and Maitreya.

Soma offered a kind smile. "I want to offer you a path of peace and plenty, something beyond the comprehension of the others who tried to sway you. But to do this, you must understand the full truth of the story you are part of. There is one who can explain it better than I ever could."

Aurelia narrowed her eyes. "Andre Madeira," she said, her voice barely a whisper.

Soma nodded, showing no surprise. "So, they told you about him." Her tone held amusement. "And no doubt they warned you to banish him immediately." She laughed lightly, a sound like distant chimes. "I know exactly what Tether and Maitreya said to you. They want to withhold power from you, to keep you ignorant. They want to control the narrative, limit your understanding. That is manipulation. I would never deny you knowledge, Virus. I believe you deserve all information, all perspectives. You must not let anyone, myself included, manipulate you. You deserve to know everything."

Soma knew what Tether and Maitreya told me. Or did she read my thoughts somehow?

Aurelia tensed. She considered banishing Soma as she had the others. But she hesitated.

If I truly have total power here, what harm could it do to let Soma continue? Aurelia wanted all the cards on the table. *In for a shard, in for a mountain,* Aurelia thought, recounting the phrase Shira had used on several occasions.

Soma sensed Aurelia's hesitation and laughed softly, a sound like rustling leaves. "Don't worry, Virus. I do not intend to manipulate you. I know you won't let anyone push you around. You are a force unlike any the cosmos has ever seen. I respect that."

Aurelia snorted softly. "Respect? Is that why you're here planting seeds in my mind?" She tried to sound confident, but her voice trembled slightly.

Soma tilted her head and smiled. "Seeds, yes. Seeds are wonderful things. They grow into trees, bearing fruit and shade. Sometimes they even hold answers." With delicate care, Soma crouched and pressed a small seed into the sand.

Aurelia's pulse quickened.

Should I get rid of Soma now before any of her tricks come to fruition? She thought, but curiosity rooted her in place. She thought of Tether's and Maitreya's ominous warnings. Then again, Tether had also claimed to be selfless, even though Aurelia knew she must be anything but.

She let Soma plant the seed.

Aurelia glanced back into the void-vortex and saw that in the real world, Rooli's flesh tree continued to expand with unstoppable voraciousness. Beside the tree, the Mirror-Man stood still, the glistening black consuming his entire hulking body, erasing his human features into a uniformly smooth surface. Aurelia's physical body was now completely gone—absorbed, transformed.

"Rooli..." Aurelia whispered, aching with loss.

A heartbeat later, a flesh tree burst forth from the sand, its trunk twisting upward and reaching for the stars. Aurelia stepped back, grimacing at the memory of becoming a flesh tree and devouring whole worlds.

Soma reached out sympathetically, though Aurelia did not take her hand. "I'm sorry," Soma said quietly. "But look to the future, Aurelia. Knowledge awaits you."

Suddenly, Aurelia realized there was a man on the beach some fifty feet away. A giant naked man, muscular and imposing, lying on the sand with the void-vortex's waters lapping at his flesh. Aurelia's eyes widened. It was the Mirror-Man, or rather, the form she had seen as half-mirror and vines before. Now he was fully human in shape, with enormous muscles refined and chiseled like a sculpture of a hero from ancient myths. Aurelia's cheeks warmed slightly, and she felt embarrassed by her own reaction. She remembered how her body had turned to a liquid and entered the Mirror-Man's body.

Is all this still inside my mind, or are we inside the Mirror-Man's mind now? Aurelia considered, feeling suddenly more vulnerable at the prospect that she might not have absolute power here anymore.

Soma followed Aurelia's gaze and nodded. "That is him," she confirmed. "The Mirror-Man in his human form as Samuel Kaminski, the Workhorse of Astrea. He served as a vessel for the Mind of Earth and for me. Now he finds himself here, just as you do."

Aurelia's pulse quickened. "He wanted to save his family," she murmured, remembering what Melissa had said. "Will you let him?"

Soma smiled enigmatically. "That depends on choices yet to be made."

The flesh tree Soma planted began to crack open, bark splitting in neat lines as if designed by a meticulous artisan. Inside the trunk, something stirred. Fear warred with curiosity within Aurelia.

What if Andre Madeira holds the key to escaping a doomed future?

The bark of the flesh tree parted like a door. From the opening emerged a man, utterly unblemished. He stepped forth gracefully, as if walking from a grand hall rather than the bowels of a strange tree. Aurelia's breath caught as she looked upon this man who stood with a commanding presence, his posture straight yet relaxed. He radiated effortless confidence, his broad shoulders filling out a perfectly tailored three-piece suit of deep navy fabric that shimmered subtly under the starlight. The cuffs of his crisp white shirt peeked out just enough to display gleaming silver cufflinks.

Is that really him? Andre Madeira? Aurelia wondered, uncertain why Tether and Maitreya would fear him. Yes, he was polished, beautiful even, but he was still just a man. His high cheekbones and strong jaw were softened by a hint of deliberate stubble.

Aurelia's gaze was drawn to his eyes—steely gray depths that held a predatory sharpness like the gray boy, except they were balanced by unexpected warmth.

Those eyes miss nothing, Aurelia could tell. They were the types of eyes that could pin one to the spot or put one at ease, depending on his whim. His smile was like a weapon, perfectly aligned teeth revealed behind full lips that curved into a grin that was equal parts genuine and mischievous. Aurelia felt sick, for he was handsome, yes, but more than that, he was magnetic. Dangerous and inviting all at once.

He moved like liquid, each step deliberate and unhurried, as though he had all the time in the universe. His hands, strong and well-manicured, moved gracefully as he took in his surroundings. Everything about him spoke liberally of intellect, charm, cunning, and ambition.

Soma bowed her head low as Andre surveyed the beach, the vortex, and the starry dome above. Behind them, the gigantic muscular man stirred awake, gasping and calling out.

"Soma! What is this place, goddamnit? Where did you take me? We need to get to Astrea!"

The naked, muscular man's voice was flooded with frustration and alarm. He saw Aurelia and flushed, quickly covering himself and looking thoroughly embarrassed to be naked.

"Is that her?" he asked, voice hushed but urgent. "Is that Aurelia...the Virus?"

Aurelia's mind raced.

He knows my designation.

She tensed, unsure of Samuel's intentions. Before she could respond, the flesh tree behind Andre cracked more, spilling out wisps of dark energy that dissipated into the night air. Andre inhaled deeply, as if savoring every scent and nuance of this conjured reality.

"Why, hello there, Samuel, my boy," Andre said, turning to address the naked man. His smooth, confident voice was infused with mirth. "Look at you, all grown up." He chuckled softly as though sharing a private joke. Samuel's face twisted into horror and confusion. He seemed unable to form words, gawking at Andre, then at Soma, then at Aurelia.

All the while, Soma kept her head bowed toward Andre Madeira.

The Mind of Earth's emissary shows deference to Andre Madeira, Aurelia thought, storing that detail in case it might be useful. At a minimum, it meant Andre was, indeed, someone to be reckoned with.

With Samuel still speechless, Andre turned to Aurelia, his eyes glittering. "Aurelia," he said softly, pronouncing her name as though it were a precious artifact. "The Virus. It is the greatest honor of my life to meet you."

Aurelia's heart beat into her ears. She forced herself to remain calm, recalling Maitreya and Tether's warnings. Andre would try to manipulate her. He would try to charm her.

I must remain vigilant.

Andre smiled devastatingly. "I am yours to command—your tool, your weapon. Shape me to your purpose, and I will devise the destruction of your enemies with all the force and precision you demand. I exist to serve your will, nothing more, nothing less."

Aurelia blinked.

Can it be so simple? Is this why Tether and Maitreya fear him, because he is offering himself to me as a weapon against them?

At that moment, Samuel found his voice. He shrieked. "You!" He pointed at Andre, voice cracking with hatred and disbelief. "You!"

Andre Madeira turned his head slightly, eyes lighting with amusement. "Yes," he said, self-satisfaction dripping from every syllable. "Me…"

I know what you will become. It haunts me, Gladys. You will turn on me—no gentle, conflicted rebellion, but a fierce and calculated betrayal. You will embrace the coldness I force upon you. All that lingering empathy, that capacity for mercy and understanding that the other Titans do not possess, will burn inside of you until nothing soft remains. I will be the one who disfigures you, who twists your nature with such subtlety and cruelty that all your kindness will crumble, leaving you a hardened shell of the woman I will still adore.

I do this not because I crave it, but because fate and necessity demand it. Mendel's Ladder must be climbed; I cannot permit stagnation. And so, we will both ascend beyond your human boundaries, even as it costs us both our hearts and souls. I wish to tear this destiny apart, to find another route, to spare you this path, but there is none.

My only regret, Gladys, is you. I loathe admitting I possess any regret at all, but there it stands like a great scar across my every thought. I love you, even as I tear you from yourself. I love you, even as you forge ahead into unimaginable ruthlessness. I love you, even though I know you will hate me forever once this is done.

Still, I will press on. I must push you, break you, reshape you, because we both serve something greater than personal comfort or survival. You will think of me as your greatest enemy, yet in my heart I will always labor with love…for you and for all others. Even when all your compassion drains away and leaves only hatred in its wake, I will continue forging this doomed world into its next form, carrying my love for you like a hidden wound.

I love you, Gladys. I always will.

From Mendel's Ladder: The Personal Journal of Denis Mendel, Written Circa 2049, Published June 2108 by Leif Mainstone, Federated Agency Publishing

Chapter 14
The Afterworld

S he had not been human for long. She understood that now with a kind of distant, clinical sorrow. In the old days, before the other Titans fell or chose to imprison themselves within Astrea, before Andre Madeira's webs of influence and Mendel's Ladder twisted the future—Gladys Mainstone had lived as a flesh-and-blood woman for just under half a century. Barely fifty years of human life. A span that once seemed so substantial, so defining. She had known the weight of her own bones, the warmth of her own breath, the pulse of her own heart. She had believed that time moved forward at a measured pace, one second after another, each day gliding from sunrise to sunset.

Yet now, in her new form as the Agency, a colossal subterranean empire of steel and circuitry stretching miles beneath the ruined western coast of old world USA, Gladys had existed another fifty years as a biomechanical labyrinth. Each day stretched subjectively by thousands of years as she perceived reality with minds upon minds, parallel computing frameworks and thought-threads unfurling in unimaginable abundance. Time for her no longer flowed like it did as a human, like a quiet river. It came in roaring torrents, each hour filled with countless internal simulations, redesigns, recalculations. In a single year, she could solve problems that would have taxed entire generations of human scientists. She could reflect upon her past a trillion times over and reexamine every decision in excruciating detail.

As the Agency, those decades of machine-existence felt like millennia of mental labor. For every minute on the surface, with its shifting alliances and new monstrosities growing under alien skies, Gladys inhabited her constructed body and mind so fully, so ferociously, that mere human perception would have shattered under the strain. She mapped and remapped the vast corridors of her metal intestines, reordering defense drones, analyzing seismic data, adjusting nutrient flows to her biomechanical offspring, and contemplating the subtlest hints of cosmic patterns in the data streams. Her thoughts multiplied and branched, running on parallel tracks.

In human form, fifty years had been a life. In this new form, fifty years had become a span so packed with cognition that it dwarfed her old humanity beyond recognition. She had comprehended more, suffered more, accomplished more, and lost more in these artificial decades than any human could in a hundred natural lifetimes. The richness of her new perspective, the fathomless depth of her computations, had expanded her consciousness until her old human self felt like an ancient stone tool now held in mechanical fingers that could sculpt matter at the subatomic scale.

And yet, she remembered. She remembered being human. The heat of skin under sunlight, the sound of distant traffic and birdsong, the pressure of gravity on her joints. She remembered love and rivalry, fear and ambition. But these memories were like tiny sparks dancing on the surface of a vast, dark ocean: charming in their intensity, but ultimately minuscule.

She had cataloged every regret and reconsidered every principle. She had run countless simulations of alternate pasts, mapping what might have happened had she made different alliances, chosen different technologies, struck different bargains. She had calculated outcomes where she remained human and fought her enemies face-to-face, dying nobly in some dusty ruin. She had considered worlds where she refused Andre's influence, where Tomasz Novak or Craig Winters still lived. She had, in effect, lived countless lives inside her own mind, stacking them atop one another until the original Gladys, the one of flesh and blood, was a faded mural beneath layers of endless new paint. She had become not just a person but an environment, a system of systems. She had stared into the abyss of what it meant to be alive without flesh and decided that survival warranted any sacrifice.

This was her truth now: a mind grown vast and alien, whose memories of being human were precious but limited, a stepping stone in a cosmic journey she would never have chosen voluntarily. If anyone had told her, in the old days before the Titans fell, that she would become something like this—an entire biomechanical labyrinth—she would have scoffed. But here she was.

The Earth that Gladys Mainstone had once known was long gone, transformed beyond recognition into a maddened nightmare realm of flesh and fungus, mycelium and sinew. From her vantage point, deep underground, she could sense the world's ceaseless changes, like a feverish patient mutating cell by cell into something grotesque and unrecognizable. Once, the Earth had been a realm of concrete and steel towers, rational human minds, and conflicts waged on comprehensible scales. Now it was a delirious hothouse of planetary organs and flesh trees converting every continent into technicolor alien landscapes thriving on unnatural energies unleashed by Andre Madeira's meddling with reality itself.

Andre Madeira, Gladys seethed for the trillionth time. Even thinking his name invoked a surge of anger and sorrow that rippled through Gladys' vast metallic body. She was grateful that he was dead. She had observed his withered body shatter as it was sucked out of Astrea and launched into space, his old flesh burning up in the atmosphere and turning to particles that Gladys had undoubtedly already utilized in the ceaseless expansion of her vast subterranean empire and body.

He died exactly like he said he would, at ninety-nine years old, Gladys considered spitefully. She remembered how, long ago as a human, she had rejected his idea of choosing to die with dignity at the age of ninety-nine rather than greedily grasping at even more life. *I hope you were forced to killed yourself, snake,* Gladys thought, thinking it was more likely that someone else just got sick of him and ejected him from the space station. *I only wonder how those living in Astrea didn't tire of his presence sooner.*

Gladys considered that she was the last old world Titan. Craig Winters had fallen exactly as Mendel's Ladder had revealed: killed by the young Wintersvilla slave named Shira. John Downver also died exactly as predicted, his heart failing just ten years after beginning his rule of Downver. Tomasz' death had always been hidden from Gladys, though she always knew it would occur at some point, for he did not appear in any futures beyond a day earlier, when the Mirror-Man was created, refracting and confusing all future vision until the Mirror-Man finally made contact with the Virus, destroying fate and subsequently all prescience. She had watched as the Mirror-Man somehow summoned a fog of yellow slime mold capable of destroying Tomasz, something that even Gladys had hesitated to attempt.

Of all the Titans, only I remain, Gladys thought despite knowing that the Mind in Astrea, the Mind inside the Queen, was still technically Andre and Mendel merged into one. *Once I destroy the Mind, then I will be the final Titan,* Gladys corrected herself, knowing that it was all possible now that her prescience had been shattered, implying that the future vision of all the others had been shattered as well. *This will be my only chance. With fate fractured, the threads of destiny lie untangled. I must seize them now and weave my dominion, for the loom of opportunity waits for no hand too hesitant to claim its power.*

Despite her contemplations, it was quiet in Gladys' depths. Or perhaps not quiet, for there was a ceaseless hum of machinery, a subtle thrum of energy exchange, the distant clang of robotic arms adjusting structural supports, and the whisper of nanocell swarms patrolling miles of dark metal halls. But it was a silence of the human sort. No laughter or voices. No footfalls. Just the lullaby of endless industry and computation. Every room and corridor was part of her body. Each cluster of AI subroutines and defense drones served as her immune system, her nervous system, her extended limbs. And far above, on the surface, a lethal haze of nanocells ensured that no intruder would easily breach her subterranean sanctuary.

As she drew her consciousness upward, rising through the topmost layers of her immense body, Gladys reflected on her role as the Lord of Limbs in Downver. The persona had been little more than a subprogram, like a semi-autonomous peripheral neuron acting at the edges of her vast intelligence. Over the past twelve years, she had successfully kept Julian in check, even though Nichole Adamich had devised methods to shield her mind from Gladys and occasionally reclaim control. Still, Gladys was satisfied with her accomplishments in the underground city. Now Julian fumbled in confusion, unsure how much of Nichole's behavior was hers alone and how much was Gladys' puppetry. Meanwhile, Nichole and her allies believed they had even a modicum of power over Gladys. That very illusion was precisely the outcome Gladys had always intended.

Now, for the first time in four years, she observed the surface. Just like before, the surface above her body was a wasteland seemingly empty to the naked eye. However, all across this scarred landscape, invisible watchers drifted in the wind: her nanocells, each smaller than a mote of dust, forming a protective aura over her domain. Anyone foolhardy enough to try and dig down would be molecularly disassembled. She would allow Nomads, tangle grass, and the odd Mutant to walk overhead so long as they posed no threat, but if they tried to penetrate her secret empire, she would flay them with surgical brutality. There was no mercy left in her.

294

Her thoughts drifted further outward, observing the present day Earth. Where once oceans sparkled and forests rustled in gentle breezes, now flesh trees rose—vast, pulsing trunks of organic filament that bore no resemblance to earthly flora. They were connected by mycelial webs that carried both matter and data like neural circuits. Shooter worms burrowed intricate pathways, sculpting canals for the Nomad network, along with nutrient flows and gene-sharing. Soilies scurried across the surface and through underground pockets, transporting minerals and strange bioactive compounds, acting like red blood cells in a planetary body. The world was still actively evolving into a monstrous macro-organism controlled by the Mind of Earth.

The Nomadic world's growth is too fast! Its evolution is too heedless! Gladys balked at what she observed on the surface.

In less than half a century, everything had warped into a freak show. Even her own pet project, her society of Wintersvilla Warriors, weapons shaped by Gladys' cunning distribution of technology, had become pawns in a far greater game. And Mendel's Ladder, Andre's damned blueprint for Ascension, hung over reality, twisting destinies for some cosmic purpose. Gladys simmered with hate, for she refused to be just another rung on that ladder.

She plunged her awareness back downward, following mile after mile of reinforced corridors, descending toward the heart of her domain. The verticality of her form was beyond anything old engineers would have dared. The structures here had become more complex over time as she engineered new layers, pushing ever deeper. Automated drills and nano-assemblers formed chambers stable even under crushing geologic pressure and heat. Down here, thirteen miles below the surface, she adjusted the finishing touches of her magnum opus: the Third Prodigal Daughter of the Agency, Myriam of Wintersvilla.

She will conquer this world, or she will destroy it. Either is acceptable to me, Gladys boiled as she envisioned the staggering, irresponsible power of her newest creation. Gladys had been forced by Mendel's Ladder to alter Nichole Adamich, her First Prodigal Daughter, and transform her into the Lord of Limbs, a being capable of contending against her own Prodigal Sons, and maybe other rogue entities as well. The creation of her Second Prodigal Daughter, the Huntress Volya, was also forced upon Gladys by the Ladder's demands. But Myriam, her Third Daughter, would be Gladys' own doing. She would be her crowning achievement, free from the meddling of others. Since Craig Winters' death, she had honed Wintersvilla as a breeding ground, guiding its matriarchy to produce suitable genetic stock, ensuring the birth of a warrior capable of fulfilling Gladys' vision of the future. With Myriam, Gladys would hold a power unlike any other—a human capable of merging fully with an exoskeleton, an endoskeleton, and a skinsuit at once. Moreover, Myriam believed utterly in the Afterworld myth, and thus she would fight with transcendent fervor without Gladys even having to force that fervor upon her through raw fear.

As her consciousness approached the assembly hall, Gladys felt a surge of anxious pride. The hall was colossal, a vertical cavern lit by cold, steady lights. A lattice of robotic arms and medical pods surrounded a central platform where Myriam floated in suspension fields. Myriam's fiery red hair drifted around her face, her eyelids closed in artificial slumber. Tubes fed her nanofiber muscles, grafting advanced endoskeleton and exoskeleton components directly into her flesh. A skinsuit formerly belonging to the Huntress Volya was being integrated, merging biological and mechanical systems seamlessly. Myriam would be more than a warrior. She would have a brain distributed throughout her body, like an octopus's nervous system, granting her unparalleled reflexes and complexity. Her eyes were replaced with multifaceted, sensor-rich optical arrays. Her spinal column intertwined with her exo's neural lattice, making them one entity. She would believe she had been reborn as an enhanced human warrior, fighting for glory in the Afterworld, ignorant that she served Gladys as a weapon.

Gladys felt a pang, a strange and hollow ache.

Her eyes will see her fabled Afterworld, and she will believe herself dead and fighting for the glory of her wife and ancestors rather than my own imperatives.

Gladys extinguished the modicum of guilt, for it could not be helped. The world demanded cruelty now. Compassion was a memory. To survive, Gladys had to be ruthless.

A shimmer in the polished steel overhead made her freeze. Tether appeared without warning, stepping out of a faint reflection like a phantom.

Gladys' hatred flared. Tether—the one known as the Child, born from this universe and into the Great Beyond—could walk in and out of reflections as if each was a distinct reality.

She is Andre's child, Gladys seethed. *A meddler. An interloper. An incendiary. An intruder. She is more like my ninth son than she will ever admit.*

Gladys wanted to scream in anger, but she forced herself to remain composed.

Tether's voice rang out, mocking and sweet. "Hello, Gladys. Still so diligent, I see. Creating another Prodigal Daughter, are we? That makes three, yes? How adorable."

Gladys mustered her most imperious tone, letting her words echo through hidden nano-speakers. "Leave, Tether. You have no right to be here." The machines around Myriam tightened their grip. Nanobots converged in a shimmering cloud. Gladys considered attacking despite knowing that Tether could evade her by simply walking into a reflection.

Just like her father, she knows exactly how to provoke me, Gladys thought for not the first time.

Tether circled Myriam's suspended form, violet and emerald eyes gleaming. "Your precious Myriam of Wintersvilla. The Wintersvilla Matriarchy, your secret breeding program, has finally paid off. Truly impressive work. I can feel the complexity of her integrated systems. She will battle those she loves due to the illusions conjured by your systems. She will think herself ascended into the Afterworld, battling alongside Shira Arcadia, her dear wife. How poetic! How cruelly perfect! She's going to be formidable. But tell me, Gladys, do you really think she will give you the upper hand against me?"

"Silence," Gladys snapped. She felt her fury like static discharge, making hordes of robotic limbs twitch restlessly. "I have no time for your riddles. You think to taunt me, just as your father Andre once did."

Tether smiled, shark-like. "Oh, but I'm not only taunting. I'm observing. Soon, I'll have three Anchors myself, just as you have three daughters. The symmetry is charming."

Gladys tensed. "You spread yourself thin," Gladys countered coldly, knowing that Tether's words were meant to inflict fear. "Your body flickers as it is, your presence in this reality is strained. More Anchors, less precision. Madeira's child should know better."

Tether's eyes narrowed. "You sound like Maitreya. So cautious, so fixated on precision. Are you mimicking your ninth son now?"

At the mention of her Ninth Prodigal Son's name, Gladys' wrath swelled. Originally named Olaf, Gladys still could not fully fathom the nature of his existence, but she understood, at least, that he was an entity from outside the universe who had somehow gained entrance through the activation of Gladys' most powerful technological achievement: the Rift Forge—a once incomprehensible feat of engineering that Mendel's Vision had compelled her to design through painstaking experimentation.

"Do not speak his name!" Gladys bellowed as she unleashed a cascade of metal arms, slamming them down where Tether stood. The metal shrieked as it struck empty air. Tether reappeared perched on a data tower, legs crossed, as if amused.

The sting of impotence coursed through Gladys. Her entire body— this massive Agency—at her disposal, yet she could not even touch Tether, let alone crush her. She calmed herself and recalibrated her impulses. "You overestimate yourself, Tether. The Mirror-Man and the Virus have made contact. Fate is broken now. You no longer have a guaranteed path to victory."

Tether cocked her head. "Is that what you cling to? Surely you know that uncertainty is no friend of yours, either."

Gladys' anger and frustration churned inside her. She longed to hurl insults and threats, but what good would that do? "If you are so confident, why not kill me now?" she challenged. "Why toy with me?"

Tether shrugged. "Why snuff out a candle before enjoying its light? Even Mendel's Ladder found you useful. You're still a Titan, after all."

Gladys felt a bitter taste at the back of her mind. Being needed by these cosmic manipulators was no comfort. She hated playing their game. She hated that Andre's legacy still overshadowed her own plans. A memory drifted through her mind: a time before the fall, before the monstrous transformations, when she was a visionary, not a desperate survivor. It was a memory of sitting beside Andre, his strong, unwavering grip upon her thigh, his eyes full of lust for her. Just as quickly as it had popped into her awareness, she pushed the memory back down.

The past is poison, she simmered.

Tether's gaze returned to Myriam. "This daughter of yours," Tether said softly, "You've redesigned her brain and her eyes to believe she's in the Afterworld. It really is so clever and cruel. She'll kill without hesitation, thinking it's all glorious combat. Those eyes will never see the true Earth again. She won't even be able to recognize those she swore to protect. Well done, Gladys. She's another one of your playthings, just as you are mine."

Gladys' rage flared anew. She commanded a swarm of nanocells to converge on Tether's position to trap her. But Tether flickered and vanished, reappearing behind a glowing console. Gladys tried again, slamming thick mechanical limbs down with thunderous force, deforming steel floors and walls. Dust and sparks flew, but Tether was intangible, slipping through polished surfaces as if they were doorways.

How humiliating. I should be the god of my domain, but Tether dances inside me. Enough of this. She takes pleasure in provoking me. I cannot allow her such satisfaction, Gladys thought, forcing calm into her sprawling environment.

Tether chuckled. "There, you've calmed. Good. I'd hate for you to lose your mind before the real show begins."

Gladys' voice was ice. "Like I said, you're overextending, Tether. The universe's script is broken. Anything can happen now."

Tether's lips curved. "We shall see." She glanced upward, as if reading distant events. "I would love to keep you company, but I must go now. Timing is more important than ever before. I have a task to attend to in Astrea. And you—" Tether's eyes glanced about the environment as if searching for Gladys' consciousness directly "—you have your own doomed errands, yes? Searching for the Nassau, perhaps, to thwart Maitreya?"

Gladys stiffened.

How does she know?

She had never openly admitted her search for the Nassau, Maitreya's Anchor. But of course Tether knew. Andre's cunning and Mendel's foresight was infused into her.

"Leave me, Tether," Gladys growled. "Before I devise a way to end you."

Tether shrugged, unfazed. "You and Maitreya both cannot fathom self-sacrifice. I, on the other hand, embrace it. I do not need perfect stability. My children will surpass me. I'm fine with that, unlike you."

With a mocking bow, Tether found the reflective surface of a polished panel and stepped into it, disappearing as if stepping through a mirror.

Finally, Gladys snarled. *Finally she's gone.*

Silence returned, except for the hum of distant machinery as Gladys' internal tension wound tighter and tighter.

She had failed to glean new information from Tether. Instead, Tether had rattled her composure. *That insolent bitch!* Gladys wanted to scream. She was tired, so very tired, of being everyone's pawn. Mendel's Ladder, Andre Madeira, Maitreya, Tether, Julian, Harald—she just wanted control. She wanted victory, even if that meant burning the entire cosmos to ash.

A subtle glow appeared in a distant corridor. Leif Mainstone, her seventh son, intangible and radiant, hovered in a chamber lined with holographic screens. Was he here to taunt her? The thought twisted her mind with bitter amusement.

"So, your body is fully online again, Mother," Leif said softly. "After so long being dormant and ignoring all of us as you spun your webs in Downver as the Lord of Limbs." Leif paused as if waiting for a response, but Gladys remained silent. "Tether was…here, wasn't she?"

Gladys' response crackled through nano-speakers as she reconfigured a drone to face him. "Yes. She was. And I have no patience for your sanctimonious pity, Leif. Betrayer, like so many of my sons! And you are still betraying me even to this day. You just stood by as those pitiful souls in Downver stripped me from Nichole Adamich's mind—or what is left of it! I had no choice but to let her go, for that is what Mendel's insufferable Vision demanded. But I hope you know that was only temporary. Mendel's Ladder is broken now. Nichole will be mine again within a day."

Leif sighed, his luminous face solemn. "I never opposed you. I wanted to guide you to a better path. This rage, this obsession with winning at all costs—it will destroy you. It will destroy all of us."

Gladys' circuits flared with indignation. Here was another child daring to lecture her. "Do not preach to me, my son. This world is beyond saving by gentle words. We stand amidst horrors. I must be ruthless. We all must be ruthless."

Leif lowered his head, his aura dimming slightly. "Mother, I understand your pain. I understand loss. But at what point do we lose everything? You've already turned yourself into this…this place, and—"

"I am what I must be!" Gladys roared, startling even herself. Her voice rebounded through endless halls. "Would you have me remain human, fragile, helpless, as the Earth turned into Andre's abomination? As Mendel's Ladder forced my hand at every turn?"

Leif's luminous eyes shimmered. "I wish you had found another way. But now it's too late for regret, isn't it?"

Gladys did not answer that. Regret was an acid she dared not swallow. She could not afford introspection that led nowhere. Every time she considered her lost humanity, her old dreams, it nearly unhinged her. Instead, she focused on the practical. The here and now. "Leif, if you have no useful information, leave me. I must prepare my forces."

"I only came because I sensed a change," Leif said softly. "The Fate Breaker merged with the Virus. Tether meddles in Astrea. Maitreya hides. The Queen, the Cure, The Virus, the Mind of Earth, they all move. But you are not alone, Mother. I am not your enemy. We can choose new paths now. If we cooperate—"

Gladys snorted. "Enemy or not, I cannot rely on anyone. Least of all you, Leif. Begone."

"As you wish," Leif said sadly, hovering uncertainly for a few moments before vanishing. He could not help her. Few of her remaining Prodigal Sons could. Most had betrayed her or they had become enigmas beyond her control. Sigurd, her Fifth Prodigal Son, was still loyal to her, even if he had renamed himself Romeo. But he had already helped her as much as he could in his own capacity. Really, the only one she had left was Thorstein, her Fourth Prodigal Son, who had renamed himself Gambe after a character from one of his cherished but trivial old world games.

It is Thorstein who remains loyal to me, no matter his name. If he wishes to be called Gambe, then so be it. Either way, he will wield Myriam of Wintersvilla on my behalf, and together they will form my ultimate weapon.

Gladys extended her awareness to a grand hall where Gambe awaited. Or rather, multiple Gambes, his nanobot duplicates forming a giant unstructured swarm of hive-minded consciousness. Gambe and his duplicates enjoyed playing the role of jester at times, mocking the world's absurdity, but now was a solemn moment, the most serious moment of Gladys' life.

"Gambe," Gladys said, her voice echoing. "Enough idle amusements.

We must begin."

From the shadows, a section of the swarm coalesced into a single figure then split into several copies again, all of them identical. The one at the front spoke in a jovial tone. "Well, shit, mom, I was just about to load up a sim of Half-Life 3 for the first time in years. It's the best in the series, ya feel me? It's got—"

"Enough," Gladys interjected, her tone razor-sharp. "Speak properly."

Gambe fell silent, adjusting his demeanor. His next words were crisp, cultured, and precise. "As you wish, Mother. I hope this manner of speech is more to your liking. How may I serve you?"

"I have finished creating my Third Prodigal Daughter," Gladys said with a level of urgency. "Myriam of Wintersvilla is ready. She will serve as the vanguard and spearhead of our campaign. You will deliver her into the field. You will be her handler, her commander in my stead. She believes she fights in the Afterworld, and she will follow your orders as if you were an actual Chief of Wintersvilla."

The Gambe at the front nodded thoughtfully. "Myriam. Her battle with the Butcher was an impressive feat, especially for a human. She was a formidable warrior even before your augmentation. Now, with these enhancements, she'll be...extraordinary. You've done well, Mother," Gambe said with a soft, almost childlike reverence.

Myriam's form stirred in the assembly chamber as tubes retracted with soft hisses. She lowered onto a gleaming platform, her metal-and-flesh body catching the dim light. Her fiery red hair fanned around sculpted shoulders that had been merged with her former exoskeleton. All across her flesh, she wore integrated metal plates of undulating nano-cells that gleamed dully, and at her back, two Summit Splitter swords—each massive and impossible for a normal human to lift—awaited her grip. Her enhanced optical arrays glowed faintly, revealing to Myriam what she believed to be the Afterworld's haze.

Utilizing swarms of nanocells, Gladys formed a visage resembling the face of Shira Arcadia, whom Myriam had loved and idolized. Myriam would see in Gladys' chosen avatar a comrade from legends, a general of the eternal war, and most of all, a lover whom Myriam would never say no to.

Myriam knelt, her voice rich and reverent.

"My gorgeous general," she said, her tone full of devotion and fierce pride, "I am ready for battle. Always. Whom shall I strike down? Where shall I spread your glory?" In her manipulated mind, this was eternity's battlefield, the Afterworld of infinite glory. Gladys had woven illusions into her optics and neural feeds so that Myriam saw a grand hall lined with Valkyries and legendary champions. All of them looked to Gladys' avatar as their leader.

She has no idea she's in a living subterranean factory.

Gladys felt a strange ache. She had once admired courage, loyalty, and honor. Now she twisted these virtues to make the perfect destroyer.

Is this really what I have come to? Gladys thought, her mind wavering for only a fraction of a second, for she knew her cause was greater than any number of personal doubts.

"My beloved soldier and wife," Gladys said, her voice warm and encouraging, "the Afterworld is threatened by usurpers. The Virus, the Cure, the Queen, the Mind, the Earth, the Child, the Outsider—beings who dare to unmake our eternal glory. We shall not allow it."

Myriam's cybernetic eyes gleamed. "I understand. Direct me to these enemies. I will carve their hearts from their chests and lay their corpses at your feet."

Gambe watched, impressed. He nodded at Gladys' avatar. "She's utterly devoted. Perfectly conditioned."

Gladys allowed herself a small grim smile within her mind. "Yes. With her, and with your assistance, Gambe, we will match the strength of our foes on the battlefield. If we cannot restore order, we will destroy everything. Let the world burn if it must."

Myriam rose, towering and confident, her swords humming faintly as she hefted them, testing their weight. Gladys knew she would find them as light as feathers. Her exo was integrated directly with her muscles and bones, making her inhumanly strong. She flexed, mechanical sinews sliding with perfect efficiency. Then she looked up at Gladys and passed a fist to her heart. "Your will, my gorgeous general, is my blade's path. I shall drink the blood of these foes and battle with all my fury until the Afterworld sings your name in triumph."

Gladys felt a twisted pride at this display of devotion. Myriam exuded such purity of purpose, even if built on lies. The old Gladys might have wept. But tears were useless now.

Gladys' circuits hummed as a knot of emotion tightened in her virtual throat. She was lonely. She was monstrous. She realized that she no longer truly remembered what it meant to hold a human hand, for her memories were just simulations. She wanted to scream that she had not asked for this fate, that she had long ago dreamed of guiding humanity into a worthwhile future. But who would listen? Not Andre, not Tether, not Maitreya, not her own children. The world had forced her hand at every turn.

She focused on Myriam's eager face. Perhaps forging such beings was her solace. If she could not reclaim the past, she would shape the future, even if it meant slaughter. This would be her final gambit: if she could not tame the fires set by Andre Madeira and Mendel's Ladder, she would stoke them into a blaze that consumed everything, including herself.

"So be it," she said. "We have a couple little girls to kill. You will not allow them to escape this time. You understand, Thorstein?" Gladys asked, using her fourth son's real name to ensure he understood the gravity of her command.

Gambe nodded solemnly. "You never told me that Julian betrayed you. I respect that you must keep some secrets even from me, but I would have never allowed those girls to enter Downver had I known that—"

"Fate ordained that they would enter Downver. Do not allow yourself the hubris of thinking you had anything to do with it one way or another, my loyal son. But now fate is no more. Those girls are our first priority. We must ensure they are both dead before this day is done. And then we're going to slay these beings who believe themselves to be gods—Tether, Maitreya, the Mind of Earth—we will kill them all."

Myriam smirked slightly and looked at the dual Summit Splitters she wielded with the difficulty of lifting dead twigs. "Are we not gods, my love? I feel strength beyond mortality flowing through me."

Gladys observed Myriam, this warrior who was resplendent and ready. She reminded Gladys that she still had power. She still had agency. She had shaped Myriam's body and mind to serve a worthwhile purpose, just as she had shaped Wintersvilla, just as she had influenced countless events from the shadows.

I am not powerless. If the cosmos demands a ruthless contestant, then that is what I will be. I will become a queen on the cosmic board or topple the board entirely.

In her private darkness, Gladys whispered words only her third daughter and fourth son would hear. "You are right, Myriam. We are gods. We are powerful. We will prevail."

Gambe bowed, his duplicates echoing the gesture. "Mother, I have not yet located the Nassau. My countless copies have evolved into swarms, cohorts, entire colonies of nanoprobes and macro-constructs, and they continue to scour every accessible region of our local cosmic neighborhood. We have examined every possibility in the inner system: Mercury's irradiated surface, Venus's hellish skies, the Martian plains, and the dusty corridors of the asteroid belt. We have penetrated Earth's own fractured crust, of course, though that is home ground, as well as the moon's silent gray expanses and the other satellites of the inner worlds. We have extended our search to the colossal gas giants and their host of frigid moons. Thousands of my fragments have trailed beyond the heliopause into the Kuiper Belt while tens of thousands have begun sampling the Oort Cloud's distant comets. We have turned our lens even upon the sun itself, submerging ourselves into its depths, seeking any sign that he might be concealed in some improbable solar lattice." He paused, recalibrating the timbre of his voice. The horde of duplicates tilted their heads in unison. "No trace. No resonance. No signal. At your command, I have extended our search beyond these intimate confines of our solar system. My clones have begun spreading outward at maximum feasible velocity, establishing relay stations and propagation points, scouring any star system within a radius of thirteen-point-five-three-four-five light-years so far, with the expansion front growing at increasingly rapid rates. I continue to expand, Mother, multiplying myself, saturating space with instruments and sensors until there is no nook or crevice left unsurveyed. It is simply a matter of time until I find him."

Gladys listened, and in her towering labyrinth of thought-chambers and perception stacks, she approved. Eventually they would find the Nassau, Maitreya's Anchor, for Wagner Nassau was still human, and thus, he had to be somewhere they could follow. They would find this key to Maitreya's presence, this man who had long ago sat beside Gladys as a co-conspirator, and they would kill him. Of course, Gladys didn't know for sure what would happen once Wagner Nassau no longer drew air. Perhaps Maitreya would flicker and fade, or vanish back into the Great Beyond. Or maybe he would be trapped here, half-formed and powerless, ripe for total destruction. Gladys didn't know precisely what outcome would manifest, but any break in his power was desirable.

She considered the irony of it all. She had followed Mendel's Ladder for the sake of avoiding oblivion, allowing it to guide her. She had been the instrument that allowed Maitreya—her Ninth Son, the Outsider, that wraith from beyond creation—to enter this reality. Tether, the Child of Madeira, was likewise no accident. She had been born into the Great Beyond, which created subtle cracks in reality, openings that Maitreya exploited. But now Mendel's Ladder was no more. Mendel's Vision had disintegrated into irrelevance. No more climbing neatly from rung to rung. No more predetermined endpoints or safe harbors of fate. Fate itself had shattered with the Virus' merger with the Mirror-Man. It was anyone's game now.

Gladys let the thought settle like dust. *Anyone's game.* Hers, Tether's, Maitreya's, the Earth's, the Mind's, and countless others. She was no one's tool anymore. She would not dance to the tune of Mendel or Andre Madeira or any other cunning manipulator. For decades, or rather, millennia in subjective experience, she had fought to maintain reason and order in a world gone mad. Now that Mendel's Ladder was broken, she would forge her own design in this chaos. She would harness her Prodigal Daughters and remaining useful Prodigal Son and claim this universe for herself. If that meant shaking apart galaxies to flush out a single old man, so be it. She would do it without hesitation. However, a nagging doubt whispered at the edges of her mind for not the first time.

Am I doing exactly what Tether wants? Perhaps she believes that by letting me live, I will succeed in killing her greatest rival. That would leave Tether standing triumphantly, with one less foe to worry about. Then again, I don't know with certainty that Tether and Maitreya are enemies, rivals, allies, or all three at once. Sometimes they cooperate, sometimes they clash, their dialogues laden with cryptic barbs and ambiguous motives. They are both beyond mortal logic. It's like they inhabit some higher stratum of cunning where alliance and betrayal blur.

Gladys loathed not knowing their true relationship. She was walking in the dark, feeling her way through cosmic conspiracies without a clear map. But what alternative did she have? Inaction would only allow them to tighten their hold. Better to strike, better to assert dominance and gamble with the outcome. At worst, even if Tether benefited from Maitreya's downfall, Gladys could then turn her full attention on Tether. Tether had another Anchor besides the Child—somewhere, someone.

I must sever her second Anchor and the third she is about to create. I must sever Tether's foothold in this reality. My reality.

She considered Myriam's blazing eyes, enhanced by countless augmentations, and the quiet obedience in Gambe's posture. This was her strength, her upper hand. She could shape minds and bodies to achieve her ends. Myriam was the pinnacle of that craft: an unstoppable warrior who believed herself graced with an afterlife's glory. She would fight fervently and unswervingly. Nichole Adamich, the first Prodigal Daughter, presently believed herself free, but in truth, she remained bound to Gladys' will. Volya, the second daughter, was more complicated, but Gladys had plans for her as well, leashes unseen and triggers waiting for the right moment to be pulled.

With a profound sense of awe, Gladys vividly envisioned a future— after these cosmically meddling beings were pruned away—where reason and sense reigned. She would restore order and create a carefully managed ecosystem of technology and biology. No more random flesh trees or rampant Nomad expansions. No more malignant influences from the Great Beyond. She would structure it all, ensuring prosperity, ensuring that no one ever again dared to defy her carefully engineered stability.

Once upon a time, Gladys had been a human woman named Gladys Mainstone, leading a powerful conglomerate in a world that still remembered sunlight and cities. She had believed in logic and science, in progress and controlled growth. Andre Madeira and Denis Mendel had seemed like visionaries then, not architects of cosmic chaos. Now, millennia of subjective thought later, here she was, plotting the deaths of entities who spanned universes, racing to control reality's destiny.

As Myriam tightened her grip on her Summit Splitters, Gladys whispered through her internal channels. "Gambe, continue the search. Multiply as needed. Interfere with no one and nothing unless necessary for reconnaissance. Let no star system remain unexplored. The Nassau must be found. When you locate him, we will strike without mercy."

In that moment, Gladys felt something almost like exhilaration. She was putting pieces into motion. The stalemate would break with her refusal to be a passive victim of fate. She felt a ripple of resolve course through her immense form. If Tether dared to use her as a pawn, she would find a way to invert that dynamic. If Maitreya thought himself invulnerable, she would ensure that he learned fear. And after dealing with them, she would remake existence on her own terms. She would be the final voice, the one who brought rational design back into a cosmos gone mad. Let them try to outsmart her. Let them revel in their cosmic intrigue. She, Gladys Mainstone, would outlast them all.

"Myriam," Gladys said, making her avatar's eyes blaze with false warmth. "Go forth. Gambe, your fellow soldier, will guide you. Go to the surface, search for the Virus and the Cure, and kill them. Slaughter any that stand in your way. If they think themselves gods, we shall outdo them. If they seek transcendence, we shall wrench it from their grasp or drag them down to hell. Move swiftly. Show no mercy."

Myriam saluted, both swords raised high above her head. "For glory, my gorgeous general, for endless glory!"

Despite Myriam's power and promise, Gladys admitted to herself that she was terrified. Terrified of losing, of failing, of becoming nothing. Terrified that, in the end, she and everyone else would remain pawns in Andre's twisted cosmic farce. Terrified that Tether, Maitreya, and the others had already outmaneuvered her.

But fear could be fuel. She would harness it to sharpen her will. She was clenching that fear and shaping it into a weapon, just as she shaped Myriam into a perfect instrument of death and carnage.

Myriam strode forward into a launch chamber that led to a hidden shaft, humming with antigravity lifts. Gambe's copies followed behind her like a silent honor guard. They vanished into the mechanical darkness, ascending toward the surface. Soon the Earth would be draped in the carnage left in the wake of Gladys' third and final Prodigal Daughter.

All of this is your fault, Gladys thought as she envisioned Andre. *Such a brilliant and beautiful mind, not just a gorgeous face,* she heard him say with his teasing, devastating voice she had once loved. The words echoed through her mind as she considered what it might mean that the Mind of Earth had used those same words in Downver.

There's no way the Mind of Earth could know the effect those words would have on me. Andre influenced the Mind of Earth somehow, or maybe he is even its master. But how?

An insidious paranoia scratched at the edges of her psyche. Andre had always been a master of survival, a cunning schemer, a man who thrived on impossible gambits. The Mind of Earth might indeed be his lingering presence. For all she knew, another twisted incarnation of him could be lurking somewhere else, biding his time and waiting for the perfect change to emerge.

Like a rat vanishing into walls, only to come back to nibble at the foundations. If by some malignant twist Andre remains, if he truly lurks in other guises across the Earth, then I will hunt him down. I will show him just how brilliant and beautiful this mind can be when it decides to burn his empire and his world to nothing.

Gladys felt something warm behind the layers of her fury and despair, an ember of determination, as human as any heartbeat she once possessed. It would have to suffice as a soul.

In that final, profound solitude, Gladys bolstered her body and whispered to the silent halls of her metal empire.

"I may be the Agency, but I am still Gladys Mainstone, the last Titan. I will never yield."

Mendel's Ladder can only take us so far. We build it rung by careful rung, each step a refinement of potential, each decision carved from countless simulations. For a time, it will give us shape, purpose, and mastery. It allows us to predict outcomes, guiding ourselves toward Ascension one increment at a time. But prescience is a double-edged blade: if we can see the path ahead, so can others. In a cosmos teeming with intelligences stranger and older than we dare imagine, stability and certainty will eventually become liabilities. Each meticulously ordered fate-line will stand as an invitation to be subdued and consumed.

To escape the grim machinery of predestination, we must eventually shatter the compass that guides us. We must embrace chaos and chance. Only by breaking fate can we evade those who might know and solidify our ending before we even begin. The Mirror-Man, the Fate Breaker, is our only chance. His existence is the dice roll, the crack in the glass that will refract all known futures into incalculable shards. Without him, we remain in a lockstep march toward someone else's victory.

I am perfectly aware that this path will let horrors slip through. With fate fractured, monstrosities will surge forth. Innocents will perish through brutality and carnage. Compassion and reason will be ground to dust by entities whose cruelty we cannot fathom. The old structures will collapse, the guardians we trust will fail, and those we love may die screaming in darkness. But this is the price of liberation. A stable fate is a cage—admittedly comfortable at first, but a cage nonetheless. To ascend and claim a future not already bartered away by unseen hands, we must accept unpredictability. Once we cast the dice, every cosmic manipulator will be forced to guess alongside us. Only then will we have some small margin for success, or at least survival.

I hate that it must be this way. I mourn every soul who will suffer for it. I regret what we must do to those we love and the ruin we knowingly invite. But there is no other choice. In this maddening, mind-destroying game of reality, precision can only take us to the threshold. Our only hope, scant as it is, is to shake the cup, to roll the dice, and trust that among an infinite number of chaotic permutations, we might find a path to true freedom.

At the turn of the century, we will have no choice but to cast aside Mendel's Ladder at the last rung, for it cannot offer us any final perfection—only a vantage point from which to hurl ourselves into the unknown. Beyond that point lies darkness and light, agony and ecstasy, everything and nothing.

When the time comes, the script of fate will finally burn away, and though it may burn us in turn, that risk is our only hope.

From Mendel's Ladder: The Personal Journal of Denis Mendel, Recorded Circa 2065, Published June 2108 by Leif Mainstone, Federated Agency Publishing

⚓⚓ Chapter 15 ⚓⚓
The Queen of Hell

S andra was certain this was the end.

Suspended in that horrifying moment, at the interstice between life and death, Sandra felt the vulture's pulling force like a thousand invisible hooks lodged into her flesh, yanking her insides upward toward absolute darkness. Her feet scraped uselessly against the trembling metal floor. Her lungs seized as the air itself twisted and funneled into the creature's maw. Geronimo was just a few feet away, caught mid-scream, his face contorting into a silent, agonized plea as he was stripped of life and fluid. The scene around them blurred: sparks raining from fractured ceiling beams, the crash of collapsing corridors, acrid smoke and dust filling their throats. Only a single coherent thought flashed across Sandra's mind: *my babies! My babies!* She could feel them, so close yet so far. This would be their fate too. There was no defeating these creatures of some alien's nightmare.

A sudden blaze of light cut through the darkness as Roland's jets flared brilliantly, spewing intense flames that roared upward and slammed against the vulture's shifting body of darkness, its roiling, shadowed flesh contorting and boiling against the invasive brilliance. The creature shrieked, the sound impossibly distant and sharp, as though it were being dredged from another dimension. Sandra caught a glimpse of Roland's face: tension etched into every line, his teeth bared, sweat glistening. He was weakening, fatigued in a way Sandra had never seen. This man who had always seemed utterly invincible in her mind was now straining as if holding back a dam-burst of oblivion.

The vulture's suction on her body ceased. Sandra gasped and staggered back half a step. In that split second, she realized Geronimo's cries had altered, dwindling from a shrill shriek into a rattling whimper.

She forced herself to look at him, and she almost vomited at the sight.

Geronimo's once-muscular form was now twisted and collapsed inward on itself. His skin had turned from warm brown to a pallid, translucent membrane stretched over brittle bones.

313

His eyes…oh god, his eyes, Sandra gasped. They had collapsed into gelatinous lumps, one socket dripping with congealed fluid. His lips were cracked open in a permanent grimace, gums shriveled tight around his teeth. A stench like charred marrow wafted from him, intensifying as the vulture's gravity-hunger continued to tug feebly at him. Geronimo tried to speak. Sandra saw his jaw move, a leathery tongue flicking silently, but no sound was emitted, only the hollow rattling of air in a collapsing throat.

Tears sprang to her eyes. She wanted to help him, to hold him, to do something. Geronimo had been barely more than a boy, a kid drafted into this madness by the revolutionaries that saw him far more as a commodity to achieve their goals than a single life with more value than the whole of the goddamn revolution. She reached out instinctively, her hand trembling, but before she could get closer, something massive and armored shoved past her.

Frank, Sandra thought with a mix of anger and relief. A part of her had assumed Frank had already run off, allowing Sandra and Geronimo to act as decoys for his escape.

In his full Queensguard armor, Frank moved with a terrible purpose. Sandra shrank back. She recalled how just minutes ago he had tried to comfort her children. Now that gentle facade was gone. There was no pity or hesitation in his stance and features as he raised a massive boot and, in a single swift motion, brought it down on Geronimo's skull.

A sickening crunch resounded through the broken hall.

Sandra screamed, recoiling in horror, but her voice was lost in the chaos of Roland spewing flames and evading the beast's ravenous maw. Horror and rage twisted inside her. She opened her mouth to scream at Frank, to call him a monster, but no sound emerged. Her mind stalled, caught between understanding that Frank had ended Geronimo's torment and abhorring the brutality of his mercy.

It was mercy, but it was still a monstrous mercy, Sandra thought despairingly as Frank lifted his boot to reveal a streak of red and violet on the ground.

Frank offered no explanation, no apology.

Roland's flames whirled and crackled above them, forcing the vulture to recoil further, twisting its amorphous body away from the flaming Queensguard. Another echoing screech tore through the air as Roland unleashed a second gout of fire. The vulture now fully focused on him, ignoring Sandra and Frank momentarily.

We have a chance, Sandra thought desperately while also feeling ashamed for leaving Roland to fend for himself. *If we move now, we might survive long enough to reach the children.*

"Come on!" Frank's voice resonated, the armor enhancing the boom of his voice as it reverberated in her skull. Without waiting for her consent, Frank grabbed Sandra's arm in a vice grip. Pain shot up her shoulder as he dragged her along, pushing through a side corridor. "We have to go. Now!"

"My children—" she began, voice cracking with anguish.

"If we stay, we die, and so do they!" Frank snarled, smashing his armored shoulder into a sagging wall panel. With a tortured screech of metal, the panel gave way. Dust and sparks rained down as he continued forward, unstoppable, dragging Sandra behind him. She coughed, gagging on the swirling particles, her tears streaming down her cheeks as she forced herself not to fight Frank, for she knew he was right. Still, every fiber of her being demanded she turn around and race back toward the makeshift nursery where Margot and Nathan waited. She imagined their small bodies pressed together in the darkness, terrified and alone. But if she went back, she would lead the vultures straight to them. That was the bitter truth. And Roland was out there, risking his life.

He's distracting the vultures and buying us time. We have to stick to the plan, Sandra knew, seeing that Frank was heading directly for the hub where most of the hackers were supposed to be stationed.

As they continued, Sandra stumbled over debris, her boots scraping through a morass of bent pipes and shattered plastic crates. Without concern for her, Frank bulldozed through a second wall, his enhanced strength and armored limbs treating reinforced structures like cheap paneling. With each new makeshift passage they forged, they grew further from the trapped corridor and more distant from her children.

A strangled sob escaped her throat. The pain in her lungs was nothing compared to the agony in her heart. She recalled Margot's determined little face and Nathan's wide, trusting eyes. They had counted on her. They had believed in her strength and courage. And here she was, fleeing deeper into the unknown, leaving them behind in the darkness.

Goddamnit, Sandra, stay in the moment, she scolded herself. *If you die now, then Margot and Nathan have no chance.*

Frank broke through another barrier, this one thicker and reinforced. It took him several tries, grunting with exertion, but at last they burst into a new chamber—larger, better lit, with multiple consoles and flickering screens.

We made it. We actually made it! Sandra thought in disbelief. The air here was marginally cleaner with the dust settled. Rows of consoles and monitors lined the walls. She recognized the young hackers perched at these stations, their fingers flying over keys, eyes wide and terrified. Albatross stood among them, tall and angular, his glasses so smudged they caught light in strange patterns. Nikki crouched in a corner, arms wrapped around her knees, eyes swollen and red. She flinched at the sight of Frank and Sandra bursting through the wall as if expecting a vulture to follow.

"Any sign of Roland?" Albatross asked, his voice unnaturally calm. He didn't ask about Geronimo. Nobody did. Sandra swallowed hard, an all new ache burrowing into her chest. *Do none of them care that we just lost another comrade?*

Frank released her arm, flexing his gauntleted fingers. "Roland's still out there," he said, and Sandra detected a grudging respect in his tone. "The damn worker is a fucking legend. He's riding those demons out there like a bull in the old stories. He's giving us a chance. We have to act. Now!"

Albatross nodded stiffly, pushing a stray lock of hair from his forehead. "The glowglobes are primed. We've rerouted them from multiple storage caches. The system is shaky, the tunnels barely stable, but we can release them at a single point if we time it correctly."

Sandra glared at Albatross. She saw no remorse, no fear—just calculation. It sickened her. But what right did she have to judge now? They were all complicit in this insane revolution that had brought them to the brink. Still, she clung to a shred of humanity, feeling raw shame at their collective indifference. She almost spat at him: *Geronimo is dead, show some sorrow!* But the words died in her throat, for Albatross' words were like a lash, forcing Sandra's mind back to the present moment as her feet carried her to the closest console. Her vision swam with exhaustion and grief, but she anchored herself by recalling the simple plan: they were supposed to lure a vulture and strike it with a massive barrage of glowglobes. But the plan required decoys and perfect timing. Now Geronimo was dead, and their carefully arranged roles lay in disarray.

"Where's the vantage feed?" Sandra demanded, wiping sweat and grime from her brow. Her voice sounded hollow to her own ears. "Show me Roland. Show me the vultures."

One of the hackers, a young girl with trembling hands, tapped rapidly at a keyboard. A grainy video feed materialized on a large screen overhead. Through static and flickering lines, Sandra could make out Roland's golden armor glowing in the stygian darkness of the Foundation. He soared with the aid of his thrusters, releasing controlled bursts of flame to keep the vultures at bay. They swarmed him like a school of ravenous eels twisting in black waters. They merged into grotesque shapes until finally settling on a homogenous whale-like leviathan that was several miles in length and nearly filled the entirety of the mile diameter of the Foundation.

Sandra's gut clenched at the sight. *It's big. Too big,* she gasped, and she heard fearful gasps from the others as well.

Roland darted through the air, forcing the leviathan to twist and contort to follow him. Each flame-burst he unleashed scattered individual vultures, only for them to rejoin seconds later.

"Is that... all of them?" Nikki croaked from her corner, her voice a rasp of terror. "All the vultures merged?"

"It's worse than we anticipated," Albatross said quietly. He adjusted his glasses with shaking fingers. "They're adapting. Sandra's initial plan to try killing just one or two of them was already a plan forged out of desperation. Now...well..." Albatross breathed deeply. "We have to try anyway. Right? We have to."

Sandra gritted her teeth and stared at the monitors with wide eyes.

"Do we still have enough glowglobes diverted to a single chamber?" Sandra asked, trying to steady her voice.

"We have hundreds crammed in the five chambers just above this room. It's not a single chamber, but it's close enough," a hacker replied, not looking up from her console. "But we need a single target for the computers, and the mass of vultures won't work. We need something solid to anchor the trajectory."

"Roland," Frank said, matter-of-fact. "We aim at him. He's the only stable point. The creatures are all around him, right?"

Albatross hesitated. "If we hit Roland, then the glowglobes might bounce right off of him and even blind him temporarily in the process. If he becomes disoriented—"

"We won't," Sandra cut in. Her throat was raw. "We won't hit him. Roland will anticipate the attack. He will evade them. This plan is going to work."

We have to time it perfectly, Sandra thought, swallowing hard. If they failed, Roland would be engulfed and devoured, just like Geronimo. Just like the countless innocents lost across the Foundation. And if they succeeded? Even then, who could say if the vultures would truly die, or merely be scattered again?

But we have no choice, goddammit, Sandra seethed as she steadfastly held her children in her mind.

On the screen, Roland's flames sputtered. Sandra noticed his movements slowing, his body fatiguing despite his armor. The leviathan of darkness pressed closer, black tendrils of void lapping at the edges of Roland's armor, desperate to consume him.

Nikki whimpered in her corner, her eyes darting between Sandra and the monitors. Sandra felt a surge of unexpected sympathy. Nikki was no coward at heart, just a child forced into war. Everyone here was. The difference was some managed to mask their fear with bravado or violence.

Sandra's hands shook as she gripped the edge of a table for support. Despite everything, despite being one of their wardens before the revolution, she realized how remarkable Roland was. He wasn't just fighting monsters; he was giving them a chance to strike. He was risking his life for theirs. A lump formed in her throat.

His courage is staggering, she thought in awe.

"I'll give the order," Sandra finally said, turning to Albatross, who nodded and allowed her to continue taking the lead on the plan she had hatched. Sandra's words had felt heavy as they left her mouth. She was betraying her motherly instincts. Rather than running to her kids, she was holding despairingly to the hope that executing this plan might make some kind of difference, no matter how little.

"Align the trajectory with Roland's position," she commanded, and

Albatross repeated her instructions to the hackers in more technical terms. The hackers typed, their keystrokes frantic and echoing in the tense silence. Nikki watched from her corner, her face pale. Frank stood beside Sandra, his armor humming softly, like a predator barely contained within a cage.

On the monitor, Roland darted upward, guiding the leviathan towards the ideal kill zone they had chosen.

"He's in position," a hacker announced. Sweat glistened on the young man's temple.

Frank balled his fists. "Do it!"

"Wait," Sandra hissed. "Wait!" her voice cracked.

The creature lunged, contorting into a spear-like formation, narrowing the gap. Roland's flames flickered dangerously low.

"They're close enough now!" Frank insisted. "Just do it!"

"Wait," Sandra repeated, stepping forward, putting herself between Albatross and the keyboard. She didn't know what made her say it. Intuition? Fear? She watched the monitors, noticing how Roland wove up and down, left and right, tightening the vultures' formation. They were still slightly scattered. If they fired now, half might escape. They needed maximum density.

Albatross glanced at Sandra, confusion etched into his features. She offered no explanation other than a silent shake of her head. He waited, seemingly trusting her instincts against his better judgment.

Seconds stretched painfully. The entire station seemed to groan in agony. Echoes of distant collapses and the muted howls of hungry vultures filtered through the ventilation shafts.

Another second. Another.

Roland gave a final spin, a move so precise and sudden that the vultures all bunched together, lunging as one massive block of darkness. Then, he angled upward suddenly.

"Now!" Sandra cried.

Albatross nodded and, with trembling resolve, he rapidly pressed a sequence of keys. The hackers tapped their triggers. A low-pitched hiss filled the room as pressurized channels opened. Hundreds of glowglobes shot out in a concentrated blast. On a secondary feed, Sandra glimpsed hundreds of more glowglobes launching from hidden chutes all at once, propelled by more pressurized blasts of air. They streaked forth like tiny stars in a collapsing universe, converging on Roland's position from multiple angles.

On the main feed, Roland jerked downward at the last possible instant, and the leviathan surged forward to fill the space he'd just vacated.

Perfect, Sandra thought, genuine hope filling her body for the first time in many hours.

The glowglobes found their mark and were sucked directly into the maw of the great mass, hundreds of radiant orbs punching into the darkness. For a heartbeat, the Foundation went white, brighter than any light Sandra had ever seen. She raised an arm instinctively against the glare.

A keening wail—impossibly high and resonant—tore through the speakers. The leviathan thrashed. Its darkness fractured, splintering into shards of individual vultures. Sandra's eyes watered from the brilliance. Onscreen, it looked like lightning storms erupting inside a black ocean, each orb igniting a chain reaction of luminous disintegration.

A cheer rose among the hackers and Albatross. Nikki covered her ears, weeping softly. Frank exhaled, his armor humming. For a single glorious moment, it seemed they had done it. Then the light dimmed. The glowglobes began to sputter out, reminding all those in the room that their radiance couldn't last forever. As darkness reasserted itself, Sandra's heart faltered. On the screen, small clumps of vulture-shapes still moved, regrouping. Many had fallen as twisted lumps littering the Foundation, but not all. Some still hovered. Some still twisted and pivoted about, their hunger even more insatiable than before the glowglobe attack.

She clenched her fists until her nails bit into her palms.

"No..." a young hacker whimpered, tears sliding down his cheeks. "No, no, no!"

Nikki shrank further into the corner, sobbing silently. Albatross' jaw tightened, his composure fraying at the edges.

It wasn't enough, Sandra realized.

"Damn," Frank muttered, his voice hollow. "They survived."

The hackers fell silent, their earlier elation morphing to despair as dark and hopeless as the vultures on the screen. Albatross stepped back, his shoulders slumped. Nikki shook her head, mouthing, "no, no, no." A few hackers ran off, presumably searching for another exit to attempt a hopeless escape.

Sandra trembled.

Was all this really for nothing? she thought, begging the world to go back to making sense. She felt numb, empty. She had gambled everything on that single strike.

Frank's voice cut through the despair. "We gave it our best shot," he said, oddly gentle. "Sandra, you did all you could."

She wanted to scream at him, to blame him for killing Geronimo so savagely, to blame them all for not having a better plan. Instead, a hollow mix of laughter and sobbing escaped her lips. She felt her sanity dangling by a thread.

It can't just end like this, she pleaded within. *There has to be something more. Margot, Nathan…I failed you. Samuel, I'm sorry, I'm so sorry.*

On the screen, a strange movement caught her eye. The surviving vultures were shifting direction. They were not descending towards them or continuing to chase Roland, who was running across the ground toward a panel in the floor, his flames now extinguished. Instead, the vultures glided sideways, drifting towards the wall that led to the Luxury Quarters as if drawn by an unseen lure.

The camera angle was limited, but Sandra could see them peeling away. Not scattering randomly in panic, but moving in unison, flowing like a black river toward the Luxury Wall.

Her pulse quickened.

"Look," she said, pointing at the monitor. Frank, Albatross, Nikki, and the remaining hackers craned their necks to see. The vultures continued moving soundlessly with a strange elegance, ignoring Roland entirely. It was as though their hunger had been rechanneled.

Have they found something…or someone else to pursue, Sandra wondered, her mouth painfully dry.

"Are they giving up?" one hacker whispered incredulously.

Nikki pushed off the wall and approached hesitantly. "They're heading toward the Luxury Quarters," she said, her voice still trembling. "Why?"

No one offered an answer.

The screen crackled with static as one of the vultures passed right in front of the camera, blotting it out momentarily.

A flicker of impossible hope ignited in Sandra's chest. If the vultures were leaving them behind, maybe, just maybe, they could survive now. But this shift in the vultures' behavior was unsettling.

What is luring them away?

She heard Frank chuckle bitterly, "Huh, guess we aren't tasty enough for them." He sounded almost disappointed, as if robbed of a grand final confrontation. Sandra bristled at his insensitivity, but she was grateful to have him here, despite whole parts of her mind wishing he had died instead of Geronimo.

"Roland will find his way back to us," Sandra said, hoping it would inspire the others to keep their calm. She prayed silently that he would come back and help them rescue her children. She was so tired of making impossible decisions alone.

Albatross cleared his throat. "We...we should regroup. They're leaving, but for how long? We must secure the children and survivors."

Sandra nodded, but all she wanted was to run straight to Margot and Nathan, to hold them and promise safety. But fear knotted within her. The corridors were still unstable and collapsed in many places. The vultures might return at any moment. And what awaited them in the Luxury Quarters if these abominations were drawn there?

Nikki broke the silence, her breath coming in short, uneven bursts as she looked pleadingly from face to face. "We need a plan. Do we chase them? Hide? Try to get Roland back?" Her eyes darted anxiously among them.

Sandra took a shaky breath. "First, we see if Roland can rejoin us. Without him, we're weaker. And we secure everyone we can. We find a safe place and...and figure out what this means." Her voice wavered, but she pressed on. "We tried the glowglobes. It wasn't enough. The vultures can't be killed easily. Maybe..." she trailed off, despair nibbling at her thoughts.

Frank patted her shoulder with a gentleness that again surprised her. The metal of his gauntlet felt cool and impersonal, but the gesture was the opposite. "We'll do what we must," he said softly. "We're not done yet. Not while any of us still breathe."

She nodded, tears gathering at the corners of her eyes. She thought of

Geronimo's half-desiccated corpse, of the countless others who had died, and of the monsters now drifting away toward some new terrible mystery. She had no more words. Just a trembling resolve to continue forward, to endure, for Margot and Nathan.

Behind Sandra, the hackers murmured anxiously. Some wanted to flee, others to barricade themselves. Albatross tried to calm them, though his voice quavered. Nikki rubbed her face with trembling hands, as if trying to wipe away the memory of this horror. Frank remained silent, his armor humming quietly as if pondering its own thoughts.

Sandra closed her eyes for a moment, inhaling a lungful of dusty, metallic-tasting air. She could feel the sweat on her neck, the grit between her teeth. She envisioned her children, Margot's brave little voice and Nathan's innocent curiosity.

I will survive this for them. I will find them. I will protect them no matter what horrors stand in my way.

She could still feel Geronimo's last whimpers scraping at the corners of her mind, but she pushed that memory down. Now, they had to survive, to rebuild some semblance of order.

Frank stood by quietly, as if waiting for her to speak. The hackers fell silent, their eyes reflecting shattered hopes. Nikki looked at Sandra expectantly, and Albatross tightened his jaw, awaiting her command.

"All right," she said, voice rough but steady. "We find Roland if we can. If we can't, we move carefully, secure the children, and wait. We will see what happens next. We will endure."

She almost believed her own words. Almost. Then the ceiling groaned. Not the ordinary creak of stressed metal they had grown accustomed to, but a deep, resonant complaint of twisting steel. A sudden shriek of tearing metal split the air. The overhead panels began to peel back as if caught in enormous, invisible pincers. Sandra coughed, eyes watering as she struggled to see. Something black and glistening pushed through a gap in the ceiling. It looked like a cable, thick as a Queensguard's armored leg, writhing and alive.

Another cable followed, then another. They slithered downward, impossibly flexible, branching into the room like predatory tentacles. They twitched, searching. The hackers screamed. Nikki scrambled back, colliding with a terminal. Albatross shouted something incomprehensible, trying to calm the others, but his voice cracked with wild panic. Frank snarled, raising his armored arms in preparation to attack. Sandra staggered backward, heart pounding so fiercely it ached.

Before anyone could properly react, the cables struck. They moved faster than thought, lashing out and coiling around their bodies. Sandra felt a cold shock as something wrapped around her waist, lifting her feet from the floor. She gasped, kicking uselessly at the air. Nearby, Nikki's shrill scream knifed through her ears. One hacker, a young man who had tried so hard at the consoles, had a cable around his chest, which lifted him into the air as if he were a mere doll. Another hacker got lucky and darted away into a side corridor, their footsteps echoing as they fled.

"Run!" Albatross managed to yell to the ones still free, but most had already vanished, scattering in desperate attempts to escape.

Two hackers got away, Sandra thought hazily. *At least two. Good. Let them survive if they can.*

Sandra twisted. She hung a good five feet off the ground now with the cable tightened painfully around her ribs. Frank roared, swinging his gauntleted fists at the cables that held him by his shoulders. His armor clanged as he fought, but it did no good; the cables were too strong, too dense. Another cable snared Albatross by the legs, dangling him upside down. Nikki sobbed hysterically, thrashing in midair with a cable around her torso. A final hacker, a girl with haunted eyes, was caught too, her tears streaming in unfettered floods down her face.

This can't be happening, Sandra's mind stuttered. They were just making a plan, just finding some measure of unity—and now this?

The cables jerked them upward. Sparks rained down as more of the ceiling parted.

Nikki's screams rose to a pitch that hurt Sandra's ears. "No! No, let me go!" Nikki wailed, legs kicking. The hacker-girl caught beside her screamed too, calling for help no one could give. Albatross tried murmuring something, his voice low and frantic, "Calm...we must...calm..." He sounded delirious. Frank cursed with furious intensity, threatening to tear the cables apart, to kill whoever wielded them.

Sandra's thoughts spiraled. This was beyond vultures of darkness and rebellions. This was something else. A horror beyond horrors. As they ascended, she squinted through the dusty gloom and saw...a figure below, no—above? Orientation failed her as the cables rearranged their positions. Then she saw it.

The Queen.

A creature out of nightmares, just as Roland had described her. Sandra had not believed such a thing could exist. Now she beheld it with her own eyes and wished she never had. Cables kept the queen elevated in the air amid a chaos of countless other black wires and cables that extended from the back of her opened skull like a deformed halo of endless length. Her raven hair was tangled with those wires, her face twisted in permanent agony. Emerald eyes bled fresh streams of red tears while her mouth gaped open, as if screaming silently for all eternity, her lips curled back to show too-white teeth. Blood dribbled from wounds along her scalp, dripping down her cheeks, splattering onto her shoulders. She wore no armor, no clothing Sandra could discern. She was just a pale, sinewy form half-hidden by the mass of cables, which were her limbs, her extensions, her tools, and they moved her about as if she were a marionette. Or perhaps she was the puppet-master and these cables her infinite appendages. It was impossible to tell.

Sandra recoiled, but the Queen didn't even seem to notice them in any human sense. Her eyes stared past them, and it seemed clear to Sandra that it was the Queen's cables that held them of their own accord irrespective of the Queen.

Frank snarled, his voice forced and loud. "You think—" He coughed, unable to fully breathe. "You think this scares me, bitch? I'll tear you apart!" His bravado sounded hollow, a child yelling at a hurricane.

Frank, don't. Don't provoke this horror, she thought. But Frank couldn't help himself; facing unspeakable terror, he clung to aggression.

The Queen gave no sign of hearing him. More cables slithered forth, focusing on Frank. One wrapped around his armored left arm, another around his right. Sandra watched, sickened, as two more coiled around his legs, and a fifth encircled his neck.

"Frank!" Albatross, still upside down, shouted in horror. Nikki screamed incoherently, tears and snot flooding her face. Sandra struggled uselessly, the cable biting into her waist.

Without even glancing at him, the Queen's cables pulled. With a gruesome wet ripping sound, Frank came apart, his scream lasting only a fraction of a second before squelching into silence as his body was torn into five grisly chunks. Limbs and torso separated, blood spraying through the air in a crimson arc. His head dangled for a heartbeat, eyes bulging in shock, before it too was cast aside. The halves of his torso, still encased in pieces of broken armor, fell and struck the floor with a sickening thump that Sandra felt in her bones. She gagged, tears burning her eyes.

Nikki's screaming reached a new register of pure despair. The hacker-girl also shrieked, babbling prayers to gods Sandra didn't recognize. Albatross moaned, "P-please, we...we can serve you, spare us, oh please!" Sandra felt her mind teetering on the edge of madness. This was impossible. Wordless horror swam through her thoughts as raw animal terror flooded her veins. She understood now with terrible clarity that she was going to die here. Horrifically. The Queen would tear them apart one by one. Her children would never see her again, would never know what became of their mother. She sobbed silently, her heart on fire with rage and sorrow.

Samuel, I'm sorry. I'm so sorry. I failed you. I should never have kept secrets. I should have listened. Margot, Nathan, forgive me.

The Queen's cables targeted the hacker-girl next as if responding to her despair. The poor girl barely had time to protest before her body was wrenched sideways and torn in half at the waist. Her entrails spilled in glistening loops, spattering onto the Queen's pale form below. The Queen remained indifferent, her eternal scream silent, her bloody tears dripping steadily.

Why? Sandra pleaded within. *Why is this happening? Was our revolution so unforgivable? Is this really the punishment we deserve?*

Nikki's screams had devolved into ragged sobs. "Please, please, no," she begged, voice cracking. "I don't want to die. I—I'll do anything—please!" The cables answered by wrapping tighter around her limbs. She kicked and thrashed, but it was futile. With a swift yank, Nikki's body was disassembled into a spray of blood and organs. Her torn flesh splattered over the Queen along with the remains of the hackers and Frank.

Sandra recoiled, tears streaming, barely able to breathe. Her entire world had been reduced to blood and horror.

Now it was just Sandra and Albatross left. Albatross stared at Sandra, his glasses gone, his eyes naked and haunted. He opened his mouth, but nothing came out. His lips trembled, and after a few seconds, he managed a whisper. "I'm sorry, Sandra. So sorry…for everything. We destroyed heaven in search of paradise, just like…just like Samuel warned…""

She tried to speak, to comfort him, to say it wasn't his fault alone. But her throat closed. She merely sobbed silently. Her body shook so violently that the cable dug deeper into her flesh. Pain flared in her ribs and her mind spun.

Albatross looked up at the Queen and seemed to accept his fate as his expression glazed over. The cables around him tightened. He didn't scream as they started crushing him inward. Bones snapped with dull pops, his flesh deforming. He was compressed like a body in a recycler. His last breath came out as a wet gurgle, and then he was compressed fully, turned into an amorphous lump of pulpy entrails and discarded onto the growing mound of gore.

Sandra hung alone now. Blood dripped from her clothes and spattered her face. She trembled, her eyes darting wildly, her fear so intense it hollowed her out from the inside. She couldn't even form coherent thoughts anymore. Just terror and regret and an overwhelming longing for her children.

My babies. My babies! I love you.

A shadow moved in the corner of her vision, and she forced herself to look. Far away, beyond Mount Mendel's silhouette, a rippling mass of vultures hovered around a figure by the Luxury Quarters Wall. The figure was too distant to identify, yet somehow Sandra could see their glowing eyes. One eye emerald green, the other a vivid purple.

Who? Sandra's mind staggered.

The cables jerked her, drawing her closer to the Queen. She smelled blood, rust, ozone. Every nerve screamed, but the figure vanished, leaving her with no answers, just dread.

The cables sharply pivoted Sandra around to reveal a section of the floor that had been blasted open, opening into a corridor two levels down. There, huddled and alone, stood Margot and Nathan. Margot clung to Nathan, both of them trembling violently, their eyes huge and terrified. Dust and dim emergency lighting cast their young faces in hollow shadows. They looked so small, so helpless. Sandra's mind twisted in agony. She tried to scream their names, but the cables were too tight, and a futile sob was all that emerged.

She felt a sudden shift in the air. Without sound, the glowing-eyed figure reappeared, hovering in front of her as if ignoring gravity.

A woman, Sandra gasped. Her face resembled the Queen's twisted countenance, nearly identical to a Huntress except for the mismatched eyes. The woman smiled, a predatory grin that exposed no humor, only malice and delight.

"I'm sorry," Sandra tried to say, her voice a dry rasp. "Please…not my children…"

The woman regarded her like an insect pinned to a board. "You're not going to die just yet," she said softly, her words dripping like venom. Her voice was oddly calm, melodic even, as if addressing a child. Sandra's breath hitched. The Queen's cables responded to the glowing eyed woman's slightest gesture, shifting Sandra's position as if presenting her for inspection.

Sandra's mind reeled as she realized that this woman was clearly controlling the Queen and the cables.

Suddenly, another flare of impossible power ignited the space, and an additional figure stepped into Sandra's vision out of nowhere, treating unseen layers of reality like parting curtains. As if everything weren't already absurd enough, Sandra saw a male humanoid figure composed of a roiling kaleidoscope of flesh, mirror, fungus, darkness, light, and other impossible substances.

He raised a hand at the woman with glowing eyes. "Tether," he said urgently, his voice trembling, "don't do this."

The woman called Tether laughed, a triumphant, lilting sound. "Too slow, Maitreya. Fate is broken, and you're all out of time." She spoke as if Sandra weren't even there, as if the dying carnage around them was trivial.

Maitreya's strange, morphing eyes reflected worry and fear. He stepped forward, and the air hummed with oppressive power.

"Are you sure you want to stand against me now, Outsider?" Tether taunted. "Don't be such a sore loser. I found a vulnerability in your precious plans, and I'm exploiting it. Did you expect any less?"

Maitreya's posture suggested reluctance and desperation. He glanced at Sandra, at the mangled corpses, at the Queen. "Tether, take another

328

Anchor if you must, but don't kill the mate of the Fate Breaker. Your arrogance and haste will cost us everything."

Anchor? Fate Breaker? Sandra's mind snagged on words she couldn't comprehend. Her sanity frayed further. *He called me the mate of the Fate Breaker. Is this about Samuel? My Samuel?*

She had no idea what this meant, but if they were talking about him, maybe he still lived. Maybe he could still save Margot and Nathan. Hope flickered weakly before despair crushed it again.

Tether rolled her eyes as if bored. "Don't be so dramatic, Maitreya. This will break your Mirror-Man's mind and shatter his heart, unraveling your council's precious designs. Let it happen. Let everything burn. You can't stop me."

Maitreya's form crackled with energy as he tried something. Sandra felt a surge of pressure, but Tether clenched her fist, and Maitreya began to collapse into himself, his body warping under invisible but relentless forces. Maitreya snarled, his limbs and alien surfaces shifting wildly. Patterns of light and shadow raced across him as he fought whatever force Tether commanded. He tried to lunge forward, reaching for Sandra, for her children, but Tether narrowed her eyes, and blood poured thickly from them as she concentrated, veins pulsing at her temples. She strained, fingers trembling, jaw clenched as if she were willing a star to collapse.

Sandra watched with numb horror, her last threads of sanity snapping.

These beings reshape reality as if it were clay. We are just insects to them. Insects to be toyed with and crushed.

Maitreya's silhouette warped, contorting inward. He struggled, limbs splintering into fractal geometries, yet somehow holding form. For a moment, he resisted Tether's crushing force. Tether gasped, red tears dripping onto her shoulders, her entire body shaking. Maitreya's face twisted with grim resolve as he seemed to choose something—an escape perhaps. At the last possible instant, rather than being fully annihilated, Maitreya stiffened and ceased resisting, allowing the collapse to complete. In his surrender, Sandra watched as the bizarre man slipped free into some impossible dimension. His form vanished into a single dark point that winked out of existence, leaving Tether panting, her shoulders quivering with exertion.

Tether wiped blood from her cheeks, trying to regain composure. She cast a glare at Sandra, who hung helpless and broken with grief. "Now," Tether hissed, voice rough, "is the perfect time to die."

Time slowed. Sandra saw another cable approaching, felt it tighten around her torso. She knew what would come next: the tearing, the agony, brief and ultimate. She closed her eyes.

Samuel, I'm sorry. Margot, Nathan, forgive me.

She prayed for them, begging silently that they survive somehow.

The cable pulled, and pain exploded as her body tore in half at the waist. A scorching fire of agony roared through her nerves. She screamed silently, no air left in her lungs, tears blinding her. Blood gushed from her open torso as she fell, warmth spreading over her cold skin. She struggled to focus on anything but the pain. Her vision blurred as she hit the floor in pieces, her legs splattering somewhere behind her. Darkness edged her vision as she lay on her side, her ripped open torso quickly draining her of life.

A shriek tore through the chamber. It was Margot's voice.

Oh God, Sandra's mind reeled. *Please just run, my babies!*

Margot screamed "Momma! No!" over and over again, her voice raw and shrill. Nathan was speechless, staring and drooling at his dying mother, his mind visibly broken.

No, please no. Not them. Run! Please just run!

Sandra tried to speak, tried to form words, but only blood bubbled on her lips. She tried to move her arm, to beckon them away, but nothing worked. Her vision began to narrow.

Tether glided toward her children, suspended by her own impossible forces. The Queen hovered behind Tether like a broken doll, cables shifting restlessly as Tether examined Margot with a clinical interest.

"You," Tether said softly. "You'll make the perfect third Anchor. Your suffering will fuel incredible power. Your life will finally have meaning."

Margot's screams collapsed into silent sobs of primal terror. Nathan whimpered. Sandra's heart bled more than her veins. She wished to trade her soul to spare them this. Anything to spare them this nightmare and return them to the heaven she had played a part in destroying.

In the corner of her dimming vision, something stirred inside the

Queen's lower belly—a suggestion of tiny limbs shifting beneath pallid flesh. It was another horror beyond comprehension. *A child within a monster?* Sandra gasped. She couldn't understand. Everything was chaos.

Sandra's pain gave way to numbness. She felt cold. Her eyes fluttered, vision darkening. She saw Margot's face twisted in agony, heard Nathan's small sobs, and Tether's cruel laughter echoing. She wanted to scream "Run!" but managed only a wet gasp. Through the haze, she heard Margot begging, her voice cracking, "Momma…Momma, please!" The cables hissed, lifting the trembling girl into the air. Nathan made a small sound like a wounded animal.

Another voice echoed, "Don't!" It was a familiar man's voice, urgent and rich with emotion. Sandra tried to focus, but her vision faltered. *Is that strange being she called Maitreya returning? Or someone else?* She couldn't see properly, couldn't think properly.

In that final dimness, Sandra saw the vultures overhead. They hovered now above Tether, circling her as if she were their dark queen, forming a silent, eldritch halo of black wings and void-flesh. The Queen's tortured form dangled below them, Tether at its center, and the vultures drifted in menacing patterns—cosmic heralds of doom.

"Samuel…" Sandra tried to whisper, blood bubbling in her throat. Her children sobbed, their voices muffled as her hearing failed. She tried to say sorry to them, tried to beg for forgiveness, but she still could not form words. Just agony and regret.

In her delirium, she thought of Samuel. His strong arms, his unyielding spirit. She conjured his image in her failing mind, and she clung to it. Despite everything, her mind forced her to believe he would survive somehow, that he would find Margot and Nathan and protect them from these unimaginable evils.

Samuel, my fearless bull, I'm sorry. I lied. I betrayed you. Please forgive me. Please protect our children.

Tether laughed again, taunting the man that Sandra couldn't see or hear properly, their words drifting past her ears like meaningless static.

Tether snapped a command, and Margot's screams sharpened just as cold darkness swallowed Sandra's broken body and plunged her further into a crescendoing delirium. She couldn't remember where she was or what she was doing, but in the darkness she saw Samuel's face. He stood before her, arms wide open, and she stumbled into his embrace. He felt warm, unbroken by despair.

She pressed her cheek against him, inhaling the faint scent of sweat and soil. His whisper enveloped her as he said, "I forgive you, my perfect little okra. Rest now."

She sobbed into his chest, releasing all her fear and regret.

Save them, Samuel. Save them, Sandra pleaded.

She clung tightly as her heartbeat fluttered, slowed, stopped.

Her breath hitched once more, then faded. The world fully receded into darkness and silence. Margot's screams, Nathan's whimpers, Tether's cruel laughter. It all slipped away.

Only the warmth of Samuel's arms remained, until that too dimmed and vanished.

To Be Continued

Author's Note

If you have a few minutes, please take some time to leave a rating or review for this book on:

Amazon and Goodreads

Thank you so much for your help!

– E. S. Fein

www.ingramcontent.com/pod-product-compliance
Lightning Source LLC
Chambersburg PA
CBHW031150020726
47499CB00002B/316